Samuel Dodson lives in America and has written a number of other books under a pseudonym.

Samuel Dodson

Majorca

Futura Publications Limited
A Futura Book

A Futura Book

First published in Great Britain 1977
by Futura Publications Limited

Copyright © Samuel Dodson 1977

ISBN 0 8600 7470 6

Printed in Great Britain by
Hazell Watson & Viney Ltd
Aylesbury, Bucks

Futura Publications Limited
110 Warner Road
Camberwell, London SE5

MAJORCA

Monday

TEN DAYS AGO ROD SHEPHERD HAD NEVER heard of Majorca. Within ten minutes he would be landing on it. The girl at the travel agency had told him it was a Spanish island about a hundred miles off the Mediterranean coast of Spain. A travel folder told him its climate was mild and warm, winter and summer, and that it was a paradise for the tourists who flocked to its smooth, sandy shores all year through. It described the island as a retreat for the wealthy and a haven for the more quiet of heart; an island shrouded in mystery, history and romance.

But Rod would have no time to explore the mystery, history and romance which the folder spoke about. Nor would he have time to luxuriate in the serenity of the little villages, the quiet grottoes or the secluded coves that hid themselves so snugly among the limestone cliffs. His schedule permitted nothing more than the time it would take to clear up the mess Lisa had gotten herself into and get back to his accounting business. It was tax time, his busiest period. It wasn't right for the owner of the firm to take off and stick the employees with all the work and responsibilities. It could cost him clients.

What kind of mess was Lisa in this time? he wondered. The last time was when she'd been arrested in the company of that nightclub owner in Columbus. "Being held," the cablegram had read. Being held for what? Only fifteen years old and already in more scrapes with the law than he cared to think about.

Where had he gone wrong? It wasn't easy being both father and mother to a daughter of fifteen. That was it, of course. As a father he'd been doing okay until Helen died. What did he know about filling the "mother" part in a young girl's life?

He stared out at a meandering cloud and looked down at the smooth blue Mediterranean far below. He ran a finger idly over his chin. The trouble with Lisa had started the night Helen died in the accident. The hostility between him and Lisa started on their way home from the funeral. He remembered trying to hold Lisa's hand and her drawing it rudely away.

"I want to go and stay with Aunt Hattie," she'd said. There were tears in her eyes, but her voice was as hard and dry as the granite of Helen's tombstone.

She had given no reason for wanting to go to Columbus,

and he could have saved all the arguments by letting her go, because in the end, when he flatly forbade her to leave home, she ran away anyway. That was when she'd gotten mixed up with that sonofabitch who ran a nightclub, which was only the beginning of the big problems. Within a week she was home and expelled from school for possession of dope. Then there was that bust in Old Town when she was arrested for smoking grass. Now she was in a Majorcan jail for God only knew what.

He shook his head. Lisa had always been a good girl, a girl any father would have been proud of. It was impossible to think that a girl like Lisa could go from good to bad in such a short period of time. But, impossible or not, it had happened. There had to be a reason. A fifteen-year-old girl who had always had a happy home life, a loving mother and father, an A-plus average in school, just didn't suddenly turn into a monster without cause. They had taught her to be decent and God-fearing; Helen had seen to that. Why had Lisa gone wrong? Why had she renounced all her moral upbringing?

A soft chime sounded; the seat-belt sign flashed on. A moment later the plane dropped slightly. Rod gripped the arms of his seat and looked toward the window. Below, resting pleasantly atop the roll of the Mediterranean, Rod saw the white-and-blue lines of a luxury yacht. It wasn't an ordinary yacht—if any yacht could be called ordinary. This one he estimated to be well over 150 feet long, complete with a seaplane moored aft and a swimming pool midship. Two sleek motor launches were anchored to port and starboard davits. He sighed, thinking how great it must be to have money enough to afford a yacht like that and to do nothing but sail from place to place without any cares. All his life he'd dreamed of having enough money to go where he pleased whenever he pleased and to buy the kind of women he needed . . . not the type of cheap tramp he'd paid for in Barcelona last night.

It wasn't that he had to buy women for sex. Lots of women found him attractive. He thought himself ordinary, not overly tall and certainly not overly handsome. Helen always told him it was his eyes that had first attracted her to him. The prostitute in Barcelona had said he had the most sensual mouth she'd ever seen. Other women he remembered claimed it was the squareness of his chin or the rugged masculinity of his face or the silver at his temples. But paying for sex gave him control over the situation. He liked to be in control, although he had never controlled his wife; he had never wanted to for some strange reason. When he paid for a woman's time he enjoyed being in command and being able to demand the kind of sex he was in the mood for.

He straightened suddenly and sat back. A twinge of guilt made him shift uncomfortably in his seat.

THE WATERS OF THE BAY ROLLED LAZILY under the late May sun. In the distance were the pale, soft beaches of Majorca with its towering mountains standing solid and formidable like pine-clad duennas. A line of white modern hotels tried to obscure the mountain backdrop, but nothing could diminish the majesty of those peaks, pointing like fingers to heaven, as if reminding all mortals that this was God's island, one of His favorite treasures. The gentle sway of the blue-and-white yacht was tempting Elaine into sleep, but a nagging pain in her chest made that impossible; the low-flying airliner only disturbed her all the more. She was naked, except for a thin coating of suntan lotion and a large floppy hat that shaded her face.

"More tourists," she said as she pushed back the hat brim and looked up at the plane, which had started its descent to Palma airport.

"Did you say something, darling?" The young man next to her rolled over on his side and put his hand on her thigh. He was more naked than she.

Elaine turned her head and smiled at him. She let her eyes roam over his tight, sculptured body. God, he's beautiful, she thought as she marveled at the smooth, bronze texture of his skin. And so very, very young, she added with a sinking feeling of despair. She studied his handsome, boyish face, then glanced down at his hand, admiring the contrast of his dark, olive skin against the suntan of her own. Everything about him radiated youth and vitality. She loved looking at his body. It was so strong, so firm, so perfect in every detail. And so generously endowed, she thought as she glanced at his crotch and felt a tingling sensation running through her. The need for him started to build in her; it always did every time she looked at him. If only the interminable pain in her chest would go away and give her the chance to enjoy him as fully as she wanted. Oh, to be nineteen and brimming with health again. Everyone said she was foolish for loving one so much younger than herself, but how could such wonderful feelings be foolish or wrong? She wasn't nineteen, but he made her feel as if she were; and he made her forget at times the terrible sickness that was eating at her insides.

A sharp stab of pain pushed back the sensuality that had been creeping up along her thighs. She sat up in an effort to camouflage it. "I just complained about more tourists," she said, nodding toward the plane in the distance. She reached for a bottle of suntan lotion and began applying another coat to her arms. "More and more come every year."

"Here, let me do that," Jorge said as he took the lotion from her. He poured some into the palms of his hands. "It is good for the economy. Besides," he added with a smile, "you were once a tourist yourself, my darling. Remember?"

How long had it been? she wondered. Five years? Six? She'd forgotten she'd had a life before coming to Majorca. It had been a life she desperately wanted to forget, a life of violence, scandal, drunkenness and, most of all, unhappiness. She'd come here on a rest cure after drying out for almost a year in a Swiss sanitarium. Majorca had seemed a paradise to her then; it never lost that appeal. She fell hopelessly in love with its broad, tree-lined avenues crossed with countless narrow cobblestoned streets with their balconied houses, quaint and old and more charming than any she'd ever seen. Thinking of it now, however, she supposed it was the purity of its churches, the grandeur of its architecture, the simpleness of its peasants that made her love Majorca so much. After all her years of fighting, clawing, lying, posturing, it seemed as though God had decreed that she should be given another chance and had transported her here to one of his private gardens where she could see beauty as beauty was intended to be seen.

It hadn't been the doctors who had cured her of her alcoholism; it hadn't been the plastic surgeons who had given her back her beauty. The wonderful island of Majorca, the bright sunlit city of Palma, had accomplished all that for her.

"I was never a tourist," Elaine chided. "I've always belonged here."

Jorge smiled as he smeared the oil over her shoulders, then lovingly down over Elaine's full, smooth breasts. She felt her nipples pout and begin to harden. She let out a shivering little moan as he toyed with them with his thumb and forefinger. "Stop that, Jorge," she said with a laugh and reluctantly pushed his hand away.

In answer he bent down and sucked one of the nipples in between his lips, nibbling it with his teeth. "I love your breasts," he said softly, his lips glistening with oil. He put his mouth over hers and pulled her into his arms.

"Jorge, behave yourself," Elaine said. She pushed him away, but not until after she'd fleetingly explored the inside of his mouth with her tongue.

"So who is to see?" he asked. "There is no other yacht but yours here in the bay." He looked around. "And there is only the skeleton crew; it is nothing they have not seen before."

Elaine felt a touch of shame for having become so flagrant about displaying her nudity of late, especially since she'd met Jorge. When she had first come to Majorca she had tried to hide the pleasure she had once had of exhibiting her naked body. She had found God here. Not the God people felt obliged to run to every Sunday, and certainly not the God her mother had revered so much; He had been a terrible God. Elaine's God was inside her, and He was good and kind and just and understanding. He acted as a constant reminder of her past immorality, and tried to teach her the rewards of humility and shame. He was the same God who had given her Jorge in all his beautiful nudity, and no God, she reasoned, could create such perfection and not be proud to have it seen.

It wasn't that she had become a completely changed woman. Far from that. Old habits, she found, were much too difficult to break. She still enjoyed uninhibited sex, parties, social drinking. None of it seemed as sinful here as it had been in her earlier life.

Elaine lay herself back on the air mattress and adjusted the brim of her hat. "You're an exhibitionist."

Jorge laughed, then shrugged, looking like an embarrassed

little boy. "I am proud to be seen making love to a beautiful woman like you, Elena."

She turned her head and gazed at him for a moment. "Am I beautiful?"

"Very beautiful," he whispered, again taking her in his arms. She let him kiss her again, this time more deeply. As he squeezed her tight she felt the pain stab at her breast. She eased him away after a moment, holding her breath until the pain subsided. When it did, she said, "Your friends aren't saying I am too old for you?" She was smiling, but there was a worried look behind her eyes as she waited for him to answer.

Again Jorge laughed. "Too old? You? You will never be old." Then, as if in an afterthought, he added, "What is a few years between two people in love?"

There it was again, Elaine thought with an anxious feeling in her heart. He really was aware of the vast difference in their ages. He said it did not matter, but he always sounded as if he were apologizing for that difference. She was too old for him, she reminded herself. She had lied to him and had told him there was only a ten-year difference in their ages. If ever he discovered the additional twenty-some years those expensive plastic surgeons had whittled away from her, Jorge would run off like a frightened rabbit. He was only a boy. She was an aging woman who had already seen and done too much in one lifetime. Jorge was basically innocent of life; she had been nothing more than a common tramp who had used her body and her beauty to gain all the luxury that now surrounded her. She had whored and connived, cheating and heartless. She had been wicked and cruel and didn't deserve the likes of Jorge Aguilar.

The nagging pain caused her to pause. But perhaps she did deserve him now. After all, she really didn't know that much about him. Although he appeared innocent and pure —like herself—perhaps there was an unattractive undersurface that made him other than what he seemed. Perhaps the others were right, that despite what he said, it was only her money he was after. Why else would a nineteen-year-old boy want a woman like her? She'd borne two children, had buried one husband and had married another before Jorge was even born. She should face facts: It was only her money he wanted, not her—a woman easily old enough to be his mother.

It was as if Jorge read her thoughts. "You Americans put too much emphasis on age and money. If you were the true Majorcan you say you are, these things would not matter at all. Age is nothing but a state of mind and money is merely a state of being."

Elaine grinned. "How did you acquire so much wisdom at nineteen?"

He rolled over on his back and put his hands behind his head, closing his eyes to the sun. "Bad upbringing, I suppose," he said with a grin.

Elaine's expression went serious. "You never talk about your upbringing, Jorge. Tell me about it."

"There is nothing to tell."

"Were you very poor?"

"See, there you go again," he said, turning toward her and opening his eyes. "If you are not concerned about age you are concerned about money." He shook his head. "I do not understand how I could have fallen in love with an American woman."

Elaine reached over and tilted his face to hers. "Are you in love with me, Jorge?"

Their eyes met and held. "Very much," he breathed as he took her hand and pressed his lips to the palm. "I have never been so much in love."

"Were you ever in love before?" The question slipped out before she could catch it. She hated people who pried into other people's pasts. She'd met too many of that type; people who pried were generally cruel, selfish people who pried only because of a wish to destroy.

"I have known a few women," he admitted. He frowned slightly and closed his eyes against the blaze of the sun again. "I do not believe I was ever in love before. At least I never felt this way before."

"Which way?" Her heart began to beat with happiness. She knew she was searching for compliments, but she didn't care.

Again he opened his eyes and looked at her. He wagged a finger.

"Ah, no, Señora Brandon. You do not trick Jorge into admitting his weaknesses." He made a grab for her. Elaine squealed as he pounced on her, covering her nakedness with his own.

A girl stepped out on deck and stood posed, cigarette in one hand, a tall drink in the other. She was wearing a hot-pink bikini that showed off her long, raven hair and flashing dark eyes to their best advantage. She looked very much like a younger copy of Elaine Brandon. The girl put an ugly sneer on her lips and shook her head at the two naked, tussling figures on the air mattress. "Don't you two ever get tired of mauling each other?" she asked through her sneer.

Elaine froze. "Oh, Cindy darling," she said, pushing Jorge away and slipping quickly into a robe.

"Don't cover up just on my account, sister dear," Cynthia said. She slurred the last two words most unattractively.

Elaine caught the slur and fidgeted uncomfortably. She saw Cynthia studying Jorge's naked body. He seemed to be enjoying the attention. "Darling," she said to Jorge, "be a dear and ask the chef to fix me a cream cheese and olive sandwich." She touched his hand to call his attention to her. "I'm famished."

"You'll get fat," Jorge said, getting to his feet. "Olives and cream cheese," he repeated with a grimace. He pretended to shiver.

Cynthia Brandon lowered herself gracefully into a deck chair. "Olives are supposed to be an aphrodisiac." She gave Elaine a smug look and added, "There are those who actually believe olives can restore one's youth."

"Cynthia," Elaine said under her breath.

"Yes, sister dear."

Jorge hesitated. He looked from one to the other, then shrugged and started toward the passageway.

Cynthia eyed his nakedness, running her tongue unconsciously across her lips. "You'd better let that thing go down a little before that new crewman sees it," she said, nodding toward Jorge's semi-erection. "I hear he eats things like that for lunch."

Jorge frowned at her. "Why do you always dig out the dirty things about people before the good ones?"

"I guess I take after my mother," she said, tossing a defiant look at Elaine. Elaine narrowed her eyes, then looked away.

"But Elaine says your mother was a very good, decent woman."

Cynthia rolled her eyes. "She would."

"That's enough, Cynthia," Elaine said tightly.

Jorge couldn't help but notice the angry look the two women flashed at each other. Ever since he'd met them there had been a constant hostility between them. He supposed he could understand it, however. Cynthia had deserved what had happened. He had met and had slept with her first. But Cynthia was a spiteful, selfish girl who never thought of anyone but herself. They had argued about something and she had told him to get out of her life. She had called him a worthless peasant, a gigolo, a beach bum. She had hurt him deeply. The truth always hurt. Elaine, on the other hand, had sympathized with him. He had told her of his hurt and she had understood and had asked him to have dinner with her. After that he and Elaine saw a lot of each other. Cynthia had fumed and raged and told him she had changed her mind and wanted him back as her lover. Jorge had come to like Elaine too much by then to hurt her. He told Cynthia he wanted nothing more to do with her, which only enraged her all the more.

In spite of himself he smiled as he looked again at Elaine and Cynthia. It flattered him to think that he could cause such friction between two such beautiful sisters. Cynthia was younger, perhaps even prettier, but Elaine had a more definite type of beauty, whereas Cynthia's was only transitory. The fact that Elaine was extremely wealthy and Cynthia dependent upon her sister's wealth and generosity wasn't the reason for his preference, he told himself. A frown creased his brow. Or was it? The thought disturbed him. He turned quickly and went to fetch Elaine's sandwich.

Elaine waited until Jorge was well out of earshot before she turned and frowned at Cynthia. "Please, Cindy, I'd appreciate your not being so sarcastic."

Cynthia rolled her eyes again. "Oh, Mother, come off it."

Elaine sat straight up. She looked cautiously around. In a lowered voice she said, "You promised not to use that word."

"Yes, sister dear," Cynthia said caustically.

A moment of silence followed, interrupted only by the sound of the dimpled waters slapping gently against the hull. Elaine lay back and fumbled in her bag for her pills. She put one into her mouth without letting Cynthia see. She had long since gotten accustomed to taking the painkilling tablets without water.

Elaine closed her eyes and waited for the pill to take effect. She'd made a mistake allowing Cynthia to come. Yet, if it hadn't been for Cynthia she might never have met Jorge. She'd benefited from her mistake, as most people do, and—thinking of Jorge—she had to admit that the benefits were well worth having to tolerate Cynthia. Still, she wished Cynthia weren't here. She was a spoiled and spiteful girl. She'd always been spoiled and spiteful. Elaine sighed. Perhaps she was to blame for that. Oh, how she wished all her pains would go away.

"Poor Elaine," Cynthia said with a malicious smile. "You've really lied yourself into a lovely problem this time."

Elaine refused to let herself get annoyed. "It wouldn't be a problem if you'd act your age and stop being so childish."

"Act my age!" Cynthia said, turning sharply. "Why don't you act *your* age? How long do you think you're going to be able to fool that boy? Do you really believe all your plastic surgery is going to hold up forever? He'll find out sooner or later, and then where will you be?"

"Jorge doesn't love me for my age," Elaine argued.

"No, just for your money," Cynthia answered with dripping sarcasm.

"No, I really don't think that either." She spoke evenly but her voice lacked the conviction she wanted to hear.

"Oh, really, Elaine. Don't kid yourself. Jorge is nineteen years old and all real flesh and blood. You're fifty-one and all silicone and plastic." She paused for a moment and looked at her mother. "Okay, I admit you don't look your real age, thanks to all those expensive doctors, but the fact remains that you're fifty-one on the inside, regardless of how young you look on the outside." She hesitated again, searching her mind for something else with which to inflict injury. A satanic glow came over her face. "And what about all those terrible scandals you ran here to escape? Jorge will find out eventually about the notorious Elaine Brandon—or should I have said the notorious Elaine Harshaw?"

Elaine winced. She had almost forgotten that part of her life. Having been the wife of Leland Harshaw was something she desperately wanted to forget. Down deep inside, however, she knew she would never be permitted to forget. There would always be people like Cynthia who would remind her—angry people, jealous people, people who genuinely enjoyed hurting others.

She found her hands were trembling slightly and turned her eyes toward the island in the distance. Palma smiled back at her, reassuring her that it was still her haven, her refuge. It was still there as long as she wanted it. She had only to stay here away from the ugliness she'd left behind and nothing would hurt her again. Elaine Harshaw had no place on Majorca; she did not exist. She was buried in those lurid headlines and court records of the outside world. Now it was only a name in the files of criminal lawyers and gossip columnists.

A sense of foreboding gripped her. Unfortunately, records and files and headlines didn't die as easily as human beings. They didn't sink into the earth and vanish into dust. They would be a reality in the world as long as the world itself existed. And being real, they would always stand in the shadows, anxious to be called forward at the slightest beckoning of a finger.

She squared her shoulders and turned back to her daughter. "The notorious Elaine Harshaw has long ceased to exist. There is no way in this world for Jorge to find out about her unless someone like you decides to tell him."

Cynthia bit down on her lower lip, biting down the hatred she wanted to fling at her mother. It was easy not to think of Elaine as her mother. After all, she'd never known the woman until after her father died and she was old enough to be pawned off as Elaine's younger sister. "You make me sick," she spat. "You and Jorge don't belong together. You not only come from two different generations, you come from two different worlds."

"I see nothing wrong with that."

"You wouldn't." Her frustration built until it exploded. "You're too damned old for him."

The pains were beginning to subside and Cynthia was beginning to lose control of herself. It all made her feel a little better. Elaine pulled the brim of her hat down over her eyes. "You yourself are older than Jorge."

"Not all that much."

"Then how about that actor you were so madly in love with a year or so ago? How old was he? Forty-nine? Fifty?" She smiled. "And you were twenty-one then. You thought that perfectly all right. Why is it so wrong for an older woman to go with a younger man but perfectly all right for an older man to go with a younger woman?"

"It just doesn't look right," Cynthia said. Her voice had lost some of its sting.

"In whose eyes?" Elaine let the trace of a smile shade her mouth. "You're just envious because you met Jorge first and then threw him aside. You don't give a damn about how things look. Your pride is hurt because an older woman took your young man away from you." She clenched her teeth, angry for having let Cynthia goad her into saying something she really had not intended saying. She knew Cynthia was furious with her, and it would serve no purpose to infuriate her further. It only made things worse.

Cynthia narrowed her eyes. "Well, at least I'm glad to hear that you admit to being an older woman."

"Oh, Cindy, please let's not keep at each other this way. I never denied that I'm an older woman. Jorge knows that I'm much older than you."

"Twenty-seven years older?" Cynthia asked mockingly.

Elaine refused to let herself be riled.

Cynthia prodded her on by laughing. She cut off her laugh as abruptly as she'd turned it on. She glared at Elaine, feeling the acrid taste of venom on her tongue. "Oh, you were always clever, Elaine. But then I've always known that. There aren't many women who can murder their husband and get away with it."

Elaine's eyes blazed. "Cynthia!"

Cynthia laughed in her face. "Any woman clever enough to do that would certainly be able to beguile a simple Majorcan hustler into her trap."

"I refuse to listen to any more of this," Elaine said. She gathered herself together and started to get up.

"I'm going to get him back, Elaine," Cynthia threatened. "And I have just the trump card that will win this little game. I'm going to take him away from you just as you took him away from me."

Elaine stood there, angry and confused. She didn't want to continue the conversation, yet part of her old self took hold of her. She turned defiantly toward her daughter. "I did not take Jorge away from you. It was the other way around. Jorge sought me out." She turned abruptly and walked to the rail, gripping it hard with both hands.

Behind her Cynthia rattled the ice cubes in her glass. "What gets me," she said as though talking to herself, "is why I've gone along with this sister act all this time. I really don't think you would carry through with all those threats you threw at me."

Elaine spun around. She felt frightened and vulnerable. It was as if Elaine Harshaw had suddenly stepped into her shoes, Elaine Harshaw, angry at the world, selfish, defiant. She glowered at Cynthia. "Don't kid yourself, Cynthia," she said, the corners of her mouth turning downward in an ugly arch. "I'm perfectly capable of carrying through with my threats, so I don't have to remind you why you will continue to play our little sister masquerade until *I* decide to take off the masks."

Cynthia drained the highball she'd been sipping and angrily threw herself back against the deck chair.

Elaine turned again and waited until Elaine Harshaw left her. She breathed deeply and tried to bring back her earlier calm. It seemed so innocent, Elaine thought, when they'd started their game of playing at being sisters. She and Cynthia had never been close, so it seemed natural somehow.

She wished now, with all her heart, that they had been closer. But that had been impossible, thanks to a husband who hated his children and refused to let Elaine see them except on rare occasions. She had married Gregory Brandon III too young, when girls thought a very rich man was worth any sacrifice. She learned only too quickly that he had never wanted her as a wife, only as another lovely possession that he could sit at the head of his table and let other men admire and envy him for possessing. The two children, Greg Jr. and Cynthia, had both been accidents, conceived during weak moments when he had had too much drink or drugs or both. To him, children were a hindrance as well as a reminder, as they grew up, that he was getting old. Elaine had begged him to let her raise her children. He had flatly refused. His reason was simple: Children were a nuisance. They got in the way of his pleasure, and nothing was permitted to interfere with Gregory Brandon's precious pleasure.

Elaine heaved a sigh. She'd been wrong to masquerade as Cynthia's sister after her complete face and body lift. In truth, it had been Cynthia's idea. But then Jorge entered the picture. Elaine wanted him more than anyone else in the world. She hated herself for actually blackmailing Cynthia into continuing the pretense when Cindy threatened to expose their true relationship to Jorge. Blackmail was an ugly word but one

Elaine was very well acquainted with; her second husband, Leland Harshaw, had been an expert at it. She supposed she had learned through association. She had panicked when Cynthia threatened her. She soothed her conscience by rationalizing that it was because her doctors had told her with certainty about her illness. She was too deeply attached to Jorge then to chance losing her last hope for happiness. She had been stupid and selfish, but she felt life owed her some small degree of contentment. She could not bear the thought of losing Jorge, so she had resorted to something she thought was against her principles; she'd threatened Cynthia, forcing her to keep silent about Elaine's real identity.

Cynthia gave her a cold look. "Yes, I guess you're right. I should have known better than to think you'd grown soft in your old age." She wanted to twist the knife now that she had it embedded in Elaine's back. "I know why I go along with this stupid game, but I wonder at times how you can sleep at night with such guilt on your conscience."

"Oh, Cindy, darling, please let's not pursue this. I know I was wrong doing what I did, but—"

"But you just had to see if you could get a boy thirty-two years younger than yourself. You should have asked me, Elaine. I could have told you that that's easy to do. Anybody can buy love, you know."

Elaine suddenly felt Elaine Harshaw slip inside her. "Not anybody, Cynthia. I certainly haven't bought yours."

"You'll never have that much money," Cynthia said spitefully. "And mark my words, you'll never have Jorge either. You'll see me dead first."

She felt the stab at her heart. Cynthia was still such a selfish child. But she was maturing in spite of herself. Fighting to keep a man she wanted, regardless of who got hurt in the struggle—including her mother—was being a woman, not a child. She found it painful, nonetheless, to see Cynthia's hatred of her. She'd never convinced Cynthia of the love she felt for her. She'd never convinced her son of that fact either.

Greg. She hadn't thought of him since Jorge had entered her life. Snatching at the straw that she hoped might change the subject of conversation, she said, "Have you heard from your brother?"

"Why?"

"I was just wondering where he was these days."

"As though you cared."

Elaine closed her eyes as she felt a cloud of sadness mist over them. "You're wrong, Cindy. I care very much. I've always tried to give you and Greg all the love I had to give."

"Whenever it was convenient," Cynthia slurred.

"That isn't true." She hesitated. "I do admit that I wasn't ever as close to you both as I would have wished. I suppose that was because you were away at school so much of the time."

"That wasn't it at all. You've always treated Greg and me like lepers."

"Oh, Cindy, how can you say that?" She felt a twinge of guilt when she added, "I did everything I could for you both." She shook her head without opening her eyes. How could she have made Cynthia and Greg understand how difficult life with their father had been? They weren't old enough to understand. She could never have brought herself to tell them that it was their father and not she who wanted them kept hidden out of sight. It was wrong to try to turn children against their own father. She herself had had enough of that from her own mother.

Greg was only seven and Cindy only four the night their father fell from the deck of the yacht. After he died she had thought that now there would be time enough to make amends, to bring up the children as she had always wanted to, close and loving. Unfortunately fate had continued to refuse to smile on her. It was on that horrible night that she had learned the devastating meaning of the word blackmail.

An uncomfortable instinct made her move back from the rail as she stared down at the dark waters far below. She hated this yacht; she hated all yachts; they brought back too many unpleasant memories. But Jorge adored the yacht. She hadn't changed much over the years, she thought. She was still sacrificing herself for those she loved, and she loved Jorge more than anyone in the world.

Almost twenty years ago she had stood near a similar rail on a similar yacht and had listened to her husband's screams for help as he floundered and finally sank into the dark, cold water. A week later they had found him washed ashore, bloated almost beyond recognition.

They had been arguing the night he died. Like all arguments, she could not remember now how it had begun—but it was about the children; they argued constantly about the children. It was incredible to her that a father could despise his offspring so much.

As she thought about it, bits and pieces of that night filtered back into her memory. President Eisenhower had won a landslide victory over Adlai Stevenson, and they were having a victory celebration aboard their yacht. It was a cold, blustery night, and she had tried to talk Gregory into having the party at their estate rather than aboard the *Trident*. No one ever changed Gregory Brandon's mind.

The party was crowded with politicians, diplomats, even many of the top people in the Democratic Party. (Gregory always contributed generously to both sides of every campaign. He hated losing.) Gregory, however, was in a foul mood. The sea was rough that night. The revelers were drinking more than usual to try to ward off seasickness.

Their argument started in the ballroom. Elaine, wanting to prevent a scene, tried to flee to the refuge of her cabin. Gregory caught up with her on deck, grabbing her by the arm and flinging her against the rail. She was shivering with cold in her low-cut strapless evening dress; Gregory, drunk as he was, didn't seem to mind the cold.

"Those goddam children. Is that all you can think about?" he swore at her. "God only knows who their father is," he raged. "You've slept with half the men in that fucking ballroom."

"Only because you forced me to," she argued. And it was true. He had insisted that she sleep with his more important friends, men whom he needed to close an important deal, men whose support he needed for some political reason. Money and power were always behind it; prostituting his wife meant very little under such circumstances.

He was drunk, of course. Gregory was always drunk or high on drugs. He slapped her hard across the face, sending her sprawling on the deck. People began coming out on deck to see what was going on. Gregory ordered everyone back inside, laughing and saying that the only way he could get his wife into bed with him was to rough her up a bit. "Only a lovers' quarrel, folks. Elaine loves it."

How she hated him that night. When they were alone on deck again he walked over to her, smiled and extended his hand. She slapped it aside and got to her feet. She had been abused and humiliated. She would never forgive him for that. She started to storm back to their quarters. He grabbed her arm. Without knowing what she was doing she swung at him with all her might, digging her nails into his face. Her claws went deep, bringing streaks of blood. Gregory yelped in pain and covered his face with his hands. He staggered backward toward the rail. He hit it with more force than he had intended, not realizing it was as close to him as it was.

At first Elaine thought he were merely leaning over it. Then, too late, she saw that he had lost his balance. He screamed as he toppled into the sea. She became hysterical and began screaming for help as she watched him thrashing about in the cold water. No one answered her cries. Everyone thought the lovers' quarrel had merely reached a peak.

No one came back out on deck except Leland Harshaw. He just stood there with his hands on his hips smiling at her. She ran to him, half dragging him to the rail, and pleaded with him to help her husband. Leland Harshaw was not a man to help anyone, especially Gregory Brandon, who owned the one thing Leland wanted more than anything else in the world: Elaine.

She shrieked at him and beat on his chest until she had exhausted her strength. When she looked down again, Gregory Brandon was gone.

When she regained consciousness many hours later, Leland Harshaw was seated in a chair beside her bed. He was still smiling his horribly sadistic smile. She loathed him.

"Everyone thinks you killed him," he said.

Terror clutched at her throat. "I killed him? But that isn't so," she stammered. "You saw. You were there. It was an accident."

He kept smiling and shook his head. "I saw nothing."

"But you must have seen. I saw you standing in the shadows when Gregory tried to help me to my feet."

Leland put his hands together and propped his chin on them. "Of course," he said evenly, "I could say that I saw everything. I could confirm your story that it was an accident."

"But it isn't a story. It *was* an accident."

"Dear Elaine. Everyone heard you two fighting that night. Everyone saw you lying on the deck. The next thing everyone knows is that Gregory drowned. Now surely you don't think the authorities are going to think he committed suicide?"

"Of course he didn't commit suicide. I'm not asking anyone to believe that. He fell. It was an accident."

"You pushed him."

"No!"

"Yes. I saw it."

"That's a lie and you know it."

Leland laughed. "And who do you suppose is going to believe you if I tell them what I saw?"

Elaine's eyes widened in fright. "You wouldn't."

Leland simply nodded. "I would. Unless . . ."

His proposition was easy to understand but extremely difficult to accept. She hated Leland Harshaw even more than she'd hated Gregory Brandon. Leland was cruel and sadistic beyond description. She had slept with him once at Gregory's insistence. It had had to do with some big land deal in California in which Gregory needed Leland's support. Gregory considered that sort of thing one of her normal duties. Leland had been harsh and uncaring. He had hurt her. Afterward she had told Gregory she was leaving him. Gregory had threatened that he would expose her as the slut everyone knew she was and would make sure she'd never see her children again. She had to back down; separation or divorce would only make things worse for her.

Elaine quickly realized that there was no way out of her predicament but to accept Leland's proposition. "And what of my children?" she had asked.

He continued to smile. "They can live with us."

That settled it. Having her children with her would more than compensate for having Leland Harshaw as a husband.

Earlier it had been Gregory's order that had sent the children away to schools. After marrying Leland, that order had come from Elaine herself. That day she had died inside, but she had no other recourse. She had, of course, heard the rumors about Leland's penchant for having sex with young girls, but she had never thought it extended to little tots of Cynthia's age. She'd almost killed him with a butcher knife the night she found him fondling her. Afterward he tried to talk Elaine into bringing both Greg and Cindy into bed with them. Elaine knew that it would only be a matter of time before Leland succeeded in sexually abusing her children. Of course the children didn't know why they were again sent away.

Over the years all they understood was that their stepfather pleaded and begged them to come and stay with him and their mother, charming them with expensive presents, tempting them with gifts of money, but their mother refused to have them.

She murdered Leland Harshaw on Christmas Day, 1965. Leland had arranged for Greg and Cynthia to come home for Christmas as a surprise for their mother. Their plane became snowbound at O'Hare Airport. Leland was gloating over how he intended seducing his two young stepchildren. After nine years of marriage Elaine had learned to drink in order to help assuage the abuse she had to take from him. She slapped him. He beat her unmercifully, breaking her jaw and one arm. Somehow she managed to get the gun out of the desk drawer in the library. She put a single shot through the center of his forehead. Her children found her standing over Leland's dead body when they arrived home.

Expensive lawyers got her off, claiming self-defense. By the time the scandal died down Greg and Cynthia were back in school and refused to come home. They hated her.

"You never cared for anyone but yourself," Cynthia said, bringing Elaine out of her reverie.

Elaine kept her eyes closed over her tears. She'd tried. She had tried so very hard. She'd lived her whole life only for Greg and Cynthia, and what had it gotten her? With all her sacrifices on their behalf she had only earned their contempt.

Again she sighed. What did it matter now? They had their whole lives ahead of them; hers was almost over. Her doctors had confirmed that fact. A year at the most, they'd told her. After that Cynthia and Greg could do what they wished. But in the meantime she was going to have some happiness for herself. Selfish as that might be, she felt she deserved as much.

She shook her head slightly to fight back her misery. Her thoughts wandered back to Greg. Suddenly she tensed. God! she thought. Suppose Greg showed up unexpectedly and let the cat out of the bag to Jorge. She could feel the fear creeping up inside her. As calmly as she could she asked Cynthia, "Did you say you'd heard from your brother?"

"Yes, we've kept in touch." She admired her nail polish.

"Is he still in the Orient?"

"Why?" She smiled. "Are you afraid he might show up here and throw a monkey wrench into your little plans?"

Her eyes glinted with devilment. "Too bad you can't black-mail Greg into keeping his mouth shut the way you did me."

Elaine kept her eyes closed and tried to keep her compo-sure, but she found herself engaged in a losing battle. "That was your doing, not mine, Cynthia. As much as I warned you, you persisted in getting yourself illegally involved with that Spanish gentleman. No one told you to smuggle him into the States. You were fortunate I had enough money and enough of the right connections to get you out of that mess or you'd be in a woman's prison right now." How she hated being spite-ful and vindictive.

"Which is where *you* should be," Cynthia said.

Elaine ignored her.

Cynthia stood up and looked out at the sea. "Is this any different from a prison?"

"No one is keeping you here. You can leave any time you wish, go anywhere you wish."

"You'd love that, wouldn't you? You'd like getting me out of your hair. You're horrible." She flung back her head, pout-ing like a willful child.

Elaine gave herself up to defeat. She felt her nerves fray. Yet hard as she tried she could not stop herself from saying, "Being horrible is a necessary trait when it comes to dealing with ungrateful children."

Cynthia glowered at her. "Bitch," she said from between her clenched teeth.

Jorge stepped on deck, carrying Elaine's sandwich. He'd taken Cynthia's advice and donned a pair of cut-off jeans. He had covered himself not out of any sense of propriety but for Elaine's sake. Although he enjoyed flaunting his beautiful nakedness in front of Cynthia, he knew that it only made Elaine suffer from Cynthia's frustrated bitterness and jealousy.

He had heard Cynthia's remark and smiled at her. "I see you are being your usual sweet, charming self, Cindy." He handed Elaine the sandwich and took her hand. "My mother would have spanked me good if I spoke disrespectfully to any of my older brothers or sisters." He shrugged and grinned at Elaine. "But then I never had to worry, because I never had any brothers or sisters."

"Our mother was always too busy to teach me and my brother better manners," Cynthia said, shooting a meaningful look at Elaine.

"Brother?" Jorge inquired.

Cynthia smiled sweetly. "Oh," she said, arching her brows in mock surprise. "Didn't Elaine tell you she has a younger brother?" The expression on her face was ugly.

Elaine tensed. "Yes," she said quickly. "Greg is traveling somewhere. We haven't heard from him in months."

"You mean *you* haven't heard from him," Cynthia said. She looked at Jorge. "Greg is in Madrid. He might be coming here, so you will have a chance to meet the rest of our little family."

Elaine gave a little nervous laugh. "Oh, I don't think Greg will come here, darling. You remember that he never got along very well with us girls."

Us girls, Cynthia thought with a shudder of disgust. The old fool. Then she forced herself to smile and lean back against the railing of the deck. "You mean he never got along with you, Elaine." She grinned, showing perfect white teeth. "But I'm sure he'll be here. I wrote and told him about you and Jorge. I'm sure he will be most anxious to get a look at his prospective brother-in-law." She slurred "brother-in-law," making it sound dirty.

Elaine nibbled at her sandwich. She noticed that her hands were trembling again. She swallowed but tasted nothing. "You never told me you and Greg were corresponding," she said in a tight voice.

Cynthia took a deep breath. She had upset Elaine, and she loved the feeling of having the upper hand. "Then I never tell you everything," she said. "After all, sisters do have secrets from one another." She glanced up at Jorge. "You'll like Greg. He's kinda wild, but one thing about him is that he always calls a spade a spade." Looking directly at Elaine, she grinned. Her eyes were asking Elaine, Well, how are you going to get out of this one?

FINALLY, ROD THOUGHT AS THE STEWARDESS walked by, checking to make sure everyone's seat belt was

fastened. The trip from New York to Majorca had been by
fits and starts. A change of planes in Lisbon for Madrid. Another change at Madrid for Barcelona. An overnight stop before connecting with a flight to Palma, the only major city
on Majorca. And all during the long, tedious trip Rod's anxiety had mounted. The young Majorca-bound passenger he'd
sat with ever since embarking in New York had been some
help in keeping his mind off his troubles, but still, the boy was
close to Lisa's age and only served as a reminder of her.

The plane banked and started toward the runway. Rod
didn't feel the motion. When he wasn't worrying about Lisa
he found himself thinking of Helen. He felt dirty and ashamed
for having picked up the whore in Barcelona the night before.
There wasn't any reason to feel guilty any more. Helen was
dead. But even so, as if through habit, the guilt remained.

"Hey, we're coming in, Mr. Shepherd." The young man
sitting next to him nudged Rod's arm and nodded toward the
window. "That's Palma down there. I sure hope it's as exciting as everybody says it is."

Helen dissolved into the noise of the engines as Rod
glanced down at the rolling landscape, the rooftops, the spires,
the sweeping beaches of Palma sitting so snug and secure at
the edge of the island. Lisa was down there somewhere, waiting for him.

"Is this your first time here, Mr. Shepherd?" the boy asked.

Rod nodded.

"Mine too." The lad smiled. "But I told you that already."
He peered down from the window. The plane suddenly leveled
off. Majorca disappeared and was replaced by a wide expanse
of puffy-clouded sky. "Man, just think," he said, relaxing back
in his seat and putting his hands behind his head. "Majorca.
The Isle of Love, they call it."

Rod had to smile. "Oh, I suppose you're an expert on love,"
he said.

"I've been around," the boy answered. Rod saw his eyes
slide away, then drop down, the way people's do when they
aren't telling a whole truth. "There isn't much I don't know,"
the boy said, keeping his eyes veiled to hide any chance of
their betraying him.

"At sixteen?" Rod said, grinning.

The boy sat straight up in his seat. "I'm eighteen and a half.

I'll be nineteen next Christmas." There was a spark of fire in his eyes.

Rod saw the hurt only youngsters can show when you guess them to be younger than they are. He'd been the same, he thought. When he was sixteen he wanted to be eighteen. At eighteen he tried to pass for twenty-one. "Sorry," he said. He glanced down at the ground that was rushing up to meet them. "We're coming in." He leaned back and closed his eyes. The worst parts about flying were the takeoff and the landing. Eighteen and a half, he thought with a smile, forcing his mind away from their descent. Even the six months were important enough to tack on when you were young enough to afford it. At forty-two he was only too willing to lose five years—ten if he thought he could get away with it.

"My dad's meeting me," the boy said. Rod didn't answer. "Is your daughter meeting you, Mr. Shepherd?"

Rod kept his eyes closed. He wished he hadn't mentioned Lisa. It brought a sudden pain. "No. No one's meeting me." He gripped the arms of the seat and tried not to concentrate on the landing.

"Dad will have the car. We could give you a lift if you like."

The boy didn't seem the least bit tense. But, Rod thought, at eighteen—eighteen and a half—one didn't think about plane crashes, death, that sort of thing. Only old people thought of such things. Despite his fling with the whore the night before, he felt very old this morning. "I'll grab a cab, thanks," he said, almost under his breath.

The boy didn't insist. "Okay, but don't forget my name. Paul Verdugo. Dad's a big wheel here, my mother tells me. I haven't seen him since I was little. My mom wasn't too happy about me seeing him even now. They're divorced. Have been for about ten years, I guess."

Rod wished he'd stop rattling on.

His heart leaped up into his throat when the plane made a sudden drop. The boy didn't seem to notice it. Then the wheels hit the ground with a screech and the plane bounced back up into the air, lurching sickeningly to one side. Rod grimaced, expecting the worst.

"Hey," Paul Verdugo said with a laugh. "What's the pilot doing, testing the ground to see if it's hard enough?"

The wheels touched the runway again; this time they grabbed and held on to it. Rod breathed a sigh of relief as

they braked and started to taxi toward the terminal. His heart
was thumping in his chest as he looked out the window. Well,
he was here at last. Majorca. Christ, why hadn't Lisa gotten
herself arrested in the United States rather than on this godforsaken little island where most likely no one spoke English?

He stepped from the plane and started across the tarmac,
head down. In his depression he was oblivious of the air, as
delicate as fine crystal, clean and bright and brimming with
the fragrances of pine and sea. He breathed it, but its intoxi-
cation had no effect on him. Everything sparkled, as though
recently washed by a soft spring rain, but he saw none of it,
none of the bustling activity of the place that acted like a
barrier against worries and problems and troubles.

The scurrying and prattle of the people inside the terminal
just served to amplify his dejection. He stood for a moment
adjusting his ears to the flood of Spanish and French chatter
going on around him as passengers uttered cries of recognition, happiness as they were claimed by waiting friends and
relatives. Some of them were speaking English, he noticed.
Well, that at least was something. The signs too, he saw, were
printed in English as well as in Spanish and French. He hadn't
expected that.

Rod glanced at young Paul Verdugo, who was standing next
to him searching the faces in the crowd of welcomers. The
boy's eyes were bright as sapphires; his whole being seemed
to shimmer with enthusiasm and anticipation.

Rod looked around the terminal. "Where's the customs
check?" he asked Paul.

"We don't have to go through customs here. We're still in
Spain. Custom checks are only when you cross from one
country to another." Paul saw a very distinguished-looking
man raise his arm hesitantly as if not sure of himself. Then the
man waved.

"There's Dad," Paul said excitedly. He started to hurry
over to the man, but checked himself and turned back to
Rod. "Are you sure we can't give you a lift, Mr. Shepherd?"

"I'm sure," Rod said, putting out his hand.

Paul took it and wrapped his hand around Rod's thumb,
then the heel of the hand.

They struggled with the handshake for a second. It always
made Rod self-conscious when youngsters wrestled with him

over the old way of shaking hands and their new way. It was like a struggle for position. He always lost.

"Don't forget to call," Paul said. "My dad's first name is Paul too, and I'm sure he's listed. He's with the American Consulate," he called as he hurried away.

Rod saw Paul and the older man stand and smile at each other for a moment. The the father's hand went out. Paul took it. Rod smiled, seeing that Paul was using the old-fashioned way of shaking hands. The next moment Paul threw himself into the man's arms and his father wrapped his arms tightly around his son.

He wondered if Lisa would greet him like that. She wouldn't. He'd be lucky if she even smiled at him.

He watched Paul and his father walk quickly toward the exit, their arms around each other's shoulders. He felt a pang of resentment toward Paul's father. The guy had run out on the boy ten years ago. He hadn't had to go through the agonies of bringing up a teen-ager. He'd escaped all of the worrying, the responsibilities. He'd hidden himself on the other side of the world and waited until he had a grown son to send for. No wonder the mother begrudged Paul's coming. But how did you get an eighteen-year-old kid to understand that? To Paul, his father represented mystery and change and excitement. His mother, on the other hand, was only a reminder of the dull, boring day-to-day existence he'd grown up with.

His resentment of Mr. Verdugo grew into a kind of pride in himself and in Helen. At least neither one of them had abandoned Lisa when she needed them. She never thought she needed them, of course. What kid ever does? From what he knew about teen-agers, parents were just another something they had to tolerate. Regardless, they'd done their best, especially Helen. He admitted that he had spoiled Lisa, whereas Helen had been harsh and strict at times.

Funny, he thought. In spite of all his spoiling, it was Helen that Lisa respected now. He was only someone she could use, as her cablegram proved. "Arrested in Palma, Majorca. Being held. Lisa." That was all it had said. No details. No call for help. No "Love, Lisa." Just "Lisa."

His shoulders sagged as he pushed himself toward the exit, to the baggage-claim area. Whether Lisa liked it or not, he'd get her out of this mess and take her back home where she belonged, even if he had to drag her by the hair of the head. And he wouldn't be so damned lenient in the future, he vowed. He'd adopt Helen's attitude and start being a little more strict, a little more demanding. He wouldn't let Lisa have her own way again. He'd straighten her out if it was the last thing he did.

His vow seemed to brace his shoulders and make his steps less heavy. He fixed a determined tilt to his chin. Things would work out, he told himself. He'd make them work out.

AT THE OTHER SIDE OF THE TERMINAL THINGS were definitely not working out for Sheila and Charlie Cranston.

"What do you mean we're holding counterfeit tickets?" Charlie boomed at the airline reservation clerk.

The young Spaniard looked apologetic. "I'm sorry, Mr. and Mrs. Cranston, but the book of airline tickets you have were among a lot of blank tickets that were stolen. The serial numbers check with those here on this list given us by the police."

Charlie puffed up his already too fat body and leaned menacingly toward the clerk. "Police, shit! I'm the police. I'm a cop in New York. Do you think a cop in New York would be carrying counterfeit or stolen airline tickets?" He reached over and snatched the list of numbers from the clerk's hand. "There's gotta be a mistake here," he said as he started to match the numbers on the illegal list with those on his and Sheila's tickets.

Sheila leaned anxiously on his shoulder and peered at the numbers printed on the page. She started to chew her gum more rapidly. "What are we gonna to, Charlie?"

Charlie saw the corresponding numbers and flipped the paper back to the clerk. "There's a mistake of some kind," he said. "Let me talk to your boss. I'll get this straightened out."

The clerk nodded politely. "Certainly, Mr. Cranston. This way, please." He came from behind the counter and led them toward a door tucked at the back of the terminal. Grabbing Sheila's arm, Charlie shoved past the Spaniard and burst through the door. His corpulent body filled the doorway completely, making it necessary for Sheila to stand behind him and peek over his shoulder at the official sitting behind the desk inside the office.

"Are you in charge here?" Charlie demanded.

The man smiled and got to his feet. *"Si, señor.* What is it I can do for you?"

Charlie strode angrily into the office. The reservation clerk eased himself around Charlie and Sheila. "Unfortunately, Señor Perez," the clerk said softly, addressing his superior, "Mr. and Mrs. Cranston are traveling on tickets that have been reported as stolen." He produced the list of illegal serial numbers together with Charlie's and Sheila's tickets.

Señor Perez merely glanced at them as they were handed to him, then waved the clerk away. "I see," he said kindly. "You may go, Juan. I'll take care of this." Señor Perez smiled. "Sit down, Mr. Cranston, Mrs. Cranston," he said, offering them chairs. The clerk withdrew, closing the door softly behind him.

Charlie hesitated, then motioned for Sheila to sit. He pulled his chair closer to hers and squeezed himself into the narrow seat. The man behind the desk looked worried for an instant; would the wooden legs manage to support this massive weight? He cleared his throat and studied the tickets for a moment. Americans, he thought. Why did they always talk and dress so loud? The woman looked as though she were dressed for a carnival. She was pretty enough, he supposed, if one could scrape through the layers of cosmetics. A splendid figure, he noticed. Very shapely; indeed, most exciting. He wished she'd stop cracking her chewing gum, however. He raised his head and smiled at them, wondering what possibly could have attracted her to this mountain of a man.

"I regret, Señor Cranston, that it does appear that the airline tickets you both hold are, without question, illegal and must be confiscated."

"Look, you," Charlie shouted, pointing a finger at the man. "I'm a detective in New York. What in hell would I be doing with illegal airline tickets?"

The man shrugged indifferently. "You are most likely innocent of any wrongdoing, naturally. But that is not the question, *señor*. No one is accusing you of having stolen these tickets, merely of possessing them. It is unfortunate that you have been victimized by some unscrupulous travel agent in New York; it is doubly unfortunate that these tickets must be taken away from you."

"Hey, wait a minute," Sheila said, jumping to her feet and making a grab for the tickets. "A very good friend of my husband's sold us those tickets."

"Shut, up, Sheila," Charlie snapped. "Sit down."

Sheila wavered on her feet for a moment, then quietly settled back into her chair.

Charlie leaned his fat arms on the edge of the desk, stretching his floral-print sport shirt across his broad shoulders. For an alarming second Señor Perez was afraid the seams of the material would split apart. Charlie narrowed his eyes. "Look. We know all about the little con jobs some of you foreigners pull in order to get dough out of us Americans. If you think you're going to take away our tickets and make us buy new ones you've got another thought comin'."

Senor Perez leaned back, unintimidated. "This is no con job, as you say, Mr. Cranston. This list was furnished to us by the airline officials in the United States. I will be pleased to put you in touch with the proper authorities at the American Consulate who will substantiate what I tell you."

Charlie heaved a sigh. He slumped down in his chair, remembering now how easily and cheaply he had acquired those tickets. He should have known there was something wrong with them. Charlie had thought the travel agent had just been doing him a favor because Charlie had politely looked the other way about the numbers racket the guy was carrying on under the counter. So their tickets were hot. Well, he'd get even with that sonofabitch. He shook his head. "Nah, I believe you," he said with resignation.

"This is not an uncommon occurrence, Señor Cranston. If the person who sold you these tickets is known to you I would sincerely suggest that you so inform the authorities in New York. In fact, I will be happy to handle it from this end if you wish."

Charlie didn't like Señor Perez on sight. He didn't like any slicked-down-hair greasers, as he called them. You couldn't trust any of them. They were cocky enough in New York; on their own home soil they were worse, he found. But then

Charlie didn't like anybody with a foreign accent or who even looked as if they might not have born and raised in New York. He hated the smug smile on the *señor*'s kisser, but there wasn't anything he could do about it. He'd been made the patsy, and he'd just have to swallow his pride. "Nah, I'll handle it myself. I'm a detective in the 17th Precinct. I'll have my boys take care of it."

"Charlie!" Sheila protested. "How are you gonna handle it? We're in Majorca." She pronounced the *j*. "If they take our tickets, how are we gonna get back to New York?"

He reached over and took her hand. "It's okay, kid. Don't worry about it."

"But Charlie—"

"I said, don't worry about it, Sheila." He let go of her hand and looked at Señor Perez, giving him a sheepish grin. "I guess we'll just have to buy new airline tickets," he said.

Señor Perez nodded and fanned out his hands. "Unfortunately, you will, *señor*. I'm sorry." He scooped up the tickets and slipped them into his desk drawer. "These will be turned over to the proper authorities."

"Where are we gonna get dough for new airline tickets?" Sheila demanded.

"We'll get it, we'll get it," Charlie said. "I said not to worry, kitten, so don't you worry, okay?" He took her hand. "Come on, kid. Let's get the hell out of here."

"But Charlie . . . "

He dragged her out of the chair and out of the office, not bothering to say goodbye to Señor Perez. Once back in the terminal he let go of her hand and shook his head. "Bastard," he muttered.

"I don't get it, Charlie," Sheila said. "Some friend you got in the travel business. What do we do now?"

"Sheila, I told you a thousand times not to worry about it. I'll straighten everything out." He ran a hand through his sparse crop of hair. "The lousy rat. Wait'll I get my hands on that sonofabitch."

"And just how are you gonna do that if you're here and he's in New York?"

"I'll do it," Charlie swore under his breath. His teeth clenched, his eyes narrowed. He slammed a fist into his palm. "The sonofabitch."

Sheila shrugged. "Well, at least I got to see Lisbon and

Madrid. That's a lot more than I ever thought I'd get to see."

"You're gonna see a lot more, kid."

"You mean we ain't goin' home yet?"

He took her arm and steered her toward a counter where a swarthy-looking woman was clearing away some cups. "Not on your life. We're gonna have the vacation we set out to have."

"How? We ain't got enough money."

"I'll get it. Look, go have yourself a cup of coffee and a doughnut or something. I've got to make a phone call. Order me a beer and a sandwich. I won't be but a couple of minutes."

"They don't have no coffee and doughnuts here," Sheila argued. "It'll be that thick brown stuff they served us back in Spain." She rolled her eyes. "I bet they never even heard of a doughnut."

"Ask for American coffee. They'll water it down or something."

"But—"

"Don't argue. Git," he said as he slapped her gently on the ass.

Sheila giggled. "I bet they won't have any beer or sandwiches either."

"They'll have them. They'll have them," Charlie said. "If they don't, ask for cold meat and cheese and rolls. I'm hungry. I'm a growing boy, remember."

"Some boy," Sheila said as she eyed him appreciatively and let her eyes roll upward again.

"Besides, I'm on a honeymoon, ain't I? I need all my strength."

Under all her makeup Sheila felt a slight flush to her cheeks. She winked at him. "I'll make that two orders of cold cuts."

"Hey," Charlie said, looking indignant. "Are you inferring that I'm petering out?"

"Not petering out, lover. Not you. It's just that the more you give me the more I want." She gave him a peck on the cheek. Suddenly her expression went serious. She looked deep into his eyes and said, "I love you, Detective Sergeant Cranston."

"And I love you, Mrs. Cranston." Without caring who was watching, he pulled her roughly into his arms and kissed her hard on the mouth. What did he care how it looked to these foreign-looking jokers?

After lingering for a moment in his embrace, Sheila shoved him away. "Charlie. People are watchin'."

"Let 'em watch." He started to pull her against him again, but she struggled out of his grasp.

She gave him a seductive smile and winked at him again. "Go make your silly phone call," she said as she started away. "But hurry it up, will ya? We don't want the hotel lousin' up our reservations." She turned and walked away, swinging her hips most provocatively.

Charlie shook his head in admiration. He clucked his tongue and gave her a loud wolf whistle. Sheila turned slightly and waved, putting a wider swing to her hips.

You're a lucky guy, Charlie Cranston, he told himself as he started toward the telephones that looked like a row of Spanish soldiers standing against the far wall. All his so-called buddies on the force had warned him against marrying a girl like Sheila. So what if she was an ex-con? He was glad he hadn't listened to any of them. At least she wasn't a cheap hooker like the lousy bitches they all wound up marrying. That was one of the many things Charlie liked about Sheila: she hated hookers almost as much as he did. Yeah, Sheila had class, all right. She'd starve before she'd sell her body for a couple of fast bucks.

It was that very principle that had gotten Sheila in trouble to begin with. She was starving and she just couldn't bring herself to whoring, so she'd stolen to keep herself alive.

Poor, dumb, high-principled doll baby. She didn't even have enough know-how to steal and get away with it. So she spent time in the slammer. So what? She'd paid her debt. She was straight as an arrow now, and she'd promised him that she'd never do anything dumb like that again. There wasn't the slightest doubt in his mind that she would keep that promise.

No sir, he wouldn't give up Sheila for anything, not even Raquel Welch. What beats all, he told himself, was that she loved him. There wasn't any doubt about that. Crazy as it seemed, it was true. He'd had too many experiences with women who'd pretended they loved him but something away back in his head always let him know they were conning him. With Sheila he just knew she loved him.

As he neared the bank of telephones he glanced over his

shoulder to make sure Sheila was out of sight. He swung left and went toward the baggage-check area. He stepped up to the counter and handed the attendant a claim check.

"I had a bag sent on here ahead which you should be holding for me," he said, giving the attendant the ticket. "I don't want to take it out, I just want to get something out of it."

Whether the attendant understood him or not he didn't know, but the guy disappeared into the dim recesses of cubbyholes and shelves, comparing the number of Charlie's claim check with the numbers printed on the tags attached to the suitcases and parcels. He came back almost immediately and handed Charlie a large brown satchel.

"That's it. Thanks." Charlie carried the satchel into a corner and snapped it open after unlocking it. He took out a stack of bills from the dozens of stacks crammed inside and stuffed the money into his inside coat pocket. He snapped shut the satchel and relocked it. He took it back to the attendant and handed it to him. "I'll pick this up in a couple of days," he said.

As he walked back to join Sheila he started to think about the lousy fink who'd sold him the bogus airline tickets. The bastard would regret that, Charlie swore. He wouldn't be able to take care of it himself, but he had a friend on the force who'd see that the sonofabitch got what was coming to him. Nobody fucked around with Charlie Cranston and got away with it.

"They only had ham and cheese," Sheila said as Charlie eased himself onto the stool next to hers. "That okay?"

"Yeah, sure. You know I like anything."

"That's your trouble, Charlie. Maybe if you started being a little more particular about what you put in that belly of yours you wouldn't put on so much weight."

He took her hand and put it on his gut. "I thought you liked fat men."

She grinned and pecked him on the cheek. "I only like you, fat man." She turned back to the cup of coffee that sat in front of her. "Did you make your call?"

"Yeah, everything's goin' to be okay. I called Tony—you know, my buddy Tony Gaventi down at the precinct. He said he'd go see that travel-agent bastard right away and there'd be new tickets wired to the hotel in a day or so."

Sheila squealed and almost upset her coffee when she threw

her arms around Charlie's neck. She stiffened slightly and eased herself away from him. "Hey, how come you got everything fixed up so quick? I heard somebody say telephoning across the ocean always took hours."

Charlie merely chewed off a part of a roll and stuffed a piece of cheese into his mouth, following that with a swig of beer right from the bottle. "Honey, when you are a cop you get certain privileges. I just told the operator it was police business—which it was," he added when he saw her suspicious look. "They put me through right away. No sweat."

Sheila put her head on his shoulder. "You're the greatest, Charlie. I always knew I'd marry a genius."

"I'm no genius, baby. Just a big fat slob who'd do anything in the world for the woman he loves."

"Meaning who?" she asked coyly, fishing for a compliment.

Charlie grinned. "Meaning Raquel Welch, of course. Who else?"

THE ELDER PAUL VERDUGO HAD HIS ARM around his son's shoulders as they started away from the sprawling airport. They were in a custom-built American car with a uniformed driver at the wheel.

"Pretty classy," Paul said, looking around the interior.

"Didn't your mother tell you that your father is a successful man?"

"Yes, she did, but she never said you were this successful," he said, admiring the built-in bar, the windows which one saw out of but no one could see in.

"Still fooling around with your piano studies?" his father asked.

"Yes. But I'm not just fooling around, Dad. I'm going to be a concert pianist someday."

"Well, there's lots of time for you to decide what you want to do with your life. You're away from your mother now— at least for a while. Maybe you'll like it here as much as I do and decide this is where you want to live."

"That's possible," Paul said enthusiastically. "From what
I've seen so far I think Majorca is just about the most beautiful place I've ever seen." He allowed his look of enthusiasm
to fade a little when he added, "But I'll never give up the
piano."

His father patted his knee. "As I said, there is plenty of
time to talk about that another time." He pointed out the
window. "This isn't exactly the most glamorous part of the
island," he said nodding to the landscape through which they
were passing.

Although the road was a bit rough, Paul Jr. was impressed
by the sweep of the terrain. One side was bordered by sea,
the other by rolling fields backed by towering mountains. The
smell of salt air and almonds greeted him as he rolled down
the window, and he could see the low rambling waves break
on the beach. Sand was blowing lazily onto the road, trying
to encroach on the marshy fields on the other side of the
highway. The place reeked of sun worship and summer vaca-
tions, long idle days, picnics and jacketless evenings. The
enchantment of the island was overpowering. Paul inhaled
deeply and wondered if he would ever want to leave Majorca.

He was hypnotized by the place. From empty fields and
stretches of shoreline Paul suddenly found they were driving
in Palma. The transition had happened so quickly he'd hardly
noticed it. They sped along the edge of the bay. Ahead the
great Cathedral of Palma loomed over them on the right.
There wasn't much to the city that Paul could see, but then
the car turned sharply to the right on Avenue Antonio Maura
and he found himself encircled by tight rows of buildings,
old and weatherbeaten by sun and salt air, their tops tilted
slightly toward one another, looking like lines of stately dow-
agers at a cotillion engaged in *tête-à-tête*.

He ignored the tall impressive new hotels that stretched
out on the left, overlooking the sea and built more for view
and convenience than for charm and romance. He liked the
older buildings, the narrow streets, the Spanish aura that
shouted at him. Even the air smelled Spanish now that they'd
left the bay behind, thick with garlic and saffron, rose wine
and fruit. He could almost feel the softness of the black lace
mantillas, the grace and poise of the flamenco dancers, dark-
skinned men in black suits plucking dreamily on ribbon-
necked guitars.

"That's Almudaina," his father said, nodding to an impressive structure they were passing. As an aside he added, "Roll up the window, Paul. We're in the city now."

Paul pushed the electric button and the window slid upward. Through it he saw Almudaina, a completely circular structure with projecting towers and a high bridge that led to the main castle, all of it surrounded by a wide moat.

His father said, "It was once the principal royal residence here in Palma."

Paul was too absorbed in the city itself to pay Almudaina too much attention. They passed into the central city with its many sidewalk cafés, its quaint stores, its glass-fronted clubs where very Spanish-looking old men sat and stared reflectively out through the glass.

"I'm glad you came at this time of year rather than later," his father said. "In the summer, this trip from the airport would have taken us twice as long. Tourists descend on us like locusts. We have about eight hundred sightseeing buses to accommodate them and they clog every road. It's a nightmare, but it's exciting."

"You don't seem to mind the tourist invasion," Paul said.

"Mind. Oh no. Majorca has been invaded by so many in its glorious history, what do a few thousand tourists matter? At least they come to enjoy themselves and not to try to rule the island."

Paul kept looking out the window. "I never saw such a well-scrubbed city."

"Yes, Palma is a pearl. But there is so much of the island that is equally clean and beautiful. Don't pay too much attention to all those modern glass hotels that run along the bay. They are only for the tourists who still want to be in New York or London. We'll go up into the mountains, or drive along the winding roads and see the cliffs, the coves, the terraced orchards. They have windmills here too, just like the Dutch." His father put back his head and gave himself up to reverie. "Yes, Palma has everything, the bright lights of Broadway, churches more beautiful than Rome's, castles more impressive than Germany's. Yet with all this, Majorca tints everything in Spanish colors. You will never mistake that you are anywhere but on Majorca." He squeezed his son's shoulder and laughed. "I'm sounding a little like the president of the chamber of commerce, aren't I?"

"A little," Paul said, laughing too. "But I don't mind. It's just about the most exciting city I've ever seen."

"And you haven't seen any of it yet. Wait. I predict you'll never want to go back to your mother again. At least I hope you won't." He took his arm from around Paul's shoulder and pointed ahead. "That's where we live," he said.

To Paul it looked like a palace. He whistled.

"And wait until you meet Laura. You're going to like your stepmother."

"I'm sure I'll love her," Paul said. He couldn't know then how foolish his polite words would seem to him later.

TWO CREWMEN STEADIED THE LAUNCH AS A third helped Elaine onto the quay. Her chauffeur quickly approached and took her tote bag from her. Speaking Spanish, the younger of the crewmen asked if the Señora Brandon would be needing them the rest of the evening. In equally fluent Spanish, she told them she might, informing them to keep themselves available. She knew what was behind the young man's question. She turned to the older of the three young men and said, "And if I hear any more gossip about the young ladies you have been entertaining aboard my yacht I will dismiss the lot of you. Is that clear?"

The man opened his mouth to protest, but seeing the stern, cold look in Elaine's eyes he closed it again and bowed his head. *"Si, señora,"* he mumbled as he toyed with the lanyard he held in his hands.

The younger crewman glanced at Jorge, who was standing beside Elaine. Jorge ignored him. He knew the men resented him. After all, if he were in their place he'd feel resentful too. They were young men he'd grown up with, known practically all his life. Jorge had bettered himself in their eyes; they had not. It didn't matter to them how Jorge had bettered himself. Methods were not important to the Majorcans. It was the final status that counted. In the course of time, naturally, one's status might quickly change. They did not think about that. They thought only of the present and of their glorious past. The future was something that would come of its own accord. It was not that they did not believe in a future; it was simply that they were a people accustomed to pirates moving in to sack their lovely island—which had happened all too frequently in bygone centuries—or to armies of other nations which felt obliged to lay siege to their shining city of Palma. Futures were for the stronger; the present and the past is what belonged to the poorer Majorcans.

Jorge didn't feel the least bit ashamed for having risen above their ranks in the manner in which he had. They had had the same opportunities as he. The only difference between them was that they took pride in their poor, peasant Majorcan lot; he detested it. When he was fourteen he had seen how the wealthy people lived. He hung around the edges of that rich world until a chance arose to break into the circle. Once inside he swore he'd never leave it regardless of the cost. He delighted in clothes that didn't scratch, and long, sleek automobiles that were converted into new ones when they were a year or so old. He liked servants who bowed and hurried to carry out his wishes, food that tasted smooth and pleasant to his palate and not thick and oily and unseasoned. Thin gold watches felt comfortable on his wrist; he liked the feel of cashmere and custom-made shoes, silk bed sheets and sunken marble bathtubs with gold faucets.

What did it matter what he did in exchange for luxuries? He knew what his friends and family said about him behind his back. It bothered him more than he cared to admit, yet it did not bother him so much that he wanted to change his ways. He'd never go back to being poor. Never. The squalor, the hunger, the smell of poverty were far more frightening than what he'd become. No, he swore he'd never be poor again.

"You seem to be upset, Elaine," Jorge said as he followed her into the back seat of the limousine.

"It's nothing," Elaine answered, reaching for his hand. The chauffeur closed the door and got behind the wheel. He turned the car away from the dock. Jorge could almost hear the crewmen laughing at him. He didn't care.

"I'm sorry I failed to mention Greg to you," Elaine said, squeezing Jorge's hand.

"Greg? Oh, your brother."

Elaine made a nervous little sound in her throat, which she meant to mean "yes." It was bad enough to have palmed Cynthia off as her sister, she could not bring herself to expand the lie. To try to alleviate her guilt feelings she made a fluttering little motion with her hand. "It's just that there was so much else to talk about," she said, hoping she sounded flippant and unconcerned. "When I'm with you I find I can't think about anyone else," she added.

"My darling," he said, taking her hand and pressing it to his lips. "You need never apologize to me for anything. I don't care if you have a hundred brothers lurking in the background. I did not fall in love with you because of your family."

"You're sweet," Elaine said, laying her hand on his cheek. She relaxed back against the seat as the car carried them along the road that skirted the bay. Behind them the Cathedral of Palma spread out its protective shadow as the city began to stir from its afternoon siesta. There was little traffic; the driver accelerated, leaving the city behind.

Elaine's pink-and-white villa sat on a peak of land that lay in the curve of Palma Bay. She had bought it for the privacy it afforded, not for its impressive size. She longed for that privacy now. She was glad Cynthia had not returned with them. Knowing Cynthia, right at this moment she was busily checking out, first-hand, the rumors about the new crewman.

The chauffeur steered the car smoothly onto a narrow stretch of road that wound its way through a sprawling orchard of gnarled olive trees. Elaine's third and last husband, Miguel, had tried to talk her into paving the winding dirt drive, but Elaine wouldn't hear of it. It seemed indecent to have a paved roadway winding its modern way through this delightfully ancient grove of olive trees.

The car hit a deep rut, jostling them on the seat. Maybe she'd made a mistake in not having the road paved. But then she'd made so many mistakes in her lifetime. Even Miguel had been a mistake. She had married him to cure her loneliness. She'd divorced him within a year when she realized Miguel had been just another of her many mistakes.

Husbands, children, life itself had all disappointed her. However, perhaps it was she who was the disappointment.

Perhaps it was she who was the failure and not her husbands or her children.

Her children. How she wished she could make them understand her. They never would. She had tried, after the trial, to explain it all to Cynthia and Greg. They were too young. Greg had laughed at her at the time. "We're not a jury," he had said. "You needn't try to win us over to your side with all your lies. You've told so many of them that you wouldn't know the truth if you fell over it."

Elaine began to toy with the straps of the tote bag, which the chauffeur had placed on the back seat. "It's because I'm self-conscious about Greg, I suppose," she said to Jorge.

Jorge's handsome brow creased. "Self-conscious? I do not understand."

"Oh, Greg and I never really got along very well. He's a strange young man. Very wild and headstrong. He's been thrown out of more schools than I care to think about."

Jorge laughed. "I can understand that. I myself hated school." He put his hand on hers. "Certainly you cannot blame yourself for his recklessness."

"No, it isn't that," Elaine said. "Being older, I tried to set an example for him, of course, but I never blamed myself for his actions."

"Then why do you feel self-conscious about Greg?"

Elaine made an awkward gesture. "I suppose it's his nature."

"His nature? What nature?"

Elaine shook her head. "I'd rather not talk about it now, Jorge. There were embarrassing things which I would just as soon forget. Do you mind?"

"Mind? No, of course I do not mind. You know how I dislike prying into other people's affairs. It is just that when something upsets you it is sometimes good to talk about it with someone."

"Promise me something, Jorge," Elaine said, gripping his hand tightly.

Jorge's eyes went serious. "Anything, my darling. Anything."

Elaine hesitated. It was as if she were searching for the courage to go on. "Well," she started, then paused again. "If Greg does show up here, please don't try to become too friendly with him."

Jorge gave a little chuckle. He shook his head. "But why? Why should I not be friendly toward my future brother-in-law?"

Elaine looked extremely agitated. "Well," she started again, then again hesitated. She licked her lips nervously. "It's just that . . . well . . . Greg is a strange sort of boy. He isn't like other boys. I just don't want you to become too closely involved with him."

Jorge laughed again. "Involved?" he said in surprise. "You sound as if you are suggesting Greg and I will fall in love or something."

Elaine jerked her hand away and turned toward the window. She put her fist to her mouth and bit down on the knuckles.

Jorge reached for her. "Elaine, what is it? What is it that you are so afraid of? Surely you know that I was only joking."

Elaine turned back to him. "That's just it, Jorge. You mustn't let anything like that happen between you and Greg."

Jorge's breath caught in his throat. "You mean your brother is . . . " He threw back his head and laughed loudly.

"Don't, Jorge. It isn't all that funny."

"Oh, my dearest, sweet, innocent Elaine," he said, taking her into his arms. "Greg is homosexual. Is that what you are trying to tell me?"

Elaine merely looked at him and couldn't bring herself to answer.

"And you are afraid he will make a pass at me and I will give in to him?"

Elaine stared at him for a moment, then quickly nodded.

Again Jorge laughed. "Oh, Elaine. Surely you should know by now that if it were men I am interested in you would have seen evidences of it in me before now. I am young, I am handsome, I am far from innocent. Many men have propositioned me. I simply am not interested in that sort of thing, not even in my weakest moments." He pulled her against him, cradling her head on his shoulder. "I am surprised at you, Elaine. I had hoped you knew me better than that."

"Oh, it isn't you that I distrust, Jorge. You don't know Greg. He is handsome, so charming, so persuasive. I love him dearly, really I do, but—"

"No amount of persuasion, charm, money or whatever, would induce me to share a bed with another man—not even this brother of yours whom you seem to think irresistible."

Elaine patted her hand on his chest. "But please, Jorge. I'm not as strong as you and I get so afraid of things at times. Stay away from Greg, for my sake, just as a favor to a silly woman like me."

"Darling, I would stay away from God if you wanted me to," he said. "So do not concern yourself any more about this brother of yours. I am sure he is a very nice fellow. After all, you did come from the same parents, so he cannot be as terrible as you think."

Elaine knew deep in her heart that she was lying again. It wasn't Greg's advances toward Jorge that she was afraid of, it was Greg's telling the truth that she feared most in the world. She'd fought for and won Jorge, but she was still not married to him. It was still possible to lose him, and Greg could easily bring about that loss. There was no doubt that Greg would come; Cynthia had obviously made sure of that.

She had to keep Greg and Jorge separated somehow. She did have some fear that Greg would make advances toward Jorge, but she felt such advances would be of no consequence, knowing Jorge as she did. In fact, she really wouldn't care if Jorge did sleep with another man. It was other women—younger women—she feared most.

"Besides," Jorge said, breaking into her thoughts. "I have known many homosexual men. Naturally I have never slept with any, but there are quite a few of my friends who are that way." He chuckled softly. "It always amuses me to learn that women are so afraid of homosexual men. They are not very different from other men outside of their sexual preferences. What one does in bed with someone does not have any direct effect on the person's character."

Elaine snuggled up close against him. His simple wisdom always impressed her.

"I have no intention of being tempted into bed with your brother Greg, my darling. That I can promise you. But I cannot promise that I will be impolite or discourteous to him. After all, he will be part of my family soon and I intend treating him as such."

"Oh, Jorge. You make me feel so ashamed," Elaine said as

she straightened up and again turned to look out the window. She could not let him see the fear in her eyes.

The limousine stopped before high grilled gates. The chauffeur pressed a button on the dashboard and they waited as the gates swung open on huge silent hinges. They drove through a high arch set in a wall twenty feet or more high, along the top of which ran a thin alarm wire that alerted them of trespassers. One of the guards patroling the grounds saluted as the limousine passed. Elaine nodded but did not look at the man. She hadn't wanted the elaborate security system that protected her and her villa, but even here on Majorca she had found that there was no escape from the prying, unfeeling intrusion of reporters and curiosity seekers. And there were those who still looked upon her as a murderess who should be disposed of, even if it meant taking the law into their own hands and dealing out the justice that the courts had refused to administer.

The fanatics had left her in peace of late. She was yesterday's headlines, and people—even the vigilantes—had short memories, preferring to fight for new causes rather than one a decade old. Still, old scars remained, and she did not exercise as much freedom as she would have wished. So, she kept the security system, more from habit than anything else. Besides, it gave employment to a few Majorcan peasant men who otherwise would have no means of supporting their families.

The driveway was wide and graveled. Palm fronds stood against a background of the mountainside to the north. Before them Elaine's sprawling villa basked in the dwindling sunlight, its pale-pink walls trying desperately to peek through the thick green vines. Terraces rose in tiers bordered with flowers and shaded by antique trees that had stood guard at their posts for centuries. Stone benches sat white and gleaming along the drive, coming into view as the car made its way slowly up the curve of the road. Beyond the villa to the south the wide expanse of the Mediterranean could be seen from the peak of the cliff on which the mansion sat like a queen's crown. The scent of the flowered valley to the north and the salt air of the sea to the south mixed into a heady, intoxicating perfume.

Elaine had always looked upon the villa as too large, too grand, but she enjoyed the way Jorge's face lit up when he looked at it, as he was looking at it now. Large and impressive as it was, she had to admit its exterior facade had an extremely satisfying and safe look about it. The main entrance was protected by a vaulted portico supported by baroque pillars, overly fancy yet majestic and impressive. This entrance was rarely used, except for formal occasions—which were few, of late. Elaine preferred the more casual entrance of the east wing, which overlooked the quiet garden with its handsome gazebo. Here a terrace of white marble and pink alabaster acted as a reception area for the less formal rooms beyond. Tall arched French doors ran the length of the terrace. The decorations topping these doors were pure Renaissance Plateresque and contrasted with the late Gothic of the upper galleries and the baroque of the main entrance. It was a confusion of styles, pitting the solid stone of the structure itself against the fragile expanse of the glass-paneled doors, the busyness of the delicate decorations and the simple, graceful curves of the Romanesque vaultings.

The main part of the house, she'd been told, had been built during the late 1700s when Majorca rivaled Venice in trade and commerce. But the Majorcan nobility, excluded from trade with the New World, withdrew their fortunes from commerce because of the increasing risks. To show off their wealth and to prove their fortunes did not depend upon ships and trade with outside nations, they invested in land and buildings. Large entrances and courtyards, elaborate staircases, wide facades embellished with loggias or galleries became quite the fashion—the more elaborate the more desirable. It was this main part of the house which Elaine liked the least because of its extravagant waste of space, yet it never failed to impress the impressionable.

The east wing was her favorite, with its three large rooms—library, drawing room and game room—facing out onto the terrace through tall French doors. The library she'd decorated to suit Miguel—rich Moroccan leather in rusts and reds, Spanish furniture, dark-paneled bookcases, an imposing mantlepiece of seventeenth-century origin commanding attention in the south wall. The room was used only sparingly now that she and Miguel were divorced, yet she enjoyed its rich, solid comfort and transacted much of her business dealings here. The larger drawing room was between the library and the game room, which was at the far eastern end of the terrace. The drawing room was the room she liked best, with its muted, soft colors, brightly bathed in the yellow sunlight that streamed through the French doors. The furnishings were simple yet exquisitely elegant, an amalgamation of classical Louis XVI and contemporary styles, Aubusson rugs, sixteenth-century tapestries. A rare D'Alcanyis hung over the fireplace. The curves, the arches, the graceful smooth lines were what she loved so much about the room. If only life were like that, smooth and clean and uncluttered; but unfortunately, for every delicate line and perfect curve life had its inevitable sharp, ugly angles. The game room was where she spent many of her evenings, trying to forget the cancer inside her by playing backgammon (at which she was very skilled) or bridge (at which she was not very expert). Jorge preferred playing billiards. She could not adapt herself to the game. She thought it ungraceful for a woman, sensual for a man. The game room had been Miguel's idea. Men liked games; they especially appreciated squareness and hard strong squares. She never cared too much for the room, although she spent time there. She never changed it, however. Men loved the room.

There were much of the grounds which she never saw or used. The tennis court was clogged with weeds, the stables empty of horses. The swimming pool, however, was currently being repaired and outfitted with the latest filtering and heating systems. Jorge loved to swim.

She had given up on life when her marriage to Miguel had ended so disastrously. Now with Jorge she wanted to start again, fixing, refurbishing, adding. She'd hire a crew for the seaplane aboard the yacht so she could show Jorge the world in the short time she had left. Money meant nothing to her. Spending it seemed to make other people much happier than it did her. She could afford to spend. Her fortune was so vast it was indecent. She had come from simple parents and a modest home. Possessing so much wealth now made her slightly uncomfortable.

The limousine stopped at the bottom of the stairway leading to the terrace of the east wing. A sudden stab of pain made her gasp, reminding her again of the uselessness of her wealth. She quickly stepped from the car unassisted and held tight to the door until the pains subsided. She took a deep breath and blinked her eyes.

She stood for a moment looking up at the high, thick walls that seemed so impregnable. Oh, she thought, how she wished these walls could keep out everyone in the world except her and Jorge. But deep in her heart she knew they wouldn't. The distant ringing of the telephone made her all the more aware that there was no way to avoid the interference of the outside world.

"ELAINE? HOW ARE YOU, DARLING? THIS IS Maggie Montgomery." The plump little woman in the expensively tailored traveling suit nervously patted at her curls with one bejeweled hand. "I'm fine, dear. Fine. But I'm having the most ghastly time here at Bahía Palace," she said, letting out a groan of exasperation.

"You're in Palma?" Elaine asked, blowing a kiss to Jorge as he trotted up the staircase.

"Of course I'm in Palma. Where else would I be? Did you get my note?"

"Note? No, Maggie. I received no note."

Maggie made a face. "Well, perhaps I forgot to write. Anyway, I'm here at the Bahía and you have simply got to put me up. This hotel is positively wretched. First they claim they received no request for a reservation from me. Then, when they did accommodate me with a suite, well, darling, I wouldn't let a servant stay in the place. Disgusting, utterly disgusting."

Elaine switched the receiver from one ear to the other to cover up her moan of despair. Maggie Mongomery was the silliest, most self-centered woman she knew. Having her in the villa would be intolerable. Still, Maggie was a very old friend and a distant relative. To deny her would be unforgivable. Elaine's reputation wasn't all that good as it was; Maggie's vicious tongue would only destroy the few social and political connections she presently had.

"Of course, Maggie, dear," Elaine said begrudgingly. "There's more than enough room for you here. Shall I send the chauffeur for you?"

"It is rather a long walk from here to there," Maggie said peevishly. It would never have occurred to Maggie Montgomery to resort to public conveyances. "Oh, Elaine," she added hesitantly. "Nancy Winston is with me."

The young girl beside Maggie shook her head frantically. She breathed a silent but emphatic "No."

"You remember Nancy," Maggie said into the mouthpiece. "Angela's little girl. Poor thing never gets to go anywhere, and I do so hate to travel alone, not that the girl is that much help to me. You have no idea of the hardships I've had to endure on this trip. Revolting, my dear. Absolutely revolting, and you know how the young people are today . . . pure selfishness, Elaine . . . pure, unadulterated selfishness."

The young girl beside her grimaced and turned away.

"What was that, Elaine?" Maggie said into the phone. "Yes, that's the one. Nancy and Cynthia went to school together for a while. Of course Angela couldn't afford to keep Nancy there, as you could Cynthia. My dear, you'll never believe how poor they are. Naturally someone had to do something for poor Nancy, and you know how generous I am, my dear." She fluttered her hand around her bleached curls again and said, "But I'll tell you everything when I see you. I'm simply dripping with the most divine gossip."

"I'll send the driver at once, Maggie. The Bahía, you say."

"That's right. I'll be waiting in the lobby, so please tell him to hurry; you know how I hate waiting."

"All right, Maggie. Goodbye."

Maggie just hung up, slamming the receiver onto the hook to prove that she was annoyed and being inconvenienced. She walked over to where her niece was standing with her back turned and spun her around. "Now what is all this headshaking and lip-pursing about not going to Elaine Brandon's villa?"

Nancy's pretty face was expressionless. She showed neither annoyance nor anger. "I'm simply not going there," she told her aunt.

"Not going? Of course you're going."

"No I'm not," Nancy said firmly. "I never cared for Cynthia Brandon when I was in school with her, and I certainly will not accept her hospitality."

Maggie looked horrified. "You won't accept their hospitality! Then what, may I ask, do you intend doing about living accommodations?"

Nancy looked unconcerned. "I have a little money of my own. I'll manage nicely, thank you, Aunt Maggie."

"Where, pray tell, did you get any money?" Maggie made it sound like the most impossible thing she'd ever heard.

"Father gave me some before I left, and I saved a little from that job I had at Carson's."

"Well, I never . . ." Maggie sputtered. "Of all the ungrateful, selfish girls I've ever met . . ."

"Please, Aunt Maggie. Don't upset yourself. I know you'll worry about me, but I'll be fine." Nancy knew her aunt only too well. "I know I'm being selfish, but please don't insist I stay with Cynthia. Besides, you'll have a much nicer time if I'm not constantly underfoot."

"That goes without saying," Maggie said. "But where on earth will you stay? You certainly cannot afford to stay here at the Bahía Palace. Surely you don't have that kind of money."

"No, I don't. But there's a small hotel I've heard about. The Jaime I. It's not far from here. Some girls from work stayed there last year when they were here. They said it was very clean and most respectable."

Maggie made a disapproving face.

"Please, Auntie. I'd like to. I'd feel very uncomfortable up at the Brandons' villa."

Maggie hesitated. Suddenly she shook her head. "No, I wouldn't hear of it, Nancy. I told your mother that I would be responsible for you. I am certainly not the kind of person who would shirk her responsibilities, especially when a member of my own family is involved."

"Oh, please, Aunt Maggie." She decided to play on one of her aunt's weaknesses. "You know how shy I am around young men," she lied. Nancy saw the flicker in her aunt's eyes at the mention of young men. They were, above all else, her greatest weakness.

"Young men," Maggie said, elevating her eyebrows. "What are you talking about?"

"You know how Elaine and Cynthia always surround themselves with young men. The villa is usually overrun by them."

"Really, Nancy!" Maggie huffed. "You're being most distasteful."

"I didn't mean it the way it sounded," Nancy said apologetically. "It's just that the society columns are always mentioning the lovely parties they give and all the young people they know. I'd feel so out of place, whereas you'd be so much at home, knowing everyone as you do."

"True, true," Maggie admitted, pursing her lips. She'd forgotten about Elaine's penchant for young men, and Nancy would be a bit of a restriction on her freedom to circulate. Her bosom heaved in resignation. "Well, I suppose I can't force you to stay at the villa," she said. "But I insist you telephone me every day to assure me that you are all right."

"Thank you, Auntie," Nancy gushed as she kissed her lightly on the cheek. "I'll be fine, really I will," she added as she picked up her suitcase and started toward the exit.

Maggie shook her head as she watched Nancy leave. Young girls today had no interest in the finer things of life. A small, insignificant hotel, indeed, she thought with a shudder of disgust. The girl would prefer that to the luxury of the Brandons' villa. It was ridiculous. Maggie tilted her head and laid a thoughtful finger against her cheek. "Young men," she said with a sigh. It was true, Elaine Brandon had always liked the company of men, and, unless she had changed drastically of late, there would be more than enough of them to go around. She smiled, thinking that that was one thing she and Elaine had in common, and Nancy Winston wouldn't be there to get in anyone's way.

Maggie looked with impatience at her diamond watch. "Where is that silly driver?" she asked irritably. "He must know I hate to be kept waiting." She wondered idly if Elaine's chauffeur were handsome.

THE AFTERNOON SUN WAS SLANTING ACROSS the wide cobblestoned street as Rod came out of the police station and stood in the shade of its facade. On first seeing it he thought it resembled a museum more than a jail. It had wide steps, carved and lettered stone arches, and delicate spires on all four corners of the building. It certainly did not have the formidable look about it that American jails had.

With Rod was a grim-looking man wearing a peaked hat and carrying a rifle in one hand. Despite the fact that Rod had accomplished nothing by coming to the *guardias civiles,* he had to admit that they were the kindest-hearted, politest police he'd ever encountered. And thank heaven they spoke English.

"I am so very sorry, Señor Shepherd," the policeman with the peaked hat and rifle said in a genuinely sympathetic voice. "But rules are rules. There is nothing we can do without permission from the Consulate."

"But why can't I at least see my daughter, talk to her?" Rod asked.

"It just is not permitted, *señor.* Your daughter is quite well, I assure you. Do as I suggest. Go and see Señor Verdugo at the Consulate. I assure you he will be very instrumental in seeing that you receive official permission to visit with your daughter."

"I don't just want to visit her," Rod argued. "I want to get her the hell out of here." He bit down on his lower lip. Losing his patience would gain him nothing. He had no fault to find with the local *policía.* They, naturally, had to abide by their rules and regulations. He could understand that. But he wanted Lisa out of there. God only knew what kind of conditions she was being forced to live under, regardless of the grandeur of the architecture.

As if the policeman had read his thoughts he said, "Your daughter is not too uncomfortable, believe me. This is not your neighboring Mexico. The food is good and the conditions are not as deplorable as you think. Your daughter has endured these past several days; she surely will endure a day or two more until you get official permission."

Rod shook his head. "I guess you're right," he said. He turned and smiled weakly at the officer. Sticking out his hand he said, "Thank you, officer. I appreciate your courtesy."

The policeman shook his hand then touched two fingers to the brim of his hat. "I am only sorry you must go away dissatisfied. Perhaps tomorrow, *señor.*"

"Yes," Rod said dejectedly. "Perhaps tomorrow."

Rod pushed his hands deep into his trouser pockets. His disappointment put a darker shadow over his depressed mood. He turned down the cobblestone street, following the officer's directions to his hotel, the Jaime I— which he had learned was pronounced "High-May Uno." He went to the right, heading for what the policeman had called El Borne, a charming cemented walkway about a hundred feet wide that ran down the center of the main thoroughfare. The trees that shaded it and the facades of ancient palaces and fine buildings that rose on either side distracted him from his disappointment a little, but not much. Women in black dresses and matching head coverings strolled along the walk. Men, dark-skinned, darkly clothed, drowsed on the benches. They all seemed to be basking, not only in the sunlight of the afternoon but in the inner contentment of their lives. There were many touristy-looking people milling about; they looked garish and out of place. The fountains' tumbling waters tried to call for his attention, the graceful beauty of the palm fronds tried to beckon to him, there was the laughter and scurrying of children, but he saw and heard little. Lisa was all he could think about. Well, at least she had been told he was in Palma. The police were nice enough to do that much for him without official permission.

A disturbing thought crossed his mind. Suppose they had told Lisa that he was there and she had said she refused to see him. Perhaps that was why official permission was required. No, Lisa knew he was the only one who would be able to secure her release. But then perhaps she did not want to be released.

That was ridiculous, he told himself as he plodded wearily along El Borne. She wouldn't have sent the cablegram in the first place if she didn't want to get out of jail.

He heaved a sigh and looked up at the soft, lovely sky. There wasn't anything he could do about it now. The Consulate was closed at this hour—he'd found that out when he tried telephoning from the police station. That was insane. What kind of business hours did they keep in this place? No wonder the place was so backward. Well, he'd just have to bide his time until tomorrow. He had hoped he'd have Lisa with him now and that they'd be on their way first thing tomorrow. It couldn't be helped. But he couldn't spend much more time away from his work.

He made a mental note to remind himself to tell the hotel clerk at the Jaime I that he planned on staying a little longer.

He turned off El Borne and headed for the hotel. He wanted a hot bath, a drink and a good dinner. He'd get to bed early, be up at the crack of dawn and get everything taken care of the first thing in the morning.

"Ah, Señor Shepherd," the desk clerk called as he came across the lobby. "One moment please, *señor.*"

"Yes," Rod said as he came toward him.

"We were made to understand that you would be checking out tomorrow," the clerk said.

Rod shook his head. "No, I'm afraid I couldn't wind up my business today. I'll most likely be here for a day or two longer."

"Ah, that is too bad," the clerk said, pursing his lips. He turned toward a young girl whom Rod had not seen standing in the shadow of a tall oak column. "In that case, Miss Winston, I do not see how we are going to be able to accommodate you." He nodded toward Rod. "Señor Shepherd's room is the only available space we have tomorrow."

The girl was pretty, Rod thought as Nancy came out of the shadow of the column and smiled at him. Too young, though, he decided. No more than seventeen, if that, but most assuredly American. He found himself smiling at her. "I'm afraid I don't understand," he said to her.

Nancy put out her hand. "My name's Nancy Winston. It seems the hotel has a small room I can occupy tonight and they were going to move me into your room tomorrow. But now that you are staying on they won't be able to accommodate me after tonight."

"I see," Rod said. There was something about the girl's eyes that disturbed him. He'd seen those eyes before on another girl. Of course! Nancy Winston had Lisa's eyes. She also had the same sweet expression that Lisa used to wear. The hair was almost the same shade too. Something told him to mutter his apologies and walk away, but he found he couldn't. He turned to the desk clerk and said, "You mean you haven't any accommodations at all?"

The clerk looked embarrassed. "Oh, we have accommodations, sir. But you see," he added in a stage whisper, "the young lady has a limited expense account and can only afford a room within a certain price range."

Rod suddenly felt very protective about the girl. Without realizing he was saying it, he said, "If you have a larger suite I'll be happy to take that and you can give this young lady my room."

Nancy put her hand on his arm. "Oh, no, Mr. Shepherd. I wouldn't dream of putting you out."

"Nonsense. My daughter will be joining me tomorrow anyway. If we stay on I will need a larger suite."

"But—"

"No buts about it," Rod insisted. "Just give me time to collect my things and you can move into my room now." He turned to the clerk. "Send up a bellboy and have him move my bags."

The clerk was all smiles. "Thank you, Mr. Shepherd. You are most accommodating."

Rod turned to Nancy. "Anything to help a fellow American in distress." He felt that he was doing it for Lisa rather than for a stranger. It was uncanny how much they resembled each other.

"How can I thank you?" Nancy said sweetly.

"That's simple," Rod said boldly, acting on an impulse. There certainly couldn't be anything wrong in asking a girl young enough to be his daughter to dine with him. It would be like dining with Lisa, which is what he'd been looking forward to this evening. "How about having dinner with me? I hate like the devil to eat alone, and unfortunately I don't know a word of Spanish."

Nancy hesitated. Being grateful to the man was one thing; letting him—a perfect stranger—pick her up was another. He certainly was good-looking, though, she thought. He had kind eyes, and the silver at his temples was devastatingly attractive. But he was a stranger, after all, even though there was something sad about the way he was smiling. "I'm afraid I can't," she said.

"That's too bad," Rod answered. "I hope I didn't offend you by my brashness." His smile faded. "I've been hassling with the local Majorcans all day and am rather desperate for some good American companionship.

Nancy wished he wouldn't look at her with that puppy-dog expression on his face. She found herself weakening. "It's just that my aunt will most likely expect me to dine with her this evening."

"Invite her along," Rod said boldly. He realized that he was being too forward. He shifted his weight from one foot to the other. "I'm sorry," he said. "I am being forward, aren't I?"

"No, not at all," Nancy said too quickly. "I understand. I

know what it's like living among strangers. I think I spent the better part of my life that way." God, he had beautiful eyes. She felt she could look at them forever.

"Well, if you can't dine with me, perhaps you could recommend a nice restaurant where I won't have trouble with the language."

"This is my first trip to Palma," Nancy said, "but I understand from what I've been told that most everyone speaks English here, so you shouldn't have any problems. As far as a good restaurant is concerned, I'm told the food at the Hotel Maricel is very good."

Rod shook his head. "I don't care much for hotel food. It always seems to taste to me like plastic."

Nancy laughed. "I know what you mean." She found herself gazing at those hypnotizing dark eyes again. "Hey, wait a minute. A girlfriend who was here last year said she ate at a marvelous, quaint little place not far from here." She quickly snapped open her handbag and began rummaging around inside it. "She gave me the name and address," she said, digging deeper into the bag. Nancy shook her head. "I guess it must be with my address book in my suitcase." She tilted her head and smiled up at him. "I'd be happy to dig it out and call your room later and give you the name and address."

"That would be most kind of you, Miss . . ."

"Winston. Nancy Winston," she said. She felt a shiver of excitement run through her when he smiled through those lovely sad eyes.

"Rod Shepherd," he said. He hesitated, trying to keep the conversation going. "May I ask what part of the States you're from, Miss Winston?"

"A little place called New York City. Ever hear of it?" She laughed.

Her laugh sounded exactly the way Lisa's once had. He felt little pin pricks rush over his skin. If he didn't know better he'd have sworn he was listening to his daughter's laughter. He felt very disconcerted, very drawn to the girl. "Yes, it's somewhere on the East Coast, isn't it?"

"Right on," Nancy said. "How about you, Mr. Shepherd?"

"I'm a hick, I'm afraid. Dayton."

"That's in Ohio."

"Right. I have a small business there, but I got to New

York once. It's only a little over an hour's flight from Dayton."

"Strangely enough I've never traveled west from New York. My aunt says anything west of Manhattan Island is un-civilized. According to her, Europe is the only sensible place to visit if you aren't fortunate enough to live here."

"I don't think your aunt and I would get along very well," Rod said.

"Don't feel badly. I don't get along with her very well myself."

Rod gave her a crooked smile. "So why not have dinner with me instead?" he asked softly. He saw the hesitation in her eyes. "Just a nice father-daughter dinner," he added.

Nancy laughed again. "Damn. Just when I was about to give in you throw me a curve. I don't think I'd much enjoy a father-daughter dinner. My father and I don't get along very well either."

"Okay," Rod said brightly, "then how about a two-strangers-from-America dinner."

"Ah, that's better," she said brightly.

"Then you'll join me?" He was unnerved to note that his heart was beating faster.

"I'll come," Nancy said emphatically. "And I won't bring Aunt Maggie."

"Bring her if you wish," Rod said. "I really wouldn't mind."

"But I would. I'll call her and tell her I met a friend from home." She tilted her head again. "That isn't telling a lie, is it?"

"No, I don't think so." He glanced at his watch. "How about seven o'clock?"

"Shall we make it eight?" she said. "People dine late in Majorca, I think. I'll meet you here in the lobby, and I'll remember to bring along the name and address of that restaurant my friend told me about."

"Good. Till eight then, Miss Winston."

"Nancy."

He took her hand. "Nancy," he said softly, repeating her name as though it were something sacred. "My first name's Rod."

"Yes," she said smiling up into his face. "It suits you."

Reluctantly she withdrew her hand and took a few steps backward toward the elevator. She smiled at him again and turned away. Rod just stood there looking after her. Suddenly he realized where he was and called, "Hey, wait up. I'm going up too. I forgot for a minute that we're both staying at the same hotel."

"My Aunt Maggie and my father would never approve," she laughed as she slipped her arm through his. It seemed like the most natural thing to do. She felt the strength of his muscles as he walked beside her, their hips touching.

Rod tried to put distance between them. He tried hard to fight down the warm feeling that was spreading through his body. To add to his discomfort he felt a quivering in his stomach when he smelled the scent of her perfume. It was very provocative.

But hell, she's only a child, he told himself. The thought disturbed him without his knowing why it should. He cleared his throat nervously. "I know I shouldn't ask this of a lady," he said, surprised that his voice came out sounding so smooth and calm. "But how old are you, may I ask?"

Nancy's eyes twinkled with amusement. "Twenty-two. Why?"

"Oh, I don't know. I suppose it doesn't look right for an older man like me to ask a young lady your age to have dinner with him."

"Why doesn't it look right? I personally think it looks fine."

Rod shook his head. "Your father and your aunt might not agree with you."

"I never cared much for what other people think, including my father and my aunt. But if it bothers you, you can still retract your invitation."

He was tempted, but he couldn't. "I wouldn't think of it," he said quickly. "After all, it is only a dinner." Deep inside his heart he didn't want it to be only a dinner date. It was because she reminded him so much of Lisa, he kept telling himself. He knew that wasn't the truth. As much as she resembled Lisa, she was still a stranger, a young lovely stranger by the name of Nancy Winston. He glanced at her out of the corner of his eye. Now that he thought of it, she really wasn't anything like Lisa, he decided. She was much older, for one thing. Also, she had larger breasts and broader hips, very womanly hips.

The elevator doors swooshed open. "Are you on this floor too?" Nancy asked.

"Yes. Two-oh-five."

"I'm just down the hall at the end."

"You're not staying here with your aunt." He made it a statement rather than a question.

"No, she's staying with some very wealthy friends of hers at their villa. I'm afraid that kind of luxury is something I don't particularly care for."

They stopped in the middle of the corridor. "See you at eight," Rod said, looking into her lovely face.

"Yes. Eight," she repeated softly. She turned and walked quickly down the hall. She found she was humming to herself.

The minute Rod stepped into his room he started to admonish himself. Already he was looking at strange women and feeling strange sensations. But it's only a dinner date, he told himself. Surely there can't be anything wrong in having dinner with a girl who reminded him of his own daughter. He pinched shut his eyes and tried to kill the feeling that he wanted it to be more than that.

GREG BRANDON WAS AS BLOND AS HIS SISTER was dark. He wore his deep tan beautifully; it set off the deep blue of his eyes, the glistening white of his perfect teeth. His hair was thick and shaggy and grew almost down to his collar. As the taxi bounced over the narrow road, Greg sat scowling at the gnarled olive trees and the sprawling green fields. How he hated coming here. He disliked Majorca almost as much as he disliked his mother. But Cynthia had begged him to come, and he never could say no to Cynthia. She was the only person in his life whom he felt he loved. He'd do anything for Cynthia, even cut off an arm. Well, no, perhaps not an arm, he told himself, admiring the trim, perfect line of his sleeve. A finger maybe. No, better the little toe. A toe wasn't very noticeable.

The taxi hit a rut and sent Greg bumping across the seat. "Damm it, watch where you're going," he yelled in Spanish to the driver. "You're not hauling cement blocks, you know."

He adjusted his suit jacket and touched his hair. He caught a glimpse of himself in the driver's rear-view mirror and smiled. He liked what he saw. Most people did, he told himself. He knew he was handsome. Why shouldn't he know? After all, hundreds of women had told him so. Everyone found him attractive; everyone but his mother. The thought brought a pout to his mouth. Elaine never told him he was handsome. She never told him anything, except to get lost. She didn't give a rat's ass about him. She never had. She'd never cared about anyone but herself. That's how he'd come to depend so much on Cynthia. Cynthia understood him. Cynthia loved him. She was always telling him how great he was, how good-looking he was, how she liked being with him. If it wasn't for their being dependent on Elaine for their money, neither of them would have anything to do with her.

Money. Christ, he'd spent almost all of his monthly allowance and it was only the middle of the month. Well, he'd hit his mother up for some bread when he got to the villa.

The taxi hit another chuckhole and Greg banged his elbow on the arm rest. "Goddamn it," he swore, rubbing at the pain in his elbow. That bruise called his attention to the bruise on his knuckles. The skin wasn't broken, but it had a puffy look. He started to think about that girl in Madrid, the one he'd been shacking up with. He wondered if he'd broken her nose when he'd hit her. If he had, she damned well deserved it. He'd met a lot of women like her, the type who purposely said things to get a guy mad enough to slap them around. They got their kicks that way. Women were a pain in the ass. But a necessary pain, he thought. Sex wasn't very satisfying without them.

He thought suddenly of Philip, one of his instructors at military school. Hell, he hadn't thought of Phil in a long time. No, that wasn't true. He thought of him more than he cared to admit to himself. Phil was a great guy. He really missed him. Like Cynthia, Phil was always telling him how handsome he was, what a great body he had. They had had a lot of great times together, and Phil had fulfilled his need for the father he had never known. It had been the night of Greg's fifteenth birthday that the head of the school had walked into Phil's quarters and found them naked in bed together. They were both kicked out, of course. But Christ, he'd only been fifteen. Lots of guys fooled around with each other at fifteen.

He squirmed uncomfortably, remembering the things that he
and Phil used to do to each other. Most guys didn't go that far
with each other. But hell, he was lonely and Phil was kind
and protective. He would have done anything for Phil.

The military school informed Elaine and his stepfather why
he was expelled. His stepfather had wanted him to stay at
home. Elaine lost no time in shipping him off to another
school—this one in Switzerland. To this day Elaine was convinced that her son was a fag. That's where Elaine and
Cynthia were worlds apart. Cynthia knew he was living with
that guy in Paris—the one who was going to make Greg into
a great actor. Cynthia didn't go around casting aspersions.
Cynthia never thought anything about it. What was there to
think? He never did anything with the guy—not the kind of
things he'd done with Phil. But Elaine was different. He
could tell by the way she looked at him and the kind of
questions she was always asking that she thought he was a
homosexual. That's what was so damned funny. If she only
knew the number of girls he'd laid. It just didn't seem natural
for him to let a day go by without screwing a woman. It was
like a contest. He wondered if there was a woman anywhere
who wouldn't go to bed with him. So far he hadn't met any.
Even Cynthia hadn't refused him. There was his mother, of
course, but he'd never asked her.

He laughed to himself, wondering if even Elaine could say
no if he propositioned her. He slumped down in the seat. It
might be amusing to find out sometime, he thought. And he
knew just how to get around her if he wanted to. She was
convinced that he was queer. Great. He'd tell her that he was
afraid of women and plead with her to help him prove that he
could enjoy a woman in bed. Oh, it might be a fun game.

No, he thought with disgust. He was being sick. He hated
his mother. Why in hell would he want to sleep with her?
Only fags wanted to have sex with their mothers. He'd read
that somewhere; or had someone told him? Whichever. It was
a known fact that all fairies loved their mothers, which was
more proof of his heterosexuality; he hated his mother.

The sun was almost just a memory when the taxi stopped
at the gates. Greg identified himself to one of the guards. It
pissed him off to have to do it, and it disgusted him to think
his mother lived like a damn empress while he had to practically beg for the pittance she sent him. They drove through

the arch and started up the drive to the villa. Greg despised the place almost as much as he despised his mother.

When they stopped in front he noticed that there were four or five cars in the garage, including Elaine's Rolls convertible and her limousine, so she was at least at home. He wondered who the new Mercedes belonged to. Most likely one of his mother's latest "tricks." He got out of the cab and paid the driver, who didn't look too pleased with the tip. Greg Brandon spent money on himself and on women, not on stupid cab drivers.

"Greg," Cynthia squealed as she raced across the terrace and down the wide steps, throwing herself into his open arms. She kissed him hard on the mouth. He tightened his arms around her and returned the kiss with equal ardor, more as a lover would rather than a brother.

"Oh, I've missed you," Greg breathed, kissing her again.

"Greg, it's so wonderful to have you here. I've been going bananas in this hellhole."

Greg smiled at her. "Where's the old bitch?"

Cynthia nodded toward the upper stories. "She's installing one of her old cronies in the west wing. Some old bag by the name of Maggie Montgomery is going to be staying here for a week."

"Yes, I remember her. She's the one with the dyed yellow curls and diamonds on every finger."

"That's the one. Mother's simply pissed for having to put her up, but she couldn't get out of it."

"Serves her right."

Cynthia tugged his arm. "Leave your bag there, I want you to meet someone."

Greg let himself be led across the terrace. "You have an evil little gleam in your eye, sister dear. What are you up to?"

"Never you mind. Just come along." She pulled him all the way across the terrace and stopped in front of the French doors of the game room. Inside Greg heard the clicking of billiard balls.

"What's this all about?" he asked, eyeing his sister suspiciously.

She gave him a little shove. "Go on in. I want you to introduce yourself to someone," she said.

"Aren't you coming with me?"

Cynthia shook her head. "No. I've got something I must

do. I'll be right back." She hurried away, leaving Greg with a puzzled expression on his face.

After a moment he adjusted the lapels of his jacket and stepped into the game room. A young, very handsome youth was bent over the billiard table concentrating on the angle of a shot. He didn't hear Greg enter the room, or if he did he pretended not to notice.

Greg waited for him to make the shot, then said, "Hi."

Jorge looked up sharply and smiled. "Hi," he said in return. He put down the cue stick and put out his hand. "I'm Jorge Aguilar," he said.

"Greg Brandon." The two men shook hands.

"Ah, the brother," Jorge said, letting one eyebrow rise higher than the other. "We have been expecting you."

Greg let his eyes roam over the young man before him. He certainly was a good-looking fellow, he thought. He supposed he was one of his mother's latest tricks. "Are you a house guest?" Greg asked, trying to make conversation. He always found it more difficult to talk to men than to women. With women a man could say just about anything and they'd respond. With men it was totally different.

"A house guest? Well, yes, I suppose you could call me that," Jorge answered with a delightful grin. "After next month I will be living here permanently," he added.

Greg frowned. "Living here permanently? I don't understand."

"I am engaged to marry your sister," Jorge said. His smile broadened with pride.

Greg stared at him, unaware that his chin had dropped and his mouth was hanging open. He glanced back toward the terrace to see if Cynthia was standing there. Oh, no, he thought. This couldn't be. Cynthia wouldn't let herself get engaged, at least not to this young fortune hunter. Besides, she'd promised him in her letter that if he'd come for a few days she'd go back to Paris with him.

"You looked surprised," Jorge said.

"Surprised isn't the word for it," Greg answered. "Cynthia never even hinted."

"But then why should she?" Jorge said. "I am not intending to marry Cynthia."

Greg's frown deepened. "But you said my sister."

Jorge was still grinning. "But you have more than one sister, don't you?"

Greg simply stared at him, unable to understand what this was all about.

"Elaine," Jorge announced, throwing open his arms.

"Elaine? Elaine isn't my sister. She's my mother," Greg said innocently.

Just outside the doors to the terrace Cynthia started to howl with laughter. She stepped into the game room, holding her sides. The stupefied, confused expressions on their faces were just too priceless for words. She pointed a finger at them, then covered her mouth to suppress her laugher.

"Cynthia," Jorge said, looking completely bewildered. "What is going on?"

"Yeah, what's the big joke, Cindy?"

"This is just too hilarious," Cynthia laughed. "I only wish I had a camera to catch both your expressions."

Greg and Jorge exchanged looks, then turned back and stared at Cynthia. "I don't get it," Greg said.

"Neither do I," Jorge said.

Cynthia calmed herself. She came toward them. "Greg, I'd like you to meet your new stepfather."

"This kid's marrying Elaine?" Greg said with disbelief as he poked a thumb at Jorge.

Cynthia nodded. They both broke out laughing.

"I fail to see what is so funny," Jorge said indignantly. "I am not going to be anybody's stepfather," he said. There was anger in his voice.

"Well, you're marrying our mother, aren't you?" Greg asked. "That would certainly make you our stepfather."

"Elaine is your sister," Jorge said, looking imploringly at Cynthia. "You told me you were sisters."

"I told you nothing of the sort," Cynthia answered. "Elaine told you we were sisters. I just didn't deny it, that's all."

"This is preposterous."

Greg shook his head. "Don't tell me you and Mother are still playing that sister game of yours? Won't she ever grow up?"

Cynthia tapped her head. "I think the older she gets the more senile she becomes."

"Stop this," Jorge shouted. "I demand to know what this is all about."

Cynthia put a finger against her lips. "My lips are sealed," she said coyly. "I'm afraid I cannot break my vow."

"What vow?" Jorge wanted to know.

Greg chuckled. "I guess I can explain, Jorge," he said. "You see, Mother and Cynthia are always passing themselves off as sisters. It was Mother's idea, and Cynthia used to go along with it because it was fun, I guess." He looked at Cynthia. "You mean to tell me Mother got herself engaged to this guy and didn't tell him the truth?"

Cynthia nodded, wearing a fiendish smirk.

Jorge's anger deepened. "I suppose you both think this is very humorous." He stood there, humiliated. Nobody laughed at Jorge Aguilar. Nobody. Besides his anger, his mind was in a blaze of confusion. It didn't actually matter all that much if Elaine was their mother, as they claimed. He didn't care about that. But the fact that Elaine had purposely deceived him and made it possible for them to make an utter fool of him this way infuriated him. He could understand female vanity, but openly deceiving and embarrassing him was something else.

He had to think this out clearly. He could not go to Elaine and demand to know the truth; that would only mortify her. She would have to come to him and tell him of her own volition. For the moment, however, he needed to get away from their jeers. He wanted to be alone to straighten out his thoughts and get back some of his Majorcan pride. It was obvious that Cynthia was trying to cause trouble. She had purposely set the whole thing up just to humiliate Elaine and him. He remembered suddenly how Elaine had asked him to promise to stay away from Greg if Greg showed up. It wasn't his homosexuality she was afraid of, it was his telling Jorge the truth about their mother-son relationship. Why had she been so foolish as to think that that would have mattered?

He saw the smug, spiteful look on Cynthia's face, and the desperate need to get out of that room overpowered him. "I'm going for a drive," he said curtly as he hurried past them and went out through the French doors. As he walked quickly across the terrace he tried to ignore their laughter; he found that he was angrier than ever, but he didn't truthfully know at whom he was angry. Elaine should not have misled him, should not have placed him in a position where Cynthia and Greg could make a fool of him. He couldn't be angry with

Greg, however. Greg had simply been an innocent pawn in Cynthia's devious little plot. He wished with all his heart that he'd never have to see Cynthia again. After he and Elaine married he'd see to it that Cynthia was sent away. If she weren't, he and Elaine would never have a moment's peace of mind.

He wasn't looking where he was going as he trotted down the steps toward where his Mercedes was parked. He almost knocked the man down when he bumped into him.

"Jorge," the man said. "Slow down. You could kill someone racing around at that speed."

Jorge looked apologetic. "Oh, hello, Miguel. Sorry. I was just in a hurry."

"I can see that," Miguel said. "Also, you look as though you were going to punch someone in the nose." He put a hand on Jorge's arm.

Jorge shrugged it off and stepped around him. "I'm in a hurry," he repeated. "See you later, Miguel."

"Is Elaine inside?" Miguel called as Jorge moved fast toward his car.

Jorge merely waved at him and sped away.

Miguel shook his head and started to climb the steps. Youth, he said to himself. Always in a hurry. He put his hand on his left knee as he climbed upward. He'd make another appointment with that doctor tomorrow. The stiffness in his knees was getting worse. But then it always did when he came out to Elaine's villa. He blamed it on being so close to the ocean. Seawater always brought on rheumatic pains. He wished she'd close this place and move back into town. Maybe after he'd persuaded her to marry him again he'd be able to talk her into it.

He should never have allowed her to divorce him in the first place. But at that time he'd needed the handsome settlement she'd given him in exchange for her freedom.

When he reached the terrace he saw Cynthia and Greg sitting on the balustrade deep in whispered conversation. "Hello there, you two," he called as he went toward them. He put out his hand. "Greg. Nice to see you, son." He didn't mean that. He didn't like Greg. He had never liked him. Greg was a spoiled, conceited, selfish brat who should have been paddled at least once a day until he was too big to be spanked. He'd tried to discipline him somewhat when he was Greg's stepfather, but Elaine always prevented it. She used to argue that Greg had had a hard enough time growing up and deserved to be whatever he wanted to be now that he was a man.

Elaine spoiled her children rotten, but they never appreciated it. They were too wrapped up in themselves to notice the good their mother did for them.

"Well, if it isn't husband number three," Greg said, sounding bored. He didn't bother to take the hand Miguel extended. "Mother is somewhere inside," he added and leaned back into his conversation with Cynthia.

Miguel shifted uncomfortably for a moment. "Yes, of course. I have some business matters to discuss with her."

"When don't you?" Greg added sarcastically.

Miguel's embarrassment grew. He forced himself to smile at Cynthia. "You are looking lovely today, Cindy." He was trying hard to be courteous; couldn't they see that? If he had any hope of remarrying Elaine he would have to do it with the children's approval. If he could only get them on his side, things would be easy.

"Thank you," Cynthia answered. There was a touch of frost on her words.

Miguel refused to be daunted. "Your arrival, Greg, is most opportune. It seems a client of mine sent me a new automobile as a sort of 'thank you' for getting him out of a very difficult position."

Greg gave him an icy look. "In America they call it a 'payoff,' I believe," he said.

Miguel swallowed. "Yes . . . well, no, it is nothing like that. You see he owed me many favors. I had intended sending the car back because it is too sporty for a man of my age. I would be happy to give it to you, Greg, if you like."

Greg wished he'd go away and leave Cynthia and him alone. "My mother has more cars than she can use right here. I'll only be staying a few days. I'm sure I have no need of a new car, Miguel, so don't try to palm off your graft money on me."

Miguel opened his mouth to protest, but Greg waved him away. "Go find Mother and stop bothering us."

Miguel clenched his fists. He was tempted to reach out and clout the young pup behind the ear. He teetered forward, then checked himself. "Yes," he said from behind tight lips. "I'll see you later."

"Not if we can help it," Greg said over his shoulder.

"Someone should teach you your manners, young man," Miguel said, fighting to control his temper.

"And someone should teach you not to be so damned bothersome, Miguel. You don't have to come out here sucking up to Cynthia and me. We know why you're here. Everybody in Palma knows that the great Miguel Montoro is losing money hand over fist on that stupid building project the Germans stuck him with. And now he wants to get back into the good graces of the Brandon family on a chance that the Brandon money might get him out of the bind he's in. Or maybe you're even planning on courting mother again." Greg laughed when he saw the flush come into Miguel's face. "That is it, isn't it, Miguel? You're thinking of hooking up with Elaine again." He laughed. "Well, forget it, unless you think you can get her out of the clutches of a young guy thirty years younger than you." He knew he was being vicious, but he didn't care. He'd never liked Miguel. He'd hated the man ever since that day he'd been slapped by him. No one ever struck Greg and got away with it.

A frightened light came into Miguel's eyes. "Elaine has no intention of marrying Jorge Aguilar."

"No? Well, I wouldn't make a bet on that," Greg said. "Didn't she tell you she was engaged to the kid?"

"She mentioned that she was thinking of getting married to him, yes, but I can assure you that we had a long talk and I convinced her that that would be a mistake."

"You convinced her?" Greg said, throwing back his head and laughing. "You've got to be kidding. You couldn't convince Elaine about anything. If anybody breaks up this impending marriage it won't be you."

"Jorge is merely a current toy as far as Elaine is concerned. A very expensive toy, I agree, but nevertheless nothing more than a passing fancy."

"Majorcan conceit," Greg said, shaking his head slowly from side to side. "Or is it Majorcan stupidity?" He chuckled again. "But don't worry, Miguel. Although we hadn't intended doing you any favors, Cynthia and I managed to throw a monkey wrench in Elaine's little romantic interlude."

Miguel shot him a questioning look. He suddenly remembered Jorge's dashing for his car, the angry look in his face. "What happened?" he asked, looking at Cynthia.

She shrugged her shoulders. "Someone burst Jorge's balloon."

"What do you mean?" Miguel asked, looking from one to the other of them.

Greg wanted Miguel to go away, yet on the other hand he took a warped kind of pleasure in what had happened and was rather proud of being responsible. "It's really very funny," Greg said. "You see, Elaine has been leading Jorge to believe that Cynthia is her sister. I guess she told him that I was her brother. But then she never let me in on any of her little games, so I knew nothing about it. I showed up, and wham! Who's the first one I run into? Jorge." Greg's expression was all innocence and light. "So naturally I introduced myself. He said he was my sister's fiancé. I assumed he meant Cynthia. I didn't intend upsetting the kid when he told me he was going to marry Elaine. I just thought he was a little young to be my stepfather."

Miguel looked worried. "Does Elaine know this happened?"

"How could she?" Cynthia said. "She's been too busy upstairs gossiping with that silly Maggie Montgomery. She doesn't even know that Greg's here."

"As if she cared," Greg said with disgust.

Cynthia put a reassuring hand on Greg's arm.

Miguel said, "She cares very much. It is you who do not care."

"Sure, sure." He turned to Cynthia. Smiling at her and speaking to Miguel he said, "Go find Her Highness. Cynthia and I have things to talk about."

Miguel eyed the back of Greg's head with contempt, then turned and went into the house. He went through the drawing room toward the central section of the house. He paused in the huge tiled foyer with its elegant marble staircase, which, halfway up, divided in two. The vaulted ceiling was adorned with scenes from antiquity by Dardone. Fluted columns with gold filigree supported the corners, and on the walls portraits of dignified nobility frowned down at him from inside heavy gilt frames. He felt at home, standing in the midst of such Spanish splendor. This sumptuous luxury could still have been his if he had not been stupid enough to let Elaine divorce him. Well, he thought, he would have it all back again. Elaine was ill. Her doctors had confided in him about her condition. She would want to be with someone when her time came to die, and he had to convince her that he was the man who should share the little time she had left. He was still handsome. She had loved him once; she would again.

He heard laughter and looked up to see Elaine start down the staircase with Maggie Montgomery in tow. Miguel stared at Elaine. She looked ravishingly beautiful in a flowing lime-green dinner gown with an exquisite emerald necklace at her throat.

He heard Maggie say, "Honestly, Elaine, this place is like an absolute morgue. You were always surrounded by the most divine men."

"I—like the times—have changed a great deal, Maggie."

Maggie grunted. "For the worse, I'd say." She shook her head. "I thought it would be like the old days, parties, men, drinking . . ." She leaned her head toward Elaine and tittered. ". . . the orgies."

Miguel cleared his throat to let them know they were being overheard.

"Ah, Miguel," Elaine called, glad for the interruption. "What brings you here?" Before he could answer she added, "You know Maggie Montgomery, don't you?"

"Yes, of course," Miguel said. "How are you, *señora?*"

Maggie would have preferred *señorita,* but she smiled anyway. "Fine, thank you. And you, Miguel?"

"Excellent." He shifted his eyes to Elaine.

Maggie, refusing to allow his attention to wander from her, said, "I was just telling Elaine that this place isn't like the old days. Why, there isn't anyone here. I really don't know how she expects me to stay in such a mausoleum. Really, Elaine, just because you did away with a few husbands is no reason to live like a nun."

"Maggie!"

Maggie grinned at Miguel. "Well, at least you're here, Miguel. You are still as handsome as I remembered." She had changed from her tailored traveling outfit to a pink ruffled dress with a high hemline and a plunging neckline. She tugged the neckline a little lower to expose more cleavage. "I never could understand where Elaine got the courage to let you out of her clutches," she said, leaning against the railing of the staircase and pushing out her more than adequate breasts. The silk of her dress stretched across her bosom, making it obvious that she was not wearing a bra.

Miguel gave a nervous laugh when he looked back at her. "I have always wondered that myself," he said.

Elaine felt uncomfortable. "Did you want to speak to me about something, Miguel?"

"Yes. It won't take long. May we go into the library?"

Maggie stepped forward. "You can have your little talk another time. I need a drink and would never think of drinking alone. Besides, Elaine will tell me everything you talked about after you leave, so why don't we all go into the library together? That way I won't have to get whatever it is second-hand."

Miguel's eyes shifted nervously. He smiled sweetly at Maggie. "I am afraid it is just some very dreary business which I must discuss with Elaine. It would bore you completely, Señora Montgomery."

"Very little bores me, Señor Montoro," Maggie said, returning his formality. "Come along." She swept past them and headed for the double oak doors on the other side of the foyer.

Elaine shrugged to show her helplessness as she followed Maggie. She really didn't want to talk to Miguel. She knew what he was going to say. She'd seen the article in the paper about the housing project he'd invested in going into receivership. He needed more money. Miguel always needed money. She had hoped that paying a high price to be rid of him would remove him from her life completely, but it hadn't. She'd sworn the last time she'd helped him that it would be the last. She intended keeping that promise. She would be marrying Jorge within the month, and this was as good a time as any to tell Miguel that she was finished with him both socially and financially. She wasn't going to tell him, however, that she intended discharging him as her business manager and attorney. He'd been stealing her blind for years, and she'd put up with it. But now that she was going to marry Jorge and in view of what the doctors had told her, it wouldn't be fair to Jorge to tolerate Miguel any longer.

"I've got to talk to you in private," Miguel said in a harsh whisper as he hurried after her.

"Maggie's just arrived. She's my guest. It would be rude to abandon her."

"But this is important," Miguel insisted as he put his hand on her arm and stopped her.

"Not now, Miguel," Elaine said, pulling herself free.

"Greg's here. He has spoken with Jorge."

Elaine stopped dead in her tracks. She turned slowly. When she looked at Miguel her eyes were wide with shock and fright. "Where? When?"

"I met Greg on the terrace. I bumped into Jorge as he was getting into his car. He tore away like a bat out of hell."

"Oh no," Elaine gasped, clutching her throat. She started to run toward the front door.

"Jorge's gone," Miguel said. "From what Greg told me, he may not be back."

Elaine's eyes widened. "You're trying to frighten me," she breathed.

"Hey, you two," Maggie called from the doorway to the library. "Are we going to have that drink or aren't we?"

"In a minute," Elaine called impatiently as she fought to keep herself under control. "I've got to speak with Greg," she said to Miguel.

"He was with Cynthia on the terrace."

Elaine turned and hurried toward the terrace. It was empty. There was no sign of Greg or Cynthia anywhere. Miguel had followed her. "Where are they?" Elaine asked, feeling the mounting terror grabbing at her insides. "I've got to find Greg."

"Hold on a minute," Miguel said as Elaine started back into the house. "From what Greg told me happened, perhaps it's for the best."

"What did Greg tell you?" Elaine demanded.

"It seems he discovered that you haven't been exactly honest with this current new lover of yours."

"Oh, no. He didn't . . ." she gasped. The pain in her chest suddenly grew worse.

Miguel nodded. "From what I understand, Jorge was under the impression that Cynthia and Greg were your sister and brother." He shook his head as though he were talking to a mischievous child. "Oh, Elaine. Why do you do these silly things? You are too old to be playing games with children."

"Mind your own business, Miguel," she snapped. "It's my life I'm playing with, not yours. I need no advice from you." She started to pace back and forth, trying to decide what she

should do. When Cynthia had told her she'd been in touch
with Greg, she should have gone to Jorge right then and told
him the truth before Greg got to him. This was all Cynthia's
doing, of course. There wasn't the slightest doubt in her mind
about that.

"I love you, Elaine," Miguel said, reaching for her. She
brushed him aside. "You would have made a terrible mistake
marrying that Aguilar boy. Why, he's younger than both
your children."

"So what?" Elaine spit.

"So it would be a mistake, that's all. Look," he said, letting
his voice go soft. "I have never loved any woman but you.
Why don't you try to forget Jorge? Let me help you forget
him. We were happy once, Elaine. We could be again."
Again he reached for her, but again she brushed him aside.
"The boy is only after the luxuries you can afford to give
him," he said. "That is the only reason he wants to marry
you."

"Is that any different from the reason you wanted to marry
me?" she asked angrily.

"You are being most unkind, Elaine. You know that is not
why I married you."

"I think that it was." She didn't want to hurt him, but she
found she suddenly couldn't help herself. She wanted to hurt
whoever came across her path. She was losing Jorge. If she
was going to suffer, then she wanted everyone to suffer. "I've
read about your money problems, Miguel. I'm not blind. I
can read you like a book. You're broke. I'm the only woman
on all Majorca who has enough money to solve those money
problems. Well, forget it, Miguel. I don't love you, and if you
were the last man on this island I wouldn't marry you again."

"Elaine, you don't know what you are saying. You're
upset."

"You're damned right I'm upset. So please go away,
Miguel, and leave me alone." She swore she would not break
into tears, but she couldn't fight them back. They welled up
from behind her eyes and streamed down her cheeks. She
buried her face in her hands and gave in to them.

Maggie came out onto the balcony carrying a highball.
"What's going on?" she wanted to know. She cocked her
head at Elaine. "Are you crying, Elaine?"

"Of course I'm crying," Elaine sobbed as she turned her back on Maggie.

"What did I do?" Maggie asked. It never occurred to Maggie Montgomery that things happened in other people's lives that did not concern or involve her.

"Elaine has had some upsetting news," Miguel explained.

"About me?"

He gave her a tolerating smile. "No, my dear, not about you."

"Then why on earth is she crying? This is absurd. All I wanted was a drink and a little conversation. I can't see why everyone is so upset."

Elaine fumbled in the pocket of her skirt for a handkerchief. She wiped her eyes, blew her nose softly and took a deep breath. Night was beginning to settle over the garden. The day was ending; she felt that her life was ending with it. Well, the damage was done. There wasn't much she could do about it. She had let Miguel upset her when he told her Jorge would most likely not be coming back. Of course he'd be back. Jorge was too much a man to run off without a fight. He'd be back, and when he returned she'd be there waiting for him. She would explain, and if he loved her—which she was certain he did—everything would be forgiven. Perhaps she was fooling herself, but something told her she wasn't. Jorge would be back because he knew how much she needed him, just as he needed her. They were two of a kind, lonely and unloved. This was the bond that held them together.

Her thoughts made her feel a trifle better. She turned and forced a tight smile. "Come on, Maggie. Drink your drink and let's have some more girl talk." She suddenly wasn't even angry at Miguel. Jorge wasn't the silly young boy they all thought him to be. She'd prove that to them all. When Jorge came back she wanted them all there to see how much of a man he was. She wanted them to see that he loved her for herself and not for her looks, her age, or her money. She'd prove to the world that she was right. "Stay for dinner," she said to Miguel, feeling her spirits rise. She was taking a gamble on Jorge, but it was a gamble she knew she wouldn't lose.

Miguel looked confused. "Thank you, but are you sure you want me to stay?"

"Of course I want you to stay." She felt most magnanimous. "Maggie, tell the maid to find Greg and Cynthia, and inform them that cocktails are being served in the drawing room. I'd like them to join us." She found that her smile was much more comfortable.

"Greg?" Maggie asked, her face lighting up. "Is he here? Oh, how delightful. I haven't seen him for months. I ran into him at the casino in Monte Carlo. Elaine, you've raised an absolute god in that boy. He's so fantastically good-looking he made me weak in the knees just looking across the room at him."

"You must be talking about me, Maggie," Greg said as he and Cynthia came out onto the terrace.

"Oh, you naughty boy, eavesdropping on a lady's conversation. Come here and give Maggie a big kiss." She giggled like a schoolgirl when Greg kissed her on both cheeks, then lightly on the lips. Maggie's pudgy little body actually shook with excitement.

"Hello, mother," Greg said, turning to Elaine. He pecked her on the cheek. "Surprised to see me?"

"Happily surprised. How are you, darling?" She put her hands on his shoulders.

"Broke."

She found herself clinging to him. She wanted desperately to put her arms around him and embrace him, but she knew it would only repulse him and embarrass her. "You should have let me know. I would have had Miguel send you more money."

"I thought I'd come and collect it in person and at the same time get a look at my new stepfather."

Elaine tried to look unperturbed. "Yes, Miguel tells me you met Jorge."

"Cynthia introduced us," Greg said with a devilish grin.

"Yes," Elaine said simply, casting a cool glance at Cynthia. Greg chuckled. "Is he old enough to marry without his mother's consent?" He and Cynthia turned to each other and snickered.

"Yes, I believe so," Elaine said, fighting hard to keep her composure. "I don't think Jorge has to rely much on his mother, which is more than I can say for you." She bit her tongue. She hadn't meant to say that. There was no reason for her to treat her children harshly now. They were out of

Leland Harshaw's reach. But in saving them from Leland she had saved them from herself as well. During all those years of being cruel to them they'd become strangers to her. She sighed. Old habits were so difficult to break. She looked at Greg and opened her mouth to apologize.

Her sarcasm put an ugly scowl on Greg's face. "I wouldn't count too heavily on my reliance," he said. "And I wouldn't count too heavily on that young stud marrying you, either."

"I hadn't meant to say what I did, Greg. I'm sorry."

"You're always sorry," he snapped. "If you want to apologize, do it with a check."

Tears clouded her eyes. "I've tried," she sighed. "I've tried so hard to—"

"You've tried, all right," Greg snarled. "Tried to get your hooks into anything that suits your aging fancy."

"Greg, please. Don't," Elaine said, turning away from him.

"Oh, turn off the waterworks, Mother dear. They don't become you. You forget, we're all on to your little tricks."

"Greg," Miguel put in. "You are being insulting."

Greg whirled on him. "Stay out of it, Miguel. Mind your own business."

Elaine put a hand on Miguel's arm when he started to say something. "Stop it, please," she said. She looked pleadingly at her son. "I just hope that someday you will understand."

"Understand what? Your insatiable lust for young beach-boys?"

Elaine stiffened her back. "It isn't like that at all between me and Jorge."

"Oh," Greg said, arching his eyebrows. "What's it like? Mother and son?" He laughed in her face.

"Jorge is none of your concern," she said weakly.

"Far be it from me to be concerned about him or you," Greg said. "I stopped caring a long, long time ago." It pleased him to see his mother wince.

Maggie rattled the ice cubes in her empty glass. "Well, I do hope you haven't stopped caring about me, Greg dear. Obviously you have, however, because I've been standing here with an empty glass for heaven only knows how long."

"Come along, Maggie," Miguel said, taking her arm. "I'll join you in a drink. Perhaps we should let the family be alone for a few minutes." When he noticed her reluctance to leave he applied a little pressure to his touch. "Besides, it has been a long time since you and I have had a chance to be alone together."

Maggie giggled. "Oh, you Latins. Are you all so horribly irresistible?"

"Not all," Miguel said as he led her into the drawing room. "Just we Majorcans." He slipped his arm around her thick waist and steered her inside.

Elaine walked over and leaned against the balustrade, studying her two children. How lovely and handsome they were. They despised her; she saw that in the way they were looking back at her.

"Now," she said, seeing that both Maggie and Miguel were out of earshot. "Would you tell me what was said between you and Jorge?"

"Said?" Greg asked, tossing her an insolent grin. "I don't know what you mean."

"Cynthia has been dying to cause trouble between Jorge and me ever since we met. I am sure she wrote you about Jorge."

"Mother, how unkind of you," Cynthia broke in, looking equally insolent. "I never mentioned Jorge's name in my letter."

Greg nodded. "She didn't. She simply asked me to come here, that she needed me to help her out." He shook his head at Elaine. "Still blaming people without reason," he said.

"What happened?" Elaine said, holding tight to the balustrade.

Greg laughed. "Nothing. When I met your young man he told me he was planning on marrying my sister. I thought he meant Cynthia." His laughter grew. "I was pretty upset thinking Cynthia was silly enough to throw herself away on such a kid. I told him as much. But he said he wasn't marrying Cynthia, that he was marrying my other sister, Elaine. I told him I didn't have a sister named Elaine but that that was my mother's name."

Elaine found that she was holding her breath. She released it slowly and clasped her hands together to keep them from shaking. How she wished the pain in her breast would go away, if only for a moment. "Go on," she said shakily.

"That was about it," Greg said. "Jorge got all excited and stormed out of the game room. A couple of seconds later we heard his car tearing down the drive."

Slowly Elaine moved her eyes to Cynthia. "Why did you do this, Cynthia? Why couldn't you have let me be happy, at least for a little while?"

Cynthia said, "But I didn't do anything." Elaine had to look away from the smug expression on her daughter's face. "I didn't say a word. It was Greg who told Jorge that we aren't sisters. I didn't break my promise to you."

Elaine's shoulders fell. She turned her back on them and looked out into the garden. She had done everything possible for them, she had even killed for them. Perhaps when they themselves became parents they would understand her. In the meantime, there was nothing for her to do but try to make herself happy.

"Why are you always blaming me for everything?" Cynthia whined.

"I don't want to lose Jorge," Elaine said softly. "I love him very much." She found in her words a renewed courage. She turned, eased herself away from the balustrade and walked past them into the drawing room. Her head was held high, her chin jutted out. The thought of her and Jorge's love for each other helped ease the terrible pain in her chest.

She wouldn't lose Jorge. She couldn't. He'd be back.

THE DARK LITTLE BAR OFF THE HOTEL LOBBY wasn't crowded. It was modern and sleek, like the hotel itself. Sheila glanced around at the empty tables and the lone customer sitting at the bar. In the corner a young man in a white ruffled shirt and black vest and trousers picked lazily at the strings of his guitar. She was glad the place wasn't jammed with people. She and Charlie had spent the better part of two hours having sex in their very American-looking hotel room, and she felt lazy and relished the tranquil mood of the place.

"This place kinda reminds me of that Mexican cocktail lounge over on Lexington Avenue," she said. "You know, the swanky one with the oak railings and the red carpeting."

"The beer was colder over on Lexington," Charlie said.

Sheila sighed. "Ah, this is the life," she said, laying her head back against the high leather booth.

He put down his beer glass and put his hand over hers. "Yeah, it sure is, sweetheart."

"I wish we could stay here forever."

"Here in the bar?" He laughed softly.

"No, you big ape. Here in Majorca." She always pronounced it exactly as it was spelled, not bothering to drop the J as was customary.

Charlie studied her for a moment, then began toying with his glass. "Maybe we could," he said. He sounded a little uncomfortable saying the words.

"What do you mean?"

He didn't look at her. "Well, I saved up a little dough, more than you think. If we find a place like this that we both really like, maybe we could settle down over here."

Sheila leaned forward. "I don't get you."

"What do you mean you don't get me?" he said, sounding a little annoyed. "I just told you."

"Where did you get to save enough money for us to live over here?"

"I saved it. That's all."

"On your salary? Oh come on, Charlie. I know better than that."

Charlie fidgeted in his seat. "If you must know, I won some money at the track a couple of years ago. I've been saving it."

"I thought you told me you didn't gamble."

"I don't," he shouted. "What do you want from me? I told you I won it a long time ago—before I met you."

"How much did you win?"

"Couple of thousand."

"A couple of thousand?" Sheila howled and slapped the table.

"What's so funny?"

"How long do you think a couple of thousand would last if we lived over here? There for a minute I thought you were serious."

"I am serious. It's enough to get us settled in a place. Then I could go out and get a job."

"Doing what?"

"Doing what I've always done. Be a detective. Maybe I'll even set up my own detective agency."

"Oh sure. You and Matt Helm."

"What's wrong with that?"

"You just ain't bein' realistic, Charlie," Sheila said calmly. "Look. What client in their right mind would hire you to investigate something if you didn't know how to speak their language or didn't know anything about the layout of the city?"

Charlie continued to toy with his glass, not chancing to look at her. "I was thinking maybe London or someplace in England where we wouldn't have any language problems."

"We haven't even seen England yet. How do you know you'll like it?"

Charlie let his annoyance show. "Okay, so if we don't like it we go someplace else."

"Where?"

"Hell, I don't know. Someplace." He banged his glass down on the table.

"You're a dreamer, Charlie Cranston." She patted his hand. "I guess that's one of the reasons I love you."

"It can work if we want it to," he said.

"Yeah, I guess it could." She sighed. "But honestly, Charlie, I bet we'd both miss New York after a couple of months. It's nice to dream like that, though, even though it ain't practical."

"It's practical," he argued.

Sheila mused for a moment. "You'd miss home just as I would," she said.

"What's to miss? Muggers, garbage in the streets, packed subways, filthy air."

"They've got all that over here too, I bet."

Charlie saw he wasn't making points. "I don't want to go back," he said petulantly.

"Yeah, sure. Tell me that after we've been over here awhile. You're already bitching about the warm beer and the lousy toilets."

They were interrupted by a young man carrying a slate on a pole on which Charlie's name was written. The page was calling Charlie, mispronouncing his name.

"Hey, kid. I'm Mr. Cranston. What's up?"

"Telephone call for you, sir," the lad said. "Overseas. Follow me, please."

Charlie grinned at Sheila. "See, I've only been gone a week and already they can't do without me." He kissed her on the forehead. "Be back in a sec." He lifted his heavy frame out of the booth and went toward the lobby, digging in his pocket for some money. He wondered how much he was expected to tip the page. He handed him sixty pesetas when he slipped into the telephone booth.

He picked up the receiver and listened to a lot of garbled conversation between operators. After a few minutes he heard a familiar voice say, "Hey, Charlie, is that you?"

"Tony? Hey, boy, how you doin'? What's going on?"

The line crackled. Charlie lost contact for a minute, then his friend at the 17th Precinct was back on the line. "Listen, Charlie. I can't talk long. There's trouble over here. Don't come back for a while. They're investigating, and they're onto something. I'll try to keep you out of it if I can, but I don't see how that's possible."

Charlie's face went gray. "Who squealed?"

"Nobody. It was just a routine check, and they started pointing fingers when some of the solid citizens started yapping about payoffs." More crackling came over the line. "I think it'll all blow over, but I'd suggest you take an extension of your trip. Say Sheila got sick or something."

"I was thinking of doing that anyway, Tony." He bit down on his lower lip. "Look, Tony. That sonofabitch that sold me our travel tickets stuck us with some bogus shit. Rack his ass for me, will you?"

"Yeah, sure, Charlie. Don't worry." He chuckled. It was a sadistic chuckle. "I'll take care of him. I heard just this morning that he pulled the same thing on another one of our boys."

"You got a copy of my itinerary. Sheila and I'll stay on schedule. You keep me informed."

"Right, Charlie. Enjoy yourself, but above all don't come home. Out of sight, out of mind, if you know what I mean. Besides, they can't question you if you aren't here, right?"

"Yeah, right, Tony. Thanks."

He replaced the receiver and leaned against the booth. He and Sheila were supposed to be gone for a month. He'd have to think of some way to stretch that out to two months, maybe three. But how? He didn't want to bring any more suspicion to himself than there already was. But Tony would cover up. After all, they were in this thing together. If he went down the tubes, so would Tony Gaventi.

When he slid back into the booth beside Sheila she smiled and said, "Everything okay, Charlie?"

"Sure, sure. That was Tony from New York. They got that little punk who stuck us with the airline tickets. He just wanted me to know everything was taken care of and not to worry."

"So fast! Wow! You guys don't lose any time."

Charlie winked. "Didn't you know you married a fast operator, kid?"

"Not that fast, I didn't." She looked impressed. "Where are we goin' to eat?"

"I took care of that. I made a reservation at a little joint the hotel manager suggested. He said the food's terrific, but it ain't cheap." He took her hand. "But I'm not worrying about money. Nothing's too good for my baby."

"Ah, Charlie. You don't have to take me to expensive restaurants and stuff like that. That's not why I married you."

He squeezed her hand. "Why *did* you marry me, Sheila?"

She sipped her martini and stirred the olive around with her finger. "Oh, I don't know; I guess 'cause you're the only guy who ever treated me like I wasn't just another piece of merchandise. You're good for me, Charlie. Why if it wasn't for you I'd most likely still be liftin' wallets out of guys' pockets and shoppin' free at Macy's and Gimbels."

"Never had any regrets about goin' straight, baby?"

"Never once since you came along. I never even think of stealing anything. That's past. I don't need to do that kind of stuff any more now that I got you."

A stab of conscience hit Charlie in the chest. It had been simple to get Sheila to go straight. He wished now that he'd done as good a job on himself. But it was too late for regrets. At least if anything ever happened to him Sheila would never have to worry about money. She'd never have to go out onto the streets to make a living for herself. She could live in comfort for the rest of her life.

He kissed her hand. "Come on, kid. Let's go eat. I'm starved." He shifted himself out of the booth with a lot of effort.

"Starved? You just had a sandwich up in the room less than an hour ago."

"That was an hour ago."

"Oh, Charlie, you really should watch your weight."

"I am watching it," he said, proudly patting his huge stomach. "And I kinda like what I see."

THE YOUNG PAUL VERDUGO WAS SITTING cross-ankled in front of the fireplace in his father's oak-paneled study. He was sipping cognac and feeling very comfortable. His father, sitting across from him, had insisted on an early dinner, for which Paul Jr. had been thankful. It had been a long, exciting day and he looked forward to a good night's sleep.

His stepmother came into the room carrying a large silver tray with coffee pot and cups. Paul Jr. thought she was the most beautiful woman he had ever seen. She wasn't like his mother at all. His stepmother—Laura, she insisted upon being called—was nothing like he expected. First she was so much younger than he'd thought she'd be. She had to be in her thirties, he figured, counting off the years she and his father had been married, but she looked closer to his own age. And he'd never known a woman who knew how to dress the way she did. Everything she put on seemed to have been molded to her skin. What he liked most about her was that she didn't treat him like a child, the way his mother did back home.

"Your father tells me you're studying piano," Laura said as she put the coffee tray down on the table in front of him. Paul Jr. gulped hard when he glanced down. Her breasts fell slightly forward and he could see almost down to her navel. She didn't have anything on under the gown.

He looked quickly away. "Yes," he said, trying to clear a frog in his throat. "I've been studying at Juilliard. I'd like to go to Paris, but Mother isn't exactly in favor of that."

"Why not?"

Paul set his glass aside. "Too far away from her apron strings, I guess."

Rather than encourage any conversation about her husband's ex-wife, Laura said, "Why don't you play something for us?" She nodded toward the grand piano sitting in the corner.

Paul shook his head. "I'd rather not, if you don't mind. I'm kinda tired. Besides, I practice long hours every day, so you'll hear enough of my banging while I'm here."

His father leaned into the conversation. "Naturally you'll visit Valdemossa while you're here?"

"Oh yes. I've already checked on that. They have daily tours to Chopin's retreat."

"Chopin?" Laura said. "Oh, yes. He's the composer-pianist who lived here with the woman who liked to dress like a man. George Sand, wasn't that her name?"

"That's the name she wrote under," Paul said.

"She wasn't very well liked by the Majorcans; she still isn't."

Laura started to pour the coffee. "Who could blame them? After all, she plunked herself down in that tiny little place and flaunted the fact that she was living in sin with a man who wasn't her husband, had two children by another man and referred to all her Majorcan neighbors as uncivilized barbarians."

Paul Jr. smiled. "I think she was a very colorful character." He took a careful sip of coffee, testing its heat. "I liked her."

Laura arched her eyebrows. "Are you normally attracted to notorious women?"

Paul flushed and quickly replaced the cup in its saucer. "I'm afraid I haven't met all that many," he said.

"But you'd like to?" She was gazing at him with cool, limpid eyes. She allowed one hand to lightly caress one bosom. It was as if she were tempting him with it.

His father was watching Laura and looked a bit ill at ease. He cleared his throat and said, "But there are so many other places to see and things to do here. There are the bullfights on Sunday, the gypsy dances, and the annual bicycle races are to be held in a few days." He noticed his wife's eyes traveling over Paul's frame. Hastily he added, "And you've got to see Deja. It's a small fishing and olive-growing village on the mountainous northwest coast. In olden times a shrine to the moon goddess was built there."

"Shades of *Norma*," his son said.

"Nowhere in all the world is moonlight as strong as in Deja," his father said.

Laura leaned forward. "Yes, it's very sexy."

Her husband fidgeted. He cleared his throat again. "You'll love Majorca, son," he said. "There's the artificial pearl factory at Manacor and the caves at Drach." He wagged his head slightly. "But it isn't anything like the old days. This used to be an absolute paradise. Unfortunately the old Majorca doesn't exist anymore. Palma's center has been eaten away by restaurants, bars, souvenir shops, travel agencies and the like. The olive trees are being cut down to make salad bowls and boxed for the tourist trade. The olives are rotting on the ground. Then there's all those new hotels strung along the coast. It reminds me of Miami Beach. The Germans have bought up the more spectacular sites on the coast nearby and have built houses in their own familiar domestic style." He sighed. "But one must always allow for progress. It's still a very beautiful island. I wouldn't live anywhere else in the world."

Laura winked and said, "And we have the most disreputable nightclubs down near the waterfront. Some even have sex shows."

Her husband flushed. "Paul might be a little young for that sort of thing, Laura." He looked back at his son. "Of course if you want a little more rustic atmosphere, by all means you should visit the other two islands, Minorca and Ibiza. They aren't as built-up as here." He reached for a cigarette and lit it. "Yes, this is a really delightful place. Good wine, cheerful, clean, friendly people. Culturally it's southern French, agriculturally it's still back in the eighteenth century. And our climate is better than anywhere in Europe."

Laura pouted. "Really, dear," she said to her husband. "You sound like a tour guide."

He dropped his eyes and stubbed out his cigarette. "Yes, I guess you're right, my dear. Sorry."

"I'm sure I'll love it here," his son said.

"I hope you do, Paul."

The ringing of the telephone interrupted them. Mr. Verdugo got out of his chair and went to answer it, apologizing that he'd let the servants go right after dinner.

Laura settled back in her seat, pushing her breasts forward. She crossed her shapely legs and Paul Jr. noticed that the side slit in her skirt went almost all the way up to the hip. "Tell me more about your interest in notorious women," she said. Her eyes, he found, were suddenly changed. It was as if a smoldering fire had recently been kindled behind them.

Paul felt uncomfortable as she gazed at him. "I'm afraid there isn't much to tell," he said. "What with eight hours of practicing every day, my experience with notorious women is rather limited."

"How about women in general? Do you have a girl, Paul?"

He wished she wouldn't look at him that way. It was very disconcerting. He normally was far from shy around women, but Laura Verdugo wasn't like other women he'd met. She seemed so sure of herself, so confident. He didn't know whether he liked that in a woman or not, especially not the bold confidence Laura was displaying.

"No, I'm afraid I never got around to having a steady girl." He suddenly realized that he might be sounding too naive, too inexperienced. "I've had girls, of course," he said and crossed his legs, ankle to knee, manly fashion.

Laura watched him pick up his cognac and take a sip. "Are you good in bed?" She looked directly into his crotch.

Paul swallowed, feeling the liquor burn its way all the way down to his stomach. To cover his nervousness he laughed. "I'm afraid I wouldn't know, but I haven't had any complaints."

"I bet you haven't," she said, winking at him.

He was glad when his father walked back into the room. "That was a friend of yours, Paul," he said.

"Oh?" Thankfully he had an excuse to look away from Laura.

"A man by the name of Rod Shepherd. He said you sat next to him on the flight in."

"Yeah, sure," Paul said. "He's here to meet his daughter." He knew that Laura was still watching him. He purposely kept his eyes averted. "What did he want? Didn't he ask to talk to me?"

"No, he was calling on business. He asked if he could come

to the office tomorrow to see if I could help him with a problem he's having."

"With his daughter?"

"I'm afraid it's confidential," his father said.

"I wasn't prying, Dad. It's just that he looked so worried on the flight in. I hope you can help him. He's a real nice guy. You'll like him." Paul thought for a moment. "You know, I don't think Mr. Shepherd knows very many people here except maybe his daughter. It might be nice if we had them over for dinner or something."

"We'll see," his father said. "Right now, though, I think you'd better hit the sack."

Paul yawned. "Yes, I am kinda beat." He got out of his chair. "Well, I'll see you both in the morning," he said as he left the room.

Mr. Verdugo looked after him. "Nice boy," he said to his wife.

"Yes," she said with a smile. "Very nice." She wondered if he'd masturbate before he fell asleep.

ELAINE'S DEPRESSION WAS GETTING WORSE as dinner ended. They had spoken hardly a word except for Maggie, who hadn't stopped talking since she'd sat down. But with all her talk Elaine hadn't heard a word she'd said.

Jorge wasn't back yet. Elaine kept thinking up excuses for him. Perhaps he'd gotten involved with some old friends and couldn't get away; or even had an automobile accident. Anything would be better than thinking he just did not want to come back—that he was finished with her.

She wanted to scream, to cry, do anything except sit quietly and pretend she wasn't upset. She had to keep up a front. She couldn't let Cynthia and Greg know she wasn't all that sure Jorge would return. She mustn't keep looking toward the door. They'd know she was worried, uncertain of him.

If she had only listened to her conscience in the first place, none of this would be happening. She'd been silly and vain.

She should have told Jorge the truth about her age right off the bat and taken her chances. It would have been easier to suffer the loss at that early stage. To lose him now would be unbearable.

When she heard Jorge's car pull into the garage, she gripped the arms of her chair to keep from jumping up. She found herself looking at Cynthia. Cynthia had heard the car too; she was looking annoyed.

"Shall we have our coffee on the terrace?" Elaine asked as she stood up. In the background she heard the front door open and shut and Jorge's footsteps crossing the tile floor of the foyer and going up the stairs. He was walking fast, most likely still angry with her. But at least he was home and she'd have the opportunity to talk to him and try to explain. She wanted to fly up the stairs and into his arms. Unfortunately, Cynthia beat her to it.

"If you'll excuse me," Cynthia said as she rose from her chair. "I really don't care for any coffee." She skirted the table and went quickly out of the room. There was no doubt in Elaine's mind where she was headed.

Let her go, Elaine thought, knowing that if Jorge was still in an angry mood he wouldn't be any more receptive to talking to Cynthia than he would to her. Besides, Jorge didn't care for Cynthia. Let her weave her little web; she wouldn't capture him in it.

They straggled out onto the terrace, Maggie talking continuously. She was moaning comfortably over her last husband, having disposed (as far as Elaine had been able to follow) of the two husbands before him, her travels to the Orient, a gigolo in Cannes, her hairdresser, her finances, and her last operation and was now settling into discussing her favorite hobby, collecting antique hatpins. Greg was mute as a stone. When they reached the terrace he isolated himself from the group and sat at the far end of the balustrade; settling himself on it, he turned and stared out into the dark, moon-washed garden. He seemed unusually upset about something. He and Cynthia had whispered all during dinner, and it was obvious that she'd said something that had disturbed him greatly.

Elaine was wondering what was going on upstairs, but her thoughts were interrupted by the sound of another car coming up the drive. Dario Avisa waved as he climbed out of his old Renault and trotted up the stairs. He had a square face, pleasant but not particularly handsome. He looked very dashing, however, in his tight white trousers and open-neck shirt. His magnificent physique made up for the plainness of his face. His thick black hair was tousled and windblown. Dario Aviso was an extremely masculine young man. For the first time in an hour Maggie stopped talking and openly stared in admiration at the young man as he came toward them.

"Dario," Elaine smiled, extending her hand. He took it and pressed it to his lips. "We haven't seen you in ages. Where have you been?"

"Unfortunately I have been kept very busy training for the races on Wednesday. Even now I cannot stay very long."

"Yes, Jorge told me you were entered in the annual Tour de Majorca bicycle races again this year. I wish you all the luck in the world," Elaine said. She motioned toward the others seated around her. "You know everyone here, I believe."

Miguel stood and shook Dario's hand. Greg nodded from his corner.

"I don't believe I've had the pleasure," Dario said, smiling at Maggie.

"My apologies," Elaine said quickly. "Maggie, I'd like to present Jorge's best friend, Dario Avisa. Dario, Maggie Montgomery, one of my oldest and dearest friends."

"*Señora*," Dario said, bowing over her hand and kissing the back of it. "I am charmed."

Maggie giggled and patted the empty seat next to her. "Please sit down, Señor Avisa, here next to me. Did I understand you to say you are a bicyclist?"

"Yes. Are you interested in bicycling, *señora?*"

"Me? Heavens yes," Maggie gushed. "I simply adore the bicycle races. I never miss the one in Paris every year." She let her eyes rove over his trim, muscled body. "You must be very strong. It is a very arduous sport."

"Dario's won our local races two years in a row now," Elaine said.

"Hail the local hero," Greg said, sounding bored as he got up from his perch and wandered back into the house. At the doorway he turned to his mother. "If I decide to go out later can I borrow one of the cars?"

"Yes, of course," Elaine said. "Take my convertible. The keys are in the ignition."

He rubbed his forefinger and thumb together to indicate that he would need some money. Elaine got up. "Oh, yes," she said, slightly embarrassed. "I'll get you some." She excused herself and went with Greg into the house.

When she was opening the library safe she caught a glimpse of Jorge and Cynthia going toward the garden. They had their heads bent together in what looked like very serious conversation. After giving Greg some money—for which he didn't bother to thank her—she walked to the window and watched Cynthia and Jorge seat themselves in the gazebo. Cynthia was gesturing frantically; Jorge looked crestfallen and very miserable.

She strained to listen but didn't hear a word. If she had she would have heard Cynthia saying, "You've got to marry me, Jorge. I don't see what else we can do."

Jorge shook his head. "Are you sure?"

"Of course I'm sure. The doctor gave me the results of the tests this afternoon. There's no doubt about it. I'm three months pregnant."

Again Jorge shook his head. "But you told me when we slept together that there was nothing to worry about, that you were taking the pill."

"Well, the pill didn't work, obviously. Look, if you think I'm lying to you we can both go and see Dr. Surado tomorrow. Or call him right now if you wish. I'm sure you can reach him at home."

"No, I believe you, I guess," Jorge said. He thought for a minute. "Does Elaine know?"

"No one knows. You're the first one I told. I thought since you're the father you should be the first to hear."

"Damn," Jorge cursed as he started pacing.

"Ah, Jorge, it isn't so terrible," Cynthia said, going over to him and wrapping her arms tightly around his waist. "I love you so. I know you don't love me now, but you'll learn to. I'll make you a good wife. We can go far away from here, away from Elaine, away from this dreary house. Greg has a place in Paris. We can stay with him until we find a place of our own."

"And live on what?"

"We'll manage. Elaine will be furious, of course. But she'll come around in time. In the meantime we can live on my allowance, and I have some jewelry I can sell. We'll manage."

Jorge was desolate. He had been furious with Elaine for having lied to him, but he still loved her regardless and had intended telling her so. Now it was too late. Cynthia had seen to that. There was always the possibility of an abortion, of course, but he couldn't bring himself to be responsible for taking a human life, young as it may be. Besides, he doubted if Cynthia would consent to an abortion. They could always put the baby up for adoption, of course, but he knew Cynthia wouldn't go along with that either. She wanted to marry him; she had always wanted to get him away from Elaine, and she was succeeding.

He eased himself away from Cynthia. "Maybe we should tell Elaine. She will know what to do."

"No," Cynthia said firmly. "Elaine has nothing to do with this. It's our problem, Jorge, yours and mine. Besides, how could you bear to go to that woman after the lies she told you?"

"The lie was a harmless one," he said. "I can understand why she lied. I was only angry because she had made it possible for you and your brother to laugh at me." He looked directly into Cynthia's eyes. "I love Elaine," he said simply. "I will always love her."

"She's an old woman." Cynthia almost shouted it.

"And you are a young woman. What is the difference between old and young? They are simply words, nothing more."

Cynthia turned on him. "I'm not going to let you get out of this, Jorge. You are going to marry me. There's nothing else you can do."

Jorge sighed. Marrying Cynthia would be a mistake. Furthermore, it would not be fair to the child to be brought up by a father who would resent it. "I can't marry you, Cynthia. I just can't."

"You can and you will. So help me God," she ranted. "If you don't you'll regret it for the rest of your life."

"You are being overly dramatic. There must be a solution to this other than our marrying."

"There is no other solution." She stood in front of him, her fists clenched so tightly together the knuckles were white. "You'll marry me, Jorge, or I'll destroy you."

"And just how do you intend doing that?"

"By killing myself."

"Oh, Cynthia, stop being so silly."

"I swear to God, Jorge. I'll kill myself. I'm not joking. I'll do it. I'll kill myself and our child. How, may I ask, are you going to be able to live knowing you were responsible for two deaths?"

"You wouldn't have the nerve."

"Try me." Her eyes were dancing crazily. "Just try me. You tell me right now that you'll never marry me and we'll see who doesn't have the nerve. Go ahead, tell me. Tell me," she shouted, waving her hands frantically through the air.

He knew she'd do it. She was just spiteful and crazy enough to carry through her threat. Cynthia was just the type of girl to destroy anything and anyone—including herself —in order to get what she wanted. He was beaten and he knew it.

Elaine couldn't help herself. She didn't want to eavesdrop, but she found herself walking toward the gazebo. Jorge had his back to her. Just as she approached it, she saw him put out his hand to Cynthia. She saw Cynthia rush into his arms. As she stepped onto the platform she heard Jorge say, "All right, Cynthia. I'll marry you."

"Oh, my darling," Cynthia cried, crushing her mouth to his.

Elaine's eyes suddenly flooded with tears and she imagined she saw Jorge's arms going around Cynthia and returning her kiss with equal passion.

A tight, agonizing moan tore from her throat. "You bastard," she shrieked. "You ungrateful little bastard."

"Elaine," Jorge said, turning sharply and pushing Cynthia away from him.

"It isn't what you think. I can explain."

"Explain? Explain what, you stupid little puppy? How are you going to explain that you intend marrying my daughter? Yes, my daughter," she raved. "Well, take her, if that's what you want." She pointed toward the driveway. "Take her and get the hell out of my sight."

The tears were streaming down her face. She turned and fled back to the house, stumbling, almost falling in her flight.

"Elaine! Elaine!" Jorge called.

But all Elaine could hear was Cynthia's almost hysterical laughter.

Dario tried to intercept her as Elaine dashed blindly across the terrace and into the house. "Elaine, what is it?" Close on her heels was Jorge. Dario grabbed his arm. "What is going on, Jorge?" Dario asked, his face creased with concern.

"Please, Dario. Excuse me, I must speak with Elaine."

Dario held fast to his arm. "I do not think it would be wise, my friend. Not in Elaine's present condition. Whatever upset her, let her be by herself for a while. Let her calm herself. She will make much more sense after she has settled down."

Jorge tried to fight down his frustration. The impetuosity of his youth told him not to listen to his friend. Yet he knew Dario was being wise. Elaine was too upset to listen to any explanation, regardless of how much he forced her to. He would wait until she was more calm. "I suppose you are right," he said finally. "Come. Let us go into the game room. I have something I want to say to you in private."

Jorge closed the doors to make sure they would not be overheard. "I have a problem, my friend," he said to Dario. "I must have been born under a bad star, Dario. Nothing ever works out for me. Why is it that whenever I think things are working out well for me the bottom always drops out and I find myself back where I started?"

"You are feeling sorry for yourself, Jorge. Why don't you tell me what has happened? Perhaps it is not as bad as you think."

"It is bad, Dario. Very bad. I played for high stakes and I've lost everything."

"You mean Elaine?"

"Yes. Elaine, happiness, wealth, everything."

"I doubt if all that is so; but even if it is you still have not lost yourself."

Jorge shook his head. "I have even lost that."

Dario had grown up with Jorge and knew his every mood. He had to admit that he had never seen Jorge so despondent before. He said nothing and waited for Jorge to go on.

Jorge slammed a fist down on the edge of the billiard table. "Damn," he swore. "Why can't things work out the way I want them to?"

"But you are wrong, Jorge. Things always work out for you." He tried to hide the touch of resentment that he felt toward his friend. It was true, however, that Jorge always had all the luck. Women were drawn to him by the mere flash of a smile or a look. Jorge had a knack for saying the right thing, doing the right thing. He had charm and poise and possessed the fortunate talent of becoming a part of whatever someone else was a part of. Jorge fit comfortably into the world of the rich. Dario, on the other hand, would always look out of place in villas like this. His only success was in bicycle racing, and like all athletes he appeared more at home in a locker room than in a drawing room.

It annoyed him more than he cared to admit to see Jorge, head in hands, wallowing in self-pity. Jorge always came out on top, while Dario picked through the ashes and basked in Jorge's shadow.

He felt ashamed for his resentment of his friend. After all, if it wasn't for the inroads Jorge made, Dario would never have met all the wealthy, fashionable people Jorge introduced him to. He should be grateful to his friend, not resent him.

Jorge ran his hand through his hair and paced about the room. He picked up the cue ball and threw it against the wall. "I can't lose Elaine," he cried. "She's everything I've ever wanted. I don't want to go back to being poor, go back to hustling the rich broads on the beach. Elaine cares for me. I'm not just some young stud she wants to have a fling with. She's not like the others, who are only out looking for a quick lay or for someone to spend a weekend with, someone to help fill a few lonely hours. Elaine doesn't treat me like those other women. To her I am not just a pretty hustler with a good bed technique. She loves me. She needs me, as I need her."

Dario smiled. "Of course she loves you. Everyone knows that. Why are you letting yourself get so upset because of a simple misunderstanding?"

Jorge shook his head. "It is more than that." His eyes looked as if they were going to leak tears. "I've lost her. I have lost my Elena." He turned and fixed a steady gaze on Dario. "I am going to marry Cynthia."

Dario had been sitting on the edge of the billiard table. He jumped to his feet. "What? Are you mad? You can't marry Cynthia." His mind raced backward. He had wanted Cynthia ever since Jorge first introduced him to her. Unfortunately, Cynthia had eyes only for Jorge then. Dario still pined for her. Cynthia was the kind of girl he had always wanted. First and foremost, she was rich. Further, she was fiery and independent and unpredictable. She was restless and demanding. She was like himself in many respects— easily bored, always looking for a good time. He could never understand why Cynthia had chosen to fall in love with Jorge rather than with him. Jorge had never really liked her. He supposed Jorge represented a challenge to her. "You can't," he repeated a little more softly. "You don't love Cynthia," he stammered.

"One does not always marry for love."

Dario tried to keep calm. He went over to Jorge and put an affectionate arm around his shoulder. "I think you had better tell me what has happened."

Jorge dropped into a chair. "It is very simple. Cynthia is going to have my child."

Dario stared at him. "Cynthia is pregnant? But you told me you had never slept with her."

Jorge bowed his head. "I told you that because I knew that you were very interested in her and I did not want to hurt your feelings. It happened only once. Obviously once is enough." He slapped his hands on his knees. "She is going to have my baby, and the only way out of it is to marry her."

"You told Elaine this?"

"No, I did not have to. Elaine heard me tell Cynthia that I would marry her. That is all she heard. She flew into a rage and called me terrible names. I was rushing after her to explain when you stopped me."

Dario put a gentle hand on his friend's shoulder. "It is not so terrible, Jorge. Once you have explained to Elaine she will find a way out for you."

Jorge looked miserable. "No. Cynthia has sworn that she will kill both herself and the baby if I do not marry her. I know her. She does not make idle threats. She will do it."

Dario knew her also. It was true; Cynthia Brandon did not make idle threats.

"Look," Dario said, patting Jorge on the back. "I would suggest you not rush into anything immediately. Why not wait a couple of days? Go and stay with Carlotta or one of our other friends. It will give both Elaine and Cynthia as well as yourself time to think things out more clearly. You would be surprised at how different problems sometimes look if they are allowed to rest for a day or two."

"Cynthia wants to leave tonight. She is planning that we elope to Paris."

"So go and tell her that it is impossible for you to leave on such short notice, that you have business you must clear up before you leave. If you cannot put her off for a few days, at least try to put her off until tomorrow." A sudden idea popped into his head. "Look. You disappear, at least for this evening. I will go to Cynthia and I will tell her that you are gone for good, that she scared you away. I will also tell her that you told me everything and that I will be willing to marry her and claim the baby as my own."

Jorge shook his head. "You are a good friend, Dario, but that will not work. Cynthia wants to marry me, no one else."

"But if you are not here she will change her mind."

"She will kill herself . . . and the baby."

"I will not give her the chance. I will take her with me tonight."

"Now it is you who are not thinking clearly, my friend. You have your bicycle races in two days. Would you throw away all your work just to marry a woman who does not want to marry you?"

Dario hesitated. Selfish vanity of youth came to the fore. He trained and waited all year for his one big opportunity to achieve the adulation of the crowd. He was too dedicated an athlete to give it all up so easily. "I will think of something," he said, but with very little conviction.

"No. I thank you, Dario, but there is nothing to do but for me to marry Cynthia." He turned toward the door. "I will go and tell her to get ready to leave."

"No, wait," Dario said. "At least let me talk to her first. Who knows, perhaps she will change her mind when I tell her how much I love her. I will charm her out of her wits. Give me a chance, Jorge. Please let me speak with her. If I cannot persuade her to choose me rather than you, then you can do as you wish."

Jorge hesitated. "I suppose it can do no harm to try. But are you certain you want to marry Cynthia?"

"Why not?" Dario said with youthful flippancy. "She is beautiful, she will inherit a lot of money one day. She is the best catch on Majorca. Besides, my father and mother are after me daily to get married. They want me to marry Isa-

bella, you know. But she is a peasant like me. I do not want
to be a peasant all my life."

No one could understand that more than Jorge. Perhaps
Dario's little plan would work. If it did, Jorge would see that
Elaine provided for them for the rest of their lives. "Very
well," he said after deliberating with his conscience. "Go and
talk to Cynthia. I will wait for you here."

Dario slapped him on the back again. "You will not regret
this, Jorge. Everything will work out. You will see."

IT WAS AFTER TEN O'CLOCK BEFORE ROD AND
Nancy finished dinner. In Palma everyone ate late. The
restaurants didn't open until eight, and no one hurried.
They sat at a wooden table in an open courtyard over which
colored electric bulbs were strung from tree to tree. There
was the smell of jasmine and the feel of a soft warm breeze
on their faces.

Nancy pushed the plate of spiny Mediterranean lobster
away from her and gave a little groan. "No more."

Rod laughed. "Well, if you're not going to finish that, give
it here," he said, reaching for her plate.

The evening was going beautifully for him. Nancy was so
like Lisa, so casual, so fun-loving, laughing, joking. He had to
keep reminding himself that this wasn't his daughter he was
with but a stranger he'd met only hours before. He couldn't
remember when he'd felt so relaxed, so totally at ease.

Across the way was built a rough wooden-plank dance
platform on which several couples in traditional folk costume were dancing the *iotas mateixas,* a dance native to
Majorca. To Rod it seemed far from Latin, accompanied, as
it was by two musicians, one playing the bagpipe, the other
the fife and drum—at least it looked and sounded like a fife
and drum.

"Not very authentic," Rod commented as he proceeded to
finish off Nancy's lobster. "I feel more as if we were in Scot-
land than in Palma."

"That instrument that looks like a bagpipe is called a *chirimies*. Bagpipes are an international instrument; didn't you know that?"

"I'm afraid music isn't one of my fortes. How come you know so much about it?"

"I took a course in ethnic music and dances when I was in college." She nodded toward the dancers. "You'll notice that the dancers are not particularly young. Only the older inhabitants do the traditional dances any more. The younger generation prefer the pop music—rock, as we call it at home." She took a sip of her wine. "You'll see later on that the traditional dancers will vanish into the night and the young set will take over, bumping and grinding just as they do at home."

"It doesn't seem right somehow. I didn't come to Majorca to hear rock and roll."

"Why did you come to Majorca, Rod?"

"Business."

"Personal or financial?"

Rod pushed the plate away. "I'd rather not discuss business tonight, young lady. I'm enjoying myself too much."

"Okay, no business." She propped her elbows on the table and thought for a moment. "If you want some typically local atmosphere, my girlfriend gave me another name and address where she says the local color is simply terrific. Want to go see?"

Before meeting Nancy at eight, Rod had promised that he'd make it an early evening, that he'd get to bed early so that he could finish with his business with Lisa first thing in the morning. Now he was only too anxious to make the night last as long as he could. "Sure. I'd love to," he said.

After settling accounts with the proprietor, they strolled arm in arm down the bustling street. Rod was amazed at the number of people crowding the sidewalks and the cafés. Palma was alive with people, young and old alike, stringy-haired beatniks (as Rod called them), well-dressed couples in furs and jewels, tourists in flowered shirts and walking shorts. The jangle of types and colors was exciting. Everywhere lights were ablaze, music blared, people laughed and chattered. Some of the chatter he understood; most of it was in foreign languages, Spanish, French, German. He heard a couple arguing in what he thought was Danish or Swedish.

"And they say New York is a melting pot," Rod laughed as they passed a young Negro speaking some African tongue to a white girl who answered back with a very broad English accent.

They turned a corner and ran headlong into a mass of people all crowding toward some activity that was going on in the middle of the street. "What's this, a parade?" Rod asked, stretching over the heads of those around him to see what the attraction was.

"The clerk at the hotel said they're having the Festival to Spring tonight. Wow, this crowd is something. Want to stay and watch, or shall we go to that place I mentioned?"

"Let's watch," Rod said, taking hold of her hand and pulling her into the crowd, closer to the street where they could get a better look.

Several young men sat on horseback, each with a cuplike vessel in one hand. One by one they were blindfolded after being allowed to assess the position of a ball that hung from a line stretched across the street. In turn, the blindfolded horsemen spurred their horses and tried to cup the ball with the vessels they carried. The crowd hooted and yelled, betting against this one or that. Rod and Nancy watched as each of the young men tried. The crowd groaned as one by one each rider failed to cup the ball.

The ball was then replaced by a live chicken, which was strung up by its feet. The vessels in the young men's hands were replaced by sharp swords. Nancy tugged Rod's arm. "Come on," she said. "I'd rather not watch this."

Rod was interested, but let himself be pulled away. "What are they going to do?" he asked.

Nancy shivered. "They're supposed to see who can cut down the chicken by slicing through the rope attached to its feet. Blindfolded as they are, there usually isn't any chicken left to cut down."

Rod shuddered. "Another one of the things you learned in your ethnic class?"

"No, my girlfriend was here last year and told me about it. She also raved about the cockfights and the bullfights. I'm afraid anything involving cruelty to animals isn't my cup of tea."

"I'm with you. The sight of blood makes me queasy. I shouldn't admit that, should I? It doesn't sound very manly."

"Nonsense. I had a boyfriend who was captain of the football team but passed out every time he was injected with a needle."

"Is that the type of guy you usually go for—captains of football teams?" He didn't know why he'd asked that, but he wanted to know.

"No, not really. I just like men to be men, whether they're athletes or accountants, like you."

Rod's heart started to beat faster. He wanted Nancy to like him. Each time he looked at her she reminded him less and less of Lisa. Oh, she resembled her physically, but he suddenly didn't want to think of her as a daughter. He was enjoying himself too much. The most disconcerting thing was that Nancy had a sexual aura about her. It attracted him more than he cared to admit.

"Where is this place you're taking me to?" he asked as they left the crowds and started along the quay.

"Down here at the waterfront. It sounds like a seedy, tough kind of place, but it isn't. It's very popular with the locals, I'm told."

It was a huge box of a place, thick with smoke, music and people. A narrow staircase climbed up one wall, at the bottom of which four trim young ladies sat at a table. They were dressed in tight shiny dresses of brilliant pink and red and green, flounced with yards and yards of ruffles. Their spines were as straight as ramrods, their heads erect. A heavy coating of mascara covered the eyelashes, the lips glistened with red. They watched the young male guitarist on stage, completely absorbed in his music and waiting for their turn to perform.

Rod and Nancy stumbled behind the waiter, squeezing their way to a table in the corner. They ordered a carafe of wine and tried to adjust their eyes to the smoke.

The guitarist launched into a brilliant coda of rippling notes, then let them fall into a single sigh. The note faded slowly into nothing. There was a long moment of absolute silence. Then the applause broke out with such intensity and volume it seemed to rattle the walls.

One of the ladies seated at the foot of the staircase—one in screaming pink—stepped up onto the stage. A young man, tall and thin with skin-tight black trousers and high-heeled boots, joined her.

"Flamenco," Nancy whispered. She watched intently as the couple began a slow, almost motionless circle around each other. They clapped their hands softly to the music of a guitar. The clapping was replaced by the clicking of castanets as the music picked up its tempo. They danced faster in a swirl of ruffles and a tapping of heels, their hands held high, their backs arched as gracefully as an archer's bow.

Rod glanced at Nancy. Her face was shining and aglow as she stared entranced at the dancers. His hand was resting atop the table. As the music increased to a still more feverish tempo, Nancy suddenly put her hand on his and squeezed it hard. She didn't turn to look at him. Her eyes were like mirrors of light, her lips half parted. He took her hand in his and leaned back in his chair.

The happiness he felt threatened to burst from inside him.

Tuesday

MORNING SPLASHED OVER PALMA IN BRIGHT,
brittle waves of color. The soft shadows of the almond trees
lay lightly across the spread of café tables at the foot of Bell-
ver Castle Hill. It was impossible to believe that so peaceful
an island had once been the site of countless bloody battles.
Greeks and Phoenicians were slaughtered by the Carthagin-
ians, who, in turn, were slaughtered by the Romans in their
zeal to spread Christianity four hundred years after Christ's
death. The Romans were devastated by Vandal domination;
the Vandals by the Byzantines. Majorca was fought over by
the Muslims, the Emirate of Cordova, Emirs of Denia, the
Catalan-Pisan crusaders. It was the scene of civil uprising,
ruthless murder of hundreds of its Jewish population, severe
floods, famine, plague. It was inconceivable that so tranquil a
place had had so violent a past.

The past was the farthest thing from Rod's mind as he sat
alone at one of the more isolated tables, ignoring the slight
morning breeze which fluttered the red-checked cloth. His
thoughts were a mixed confusion of bright and dark. His
evening with Nancy the night before had made him happier
than he'd been in a long, long time. On the other hand, his
scheduled ten-o'clock appointment with Mr. Verdugo at the
Consulate made him feel guilty about his happiness.

Last evening there had been moments—too many of them
—when he'd not thought about his daughter at all. Nancy had
miraculously lifted him out of his depression and had proved
to him that he could be happy again. After leaving the
taverna and the flamenco dancing, they had taken a moonlit
buggy ride through the parks and narrow, sleepy streets. He
tingled at the thought of her kiss. He had put out his hand
and had thanked her for a delightful evening. She took his
breath away when she suddenly stretched up on tiptoe and
planted her mouth, warm and soft and moist, tightly against
his. It had thrown his mind into such turmoil that it took
every ounce of his willpower to ease her away.

He kept telling himself that his attraction to Nancy was
due only to her strong resemblance to Lisa. But in the bright,
crystal light of morning he knew that wasn't the case. It
hadn't been Lisa who'd looked longingly across the table at
him. It hadn't been Lisa who'd slipped her hand in his. He
thought it all harmless enough at first; now he must face the
reality of it all.

He looked up at the great crust of mountains in the distance and wished Nancy were sitting here with him. Stop it, a little voice inside his head exclaimed. Nancy Winston is only a girl who reminded you of your daughter. The goodnight kiss meant nothing. You certainly aren't going to start an affair with Nancy.

An affair! Where in hell did that thought come from? He sat straighter in his chair. He wasn't starting an affair with Nancy. They had only spent a harmless evening together. What was wrong with that?

He sensed a familiar ache in his groin. He ignored it, telling himself that it wasn't Nancy Winston who was causing the ache. In his heart he knew he was lying to himself.

It was insane. He couldn't possibly be sexually attracted to a girl Nancy's age.

But you are, a little voice told him.

I'm not. It's just that there were moments last night when Nancy had acted more like Helen than Lisa. But Helen certainly would never have been forward enough to slip her hand in his on a first date, let alone brazen enough to kiss him goodnight.

The ache in his groin got more intense. He wondered what it would be like to have sex with someone as young as Nancy. Oh, he supposed he had had prostitutes her age, but prostitutes didn't have ages—they were always old, even the young ones. Besides, he hadn't had all that many. He frowned. Was he equating Nancy with prostitutes? No, of course not. Nancy was a clean, decent girl. A bit forward perhaps, something he wasn't very accustomed to except in those women he'd paid. But they were expected to be forward; it was included in the price. Nancy's forwardness wasn't of that kind. She was from a younger generation that didn't have the reservations older people carried around with them. Forwardness in Nancy was rather refreshing. It fit her well. On her it sparkled; on prostitutes it lay like cheap jewelry.

He shivered, suddenly thinking about the exciting things the whore in Barcelona—and others like her—had done to him. Nancy, for all her forwardness, would never do things like that, he was sure. Such things had no place in a husband-and-wife relationship.

Husband-and-wife? Now he was equating Nancy with a husband-and-wife relationship. Christ, they'd only had one date, he reminded himself. Slow down, Rod. You're letting yourself get a bit carried away. Yet, he found himself smiling as he remembered how she'd laughed, the way she'd hung on his every word. She'd acted so much like Helen last night, sweet, pure, thoughtful, making him feel as if he were the most important person in the world. She was like Helen in so many ways it was uncanny. He wondered if Nancy would be like Helen in bed too. He and Helen had had a good sex life, the type of relations that they'd been brought up to perform . . . normal, correct relations and not the perverted, unnatural acts that belonged in the catalog of every prostitute. Nancy being as young as she was, she most likely didn't know women did those things to men. He was glad she didn't. Chaste innocence suited her so well. It was one of the things that attracted him to her.

He rubbed his hands over his face to clear away the thoughts of sex and Nancy Winston.

He stirred his coffee. Its dark, murky color chased Nancy away and replaced her with Lisa. He closed his eyes and could picture Lisa sitting alone and frightened in the dark, cold light of her jail cell. He would get her out of there today if he had to break down the stone walls to do it. Mr. Verdugo had sounded encouraging on the telephone last evening. He was sure he'd be able to help him free Lisa. Yes, it would only be a matter of time now until he could get Lisa free and they'd be on their way.

Tonight he would be having dinner with his daughter. The thought made him happy. But what about Nancy? He sighed. He reminded himself of his resolve to forget about other women. Lisa was the reason he had come to Majorca, not other women, especially a woman as young as Nancy. He just wouldn't see Nancy again. It would be for the best. He couldn't afford to do something foolish. It would be a mistake to encourage a relationship with Nancy. If he had any sense at all he'd get Lisa out of jail and get on the first plane for home.

He glanced at his watch. There was still over half an hour before he was due at the Consulate. He stood up and put twenty-five pesetas under the saucer. That certainly would be enough for one cup of coffee, he thought, seeing that the waiter was busy with several other customers.

He strolled down one of the twisting streets with its balconied houses with potted geraniums bursting through the slats of wrought iron. Very early this morning he and Nancy had driven through streets like this one; then they had been absent of people. Now everything was alive. It was as if a painter had taken a brush and had added activity to his street scene.

He walked on until he reached the main thoroughfare of Paseo Generalissimo Franco, a vaulted arcade of leafy shade trees and pavements as smooth and shiny as polished marble. People were laughing and gesturing as they lingered over breakfasts of coffee and rolls and meats and cheeses. Through the windows of the shops Rod noticed the shopkeepers busy with their morning trade. He paused before one of the display windows and admired the handsome leather, the exquisite glassware for which the Majorcans were so famous. (He'd read that in one of the travel brochures.) A particular leather handbag caught his eye. He decided he'd buy it for Nancy. He caught himself just as he was entering the shop. Buying a gift for Nancy would only prove that he wanted to start something. He was glad the shop clerk was busy with customers and hadn't seen him enter. He turned and walked quickly away.

As he walked he couldn't stop thinking about the beautiful young girl he'd been with last night. She had made him feel so young. Everything seemed so different this morning. Even the city itself was different. It was as if he were seeing Palma for the first time. Everything had changed since yesterday. He felt almost like a boy again, when nothing was crowded, nothing complex, when everything merely consisted of soft shades and uncomplicated lives.

He strolled on, his footsteps lighter than he remembered them ever being. There was a sense of freedom, of space, of openness all around him. He could almost imagine the exhilaration a butterfly must experience when it first emerges from its cocoon. He was a stranger in a strange land, yet he did not feel the least bit strange. He couldn't, for the moment, identify exactly how he felt. Then it came to him. He raised his head and looked about. It was excitement; a sensation so foreign to him he'd almost forgotten what it felt like. It was like that afternoon he'd stepped off the bus in Dayton years and years ago, alone, determined to make it on his own so he'd never have to go back to that isolated life on the farm.

A few days ago he was sure that Majorca would turn out to be some sordid little Spanish province where all the women dressed in mourning and all the men looked like shabby replicas of aging matadors. But it wasn't like that at all. If it wasn't for Lisa being in jail he thought he might enjoy his visit.

He thought of Nancy and forcibly shoved the thought away.

How he wished Helen were here with him now. No, that wasn't true. He was glad he was alone—at least for a little while. He wanted to be alone; he always had. Ever since he could remember he had enjoyed experiencing new adventures on his own. He liked to interpret new sights and sounds the way he wanted them to be and not have them distorted by someone else's interpretations. As much as it disturbed him to admit it, he never actually enjoyed traveling with Helen. She had always been so practical, so unromantic about things and places. To her a landmark or a historical building was nothing more than a compilation of dates and facts and architectural lines. Rod, on the other hand, preferred to look at a place or a structure and imagine the excitement and the events and interesting people that lurked in its past. Lisa was a lot like him in that respect. At least she used to be.

His excitement dimmed slightly as he thought of Lisa. He had always tried to be a good father to her. A feeling of discomfort made him shrug as he thought of the times when he had not been a good father, but Lisa certainly did not know about those times. No man is perfect, he told himself, trying to dislodge his guilt feelings. He'd raised his daughter as well as any man could. It hadn't been his fault that she'd gone off on a wrong track.

He and Lisa were so much alike, though. Perhaps she was discovering that she had the same sinful weakness as himself.

He shook his head. No. Impossible. Lisa wasn't old enough to understand such feelings. She was only fifteen. What could she possibly know about that kind of physical need at fifteen?

He shook off the thought. He wouldn't think about such things now. He was in a strange and exciting new place. He'd arrange for Lisa's release, and then he'd make the trip into a holiday for them. Perhaps here he and Lisa would find each other again.

A holiday! Sure, why not? To hell with the office and tax

time. To hell with the clients. Wasn't his daughter far more important to him than his work? He hadn't had a vacation in God only knew how long. He was certainly far from rich, but he could afford a well-deserved vacation. His employees could get along without him for a week.

He patted the wallet of traveler's checks in his inside pocket, also touched the thick wallet of money in his hip pocket. There were an awful lot of people milling around. Everyone knew that pickpockets ran rampant in these resort places. Not knowing what it would cost to secure Lisa's release, he'd brought a lot of money with him.

He'd come a long way from that bright day he'd stepped off the bus in Dayton with nothing but his ambition. He'd worked hard and found he was good at figures. No job had been too menial or too hard. He did anything and everything he could to keep from having to go back to that dismal farm and his strict, puritanical parents, who thought happiness was found only in God. He'd made a small success of himself. Oh, not a very large success, but his accounting firm was one of the most respected in Ohio. He was proud of Shepherd & Company.

Yet while making his company a success he'd never traveled much for pleasure. He never had the time and Helen never had the desire, always giving Lisa and her church work as excuses for staying at home. Helen was very dedicated to the church and expected him to be as well. To her a vacation meant driving up to her folks' farm in Celina for a week. He'd taken her with him to a convention in New York once. Rod had found it exciting; Helen had hated it. New York, she'd said, was a modern-day Sodom and Gomorrah. The same thing was true about their trip to Hawaii. After those two times he went to the conventions alone. Perhaps he never should have married Helen. No, that was wrong. He was glad he'd married her. She'd been good for him. She'd set a good example, and there wasn't a woman alive who would have been more thoughtful and understanding. Helen had been good, there was no other word to describe her. Her strict religious beliefs, her need to do what was right, had forced him to see the error in his old ways. He had always had a weakness for women. She'd recognized that in him and had taught him how to strengthen that weakness. She'd proved to him that a good, moral woman could be far more satisfying than the faster models he had once preferred.

His conscience started to bother him as he recalled the number of times he'd slipped back into his old ways. He'd always been careful; Helen never found out about his slight digressions. He couldn't understand the urges that overpowered him occasionally. Hard as he'd tried to rid himself of them, they continued to itch until he was forced to scratch the itch.

He loosened the collar of his shirt slightly. He mustn't let himself fall into that trap, not ever again. But oh, how often had he made that resolution? He remembered again the prostitute in Barcelona, and it made him fidget uncomfortably. He must try to stay away from temptations like that. If it hadn't been for that weakness in him, Helen might be alive today. Yet hard as he tried, he had never been able to resist those temptations. If only Helen had understood him better— if only he had found the courage to be completely honest with her about sex—he never would have had to resort to other women. But she hadn't understood those occasional needs that plagued him. It was too late now to hope that she might. Helen was dead, and it had been his strange urges that had indirectly been responsible for her death.

To him it was a paradox. He had loved Helen for her puritanism in bed. She was so simple, so trusting, so loving. Still, a deeply ingrained need for the unconventional drove him away from her on occasion.

He must change, he vowed. He had lost Helen because of his weakness, and now there was a chance that he might lose Lisa as well. He must not let that happen. He could change. It wasn't too late. He would become more like Helen— reserved and conventional and strict, both with himself and with Lisa.

How would Helen have handled this mess Lisa had gotten herself into? He thought for a moment, conjuring up Helen's lovely yet determined face. Helen would be unbending and demanding. She would come for Lisa and would take her home where she belonged, even if it meant dragging the girl there by the hair of the head. He'd force himself to be like that. He was finished with pampering Lisa. After all, what had it gotten him? He'd always been soft and understanding; Helen, on the other hand, had always been firm and unyield-

ing. And in the end it was Helen Lisa longed for, not him.
Yes, he'd adopt Helen's attitude. He would not let Lisa have
her own way again. He would straighten her out if it was the
last thing he did.

His vow seemed to brace his shoulders. His chin firmed as
the soft sea air beat gently against his face. Things would
work out here on Majorca, he told himself. He would make
them work out.

He and Lisa would have a vacation. He'd forget business.
Business seemed out of place here anyway. He'd forget Shepherd & Company. Twenty-four hours ago he would never
have entertained such a notion, but in Palma it seemed
natural.

And he wouldn't encourage Nancy, either. In spite of the
strength of his newfound purpose, the thought of Nancy
made him weak. He liked her very much—more than he
wanted to admit.

He wondered if it had been his date with Nancy that had
caused such a change in him this morning. He couldn't kid
himself; Nancy had a lot to do with it, of course. But she
wasn't all of it. He'd changed overnight because he knew that
today would be the day he'd have Lisa with him again. That
was why he was so happy. That, and Nancy, of course. But
Nancy was just a small part of it.

He knew he was lying to himself again.

He was early for his appointment but found Mr. Verdugo
waiting for him when he walked into his office. The two men
shook hands.

"My son, Paul, was quite taken with you, Mr. Shepherd,"
Mr. Verdugo said as they seated themselves around the desk.

Rod had forgotten his original resentment of Paul's father.
Seeing him now and hearing him speak of his son brought
that resentment back. There was something about him—the
thick, horn-rimmed glasses, the pinched face—that branded
him as the type of man who would walk away from an infant
son and not bother about him until the son was old enough to
fend for himself. Paul Jr. didn't look like his father at all; he
didn't have the selfish, independent air about him that his
father had.

"Paul's a very nice boy," Rod said. "I liked him immensely.
One doesn't find too many good, level-headed kids like that
around nowadays."

"That was one of the reasons I wanted him to come over here for a while. I'm afraid his mother was turning him into too serious a young man. A boy Paul's age should have fun. We both know how easily age supplants youth."

There was something irritating about the way Mr. Verdugo spoke of his son. It was as if Paul Jr. were a toy someone had given him, a toy he found amusing but would tire of before long. Rather than pursue the subject of Paul Jr., Rod said, "I mentioned on the telephone last evening that I was having a problem getting my daughter released from custody. She's being held at the Palma jail. I went there yesterday, but they said I would not be able to see her without official permission. I'll not pretend that I'm not annoyed and more than a little concerned about her."

Mr. Verdugo smiled and nodded. "I'm familiar with the case. I'm sorry our local police gave you a hard time, but if you were to stay here for any length of time you would get used to the Majorcan ways of doing things. Everything must be by the book, so to speak. They are a people who respect authority and never go against it."

"Can you give me permission to at least see Lisa?" Rod asked as he leaned forward in his chair.

Again Mr. Verdugo nodded. "Yes, I can grant that permission. Unfortunately, I am in no position to effect her release, however."

Rod frowned. "Why not?"

Mr. Verdugo opened a file that had been sitting in front of him. He adjusted his eyeglasses. "I've been reacquainting myself with your daughter's case. Naturally I was apprised of Lisa's arrest when it occurred. In fact, I was instrumental in getting her to cable you. She didn't want to at first," he said, looking over the rims of his spectacles at Rod. He removed the glasses and laid them aside. He leaned back in his chair and crossed his arms in front of him. "Possession of hard drugs is a very serious charge here on Majorca."

"What? Hard drugs?" Rod started out of his chair.

Mr. Verdugo waved him back into his seat. "Your daughter was arrested for possession of drugs. A search of her purse showed a rather large supply of both heroin and cocaine."

"Oh, no," Rod breathed, his face going white. He wiped his hand across his eyes. "I can't believe it," he said, shaking his head. "Lisa doesn't take that stuff. It must have been planted on her."

"No. In fact, your daughter was foolish enough to admit to the police that she'd carried the drugs with her when she entered Majorca. That was a mistake." He studied Rod for a moment, then asked, "Didn't you know that Lisa was on hard drugs?"

"But she isn't," Rod argued. "Oh, there was a little trouble about marijuana back in the States, but she told me she had stopped using it."

"They all say that," Mr. Verdugo said with a look of contempt. "The kids today lie so much they wouldn't know what telling the truth is all about."

Rod's resentment took hold of him again. "I disagree. I think the young people of today are a lot more honest than we were when we were their age."

"I don't know where you were brought up, Mr. Shepherd, but I never smoked marijuana or indulged in the free sex practices that go on among the young today."

Rod gave him a cold look. "I was raised on a farm in Ohio, and I can assure you we had drugs and booze and sex. And we had to lie in our teeth to cover it all up because things just weren't as honest and open as they are now." He couldn't stop himself from adding, "You must have been raised in a very sheltered atmosphere, Mr. Verdugo."

Mr. Verdugo cleared his throat and replaced his spectacles. "Yes, well . . ." he said, again glancing at Lisa's dossier. "Lisa's case isn't completely hopeless, of course."

"What do I have to do?"

"Fortunately there are certain higher-ups here who are not quite as honest as one would hope them to be, Mr. Shepherd. I, naturally, would have no dealings with such people, but you being a more worldly, realistic man might consider asking their help."

"Can they get Lisa out of jail?"

Mr. Verdugo put his hands together and propped his chin on them. He nodded. "Lisa's release would simply be a matter of contacting the right person with the right amount of cash."

Rod's gaze was icy. "Can you arrange this?"

"Officially, no. Unofficially, and as a favor to a man who befriended my son, yes." He hesitated. Rod saw a wicked sort of gleam come into his eyes. "Incidentally, you might be interested to know that your daughter was not traveling alone. She was with an older man, a man who ran off when Lisa was arrested. The man is a notorious drug smuggler and is wanted in practically every country in Europe. Lisa admitted she was with this man, but refuses to tell us where we can find him—if she knows. It would be advisable to try to find out the whereabouts of your daughter's . . . er . . . friend. It would be a great service to many people."

Rod tried hard not to show his shock. "Do you know the man's name?"

Mr. Verdugo made a vague gesture. "He goes by many names. Here we know him as George Petrik. A Bulgarian, I believe."

"If my daughter knows where this man is, I'm sure she'll tell me."

Mr. Verdugo smiled. "I'm afraid I don't agree with you. A father is sometimes the last to know what his child is really like."

"Not if he makes the effort," Rod answered, trying to hold a check on his temper.

"Well, if she does tell you where this Petrik character is, we would be most appreciative if you informed us." He opened a desk drawer and pulled out a business card. "Now. This is the name and address of a very prominent lawyer here in Palma. His name is Miguel Montoro. If anyone can secure Lisa's release, he can, but I warn you, he doesn't come cheap."

Rod took the card and glanced at it. Then he slipped it into his pocket. "I'll call him."

Mr. Verdugo reached for the telephone. "If you're certain you want to see him, perhaps it would be best if I called and made the appointment for you."

"I want to take my daughter home, regardless of cost."

Mr. Verdugo dialed. Rod noticed that he didn't have to look up the number. He spoke for several minutes in Spanish, which made Rod wonder what they were talking about. Most likely they were deciding how to split the fee, he decided.

JORGE SAW THAT THE NEEDLE OF THE GAS gauge was touching the empty mark as he drove into the neighboring town of Andraitx. His muscles ached, and his eyelids felt too heavy to hold open much longer. He'd driven aimlessly most of the night, trying to decide what he should do.

He'd waited in the billiard room for over three-quarters of an hour, but Dario had never come back. When he'd gone to search for Cynthia and Dario he'd found no one, only Maggie and Miguel getting more than a little drunk on brandy. He had tapped on Elaine's door, but she had only ranted at him and repeated that she never wanted to see him again. And so he had packed his few belongings, made one last search for Cynthia and Dario and left the villa. He hadn't intended taking the sports car Elaine had given him, but he wanted to get away as quickly as possible.

He kept telling himself that Dario had been successful. He hoped Dario hadn't lost that terrible temper of his and done something foolish. No, Dario knew what was at stake. Everything would work out all right. He would stay with Carlotta and give Elaine time to simmer down. Carlotta would put him up for a few days, he was sure.

He had thought he loved Carlotta once. But he had been a child then; they both had been children, simple and innocent and filled with the dreams of children. They had different dreams, though. His had been for wealth and success, hers for a modest house and a loving husband and children. As Jorge grew older, ambition and discontent grew with him. Carlotta had never understood his need to better himself. She could not imagine any life better than the life they'd always known. She saw nothing wrong with being poor. It was an honest and respectable status. In her mind, wealth represented evil, decadence and corruption. That fact was proved to her when her mother died and she became responsible for a brood of younger brothers and sisters and a father too infirm to support them. She had taken work as a domestic for one of the very rich families of Palma. She saw their wickedness, their selfishness, their sinfulness. One of the men of that great and noble house had forced himself upon her, raping her during one of his drunken rampages. When she became pregnant with his child, he denied everything, laughed in her face, called her a slut and kicked her out. She could not go home carrying her shame. Jorge and Dario had understood and had helped her as best they could. But Carlotta had no place in the world Jorge and Dario sought, the world of wealth and luxury. She bore the child; blessedly it was born dead. Her family still needed her financial support. She'd been branded a common woman and, out of desperation, began to live as one. She had never thought herself capable of hating. But she hated now. She hated all people of wealth and power. She hated the rich with every fiber of her being.

Jorge sighed as past memories crept back to him. Carlotta would let him stay with her for a few days. She would not turn him away when he needed her. She would remember how he had helped her when she was in need. He couldn't stay long, however, and he'd pay for his time. Living with Carlotta would cut off her trade; a prostitute couldn't afford to have a male friend staying with her for any length of time. It discouraged customers. But Carlotta wouldn't refuse him; Carlotta never refused him anything.

He crossed over the narrow river that flowed down through the mountain gorge into a valley filled with orange, almond and lemon trees. He drove past the pastel facades of the little houses, each surrounded by balustraded platforms inclined slightly inward to channel the rainfall into the cisterns below. Carlotta's house was the last in the row, looking as neat and respectable as the others. She'd be asleep and alone at this hour. From past experience he knew that Carlotta never permitted anyone to stay overnight—at least none of her paying guests.

He rapped rather loudly and was surprised when the door opened almost at once. "I thought you'd be asleep," he said to the lovely young girl who stood before him, a colored wrapper tied tightly around her middle.

"Jorge," Carlotta squealed as she threw herself into his arms. "Oh, Jorge, I am so glad to see you."

He laughed and swung her around.

"I thought you had forgotten me," Carlotta said as he put her down on her feet. She put her hands alongside his face. "You are looking tired, my love."

"I am, a little."

She reached up and touched her lips to his eyes. "Then you must rest. Come in. Come in." She took his hand and led him into the little house. When the door closed behind them she threw her arms around his neck again. "Oh, my dearest Jorge. How I've missed you." Suddenly she became self-conscious and released him, her face flushed with embarrassment. She rubbed her hands together. "But I am forgetting myself. It is not right for a woman to throw herself into the arms of another woman's fiancé."

Jorge reached for her and pulled her against him. "We are friends, no?" he said, touching his lips softly to hers. "Since when cannot friends show their affection one for the other?"

"Friends," Carlotta repeated, not wanting to show the stab of pain that pierced her heart. Friends. Lovers no more, she thought. "Are you hungry, Jorge?" she asked, again pulling herself from his embrace.

"No. Perhaps some coffee, if it is not too much trouble."

"Nothing is too much trouble as far as you are concerned." Carlotta padded toward an alcove in which a small stove, sink and ice box sat behind folding shutters.

Jorge glanced around the room at the miscellany of painted Majorcan country furniture and plain walls. He'd seen the four white, flat walls before, and yet they looked back at him as if he were a stranger to them. He supposed they were so accustomed to seeing strangers that no one was familiar any more.

"How is your family?" Jorge asked politely.

"They are fine," Carlotta called to him amid the clatter of dishes. "They have moved to a little village near Benisalem. It is better that my father be away from the damp sea air. They seem to like it there. I have been able to afford a very nice house for them, and the children are in school. They are happy." She came hurrying back, carrying two cups of steaming coffee. "Do you still take it black, Jorge?"

"Yes."

She handed him one cup. "Well, at least you have not changed in that respect," she said, settling herself on the couch in the corner.

"Oh? Do you think I have changed much?"

She cocked her head at him and studied his face. "You have gotten a little older, I think, but you are still as handsome as ever."

"As are you," he said, letting his eyes travel over her sweet, girlish face, her long shimmering black hair that hung loose over her shoulders. "Yes, you are still the most beautiful woman on Majorca."

Carlotta laughed and slapped her hip. "I am getting fat," she said. She smiled with her eyes as she watched him over the rim of her coffee cup. "So what brings you here to me, Jorge? You look worried about something."

"I have a favor to ask of you, Carlotta."

"Anything. You know that."

"Can I stay with you for a day, perhaps two?"

"You can stay as long as you like, dearest Jorge," she said without hesitating. She reached out and put her hand in his, and pulled him down beside her on the couch. "But you must tell me why. Are you in trouble?"

Jorge shook his head. "No, no trouble. It is just that I have some serious thinking to do."

"About the Brandon woman?" Her eyes flashed with hatred.

"About both Brandon women." He lay back against the couch and closed his eyes. "You heard I was engaged to marry Elaine Brandon?"

"Yes. Everyone knows. It is common gossip here where you and Dario grew up. She is a very rich lady." She gripped his hand more tightly. "Are you sure you know what you are doing, Jorge? You, like me, are a *Chueta*. Have you forgotten how much contempt the nobility holds for us Jews?"

"Why do you insist upon living in the past?"

"I do not live in the past, I only remember it. Have you forgotten that Majorca belongs to the Jews? How can you marry into the wealthy Christian class, knowing many of your ancestors were burned alive or beheaded if they did not embrace the Christian religion? Do you forget how they forced us to eat pork in public to prove that we renounced our birthright?"

"Oh, Carlotta. That was centuries ago. The Inquisition is long since past. I am more Spanish than Jew, as you are."

"I am *Chueta*. Majorca rightfully belongs to us and not to the rich nobles who stole it from us and forced us into slavery. You are one of us, Jorge. You should be fighting these wealthy interlopers and not joining them."

"I am Spanish and I am Christian," Jorge insisted. "Let the past die, Carlotta. Look to the future."

Carlotta opened her mouth to argue, but caught herself. Her expression softened suddenly. "Ah, here you come to me with your troubles and I lecture you. I am sorry, Jorge." She put her hand in his again. "I suppose I should be happy for you if you think you are in love with this Elaine Brandon woman."

Jorge sat forward and clasped his hands between his knees. "I believe I am in love with her, but I cannot marry her yet. In fact, I should not marry her at all. I should be the one to marry Cynthia and not Dario."

"Whoa," Carlotta said, putting down her cup and holding up both her hands. "I think you had better start at the beginning. Cynthia? She is the younger sister, no?"

"No. Cynthia is Elaine's daughter."

Carlotta's eyes widened. "But I thought . . ."

"Yes, so did I," Jorge said. Then he told her everything from the beginning.

When he finished the coffee cups were cold and empty. Carlotta's face was grim. "The rich," she said with distaste. "Do they do nothing but lie and deceive? They are all a despicable lot in my eyes." She saw Jorge turn away from her. She knew Jorge would never let himself see all the evils of the rich. Wealth had blinded him beyond hope. She sighed. If that was what Jorge wanted, if that was what would make him happy, then that is what she wanted for him.

Jorge leaned back. "I suppose Dario convinced Cynthia she should run off with him, but it isn't like Dario to simply go off without saying a word to anyone, especially to me, knowing that I was waiting for him in the billiard room."

"That is not like Dario," Carlotta agreed. "Dario is never sure of himself. He is always afraid of failing. Perhaps he thought if Cynthia confronted you again, you and she would change your minds, and so he swept her off before she could see you."

"Yes, perhaps," Jorge said. "My presence at the villa was upsetting Elaine greatly, so I had to get away. I packed a few things and came here."

"You did the right thing, Jorge. Now," she said, rising to

her feet, "before anything more is discussed I think you should sleep. After that I will fix you your favorite dinner of onion soup and shrimps Bilbao—the way you like it with olive oil and lots of garlic."

He held her hands. "You are a good friend, Carlotta," he said as he smiled up into her face.

She wished he would stop using that word. She did not want to be just a friend. Couldn't he see how much she loved him? She could disguise her feelings with every other man, but never with Jorge.

He let Carlotta fuss over him, tucking him into bed as she might a young child. He thought sleep would come easily, but it did not. All he could think about was Elaine. He was not too concerned about Cynthia. She was capable of taking care of herself; Elaine needed a man to look after her. He wondered what she was doing at that precise moment.

THE LUNCHEON TABLE WAS LAID ON THE SEAward terrace overlooking the Mediterranean. The sea stretched its long, dimpled hand as far as the eye could see. Below, tiny enchanted inlets dented the shore. The centuries had washed clean the blood from the sand. No invading ships stood offshore, no armed warriors stood on the land, braced to repel attempts at invasion. A soft breeze sighed as though mourning the thousands who had given their lives for this tiny island. With the sigh the air was perfumed with the scent from the pine groves that ran like an unending backdrop along the beaches.

Maggie had shoved the luncheon dishes aside to make room for a large, square velvet-lined box which she was in the process of opening. Elaine put one of her painkilling tablets into her mouth and washed it down with water. She began toying with a salad of fresh fruit and lobster, her mind far removed from the talkative, lumpy woman seated across from her.

"You will simply adore the new items I've added to my

collection," Maggie said as she raised the lid of the box and smiled down at her collection of hatpins. "Now take this one, for instance," she said, picking up a long gold pin, its head a massive rosette of ruby and pearl. "This one belonged to Czarina Catherine." She held it out to Elaine.

Elaine hadn't heard her, nor did she acknowledge the pin that was thrust under her nose.

"Isn't it positively gorgeous? And believe me, I paid plenty for this little trifle." When she received no reaction from Elaine, she tightened her mouth in an irritable line. "What's wrong with you, Elaine? You're not interested in a word I've said. You're as bad as that worthless niece of mine. Imagine Nancy calling at six o'clock to tell me she was having dinner with a friend and not having the manners to invite me—as if I would have gone. But that isn't the point. Nancy could at least have asked me to join them. Ungrateful, just plain selfish and ungrateful. Elaine," she added sharply. "I'm talking to you."

Elaine looked up, struggling out of her troubled thoughts. "Oh, I am sorry, Maggie. I was just wondering about Jorge."

"What's to wonder about? I've known plenty of young men like that before. He'll come back with his tail between his legs when his money starts running low." She replaced the hatpin and snapped shut the lid. "I see no sense in my trying to keep you amused if you are going to persist in mooning about a little fortune hunter."

"Oh, Maggie. Please don't. Jorge is not what you think."

"Say what you will, Elaine, but I am far from being a babe in the woods. These boys come out of the woodwork when a rich, single woman walks on the scene. My dear, you should have seen the divine number I met in 'Cannes last summer. Simply ravishing. A young god, and hung like a bull." She giggled. "I remember one night, the first night I allowed him to come to my suite. Well, we were in bed and I touched that gigantic prong of his for the first time. Well! I . . ."

"Maggie, please don't go on. I'd rather not hear, if you don't mind." She rubbed at her temples. "I'm getting a slight headache. I think I'll lie down for a while."

She started to get up just as Greg walked out on the terrace. "Hello, ladies," he said gaily. "Mother," he said in greeting and bent to kiss the top of her head. Elaine was so astonished she sank back into her chair.

"You're in a bright mood today, Greg," Elaine commented.

"A bright day like this deserves a bright mood. Has anyone seen my darling sister?"

Elaine shook her head. "Not since last night."

"Me neither," Greg answered. He smiled coyly. "And I see your little peacock has flown the nest."

Elaine picked up her fork and began playing with her salad again. "Yes," she said in a meek little voice. Oh, why had she sent him away? She'd been a fool, as always.

Maggie pulled her salad toward her and began bolting the slices of orange. "Cynthia and that Jorge person most likely flew off together," she said.

Elaine felt the pain in her breast grow worse. She couldn't trust herself to look up and let them see how much hurt she was suffering.

Greg smirked. "Could be, but Cynthia would be crazy to run off with that character," he said, helping himself to some coffee. Elaine glanced at him. He seemed so pleased with himself about something, yet his eyes made that a lie.

"Oh, I don't know," Maggie said. She swallowed a large piece of lobster. "You two didn't see the way they were goo-goo-eyeing each other when I arrived here yesterday. I thought they were on their honeymoon until Elaine straightened me out. Really, Elaine, I don't know why you're drooling over that boy. I don't think he gives a rap about anyone but himself."

Elaine fought to control herself. "I don't agree with you, Maggie. You just don't know Jorge as I know him."

Maggie swallowed another piece of fruit dripping with dressing, which ran out of the corner of her mouth. "I don't think I could afford to know him. Too expensive for my small fortune. Of course, you don't have to worry about that, Elaine. You have more money than you'll ever need."

"And she isn't parting with any of it, either," Greg said, letting his eyes slide toward his mother.

She wished they'd stop picking on her, Elaine thought. Her head was beginning to throb for real. "How much money I have and how I spend it is my concern," she said, keeping her voice casual and even.

"You should give more to the needy," Greg said with a half-laugh.

"I suppose you mean yourself?" his mother said. She felt

suddenly annoyed with his pleased expression. Giving in to her own self-pity, she said, "Why should I give you any more money than I do? You'd only squander it on drink and God only knows what other terrible pastimes you indulge in."

Greg snickered. "I eat little boys under the full of the moon," he said, to torment her.

"Don't be disgusting, Greg."

"Well, that's what you think, isn't it?"

She found herself eating faster, but she wasn't tasting anything that slid over her tongue. "I just don't know what to think about you any more, Greg."

Maggie giggled, her mind still on Greg's remark. "Eat little boys under a full moon," she said. "Oh, it sounds delightful." She giggled again and added, "You must take me with you some night, dear," she said to Greg.

"Not on your life, dear lady. You'd charm everyone up into your tree and leave nothing for me."

Maggie howled. "Oh, go on. I'd be kind. I'd let you have at least one." She laughed again and slapped her hand down on her fat knee.

"If you'll excuse me," Elaine said, touching her fingertips to her temples. "My headache is getting worse. I think I'll lie down for a while." She got up and left them, ignoring Greg's comment that women always seemed to suffer from so many headaches, and Maggie's remark that she was as healthy as a horse—never having had a headache in her life—because of her active sex life.

Just as Elaine started up the stairs to her room, her maid came hurrying down. There was a very distressed look on the older woman's face. "What is wrong, Teresa?"

"Oh, *señora*. Something terrible has happened."

Oh, no, Elaine thought. Not something else. There were enough things wrong without adding to them.

"The emerald necklace you wore to dinner last evening," Teresa said.

"Yes, what about it?"

"It is gone, *señora*. I have searched everywhere. It was on your dressing table when you went to bed last night. I was going to put it away then, but if you remember you told me to leave you alone. So now, when I was straightening up your room, I looked and looked for the emeralds, but I cannot find them anywhere. Did you perhaps put them in the safe yourself?"

Elaine shook her head and tried not to frown, remembering what the plastic surgeon had said about how damaging frown lines can be. "No. It was on the dressing table when I went to sleep. It wasn't there when I got up. I thought perhaps you'd crept in and locked it away."

"No, *señora*. You did not want me puttering around your room this morning either. You were in a bad humor, so I left you alone."

Teresa had been with her for years, but still her bluntness always surprised Elaine. "Yes, yes," she said, dismissing her. There had been no one in her room either last night or this morning. Teresa certainly wouldn't take the necklace. The woman might be a little lazy, but she certainly was not a thief. "It must be around somewhere," she said as the maid scurried back up the stairs. "Look again, Teresa. Perhaps it fell to the floor or something."

Elaine started to follow, but something stopped her. Maggie, she thought. Maggie had been in her room earlier that morning. And sweet as Maggie was, she adored borrowing things that attracted her. She loved jewelry and on more than one occasion had borrowed things from Elaine without asking permission. She'd most likely taken it and forgotten to mention it.

She turned and went back out onto the terrace. Greg and Maggie was poring over her collection of hatpins. Greg was holding a long daggerlike pin up to the light and admiring the slim, sharp point of the blade.

"Maggie?" Elaine said as she approached them. "It seems my emerald necklace was misplaced. You didn't by any chance borrow it this morning?"

"Borrow your emerald necklace?" Maggie said, sounding aghast, as though she were being accused of stealing. "Of course I didn't. I certainly would have told you if I had." She looked hurt.

"Oh, darling, I'm not accusing you of anything. I simply thought you might have picked it up and put it down somewhere other than on my dressing table."

"But I didn't see it on your dressing table," Maggie said with a pout. She took the daggerlike hatpin from Greg and replaced it in the velvet-lined box. "If it's missing, perhaps you should ask that Jorge person about it. He most likely stole it to finance his elopement with Cynthia."

ALL DURING THE RIDE IN THE TAXI ROD WAS trying to think what he was going to say to Lisa. He couldn't believe that she was addicted to hard drugs. Not Lisa. Not his little girl. Regardless of the evidence against her, regardless of what she admitted to the police, he couldn't bring himself to believe it. But what if it was true? No, he couldn't, he wouldn't believe it. If it was true he'd have to face it, however. He'd not play ostrich and stick his head in the sand.

Rod glanced at his watch. He didn't have all that much time to spend with Lisa before keeping his appointment with this Montoro fellow. But he had to talk to Lisa first to see what he was up against. It was possible that they wouldn't release her at all if they could prove a definite link between her and George Petrik.

A drug smuggler. Christ, how did she get connected with someone like that? And better still, why?

The cab pulled up before the little police station. Rod got out, paid and trotted up the steps. He showed Verdugo's authorization to the policeman behind the desk and was told to wait. A few minutes later he was being led toward Lisa's cell, his mind still struggling with what he was going to say to her. He decided, on the spur of the moment, that perhaps it would be wise to wait and let her make the first move.

She was standing with her back to him when they unlocked the cell door and allowed him to enter. He waited until they locked him inside before he spoke.

"How are you, Lisa?" he said. He could hardly control himself from grabbing her and pulling her into his arms. He wanted desperately for her to throw her arms around his neck and kiss his cheek, as she once used to do. But she didn't move. She didn't say a word.

"Lisa?" He walked over to her and touched her shoulder.

She shrugged off his hand. "I don't want you here," she said. Her voice was bitter.

"Then why did you cable me?"

She shrugged again. "I don't know. I wish I hadn't."

He put his hands on her shoulders again and turned her around. "You don't mean that."

He saw the tears in her eyes and tried to pull her against him. She shoved him away. "Don't touch me." She backed away from him, her angry eyes blazing behind their tears.

"You were always glad to see me in the past. Why have things changed so between us?"

"That was in the past," she said, turning away from him. "I didn't know any better then."

He tried not to let her upset him. "I'm still your father, you know."

"I don't want you as my father," she said spitefully. "I don't ever want to see you again."

The resolve he'd made when he'd landed at the airport came back to him. He was being the old soft, sweet guy he once was. He'd have to be tougher, less lenient. He stiffened his jaw. "Now you look here, young lady," he said in a hard, angry tone. "Regardless of what you want or what you don't want, I'm your father and I'm responsible for you, so you sit down on that cot over there and listen to what I have to say."

He saw the surprised look on her face. He saw her falter, then hesitate, then finally sink down on the edge of the cot. "Whatever you say won't make any difference," she said.

"Whether you like it or not, I'm going to get you out of here," Rod said, shaking a finger at her. "I'm getting you out, and you're coming back to Ohio and going back to school. I promised your mother before she died that I'd look after you. I haven't done a very good job of it so far, but that's all going to change. I've let you have your own way too long."

"My mother," Lisa said with a slur. "A lot you cared about her."

Rod's eyes opened in surprise. "I cared very much about your mother."

"Is that why you killed her?" Lisa asked, flashing her eyes contemptuously.

Rod's shock took his voice away for a moment. "Killed her? Are you nuts? You know very well that your mother was killed in an automobile accident."

"While on her way to meet you."

"Yes, that's true enough."

"Then I hold you responsible for her death."

Rod stared at her for a minute. He shook his head. "You're wrong, Lisa. I specifically told Helen to stay at home that night. I had no idea that she'd follow me."

"Of course you didn't." Lisa's mouth was turned down at the corners. There was genuine hate in her eyes. "What man would expect his wife to go along with him to that place you went to?"

"What place? What are you talking about?"

"Oh, come off it, Dad. I found out where you'd gone that night. I know all about it. Mother was just trying to save you from yourself, and got herself killed for it."

Rod's eyes went wide, his mouth dropped open. "You don't know anything about that night," he managed to say.

"I know all about it. I even know the name of the woman you went to see. Rose Mallory, isn't that it?"

Rod suddenly reached out and grabbed her. "How did you know about that woman?" He found himself shaking her. "Tell me!"

Lisa was looking up at him, her eyes misted over with a detached kind of haze. She wrenched herself free. "Stop shaking me." She turned away from him again and began rubbing the hurt in her arms.

"I'm sorry, honey," Rod said helplessly. "I didn't mean to hurt you."

"You never mean to hurt anyone, do you, Dad?"

Rod stood there, his shoulders slumped down, the taste of frightened desperation in his mouth. "How much do you know about me and Rose Mallory?"

Lisa gave him an indifferent glance. "Does it matter? I know who she is."

Rod's heart was thumping wildly in his chest. "Who is she?" He felt suddenly like a condemned man waiting for the trap door to fall out from under him.

"She's a prostitute. She owns that brothel outside of town."

"What else?" The pounding in his temples almost blotted out Lisa's words.

"What do you mean, what else? I know you've been sleeping with her, if that's what you mean."

In spite of the terrible accusation, Rod found his muscles

relaxing. He breathed a sigh of relief. It was as if a tremendous weight had been lifted from his shoulders. Lisa must never know the truth about Rose Mallory. Let her think what she wants to, it didn't matter. Just as long as she didn't know the truth about Rose.

His silence angered her all the more. "You don't deny it, do you?"

Rod looked beaten. "No, I don't deny it. I've slept with Rose Mallory."

The tears streamed out of Lisa's eyes and ran unchecked down her cheeks. "You disgust me," she wailed and threw herself down on the cot.

He wanted to go to her. He wanted to take her in his arms and explain everything, but he couldn't. He would never be able to explain, regardless of what it cost. Later perhaps she'd understand, but not now.

"Look, Lisa. I don't care what you think of me or how much I disgust you. I'm still your father, whether you like it or not, and I've come all the way here to this godforsaken place to get you out of jail. I intend doing just that. So let's forget for the moment that you hate me as much as you do and let's talk about this trouble you've gotten yourself into."

"It's none of your business," Lisa said, sitting up and wiping the tears from her face. "I don't want you to do anything for me . . . ever."

"Well, I'm going to, so you'd better get used to it. Now, who is the man you were traveling with, and what's this I hear about you being caught with hard drugs in your possession?"

Lisa shrugged. "They found them on me, so I guess I was carrying them, right?"

"Wrong. I know you too well, young lady. You were carrying them for someone else, weren't you?"

"No."

"Don't lie to me, Lisa. I can tell by your eyes that you're lying."

Lisa felt suddenly caged. "I'm not. I had them and they were mine."

"You're protecting someone. I can read it in your face. You're not fooling me, Lisa. You were carrying them for that Petrik character, weren't you?"

Lisa stared at him. "Who told you about George?" she blurted out.

"The authorities know all about your friend George Petrik.
Everything, that is, but where they can find him. He's a bad
man, Lisa. He's wanted by every country in Europe for
smuggling dope. Surely you can understand how dangerous
it might be for you if you continue protecting a man like that.
You could easily spend the rest of your life in one of these
foreign prisons." He went over and knelt beside her on the
cot. "Tell me where he is, angel. It'll make it so much easier
on both of us."

"I don't know where he is."

He put his finger under her chin and tilted her face up to
his. "Is that the truth?"

Lisa hesitated for a moment, then quickly nodded her head.
"I met him in New York. He asked me to come with him to
Spain. After they arrested me, he split. I don't know where
he is."

Rod let out the breath he was holding. "Okay, I believe
you."

Lisa rallied out of her moment of weakness. She pushed
herself up from the cot. "That doesn't mean I don't intend
trying to find him myself. And although I don't know where
he is exactly, I have a good idea where to look."

"Oh, no," Rod said with a firmness he didn't think himself
capable of. "You're not going to get out of my sight again.
You're going home with me and you're going to stay there
until you're old enough to think sensibly."

Lisa knew better than to argue. She'd run away from him
before they got on the plane—if he succeeded in getting her
out of jail.

He put his arm around her and was surprised to see that
she didn't knock it away. "I guess I can understand why you've
grown to hate me. I don't know who told you about Rose
Mallory, but it wasn't what you think it was. Someday maybe
I'll explain. Right now I'm more interested in you, not myself, our relationship or what you think of me. You're the
most important thing in my life, Lisa; everything else comes
second. I want you to be happy, whether it is with me or with
someone else, but your happiness is foremost in my mind. I
can't help you if you don't tell me the truth. So tell me again,
Lisa. Are you using drugs? Were those hard drugs they found
on you yours?"

Another moment of weakness swept over her. She'd been

alone ever since George ran out on her. She wanted desperately to love her father again, just the way she had when she was a little girl. She found herself leaning against him. Without realizing what she was saying, she said, "They weren't mine. They were George's. I was carrying them for him."

Rod hugged her. "That's what I thought," he said. He thought he'd burst with happiness. At least he'd successfully hurdled the first obstacle.

"Okay. Now I think I can work a deal to get you released. I have an appointment to see a man in about half an hour. Don't worry about anything," he said, kissing her on the temple. "Everything is going to work out just fine."

Her bitterness returned from out of nowhere. She remembered him as the murderer of her beautiful mother. She didn't want him to do anything for her. She wasn't going anywhere, not with him. What kind of life would she lead shackled to a little house in Dayton, Ohio? No, she had to be on her own. She didn't want to have anything more to do with this man who claimed to be her father. She shoved herself away from him again. "I don't want you to do anything for me." Out of pure spite she added, "I'd rather live with a drug dealer than a murderer."

"Oh, Lisa, stop that. I'm really not responsible for your mother's death. Someday I'll explain it all."

"Explain it now," she challenged.

Rod looked at her hopelessly. "I can't. Not now. You wouldn't understand."

"I'm not quite as naive as you think, Father. Lots of my male friends boast about sleeping with whores."

Before Rod knew what he was doing, his hand slashed out and slapped her hard across the face. "I won't permit you to use words like that."

Lisa laughed at him in spite of the hurt on her cheek. "Oh, you kill me, Dad. You really do. Why does the word 'whore' bother you? 'Prostitute' doesn't seem to offend you at all."

"It isn't the word, it's the person who used it. I'm sorry I slapped you," he said with sincere apology.

Something inside her urged her on to goad him further. "I know all about prostitutes and whores, father dear. And why shouldn't I, having been born to a man who so enjoys frequenting them."

"That's a lie, and I want you to stop talking this way."

"Is it a lie?" she asked, seeing that she was making him most uncomfortable. "Tell me, Daddy. When was the last time you slept with a prostitute? Last night? The night before?"

Visions of the dark-haired, dark-eyed woman in Barcelona flashed on the screen behind his eyes. A sick feeling clutched at the pit of his stomach. His mouth was dry as cotton. His voice, he found, had abandoned him.

Lisa laughed in his face. "Rather than worry about taking care of me," she said, "I'd suggest you take care of yourself first."

"I've got to go," he said hastily as he glanced at his watch for want of something to do to get out from under the accusing eyes of his daughter.

"Don't go to any trouble for me," she said as Rod rattled the cell door to let the attendant know he was ready to leave. "I don't want your help."

"Well, you're going to get it whether you want it or not." He kept his back turned so she wouldn't see the hurt, the guilt, the anger that was in his face. He'd made a mess of everything. Nothing had gone as he had hoped it would go. He waited while the jailor unlocked the door. Outside the cell he looked back through the bars at the small, fragile little girl leaning against the far wall. "Don't worry about anything. I'll be back as soon as I can," he said.

"I'm not going anywhere."

She waited for his footsteps to retreat down the corridor before she let the tears come again. She buried her face in her hands and tried to keep from thinking how much George Petrik looked like her father. The resemblance was more pronounced now than she'd first thought. And she loved George Petrik more than any man she'd ever met.

She suddenly felt dirty and ashamed. She threw herself down on the cot and let her tears bubble out through her sobs.

ELAINE SLAMMED CLOSED THE SHUTTERS,
barring the sunlight as though it held pestilence. Her head
was aching dully, but the ache was lost in the overpowering
pain in her legs and arms. The cancer was eating at the
marrow of her bones; she could feel it. Beads of perspiration
seeped from her pores as the chilling fear took hold of her
again. It wasn't so much that she was afraid to die; it was
dying without Jorge. The thought of not having his love was
more painful than the cancer itself.

She laid down on the chaise near the windows and put a
cold towel on her brow. She pinched shut her eyes and tried
to hold back the tears. She had lost him. She had to face that
fact. He'd gone with Cynthia, and he was not coming back.
Hard as it may be, she had to resign herself to it, just as she
had resigned herself to dying. It seemed such an unfair
waste, but there was little she could do about it. Jorge had to
do whatever made him happy. She knew only too well the
futility of sacrificing for the sake of others. She'd done that
all her life, and what had it gained her?

The tears rushed down her cheeks. Oh, God, she sobbed,
covering her face with her hands. Why? Why couldn't I have
just this one last little bit of happiness?

She wiped away the tears and stiffened her shoulders. No,
it just wasn't meant to be, she thought. She'd done too much
wrong in her lifetime, and this was her punishment. She was
being selfish in thinking only of her own wants and desires and
not Jorge's. But then, everyone is selfish, and who can blame
them for that? You live for yourself, and anyone who says
otherwise is a liar. And no one really changes. Even in the
most devoted act of penitence they remain as they were.

Well, she thought with a sigh, if this was what fate had in
store for her, then there was nothing she could do about it.
Jorge was gone. She was left alone. But that was nothing new
to her. She had always been alone, even with three husbands,
children, friends and acquaintances, she had always been

alone. From now on, however, things would be different, she promised herself. She would stop being understanding of Greg and Cynthia and everyone else. No one really liked her. Her children despised her. She couldn't blame them, however. She remembered refusing them everything, slamming doors in their faces—anything to make them keep away for fear their demented stepfather would get his filthy hands on them when they wouldn't know how to stop him. She had sacrificed herself for her children. She wasn't the first mother to make such a sacrifice. She didn't feel she deserved their hatred, but she could understand it. There was no way of ever finding a solution to their dislike of her. So, she'd fight now for her own happiness. She'd lost her children. She'd make everything up to them after her death. In the meantime she'd do whatever she had to do to make herself happy. She had killed a man, and now God was accomplishing what the judge and jury had not. She was dying. Impending death brought on desperation.

She turned her head slowly toward the bedroom door when she heard the tap. *"Si?"* she said weakly.

Miguel Montoro peeked around the door. "Teresa said you were not feeling well. Am I bothering you, my dear?"

"No, come in, Miguel. It is just a slight headache. Nothing more."

"I thought perhaps it was the pains again."

"No," she lied. She had been angry with the doctors for having told Miguel about her cancer. But there was nothing she could do about that now. Like everything else, it was too late. "I've learned to live with the pains. I just have a headache."

"Good." He entered the dimly lighted bedroom and came to sit beside her. "Worried still about your young lover?"

"You know he's gone?"

"Yes, I spoke with the very talkative Maggie Montgomery just before I came up. That woman has a tongue like a running brook. It never seems to grow tired of running on."

"Maggie is harmless enough," Elaine said. "She's a lonely woman, really. That's why other people's affairs and troubles hold such great interest for her. She means no malice."

"Being a good friend of yours, I'm sure that she doesn't. Do you mind if I smoke?" he asked, pulling a cigar from his pocket.

She did mind, but she shook her head.

Miguel lit his cigar and settled himself more comfortably. "I was wondering if you knew an American who is here in Palma by the name of Rod Shepherd. The Consulate tells me he is from a place called Dayton, Ohio."

Elaine thought for a moment. "No, I don't think so. Why do you ask?"

"No reason. I just thought he was a friend, or a friend of a friend. He's having a little trouble with his daughter and I have an appointment to see him in a little while."

"Sorry, Miguel. I don't know the man."

Miguel puffed on his cigar for a moment, thoughtfully fanning the smoke away from Elaine's face. "So, young Jorge has run off to pout. If you are lucky he will not return."

"Don't, please, Miguel," Elaine said, pressing the cold cloth tighter to her forehead. "I'd rather not discuss Jorge right now."

"I realize that you aren't feeling well, Elaine, but perhaps this is the perfect time to speak of this young rascal." He chuckled. "At least you cannot run away from me and lock yourself in your bedroom as you usually do whenever I broach the subject."

"Please, Miguel, not now."

But Miguel would not be put off. "I am sorry, Elaine, but I must insist that you listen to reason."

Elaine closed her eyes and resigned herself to the lecture she knew she was going to have to endure. She promised herself that she'd not utter a word, just wait until he was finished. Let him get it all said, and then perhaps he'd not bring it up again.

"Elaine, my darling," he said as he took her hand in his. She waved a hand in front of her face to dislodge the drifting smoke from his cigar. He quickly stubbed the cigar out in a convenient ashtray, muttering an apology. He took her hand again and gently massaged the fingers. "Everyone has told you this before, I am sure," he started. "This young man of yours is just not right for you. He is much too young. I am the only man alive, other than your doctors, who knows the true state of your health. The excitement of a marriage and a honeymoon with one so young and vibrant might bring on too fast a conclusion for you, if you know what I mean."

She felt him watching her face, but she kept to her resolve

and said nothing. She wished he'd hurry up and go. No one had to remind her how short a time she had left.

"I made you a promise once that I would never mention to anyone about the cancer that is eating you alive. I am tempted to break that promise and tell Jorge."

She sat up with a start, catching the cold cloth as it slid down her face. "You wouldn't dare," she said, breaking her resolve. Her face was a mask of fear. "I won't have Jorge loving me out of pity," she swore.

"Still, I think he should know."

"I am warning you again, Miguel. You say one word to anyone about what the doctors told you and I swear to heaven I'll see that you are completely ruined. And I can do it, too, so don't forget it. It is my money you operate on, and I'll pull that away from you in a minute if you ever so much as hint at my problems."

Miguel blanched. He could tell by her expression that she would carry out her threat. A quiver of fear shook the pit of his stomach. Elaine Brandon was not a woman to be trifled with. True, she knew very little about her vast fortune; he never had thought her very good at business affairs. She was, after all, a woman, and few women had a head for business. But Elaine was dangerous when aroused. It would be the end of him if she took away the control he had over her money. If his accounts were subjected to a careful audit, his manipulations with the figures would be discovered. He needed her money. He needed her power and her connections. The advisory board at the bank were his pawns, even though Elaine thought it was they who held the reins of her vast empire. He had to appease her sudden anger.

"All right, all right. Calm yourself. I'll say nothing to Jorge or to anyone else, but I think it is wrong to keep this from him."

"Wrong or right it is not your decision to make. It is mine. I forbid you to say a word, is that understood?"

Miguel nodded. "But think of yourself, Elaine. It will prove disastrous to marry this young pup."

The look of fear on his face pleased her. Miguel thought her stupid about her fortune. She knew all about his juggling of figures, his paying off the members of the bank's advisory board, his illegal manipulations of her holdings. Before Jorge it hadn't really mattered how Miguel cheated her. She had more money than she'd ever be able to spend, even more than Cynthia or Greg could spend after her death, so the meager funds Miguel pilfered were of no consequence.

She readjusted the cold cloth to her forehead. "I fail to see how."

"The relationship just would not work. What about the times after you two are married that Jorge will want to go out with friends and you will be too tired or you simply will not be invited to go along with him? What then, Elaine? Will you be content to just sit home and watch the television or read a book night after night, waiting, hoping, looking forward to his coming through the door and crawling into bed with you for twenty minutes?" He scoffed. "Twenty minutes, did I say? With a young stallion like Jorge I am sure he would reach his orgasm in less than five minutes and then he'd be off to sleep, leaving you frustrated out of your mind."

Elaine closed her eyes again and refused to let him upset her. "You are wrong, Miguel. It isn't like that at all between Jorge and me. He is a very thoughtful, considerate man."

"Man? He's a child, Elaine. Do you think I am blind to what he is? I remember only too well when you bought him that new sports car for his birthday. The day it was delivered he drove into Palma to show it to Dario and the rest of his friends. He left you alone here for hours. You invited me to have dinner with you. Your invitation wasn't out of courtesy, Elaine; you just did not want to be alone. You weren't kidding anyone, let alone me. Then Cynthia and I played backgammon while you spent hours in your room primping and bathing and making yourself so very seductive with your most expensive scents, waiting for Jorge to come home and thank you properly for his very costly birthday gift. And when did he come home, Elaine? Four? Five? Six o'clock the next morning? And from what Cynthia told me he went straight to his room and didn't get up until after three the next afternoon, when he promptly took off in his new car again to spend more time with his young friends." He gave her an impatient sneer. "Wise up, my dear Elaine. You are not in his class at all. You just do not fit in. If you must marry, marry me, or marry someone at least closer to your own age."

Elaine moved her head from side to side. "And slowly sink into quiet, refined old age? No, Miguel. I may be foolish and silly, but I would rather have a few minutes basking in Jorge's youth and exuberance than be reminded that I am old."

"So have your youthful moments with Jorge, or someone like him, but God, Elaine, you do not have to marry to gain moments like that. Borrow them, buy them, anything, but do not marry for them. You will be lonelier afterward than you have ever been in your life."

Elaine repositioned the cold towel down over her eyes. "I don't have much longer to live," she said. "You know that. And for the short time I have left I would rather be around Jorge—married to him—than pass away in the quiet company of someone dull and old and retired."

"It is easy for you to say that, Elaine. You are dying." With financial ruin at his heels he almost envied her her cancer.

Elaine flinched under his frankness.

"Not all of us can be so free with our desires," Miguel argued. "If the cancer inside you were not fatal, would you be doing the same thing as you are doing now? If you knew you were to live for years and years and years, would you even consider marriage to Jorge, or someone like him?"

Elaine hesitated. She thought for a moment and then said, "Yes, I would." She pressed the cloth more tightly against her eyes. "I love him, Miguel. But I suppose you can't understand that." To be honest, she wasn't completely certain that that was true. She thought she loved Jorge—but perhaps she merely wanted to possess him. She guessed it was because she'd never owned anyone's love. Or perhaps it was that she had learned to love despair.

"No, I can't."

"I just can't seem to relate to people of my own age any more. They all seem so boring, so resigned to the fate of growing old. I've heard everything that they have to say. They aren't interested in the world outside their own; they're only interested in themselves and their dull existences."

Miguel clucked his tongue. "And I suppose you can relate to Jorge and Dario and young people of that age? Just how do you relate, Elaine? And what do they have to offer that is so much more exciting? They don't know anything, they can talk only about cars and clothes and the new dances. I bet no one in Jorge's circle, including Jorge himself, has ever been to a museum or an opera or even cracked open a book.

They only know Beethoven because it's a name seen on a T-shirt. They wouldn't know how to spell 'philosophy,' let alone what it means. So what do they have to offer? They are badly educated, they have no culture, they aren't traveled. So what is it?"

"Youth," Elaine said simply.

"Youth." He pretended to spit on the floor. "I spit on youth. It is the curse of our society."

Her headache seemed to be getting worse. She wished he'd stop. One nice thing about Jorge was that he wasn't as verbose as Miguel. She smiled to herself, remembering an old quotation: *Boasting youth and narrative old age.* She blanked out Miguel by trying to remember where she'd read or heard those lines.

Unfortunately her attention was arrested again when Miguel made a comment about Jorge's intention to steal her blind. It sparked a reminder of her missing emerald necklace. She waited for him to finish the rest of his speech, then said, "If I may change the subject, Miguel, you do have my insurance policies in the vault in your office?"

He gave her a quizzical look. "Yes, of course. Why do you ask?"

"Oh, Teresa and I can't find the emerald necklace I was wearing at dinner last night. You might contact the insurance company about filing a claim."

"Your emerald necklace was stolen?"

"I didn't say stolen, Miguel. I said it was missing."

Miguel knit his brows together and ran a thoughtful finger across his chin. "Your young lover runs off, your emerald necklace disappears. Is it possible that the two have a connection?"

"No, of course not," Elaine said much too quickly. She was glad the cloth was covering her eyes so that he couldn't see the anxiety that she was sure was reflected there.

"But if I call in an insurance investigator he is sure to make a connection."

The cord in her neck started to twitch nervously. "Well, perhaps we'd best not call in the insurance people just yet. We'll wait until Jorge comes back."

"And if he doesn't come back?"

The twitch became more noticeable. "He'll be back. I have no doubt of that."

"Not according to what your friend Maggie says," he said, letting his eyes slide over to her. "She says she thinks Jorge and Cynthia ran off together last night."

"Maggie talks too much."

"But there is that possibility?" Miguel persisted.

"I don't deny that the possibility exists, but I doubt it very much. Jorge would not have gone off without talking to me about it." She remembered Jorge's tapping on her bedroom door and her shouting for him to go away. Yes, the possibility of his having gone off with Cynthia was a good one, but he wouldn't have taken her emeralds. Besides, he didn't have access to them. A little gasp caught in her throat when she remembered the long, long time she'd spent soaking in her tub before going to bed last night. Jorge could have sneaked into her room and she would never have known. She had hoped then that Jorge would force himself onto her, and she hadn't bothered to lock her bedroom door. Anyone could have come in and taken the necklace. The thought brought worry in its wake. But Jorge was no thief. Yet she must not discount the powers of persuasion Cynthia might have exercised on him. She could have pleaded and cajoled until he couldn't resist.

She was suddenly frightened. "Perhaps it would be wise to know exactly what did happen last night," she said to Miguel. "See what you can find out about Jorge and Cynthia. Start asking around. Surely someone saw them leave or knows where they are."

"So you are worried that they may be together?" He sounded like a man who had just fought and won.

"I just want to know the truth," Elaine answered. "I'd rather know the truth about what happened than endure this seemingly interminable uncertainty."

"All right. I will check around, if that is what you wish." He stood up. "I am pleased to see that you are smart enough to realize that this diamond you call Jorge might have a flaw."

"He has many flaws, as do most of us. I may love him, but I am not blind to his faults. I may be a silly old woman, but I am still a practical one." She held out her hand.

Miguel bent over it and pressed it to his lips. "Stay well, my lovely Elaine. I will come again as soon as I can." He looked at his wristwatch. "Heavens, it is later than I thought. I am off to see the American to try to help him get his daughter out of jail."

The word "jail" hit a raw nerve. Elaine gritted her teeth. The laws on Majorca were very strict when it came to thievery. Jorge mustn't be involved with the missing emeralds. The thought of so handsome a young man having to go to jail was unbearable.

After Miguel left, she lay musing about what he'd said to her. How could she explain to him the need she felt for Jorge? She didn't understand it herself, yet it was there. It wasn't the ordinary kind of love, not the kind of love she felt when she herself was young and frivolous. She wasn't enmeshed in the romantic foolishness she permitted herself years ago. She was convinced that Jorge loved her, but it was a sensible, mature kind of love, the same kind of mature love she returned. Miguel wouldn't understand. No one could understand unless they themselves were experiencing it.

If she were to be truthful to herself, brutally frank, she would have to admit that it was more "concern" she felt for Jorge than love. No one had ever shown him any real affection before. She was certain other women had loved him, but it had been love without affection—real affection.

She sighed. She wished with all her heart that he would walk through the door right now and take her in his arms. She'd forgive anything if she could only see him, talk to him again. Yes, she could even forgive his wanting to marry Cynthia if he would only come and talk to her.

THE HOT SUN WAS HANGING FLAT AGAINST the sky as Charlie and Sheila trudged their way up the narrow winding street toward Palma's massive Gothic cathedral. The Cathedral of Palma crowned the dignity and quality of the older part of the city like a great fortress of stone lace. Here on its site during the Arab domination a great mosque had once stood. It was believed by many that the cathedral was the fabric of that magnificent Muslim temple and was merely purified and adapted to Catholic usage.

Charlie and Sheila walked out of the little Garden of the Queen and started up the stepped pathway, leaving behind the small bronze statue dedicated to Juan Alcover, the Majorcan lyric poet of the last century. They climbed up, passing between the walls of the March Palace and the Aludaina. The sea came into view, looking like a dazzling haze of blue in the bright of the day. Pine trees and oleanders cast shade across the steps from either side. They had strolled through the antique shops and had seen the solid thirteenth-century Catalan Gothic bell tower beckoning to them. Sweat plastered Charlie's shirt to his back and beaded his forehead as he climbed upward, swinging the camera and paraphernalia bag from one shoulder to the other. Sheila looked cool and unwrinkled in her summer chiffon and large picture hat, the ribbons of which fluttered behind her in the breeze.

As they stepped into the shadow of the gigantic old church, Sheila looked up with awe at the sturdy square phalanxes of the outer buttresses rising from a solid wall and ending, like fingers of God, in little Gothic spires. The buttresses soared as high as the roof, and the whole building radiated strength rather than beauty.

She glanced at the guidebook, which was broken open in her hand. "Gothic art never appeared more intelligent, more correct, or more impressive," she read. She tilted her head at Charlie. "I can understand the impressive, but what do they mean by more intelligent, more correct?"

"You're asking me?" Charlie said, trying to catch his breath. "I guess they mean that the guy who piled all these stones together was smart and didn't make any mistakes."

"Oh, Charlie, I don't think that's what they mean at all."

"Then you figure it out, kid. Me, I'm going to sit down on those steps over there. That climb was murder."

"If you hadn't eaten so much at lunch you wouldn't have minded it so much."

"I've worn off everything I had for lunch walking up here." He lowered himself onto the steps, pulled out a colored handkerchief and wiped his brow. "We ought to be taking a siesta like everybody else," he commented.

Sheila stood gazing up at the beautiful cathedral. She glanced at the guidebook again. "Funny," she said, frowning at the page. "They don't give it any name. They just call it the cathedral. I thought all churches and cathedrals were named for some saint."

"The Immaculate Conception in the Bronx ain't the name of any saint."

"Yeah, but it's a religious thing, ain't it? This place just doesn't have any name at all." She sighed. "That's kinda sad when you think about it. Here is this beautiful church and it don't have a name."

"It's gotta have a name," Charlie said, making a grab for the guidebook.

Sheila wandered over toward the vaulted doorway and stood admiring the handsome, saintly statues sitting in their niches. High above was the huge rose window tatted in stone and marble. Centuries before, James the Conqueror had stood where she was standing, making his farewells to his staff at the end of his first campaign. "Since God has done me such grace," he had said (according to his Chronicle), "and has given me such a Kingdom in the seas as no King of Spain was able to conquer, and I have built here a church to Our Lady Saint Mary, besides other churches, be sure I will never desert you . . . "

She turned and went back and sat down next to Charlie.

"Yeah," Charlie said, resting back on his elbows. "This is the life, huh, kid? You know, maybe we should forget about the rest of the tour and just settle down here. I kinda like this place."

"You've liked every place we've been so far. And, if I remember, you said the very same thing about all of them." She poked a finger into his flabby chest. "I bet you say that about every place we're goin' to, too."

"I like it here. I shoulda come to Europe a long time ago. I bet I'd've never gone home."

"Then you'd never have met me."

He smiled at her. "Yeah, that's right. Well, now that I've met you and now that we're over here, maybe we should think about staying."

"There you go again. We've been all over this before, Charlie Cranston. It just don't make any sense settling down over here when we belong home in New York."

"Why not? It makes good sense to me."

She rolled her eyes heavenward. "You're nuts, Charlie, d'ya know that?"

"About you, maybe. About living back in New York, no."

"And you're gonna bring up our kids speaking some foreign language." She thought about having missed her period this month. She felt she'd better test him without coming right out and mentioning it.

"Kids?" He looked at her in surprise, snapping at her bait.

"Sure, kids. I'm not too old to have kids, you know. We can have kids. At least I intend having some if you aren't too old to provide the necessary ingredient." She jabbed him with her elbow.

"Hey, I never thought of us having kids right away." He puffed out his chest. "Sure, why not? Gee, kids," he reflected. "That really would be great." His expression changed. "Then that's more reason for us to settle down over here. I don't want no kid of mine growing up in that hellhole of New York. No siree."

"So we won't live in New York. We'll take a place out on the island."

"On the island? You're off your rocker. That's worse. There ain't nothing out there but hoods and Mafia."

"And I suppose they don't have crime and killings and stuff over here." She cocked her head at him again. "You know, Charlie, I think there's something fishy goin' on, which you ain't telling me about."

"What do you mean, fishy?" he asked, feeling apprehensive.

"Like you getting the money so quick for those new airline tickets and all. And this wanting to live over here and not wanting to go back to New York. There isn't anything funny goin' on that you ain't telling me about, is there, Charlie?"

He sat forward, putting his elbows on his knees and staring down at the ground. He picked up a pebble and tossed it down the steps. "No, there ain't nothing funny going on."

"Well, how come you had those phony tickets in the first place, tell me that?"

"I told you," he shouted.

She frowned at him and poked a finger toward the cathedral.

"I told you," he repeated in a softer voice. "The guy was recommended to me by Tony. He said he'd give me cut rates. I never pass up a bargain, you know that." He showed her his most innocent expression. "Would I have bought them if I'd known they were hot?"

"No, I guess not," Sheila admitted. "But I still think there's somethin' fishy goin' on."

"Fishy, schmishy . . . Come on, let's go inside and have a look at this fancy mausoleum."

"It ain't a mausoleum. That's where they bury dead people."

"They bury them in cathedrals too, don't they?" He heaved himself to his feet. "Come on, let's take a look, then we'll go someplace and have something to eat."

"Charlie," she said, putting her hands on her hips. "Don't you ever think about anything but eating?"

"What do you want from me? I said we'd look at the church first, then eat. Doesn't that prove that I'm interested in something besides food?"

She shook her head at him, then hurried to catch up as he started through the vaulted doorway and on into the dim, lofty recesses of the massive cathedral.

Their eyes were drawn immediately to the great rose window at the east end of the nave over the Chapel Royal and the two smaller rose windows over the east end of each aisle, all three bursting in red, blue, yellow and green glass. Behind the screen at the east end of the apse lay entombed the mortal remains of James II and James III of Majorca.

"See," Charlie whispered. "Didn't I tell you it was a mausoleum?"

Sheila nudged him with her elbow and walked on. They saw the Treasury with its rich collection of the relics for which men in the Middle Ages had fought and died. They saw the simple tombstone to the Majorcan Gil Muñoz, who surrendered his title of Pope in order to accept the bishopric of Majorca. They paused before the tomb of the distinguished General Don Pedro Caro y Sureda, who died during the Peninsular War against Napoleon.

"Beautiful, ain't it, Charlie?" Sheila said wistfully, looking up at the exceedingly beautiful paintings, statuary, the lofty, lacy ceiling, the Mediterranean light pouring through the windows.

Charlie stood deep in thought. His face was creased, giving him a troubled look. He shook himself slightly. "Come on, Sheila. Let's get out of here. I'm hungry."

IN A LARGE, ISOLATED HOUSE ON THE OUT-
skirts of Palma, Miguel Montoro unlocked the front door
and stepped into the cool interior. He tossed his white straw
hat onto the console and started to undo his necktie and shirt
collar. He stopped under the large crystal chandelier and
looked toward the curving staircase. "Are you home, Margarita?" His voice sounded too loud for the elegant foyer; it
seemed to disturb its elegance.

"In the bedroom," a woman answered from somewhere
upstairs.

The door at the top of the stairs stood open. Miguel leaned
against the framework, admiring the lovely, naked creature
stretched out so seductively on top of the silk spread. A drop-
let of spittle seeped out of one corner of his mouth. "You
have been waiting for me, I see," he said as he watched the
beautiful girl ease her thighs apart and rub the mound of her
vagina.

"You took so long getting home I thought you weren't
coming at all. I almost started without you," she said as she
began toying with her clitoris.

Miguel kicked off his shoes and started to strip out of his
clothing. "I'm sorry, my dear, but I had to attend to some
rather profitable business."

"How profitable?"

He chuckled. "Very. An American with a daughter in jail.
I quoted him a high price, but he was willing to pay it. I was
sorry I had not doubled my price. I'm sure he would have
paid anything to get his daughter freed."

"And did you arrange to have her freed?"

He wagged a finger at her as he climbed naked onto the
bed. "You do not grant favors without first receiving your due
reward. The girl will be freed tomorrow, after Mr. Shepherd
has delivered the necessary cash to, shall we say, cover the
legal aspects and expenses involved." He stretched out beside

her and put his hands behind his head. "I have had a very rewarding day, Margarita. Very rewarding."

"Yes, I can see you look very pleased with yourself. Did you speak with Elaine Brandon again?"

"Yes. Everything is going well on that score too. I think she is convinced that her young stud has run off with her daughter. I think my plan to break her and Jorge up is working out."

"What plan?"

"You mustn't question me, because I don't think I should tell you everything right now, but I can tell you this much. You remember my mentioning that Elaine's days are numbered?"

Margarita nodded her head gravely.

"Well, I have a plan to make sure she never marries that stupid Jorge she thinks she wants. After she realizes she can't have Jorge, she'll turn back to me. I'm convinced of that. Then Elaine and I will get married."

"Married?" Margarita said, pushing herself up on one elbow and glaring at him.

"Patience, my dear, patience." He kissed her lightly on the forehead. "Elaine and I will marry," he continued, speaking more quickly. "Then Elaine will conveniently pass on, leaving me—her grieving husband—sole heir to her estates. Then, my love," he said, taking her roughly into his arms, "you will become Señora Montoro, one of the richest women in the world."

Margarita's eyes sparkled with greed. "The richest woman in the world. That has a very nice sound to it, Miguel."

"And how does pretty little Margarita thank her Miguel for making her such a grand lady?" He pinched her breasts hard, leaving marks on her skin.

"You know I do not like it when you cause pain," she said angrily, shoving his hands away.

Purposely Miguel again reached for the nipples and pinched, this time much harder.

Margarita yelled at him to stop. When he would not, she slapped him with all her might.

Miguel sighed and lay back. His penis was getting harder. That was what he liked so much about Margarita. She understood him. She understood the need that gnawed inside him. She wasn't like Elaine. Elaine had never been the woman he

wanted. It had been her money, not her body, that had
excited him. He had thought she would be a dominating
woman, as his mother had been. But Elaine Brandon was
weak, feminine, totally submissive. He hated her for that. His
earliest memories of sexual arousal were when he was very
young and his mother used to paddle him for being naughty.
He found himself looking forward to her paddlings and went
out of his way to be mischievous. He never understood—and
still did not understand—why the sting of the paddle aroused
him sexually. He would masturbate when the paddling was
finished and sometimes achieved an orgasm during the paddling. His father punished him once when he had misbehaved,
but it wasn't the same. He felt nothing except the pain of the
punishment. He was glad when his father and mother separated and his punishments were inflicted solely by her.

"Again," Miguel moaned.

Margarita had known Miguel a long time, ever since his
mother died. She knew his moods and his needs. She slapped
him again, then again.

"Yes, my darling, Margarita. Hurt me. Hit me. Paddle me.
I have been a very bad boy today and I should be punished."

Miguel never tried to understand these masochistic needs
within him. They were far too pleasurable for serious thought.

Margarita grabbed him by the hair of the head, digging her
nails into his scalp. "Bastard," she snarled and aimed a fist at
his eye.

Miguel grabbed her arm. "Not the face," he said. "You
know better than to hit where it would show."

Margarita dug her nails into his chest and left long, deep
scratches.

"Yes, yes," Miguel murmured, hardly audibly. "Hurry. I am
in the mood for something wild and terrible. Get the equip-
ment out of the nightstand. Put on the heels and the leather.
I want you to work me over good today. I deserve it," he
whispered, fondling himself, trying to keep back the orgasm
that was building up in his groin. "Hurry up. Beat me. Hurt
me. Make me crawl. I can't hold back too much longer.
I'm ready to come just thinking about what you're going to
do to me."

IT TOOK JORGE A FEW MINUTES TO REMEM-
ber where he was when he opened his eyes. The sound of
clattering dishes and the shuffling of Carlotta identified the
place after a moment. He stretched his arms over his head
and yawned. He felt better, but he was ravenous. The smell of
onion soup and shrimp tickled his nostrils and made his
stomach rumble. He kicked back the coverlet and got out of
bed. Just as he drew back the draperies that hid the tiny
bedroom alcove from the larger living room, the front door
burst open and a man stood there. He looked first at Jorge,
then at Carlotta, then back at Jorge.

"Who have we here?" he said with a sneer. "Well, if it
isn't the handsome and dashing Jorge Aguilar. Slumming,
Jorge? Or did the grand Señora Brandon finally find out what
a dud you are?"

"Hello, Alfredo," Jorge said, ignoring his insults. He smiled
at Carlotta, who was looking at the two men, her eyes darting
nervously from one to the other. "I'm starved, Carlotta.
When's dinner?" Jorge asked.

"Dinner?" Alfredo railed. "What is going on here? Since
when do you give dinner to your customers, Carlotta?"

"Don't be disgusting, Alfredo," she answered, placing plates
and silverware on the table. "Jorge is staying with me for a
few days. He is not a customer."

"You're kidding. How do you expect me to refer customers
to you if you have this character staying here? Or is he going
to sit beside the bed and make notes?"

"I don't want you to refer any customers to me for a few
days, Alfredo. Tell them I'm sick or that I had to go away for
a few days. I deserve a vacation anyway."

"*You* deserve a vacation. What about me? Oh, no, Carlotta. If you won't work I don't get my commission, and
without a commission I don't pay my bills or buy the little
luxuries I like to buy."

"Like those little boys you like so much," Jorge inserted with a sneer.

Alfredo glowered at him. "You keep out of this, hotshot. Go back to your fancy lady and leave me and Carlotta alone. You don't belong in this town anymore. You outgrew it, just as we outgrew you. So get lost."

"Stop it, you two," Carlotta said. "Look," she said to Alfredo as she went over to him. "I would like a few days off. Just two days. That won't hurt business very much. I'll pay you something for the two days I'm not working so you won't starve. What do you say, Alfredo? Just let me have two days alone."

"Alone? You mean two days with joy-boy here."

"So what's so wrong with two old friends wanting to spend some time together?" she asked.

"Two old friends. Hah, that's a laugh." He scowled at her. "I say, no. No two days off. No little romantic fling with an old heart-throb. No. No. No."

"Ah, please, Alfredo. I'll work twice as hard afterward. You can double the traffic if you like. Just let me alone for two short days."

Alfredo folded his arms across his chest and took a firm stance. "I said no and I mean just that. No!"

Carlotta tossed her head and flounced away from him. "Well, I'm taking them, whether you like it or not," she said.

"You'll do as I tell you to do," Alfredo shouted.

"Go to hell," she spat back at him.

He started menacingly toward her, showing a clenched fist.

"I don't need you, Alfredo," she yelled. "I never did need you. So leave me alone and get out of my house. I'll do as I wish. They pay for me," she said, poking a thumb into her chest. "Me. Not you." She tossed her head again and laughed up at the ceiling. "Who would pay for you?"

He hit her so hard she went flying across the room and banged into the opposite wall. Jorge was on him in an instant.

"You rotten bastard," Jorge snarled as he punched Alfredo on the side of the head. Another fist caught Alfredo under the chin, sending him backward over a wooden chair. As he struggled to keep his balance, Jorge hit him again, this time delivering an uppercut that shot Alfredo's head backward, almost snapping it from his spine. Alfredo teetered and fell to one knee. Jorge closed in on him.

Alfredo's fist shot out and caught Jorge in the midsection. Jorge clutched at the pain and Alfredo straightened up and connected with a fist to Jorge's jaw. Jorge staggered backward, grabbing the edge of the table for support. He stood for a moment trying to clear his vision. Just as Alfredo closed in to strike another painful blow Jorge shot out with a left, followed by a right to the head. He heard something crack and saw blood begin to flow from Alfredo's nose. He hit him again, pitching Alfredo back, flattening him onto the floor on his belly.

Alfredo lay quite still. Jorge staggered over to him, grabbed him by the collar of his jacket and dragged him toward the front door. He motioned for Carlotta to open the door, which she hurried to do. Jorge threw Alfredo bodily out onto the stoop and slammed the door. Carlotta threw herself into his arms.

"Oh, Jorge. You are so wonderful. I have wanted to be rid of Alfredo for a long time. I am glad this happened."

Jorge pressed her to him. "Did he hurt you?"

She shook her head. "No." Jorge looked down and saw the dark bruise at the curve of her chin. He touched it lightly with the tips of his fingers. "It is nothing," she said as she reached up to kiss his mouth. She saw a spot of blood on his lip. "Oh, but you are bleeding." She hurried from him to get something with which to tend the cut.

"What will you do now without Alfredo?" he asked as she dabbed at the cut.

"Good riddance to bad rubbish. Alfredo was more trouble than he was worth."

"If you have trouble with him . . ."

"I will have no trouble. There is too much I know about Alfredo that would cause him many problems with the *guardias civiles*. The police would be happy to put him away if they were aware of what he does with those young boys he is so fond of picking up, to say nothing of his pimping and his dope pushing. That was the first time he has ever hit me, and it will be the last."

As she talked, Jorge found himself only half listening to what she was saying. He felt a stirring in his groin. The clean, fresh smell of her permeated his nostrils, sending reason out of his head. He couldn't explain what was happening to him. He tried to tell himself that he loved Elaine and only Elaine, but the hardening in his loins erased everything from his mind, and all he could think of was the need for Carlotta. But it was insane. He and Carlotta were just friends. What then was this crazy sensation that was building up inside him? He felt an overwhelming urge to protect her, to harbor her from the Alfredoes in her life, the sordid, seedy customers to whom she gave herself.

He could well understand her popularity. She was beautiful, beautiful beyond description . . . so young and clean and innocent. She was far from innocent, of course, but when he looked down at her, none of that mattered.

"There," she said, examining her handiwork with the cut. "It will hardly show. Now, I will get you your dinner." She started away from him, but Jorge, on impulse, caught hold of her and pulled her against him. Carlotta felt his hardness and looked at him with a confused little frown creasing her brow.

"Let's go to bed," Jorge whispered as he pressed his mouth to hers.

She let herself be lifted up into his arms and carried to the little bed in the alcove. She wanted to question him, but reminded herself that she must never question supreme happiness. She didn't know why he suddenly wanted her, needed her, but she didn't care.

Jorge, on the other hand, kept telling himself he wasn't playing fair. He mustn't do this to Carlotta. He didn't love her. He was being cruel and selfish, and yet he couldn't stop himself from gently, swiftly removing her clothes as well as his own and pressing his hard, hot body against hers. It was as if he were caught in the wild, swirling current of a rapids, from which he could not swim free. His mouth found the pouting nipples of her breasts. He nibbled lovingly, tenderly, feeling Carlotta's fingers tug and pull at his thick, curly hair.

She stifled a little groan as the need for him grew to such proportions she thought her body would burst into flame. "Oh, Jorge. I love you so," she murmured.

THE TELEPHONE BESIDE HIS BED JANGLED.
Rod picked up the receiver. *"Si,"* he said.

"Hey, I thought you said you didn't know a word of Spanish," Nancy laughed.

"Hello there," he said as he stretched out contentedly on the bed and groped for a cigarette. The mere sound of her voice made him forget his troubled day.

"I hadn't heard from you. I thought perhaps you'd call."

"Sorry. I just got in. I've had a rotten afternoon."

"How about telling me all about it over a cocktail and some dinner?" She laughed again. "I know it isn't supposed to be proper for a girl to invite a man to dinner, but I happen to be all for the women's liberation movement."

"Sounds great," Rod said, but as soon as the words slipped out he cursed himself, remembering the resolutions he'd made to himself earlier. He mustn't encourage her. Much as he wanted to, he felt it wasn't right. Besides, to be honest, she made him feel vulnerable and afraid. His scene with Lisa had brought back his guilt. She'd been right about his need for sex with other women. But he mustn't give in to those urges any more. He'd thought about calling Nancy when he returned to the hotel, but refused to let himself do it. Nancy was a beautiful stranger, and he was frank enough to admit now that he wanted to go to bed with her. He supposed it was her forwardness that convinced him she'd be an easy mark. He mustn't weaken. He mustn't give in. This time he'd be strong and resist the temptation.

He checked himself. "I don't think I can, however," he said, turning his voice a little cool.

"I'll scratch her eyes out," Nancy kidded. "What's her name?"

"Oh, nothing like that, Nancy. It's just that I'm kinda beat and I don't think I'd make very good company tonight. Later in the week, perhaps."

"You'll be gone later in the week," she argued. "Come on,

Rod. Give a girl a break. I promise I'll be bubbly and spar-
kling and a bundle of laughs so as to take your mind off your
troubles. What do you say?"

No, a voice told him. But then what harm would there be
in it? She was right. He'd be gone tomorrow and never see
her again. The thought hurt without his knowing why it
should. She was a stranger, after all. Just a girl he'd met. She
meant nothing to him.

What the hell, he thought. Why not? It was only another
dinner date. After all, he had to eat and he hated eating alone.
He shook his head. That was the excuse he'd made yesterday.

When she sensed his hesitation Nancy said, "Ah, come on.
I've just gotten off the phone with Aunt Maggie and she's
p.o.'d at me for some reason. I don't feel like being alone.
I gave in last night, so how about returning the favor? Please."

Oh, what the hell, he thought again. He knew when he was
licked. He knew he shouldn't, but he said, "Okay. I'll tap on
your door in about an hour."

"Make it forty-five minutes. I'm hungry as a bear."

It was just over thirty minutes later when he called for her.
Two hours later they were lingering over coffee and brandy
in a cozy little restaurant in the older part of the city. It wasn't
a very fashionable place—in fact, it was a bit run-down and
shoddy—but the food was excellent and the atmosphere en-
chanting. They were fussed over by the owner and his wife,
two fat, jolly people who spoke broken English and who
watched them all the time to make sure they were enjoying the
food. There was no entertainment or music, just dim lights,
yellow tablecloths and fresh arrangements of flowers everywhere.

Nancy sipped her coffee and smiled at him. "How does a
good-looking man like you stay out of the clutches of marry-
minded females?"

Rod grinned and looked embarrassed. "I just don't encourage them."

"Is that why you were so reluctant to go out on a second
date with me?"

The flush on his cheeks darkened. "Do you always say
what's on your mind?"

"Sure. Why not? It's the only way to be: honest. To be totally honest is the test of a person's sincerity." She took a sip
of her brandy and waited for him to say something. When he

didn't, she pursued the subject with, "Well, tell me the truth. Do you think I have designs on you?"

Rod shrugged to hide his embarrassment. "I don't know. Do you?"

She smiled and propped her elbows on the table. "I'd like to go to bed with you. After that, I'll decide."

Rod squirmed in his chair. His cheeks were red hot. "You don't beat around the bush."

"Why should I? I'm a liberated woman."

Rod frowned into his drink. She was being crude the way Rose Mallory was crude. He didn't like it. "It doesn't suit you," he told her, finding he could not bring himself to look at her.

She reached across the table and touched his hand. "I'm sorry, Rod. I guess I'm just too used to dealing with the guys I went to school with. They expect a girl to be forward."

"You needn't remind me that we come from two different generations," he said, sounding hurt.

"Oh, please, Rod. I didn't mean that." She squeezed his hand. "I've hurt you. Forgive me." She paused. "It's just that I guess my aunt upset me with all her nasty talk on the telephone a little while ago. I'm just trying to prove that I have a tough hide and that nothing bothers me. If you want to know the truth, that isn't so. I have feelings just like everyone else; I just don't like to show them very often."

Rod smiled at her. "I'm just being sensitive. I should be the one to apologize."

Nancy breathed a sigh. "There for a minute I thought the evening was over before it started. Now, let's start again. How about going to bed with me?"

Rod burst out laughing. "You're impossible."

"Don't you like me?" she asked.

"Of course I like you. I like all women." It slipped out before he could catch it.

"Is that why you don't want to remarry?"

"What do you mean?"

"You said you liked *all* women. I thought maybe you found one wife insufficient."

Rod ran his fingers through his hair to hide his discomfort. "I'm not ready for marriage just yet. My wife just died recently. I told you that last night."

"But you think you'll remarry someday, right?"

Rod shook his head. "I doubt if I'll ever marry again."
"Why?"

Rod straightened in his chair and tried to assume an air of
sophistication. He thought of her remarks about honesty and
decided to try it. "I told you. I like women—plural."

"Good. That makes you solidly heterosexual. I approve."
She put down her brandy. "But what has that to do with not
getting married again?"

"I don't think it would be fair to my wife if I saw other
women on the side."

"Is that how it was with your first wife?"

Rod flushed again. He felt infected with Nancy's honesty.
"Yes," he said. "I'm not proud of it, but it's true."

"You don't have to be proud of it, but you don't have to be
ashamed of it either. It's healthy to have an occasional fling
with someone other than your spouse."

Rod shook his head. "That's not the way I was taught. As
you said, we come from two different schools." He toyed with
his drink. "To be perfectly honest, I think it was my extramari-
tal affairs that caused Helen's death."

"That's idiotic."

"It's true. If I hadn't been fooling around she possibly would
still be alive today."

"How many times did you fool around?"

"Four, five maybe."

"In how many years of marriage?"

"Fifteen."

"Oh, man. That's nothing. There for a moment I thought
you were looking for something different every week."

"I still think those four or five times are what killed
Helen."

"You don't know women. Chances are she knew all about
your little escapades and was intelligent enough not to let
them bother her. If you had threatened to leave her—which
I assume you never did—then I could understand her going
off half-cocked."

"Helen would never have understood."

"Well, be that as it may, I still disagree with you." A quiet
fell over the table. "So you aren't going to marry again because you are afraid it will prove fatal to a second wife."

Rod fidgeted. "Something like that," he said, trying to
match her truthfulness.

"I have a different concept of marriage," she said. "Now, I honestly believe in the modern approach to marriage. Oh, I'm not for common-law marriages or living in a commune, but I do believe that a man and a woman should continue to live their own lives after marriage. One should not hamper the other."

"You're saying that the husband and the wife should both be free to have other sex partners?"

"Sure, why not?"

"I wouldn't want any wife of mine sleeping with other men."

"But it would be okay if you slept with other women, right?"

"I guess that's selfish of me, but honestly, yes, that's right."

Nancy shook her head. "You're a male chauvinist, do you know that?"

Rod gulped down the rest of his brandy and motioned to the fat proprietor. "It's getting late," he said and asked for the check.

Outside she slipped her arm in his as they started back toward their hotel. Nancy sensed his discomfort and gave his arm a little tug. "I know where you can see a sex exhibition, if you're interested."

Just out of curiosity and glad for a change in the conversation, he said, "Where?"

Nancy giggled and squeezed close to him. "My hotel room."

Rod laughed. "You're crazy, do you know that?"

They walked along in silence for several yards. "I've put a damper on your evening, haven't I?" Nancy said.

"No, not really. It's just that I've been in a rather low mood all day."

"Tell me about it."

He blamed it on the warmth of the night, the brightness of the stars, the gentle weight of her arm on his. He didn't want to burden anyone with his problems, but he liked talking to Nancy. It was easy and open and honest and seemed the most natural thing in the world. "Maybe it would help," he said as he looked around. "But let's have another brandy someplace quiet."

"Only if I pay. The dinner was supposed to be my treat."

"Then we'd better find someplace American-looking. I think the Majorcans would be shocked out of their gourds if they saw a woman paying for a man's drink."

"You know, you have some pretty old-fashioned ideas, Mr.

Shepherd. I'll have to do something about them." She pointed to a little café across the street. "That place looks nice and quiet."

Zorrilla's was an intimate, small café hidden behind a respectable facade of frosted glass and oak paneling. An attendant in white jacket and black trousers, lace shirt and string tie ushered them to a small table in the corner. Through an archway Nancy spotted a little patio beyond.

"Let's sit out there," she said to Rod.

The waiter smiled but shook his head. "If I may, *señorita*, I would advise against it. Unfortunately the mosquitoes will be out in droves. You will be much more comfortable in here." He handed them menus with a flourish.

"Just brandy for two," he said, waving aside the cards.

He sat collecting his thoughts, wondering if he was doing the right thing in telling Nancy his troubles. When the brandies were set before them he had just about reached the decision to keep his troubles to himself.

"Now," Nancy said, leaning toward him. "What kind of trouble did you get yourself into today?"

"Maybe we should let it ride," Rod said, sipping his brandy.

"It's generally best to talk problems over with someone. I'm a very good listener." She urged him on. "Strangers sometimes can see things more clearly and a lot more objectively." When he still sat reflecting, she added, "What kind of trouble is your daughter in?"

The key word pushed him into talking. He began by telling her all about Verdugo, Montoro and Lisa, and she listened with genuine concern.

"Poor Lisa," Nancy said. "How did she get hooked up with this Petrik fellow?"

"Who knows?" Rod answered, swirling the brandy around in the bottom of the glass. "She said she met him in New York. Christ, according to what that lawyer, Montoro, knows about him, Petrik is old enough to be her father."

"I see nothing wrong with that," Nancy said. "What concerns me is that he's so deep into the drug business. That could spell a lot of trouble if Lisa gets too involved with him."

"She won't. I'll see to that."

"Don't be too sure. She's a woman, after all. Perhaps a very young, immature woman, but a woman nevertheless. If she thinks she's in love with the guy she'll go to him regardless of who stands in her way." She smiled at him. "I have a feeling Lisa is very much like her old man."

"I just can't understand her anymore. She was such a nice, quiet, sedate little girl. Now she's turning into a veritable monster."

"She's just going through a stage. All girls do at fifteen."

Rod shook his head. "I don't think that's it. She used to be very fond of me; now she absolutely despises me. I can tell by looking at her that she hates me with a passion."

"I'm sure that isn't true," she said, laying a sympathetic hand over his. "She's hurt and confused and misses her mother very much. It isn't easy, I'm sure, for a girl of fifteen to suddenly find she's without a mother at a time when she needs one the most."

"Lisa blames me for that."

"For what? The loss of her mother? I don't understand."

Rod downed the rest of his brandy and heaved a deep sigh. "I've told you most of the story, I might just as well tell you all of it. God knows I've kept it to myself long enough. Maybe I'll feel better if I talk it out with someone like you."

"Try me." She took his hand and held it.

He took a deep breath and let it out slowly. "Helen wasn't Lisa's mother." He looked at her, expecting to see shock registered on Nancy's face. But she was simply sitting there calmly, waiting for him to continue.

When he faltered she said, "So?"

"This isn't a very nice story, I'm afraid. I was a heel and a louse, but I'm paying the piper now for all my indiscretions."

"Why don't you tell me and let me decide that?"

"Well," Rod started, "before Helen and I got married I'd been running around with a pretty fast little number by the name of Rose Mallory. When I told Rose I was thinking of marrying Helen, she told me I had another think coming because she was going to have my baby. So I went to Helen, and at least I was man enough to tell her I loved her and I wanted to marry her but I had this problem with Rose. I thought that would be the end of me and Helen. But to my surprise, Helen went to see Rose and made her a proposition. She told Rose she'd take the baby and raise it as her own if Rose would give it up. To make a long, sordid story short, Rose quoted a price, Helen and I agreed to pay it, and when Lisa was born Rose disappeared.

"We didn't hear from her again until just last year. She'd started up a roadhouse in the suburbs of Dayton. It was a brothel, actually. Everybody knew what kind of business went on at Rose's, but even the cops smiled and looked the other way. Then, out of nowhere, Rose called me one night. She said she wanted to see me. I hadn't the least idea what she wanted to say, but I went to see her. She said she wanted Lisa back. We'd never adopted her legally, so Helen and I didn't have a leg to stand on. Rose said if we didn't give her Lisa she'd make a stink and get Lisa back if she had to do it through the courts.

"I came home and told Helen. She suggested we get rid of Rose as we had before, by offering her money. I called Rose and offered her a sum she couldn't refuse." Rod grinned boyishly. "I'm not exactly a rich man, but I have some money."

"Go on," Nancy said, leaning forward with interest.

"So, Rose took the money. I drove out that night and delivered it to her. It was raining like hell. Helen had wanted to come with me and give Rose a piece of her mind. I didn't want to create an unpleasant scene, so I told Helen to stay home, that I'd go alone. After I left, Helen must have changed her mind, because she got in her car and followed me. I guess she just wanted to get the anger off her chest. Well, that's when the accident happened, and Helen was killed.

"Someone told Lisa that I'd gone to Rose's. She thought her mother was on her way to confront me with the fact that she knew I was frequenting prostitutes. When Helen was killed, Lisa began to hate me, thinking that while I was sleeping with Rose, Helen was lying dead in a wrecked car."

Nancy squeezed his hand. "Why don't you tell Lisa the truth?"

"I can't. Lisa's just a child. She wouldn't understand."

"She's not a child. She's fifteen," Nancy argued. "Tell her, Rod."

"No. I know my little girl. You said before that she was like me. Well, she is. If I know Lisa, she'd feel it was her duty to be with her real mother. I just couldn't live knowing that Lisa had gone to Rose. She'd wind up a prostitute just like her real mother." He motioned to the waiter to refill their brandy glasses. "I just wouldn't be able to live with myself if she did that."

"Give the girl some credit, Rod. I don't know Lisa, but I don't believe she'd forget so quickly who raised her."

"In Lisa's mind, that wouldn't be the point. She would do what she thought was just and honorable. She'd go to her real mother. I know she would."

Nancy pulled her hand away when the waiter brought the brandy. "Well, do it your way, Rod, but I think you are making a terrible mistake."

"I don't think so."

There was a moment of silence. Then Nancy said, "What do you intend doing now?"

"Now," Rod answered, swallowing his brandy, "I'm going to give this Montoro character the money he's asked for and then I'll fly home with Lisa neatly tucked under my wing."

"Back to Dayton and Rose Mallory?"

"Back to Dayton, anyway. As for Rose Mallory, people aren't looking as kindly as they once did on Rose's roadhouse. I think before long Rose will be asked quietly to take her business someplace else. I have a lot of connections in Dayton. It would be simple for me to whisper the right words in the right ears and get her ousted."

Nancy studied his face. "You're a strange man, Rod Shepherd. At times you sound like the sweetest, nicest guy in the world, and then you turn around and show a mean streak a mile wide." She smiled. "I like that. Most men are easy to figure out. You're very different. I think I'd like to get to know you much better," she added, leaning across the table and giving him a very seductive look.

Rod stirred uneasily on his chair. "Don't tempt me, young lady. I am in a particularly vulnerable mood this evening."

"Good. Your room or mine?"

Rod laughed, but when he looked at Nancy he saw that she wasn't smiling.

"I'm dead serious," she said.

Reason told him to change the subject. How or where the words came he didn't know. "I think my bed is bigger."

The minute the door to the hotel room closed, Nancy was in his arms, kissing him passionately on the mouth. "I know I'm being brazen and wanton, but I don't care. I want you, Rod. I want you more than I've ever wanted any man before."

This wasn't happening to him, he kept telling himself. Get her out of here. Tell her to go back to her own room. Yet, as much as he argued with himself he found he could not stop kissing her mouth, her eyes, her throat. With dreamlike helplessness he found they were taking off their clothes, then lying naked on the wide bed.

Rod pulled her into his arms and crushed his mouth over hers. He pressed down, hot and urgent.

Nancy pushed back hard against him. She arched upward, and her young, full breasts crushed into his chest. Her body tingled as his hands caressed and soothed the creamy softness of her skin.

Nancy's mouth left his and seared a torrid trail down to his neck, nibbling at his earlobes as it passed. It continued down, resting finally at the hard points of his chest. The nipples hardened as her lips covered them, one by one, drawing them gently into her mouth. His whole body was trembling.

His hands locked into her hair, pulling gently, pressing her mouth still harder against the desire that was building inside him. A soft, quiet moan escaped his lips as his tongue flicked out, moistening the already wet corners.

Nancy teased and fondled, sending shivers of pleasure through the hard muscled body beneath her. Her mouth abandoned his chest. She licked and kissed her way through the hair on his chest, pausing, searching, feeling her way toward a pulsing need that had to be satisfied.

His penis was hard as steel as he felt the throbbing sensations forming into an uncontrolled readiness. His hands tugged at her hair, reaching, stretching, scratching at the torture to which she was subjecting him. He looked down at her just as her lips touched the head of his engorged cock.

Rod froze. He felt a sudden icy chill rush through him. This was Nancy. This wasn't some woman he'd paid to do this to him. This was a girl he knew and one he liked more than he wanted to admit, a girl who was like Lisa or any other decent girl. He felt filled with loathing and disgust, but he didn't know whether it was disgust at Nancy and women like her or disgust at himself.

Roughly he shoved her away and swung his feet over the side of the bed. Nancy stared at him, but he avoided her eyes. She was a whore, a prostitute, no better than all those other whores he'd frequented. She was just like those other women who'd been responsible for Helen's death.

He got up and stormed into the bathroom, slamming the door behind him.

"Rod? What's wrong?" Nancy called helplessly.

He shut out her voice by angrily twisting on the water taps. He stared at himself in the mirror.

ALTHOUGH BORN IN THE LITTLE TOWN OF Andraitx, Dario Avisa considered Palma his home. He was a somebody in Palma, and just another poor, struggling peasant in Andraitx. As he pulled into the driveway of Elaine's villa after being cleared by the guard at the gate, he looked at the magnificent house and felt that he belonged here. This was the way he wanted to live—in splendor like this, with a staff of servants and an endless stream of money flowing through his fingers. This was what Dario Aviso was meant for, not a farm, a plow and a team of donkeys.

Someday he'd live like Elaine Brandon. He shook his head. He certainly would not do it by riding bicycles. But it was a start. At least he was meeting people with money and position. For the poor like himself, sports was the only way to get a toehold on the rich of the world. He wished he were more like Jorge, able to attract any woman, not just the ones who wanted a body to show off for a few days. Rich women fell in love with Jorge; they only paid guys like himself for their services and then dismissed them. He wanted to be kept. He did not care by whom, just so he'd have enough money to set himself up in a nice place, have good clothes, a sporty new car and lots of cash to flash around. He could pretend to love them if that was what they wanted. He was good at pretending. He had convinced that silly Isabella that he loved her. It was the only way he could get her to go to bed with him.

He had been a fool to sleep with Isabella. She was such a dumb peasant. The fuss she was now kicking up was not worth it. So she had lost her virginity. So what? It had taken two to accomplish that. If it had not been him it would have been some other guy, so why should he be expected to marry her and live in that lousy village for the rest of his life just because Isabella had been hot for a man? He was the one whom the family wanted to put the screws to now. Stupid peasant broad. He should never have fooled around with her. She had known the consequences as well as he. She had known the people in the village would brand her as an outcast if they found out. So why did she have to shoot off her mouth to her family and friends? Why should he worry about her? He would get the hell out of Majorca the first chance he got. He would not let himself be pressured by her father and brothers into marriage. Not to a peasant like Isabella.

Why hadn't Cynthia liked him as Isabella did? It would have been perfect to marry someone like Cynthia Brandon.

He noticed that every light seemed to be burning in the windows of the Brandon villa. The Brandons did not have to worry about electric bills; there was no necessity to economize. And they did not have to think about turning the lights on or turning them off; they had hired help to do that sort of thing. Cynthia Brandon, he thought. If he could only marry Cynthia he wouldn't have to worry about anything ever again.

Maggie and Greg were sitting at the coffee table in front of the fireplace when the butler ushered Dario into the drawing room. The opulent good taste of the room overpowered him as he entered it. He felt a little out of place, feeling his awkward bulk too large in proportion to the delicate lines of the furniture. Yet he tilted his head arrogantly high as he smiled and walked toward them.

"Dario," Maggie gushed. She held out her bejeweled hand for him to kiss. She was wearing a kewpie-doll smile and a kewpie-doll dress. "What a delicious surprise. I was just showing Greg again an item I recently added to my collection." She picked a long silver hatpin up from the velvet cloth and held it out for Dario to admire. "I found it in the most divine little shop in Palma this afternoon. Exquisite, isn't it? And very expensive, I might add. Oh, these local Majorcans would steal a woman blind if she'd let them."

"Handsome," Dario said, not bothering to take the hatpin from her fingers. "Hello, Greg. Nice to see you again."

Greg shook his hand politely, which surprised Dario. Greg was usually so surly and uncommunicative. Dario didn't particularly care for the fellow. He was amazed to see Greg so fascinated by Maggie's collection of antique hatpins.

"Is Cynthia around?" Dario asked Greg.

"No," Greg answered, picking up the daggerlike hatpin he'd admired yesterday noon and turning it over and over in his fingers. "From what I understand, she and that Jorge fellow took off last night and no one has heard from them since." He spoke with a touch of malice.

"That's odd," Dario said. He considered mentioning his conversation with Jorge the evening before, but decided he'd best keep still.

"What's odd about it?" Maggie wanted to know. "I personally saw the two of them billing and cooing in the gazebo last night. If you ask me, I think they eloped." Maggie laid a thoughtful finger on her cheek. "Hold on," she said as she tapped the finger against the sagging flesh. "Didn't I see you talking to Cynthia on the stairs last night, Dario?"

Dario flushed under his deep tan. "I spoke to her only briefly. She said she was in a hurry and ran on up to her room."

"But you followed her," Maggie said. "I saw you go up the stairs."

"There was something very important I had to speak to her about, but I found her with Greg and didn't want to interrupt them. I waited in Jorge's room for a while, but when I searched her out again she wasn't anywhere to be found."

"Well, it's all too confusing for me," Maggie said. "Everyone rushing in and out, appearing, disappearing, I'm sure I don't understand any of it." She fluttered her hands. "But then I'm not expected to understand any of it; it isn't any of my business, I've been told."

Greg looked amused. "And who told you that?"

Maggie pouted prettily. "Elaine as much as said so."

"Elaine said what?" Elaine asked as she strolled into the drawing room.

Maggie fluttered her hands again. "Oh, we were just speaking about Cynthia and Jorge and how you told me not to concern myself about them." She bent over her collection of hatpins and pretended she was alone in the room.

"You are looking extremely ravishing this evening, Elaine," Dario said, taking her hand and kissing the back of it.

"I've had a dreadful bout with a headache all day, but it

seems to have disappeared. I'm feeling much better now. I'm afraid I've allowed this Cynthia-Jorge business to upset me."

"That's understandable," Dario said. Again he wondered if he should speak of his conversation with Jorge the night before, but decided it was not his place to interfere in Jorge's and Elaine's private affairs. He did venture to say, however, "Jorge too was very upset last night."

Elaine dismissed the remark with a wave of her hand. She didn't want to think about Jorge and Cynthia. She forced herself to face the obvious. Jorge and Cynthia had run away together. She had lost and Cynthia had won, it was as simple as that. She dearly wished things hadn't turned out as they had, but there was nothing she could do about it but try to forget. Making herself sick over the matter wouldn't accomplish anything. After all, no one was to blame but herself. She had created her own unhappiness by her lies and her deceit. She'd fretted about it all day and all of last night, deciding finally that she had no other recourse but to put it out of her mind and hope and pray that Cynthia would make him happy. After all, the only thing that mattered was Jorge's happiness. If he found it with Cynthia, then she would be content.

Elaine wandered toward the windows. "Jorge will get over being upset," she said over her shoulder to Dario. It hurt just to speak his name, she found.

Greg didn't want to sit around talking about that stupid Jorge and his sister. He was bored. He had used up the last of his coke to fight off his boredom, and now the boredom was getting worse than before. He was tempted to ask Dario where the action was in town, but decided against it. Dario was a hustler and a jerk of an athlete. He most likely thought Mary Jane was a girl's name. He pushed himself out of his chair and started for the door. "I'm going out," he said.

"Try to get home at a decent hour, not like last night," Elaine said.

Greg frowned. "You heard me come in last night?"

"This morning," Elaine corrected. "Yes, I couldn't sleep. It was about four o'clock when you drove up."

"Always the devoted mother keeping watch over her young," Greg said sarcastically. "Too bad you didn't keep a closer watch over Jorge."

He bumped into Miguel just as he was leaving the room. "You again?" he said angrily to Miguel. "Why don't you move in? You're here more than any of us."

Miguel ignored the remark. He stepped aside and let Greg leave.

"Miguel," Elaine said, hurrying over to him. "Any news?"

Miguel greeted the others, then said, "I'm afraid not, Elaine. We've checked everywhere. There isn't a trace of them. They must have driven somewhere. No one has seen or heard from them since yesterday."

"Check the pawn shops," Maggie said. "If Jorge stole Elaine's emeralds he'll try to hock them somewhere along the line."

Elaine felt every nerve in her body grow taut.

"Jorge stole your emeralds?" Dario asked Elaine with concern. "But that isn't possible. Whatever Jorge is he is not a thief. That I would stake my life on."

Elaine laid a hand on his arm. "No one is accusing Jorge of taking my necklace, Dario. It's just that the necklace disappeared at the same time as Cynthia and Jorge."

Maggie wouldn't be put off. "They took it, I'll bet my bottom dollar on it."

"Oh, Maggie, please don't say that." Elaine tried to keep her voice sweet. "We don't know if the necklace was even stolen. It just hasn't turned up, that's all."

Miguel helped himself to some cognac from the decanter on the table. "I thought I'd come out, Elaine, and take you out for some diversion."

"At this hour?"

"It's early. Oh, come on, Elaine. It will do you good to get out of this house. We can dance and have a few glasses of wine and perhaps a midnight supper somewhere. What do you say?"

"Thank you, Miguel. But I really don't wish to. Why don't you take Maggie?"

"Ah, but I was going to ask for that honor," Dario said, flashing his most beguiling smile at Maggie. "*Señora?*" he said, bowing to her.

Maggie clapped her hands together. "I couldn't think of anything I'd like more," she gushed as she quickly closed the lid on her hatpin collection and tucked it under her fleshy arm. "I won't be a moment, Dario. Oh, I haven't been dancing since I left Monte Carlo. It will be such fun, especially with you, young man," she said as she hurried out of the room.

Miguel took Elaine's hand. "Then how about you and me indulging in a very spirited game of backgammon, Elaine."

"Yes, thank you. I think that is more along the lines of what I had in mind for this evening," she said.

He laughed softly. "We will be alone here. I hope I can trust myself with you."

THERE WAS A SINGLE LIGHT BURNING OVER the doorway of the bar. The street was shabby and littered with trash and garbage. Two aging prostitutes sauntered along the dark street, arms linked, hips swaying in an exaggerated motion from side to side. In a doorway a drunk was sleeping off his wine, the bottle still clasped tightly in his hand. One of the old prostitutes stopped and ran her hand over the drunk's crotch. She rolled her eyes and laughed. She inched her finger and thumb apart to show her girlfriend how large the guy's penis felt.

Inside the seedy little bar, Greg Brandon sat hunched over a whiskey glass. He banged the glass on the bar, then fished in his pockets for his package of cigarettes. It, like the whiskey glass, was empty. He crumpled it up and threw it on the sawdust-covered floor. "Whiskey," he shouted to the bartender. Greg got up and staggered over to a battered cigarette machine in the corner. He didn't bother selecting a brand. He didn't care about anything at this point. He was spaced out on too much grass, coke and pills.

Out of nowhere he heard Cynthia's words echoing inside his head, and he put his hands over his ears. He didn't want to hear them. Why had she said such rotten things? She knew him better than that. It was Elaine who'd warped Cynthia's opinion of him. Now Cynthia believed as his mother did—that he was a fag, a conceited homosexual who beat up women to show his contempt for them. He wasn't queer. He'd prove it to them all. He felt a sudden nausea. Cynthia and Elaine, between them, had most likely told that pretty hustler, Jorge, that their brother was a fag.

He hated them all. He staggered back to the bar.

"Where in hell is everyone?" Greg yelled at the bartender. "Hell, it's almost midnight." He needed people around to get him out of his depression. He wished he were in Paris. In Paris things would be really starting to swing. But this wasn't Paris, he reminded himself. This was Majorca, with its "not before midnight" policy. Nothing ever started anywhere in Spain until after twelve o'clock. It was like a perverse Cinderella story. After midnight the church went to sleep and the devil took over until sunrise.

He tapped out a cigarette and impatiently fished for a match. The bartender supplied it.

Paris. Yes, that's where he should be, in Paris. Why had he let Cynthia talk him into coming to this goddam place? He hated her. He hated Palma. At least in Paris they had the decency to keep the bars dim. Not so here. The Spanish seemed to have a thing for brightly lighted bars—at least until midnight.

He caught a reflection of himself in the mirror behind the bar. What the hell difference did it make what Elaine and Cynthia thought about him? So what if he'd stayed with that movie producer in Paris? He hadn't done anything but lie back and let himself get sucked off. How could Cynthia get the wrong impression? He met his own eyes; he studied his handsome reflection. Why hadn't she understood?

He jerked his drink off the bar and took a deep swig. Christ! Why did he stay here? Why didn't he go to Paris? At least there they played the music so loud a body couldn't think.

The door behind him swung open and a dark Spaniard strolled in. Greg turned his head and eyed him for a moment. A pimp or a fag, Greg decided, seeing the flashy suit, the too-tight trousers, the slicked-down hair. It was strange that a guy would show up just now when his thoughts were running along that line. He'd read somewhere that thoughts acted like a magnet sometimes.

The newcomer sat down on a stool two away from Greg. Greg did not feel like conversation with a guy like that and knew he'd be courting it if he stayed where he was. Fairies were always trying to pick him up, always drooling over him.

He lumbered up off his stool, dragged his drink from the bar and settled himself at a small table in the corner.

The guy and the bartender said something to each other in Spanish. From what Greg could gather, the newcomer had said, "Not the sociable type," and had laughed.

Fuck 'em, Greg thought as he pulled a small pill box from his inside pocket and popped two of the yellowjackets into his mouth. He wished he hadn't smoked the last of his grass on the way here . . . and he was completely out of coke. He could sure use a joint right now. The booze wasn't helping at all.

Cynthia's lovely face misted before his eyes again. Why? Why had she turned against him? She'd fallen for that lousy stud, obviously. She didn't need a stupid jerk like that. He shook his head to dislodge the vision. It wouldn't go away. Greg picked up his whiskey glass and drained it. He banged it down on the table. "Whiskey," he yelled at the bartender.

The pills were starting to hit him. He could feel the sweat dripping from his armpits, the blood rushing to his head. The place was suddenly hot and the air too thick to breathe. He yanked open the collar of his shirt and ran his hand around the back of his neck.

"Señor," a voice said. Greg looked up and saw the guy in the flashy suit and tight pants standing in front of him holding Greg's drink.

"Thanks," Greg muttered and dragged his billfold from his pocket. He tossed some money on the table.

"Would you like some company?" the young man asked.

"I have all the company I need," Greg answered as he took a swallow of his drink.

"You look to me like a man with troubles."

Greg ignored him.

Alfredo touched the bandage across the bridge of his nose and studied Greg. "You are a very good-looking man," he said, letting his eyes move hungrily over Greg.

"Get lost."

"It embarrasses you to be admired by another man?"

Of course it did not embarrass him, Greg thought. In fact, he never got enough admiration, often as he received it. He was conceited. Sure. He admitted that. Why shouldn't he be? He had a lot to be conceited about. He fought against encouraging the guy. "Nothing embarrasses me," he said, taking another swallow of whiskey.

"Good. I like conceited people, especially men. They are such a challenge to me."

"A challenge?" Christ, why did he answer. He was encouraging conversation with this fruit. Oh, shit, he thought, why not? What in hell else is there to do in this crummy dump? Besides, maybe the guy knew where he could get some grass.

"Sure a challenge. Humble people succumb too easily to flattery." He sat down in the chair opposite Greg. "You, above all others, should know that."

"I didn't invite you to sit down."

"Sorry. Do you want me to leave?" Alfredo remained seated and fixed a smile on his lips.

Greg took another gulp from his glass. "I don't give a damn what you do." And he didn't. Talking was helping him to forget he was in this lousy place and to take his mind off Cynthia.

"My name is Alfredo Lorenzo," the young man said. He put out his hand. Greg ignored it.

"So?" Greg said drunkenly, trying to focus his eyes. His head suddenly felt as though it weighed a ton. He didn't think he was going to be able to hold it up. He swayed in his chair. His eyes rolled lazily in their sockets. Greg's head pitched forward, but he caught it before it bumped the table top.

"I think you are very drunk," Alfredo said. "Perhaps you should think about going home. Come. I will help you." He touched Greg's arm.

Greg swung his arm and sat up straight. "I don't need any help," he slurred. He tried to make out the guy's features. His eyes came into focus for a moment and he saw the bandage across the bridge of the man's nose. "Somebody beat you up?" he asked. He found that quite funny and started to laugh.

Alfredo touched the bandage gingerly. "Just a misunderstanding with a friend."

"Some friend," Greg said, noticing now the dark bruises on the man's chin and cheeks, the cut over his eye. "What was he, a hippopotamus?" He staggered over the word, tripping himself up in the consonants. That too he found extremely funny and went into gales of laughter.

"I haven't seen you in here before tonight," Alfredo said.

"I've never been in here," Greg said, his voice heavy with

drink and still shaky from his laughing. "I was told I could get some Mary Jane," he said in a confidential whisper that could be heard across the room. He teetered over the table, his head almost falling down on it again.

Alfred smiled. "Mary Jane? Oh," he said, having heard the American slang word before. "You are out of grass, my friend? That is too bad. But perhaps I can help you. I have friends who will supply you with all you want if you have the money to pay."

"I've got the money," Greg boasted, pulling out his wallet and showing Alfredo the wad of bills. Alfredo was impressed. He eyed the bundle greedily.

"Come with me," Alfredo said, again touching his arm. "I will fix you up."

Greg swayed on the chair. He started to get up and then sank back down again. "Gotta go take a piss first," he said. Again he tried to get up, but couldn't quite manage it. Christ, why had he let himself get so drunk? But then he hadn't had that much to drink. The pills and the grass and the little bit of coke he'd taken earlier were what was doing him in. Shit. What the hell did he care? Without Cynthia he didn't give a shit about anything, not even himself.

"Come, my friend. I will help you," Alfredo said. He put his hands under Greg's arms and lifted him off the chair. "This way," he said, steering Greg toward the men's room.

The nauseating smell of stale urine and unwashed toilets made him choke as he staggered into the room with Alfredo's support. He tried not to breathe. He found himself standing in front of the urinal. He propped his hands against the wall to keep himself from falling. He heard Alfredo laugh and say, "You'd better take it out, my friend, unless you want to ruin your expensive trousers."

"Huh?"

"Here, I will help you." Boldly Alfredo reached for the zipper of his fly and pulled it down. Greg just stood there, weaving back and forth in a drunken stupor. He felt Alfredo's fingers wrap around his cock and yank it out of his pants. Greg turned his head and saw Alfredo's smile. Greg had seen that smile of desire before. Lots of guys had looked at him with that same expression of yearning on their faces.

"Want to blow me?" Greg asked, not really knowing what he was saying. He started to urinate.

He heard Alfredo laugh again and saw him nod toward the partition that separated the urinal from the toilet. "If you want that, my friend, there is someone sitting on the other side of that partition who will be glad to accommodate you."

Greg turned and looked toward where Alfredo had nodded. Beneath the partition was a pair of men's shoes, trousers hanging down around them. Greg frowned.

"You see that hole in the partition, my friend? Well, if you will put your cock through there the man on the other side will suck it for you. I know him. He spends most of his evenings that way." Alfredo leaned closer to Greg. "I use him myself many times when I need release from my tensions. Try it, my friend. I can guarantee that the man sitting on the other side is quite expert."

Greg found himself sobering up. He couldn't understand what was sobering him, but the thought of putting his cock through a glory hole repulsed him very much. All those sordid thoughts about Phil at the military school flooded back into his mind. He saw his mother's face accusing him of being queer, the eyes wide with shock and disappointment.

"I'm not queer," Greg yelled as he finished urinating and pushed away from Alfredo, staggering toward the door.

"Better put that thing away before you go out there," Alfredo laughed, as he hurried after Greg.

Greg pushed himself back into his pants and went out, back to his table in the corner.

There were several more customers there now, and there was music, loud music. The lights too seemed to have dimmed. He fell into his chair and called to the bartender to bring him another whiskey.

"I thought we were going to see my friend about the grass you wanted," Alfredo said as he reseated himself at Greg's table.

"In a minute. Let's have another drink first. Bring a drink for my friend," Greg called to the bartender.

The place was filling up fast. Greg felt much better now that there was motion and noise around him. It helped blot out the memory of Cynthia and his mother's disapproving eyes. He found himself floating with the music. Why he was talking to this Alfredo character he didn't know, but it helped keep his mind off those other things he wanted so badly to forget. The guy was queer, there wasn't any doubt in Greg's mind about that. Didn't he say he frequented that glory hole in the men's room all the time? And the way he'd pulled Greg's cock out of his pants. It was as if he were making love to it with his fingers. Greg had to admit that it had felt pretty good. To his surprise he felt a hardening in his crotch.

"Come on, let's go see about that grass," Greg said, feeling uneasy. "My car's just outside."

"I think I'd better drive," Alfredo said as he steered Greg toward the beat-up old Fiat parked a little way down the street. "I'll drive you back here after we've seen my friend."

Greg laid his head back against the seat as Alfredo put the car in gear and drove quickly through the half-deserted streets. He found himself fighting to keep from passing out. The uneven streets supplied enough holes and bumps to keep him conscious.

"Where in hell are we going?" Greg asked as he forced himself to concentrate on the houses and buildings they were speeding past.

"It is not far. My friend has an apartment just down this street."

Alfredo pulled the car to the curb before a dismal dark and shuttered building. The basement apartment he and Greg walked into was just as dark and dismal. The air was thick with the smell of marijuana and incense. A single candle burned in the center of a large round table, around which five or six people were sprawled on the floor.

A young girl with huge eyes and a blood-red mouth swayed toward them. She smiled up into Greg's face and touched her lips lightly to his. He pushed her away.

The girl giggled and winked at Alfredo. "He does not like girls, Alfredo?"

"I do not know," Alfredo said. He put his arm around Greg's shoulders and leaned into his face. "Do you like girls, my friend?"

Greg yanked Alfredo's arm away. "Yes," he spat. "And don't touch me again."

Alfredo grinned and made his eyes larger.

The girl took Greg's hand. "Come with me, beautiful man. Perhaps you need only to relax to show me how much you like girls." She led him toward the table. Someone handed him a pipe. Greg put the stem into his mouth and took a deep drag. The smoke burned his lungs. He held it down, feeling his face getting hot. After a few moments he released his breath. "Good grass," he said to the girl.

"There is plenty," she answered as she steered him to a pillow on the floor. Greg lowered himself onto it; the girl snuggled close to him, putting her hand inside his shirt. "Blond men are my weakness," she purred, tickling the hair on his chest.

The grass was strong. He felt his spirits begin to soar. He felt light and silly and happy. He grinned a lopsided grin at the girl and took her face in his hands. He planted his lips firmly against hers, darting his tongue into her mouth.

"You would like to make love?" she asked, under his mouth.

"Very much," he answered.

"Wait," Alfredo said to the girl. "I did not bring him here for you, Francie."

"But he does not want you, Alfredo." She smiled at Greg. "You do not want him, you want me, do you not?"

In answer Greg grabbed her and kissed her hard, groping for her breasts. After a moment he released her. Alfredo stood over them glowering down. "Get lost," Greg said, returning his attention to the girl, slipping his hand up under her skirt. Greg did not see Francie and Alfredo wink at each other when Alfredo motioned with his head toward the door to the bedroom.

"That feels so nice," Francie cooed as she let Greg fondle her crotch. "But let us get more comfortable." She got up and held out her hand to Greg. She helped him to his feet and steered him toward the room beyond.

Greg fell heavily on the bed. His head was swimming. He thought he felt Francie starting to remove his shoes and socks, then his jacket and shirt. He lay there, reveling in the beautiful high the grass had given him. Everything was so brilliantly colored, so vibrant. He was back at military school running through the tall grass with Phil. The smell of the spring flowers was overpowering; he could almost hear the roots of the trees stretching out their tentacles and digging deeper into the earth.

All of a sudden he focused, finding that his mouth was dry as cotton. "Drink," he mumbled as he tried to sit up.

Francie eased him back onto the bed as she stripped away the last of his clothing. "I will get you something," she said and skirted around Alfredo, who was standing in the doorway admiring Greg's naked body.

Alfredo walked over to the bed and sat on the edge of it. He ran his hand over Greg's chest. "Are you sure you want only Francie?" he asked softly.

"Go 'way," Greg muttered.

Alfredo did not move. He glanced up when Francie came back into the room and took the glass she carried. "Here, handsome," Alfredo said, holding Greg's head up so that he could drink. "After this I do not think you will be so particular about what or who you want."

Greg only barely heard the words. They buzzed around inside his head, making no sense. The drink was sharp to the taste, but it quenched his thirst, and that was all he cared about at the moment.

"I also brought this," Francie said, putting a cigarette between Greg's lips.

He dragged the smoke deep into his lungs again, gulping air with it. He felt weightless, floating free without a care in the world. He felt hands all over him, fluttering like wings of birds over his burning flesh. His mind kept telling him that they'd put something in the drink, acid most likely, and the cigarette wasn't just grass, it was opium. But Greg didn't care. He felt so relaxed, so at peace with the world, that nothing mattered at all.

He felt himself sinking deeper and deeper into the softness of the bed. Through the haze he heard Francie's voice, but he couldn't make out the words.

"He's had too much," she'd said. "He can't get it up." She bent over him, sucking his penis into her mouth. She ran her tongue around it, then straightened up. She giggled. "No, he's just out of it."

"Roll him over," Alfredo said. "That's the nice thing about liking men, there's always many routes to travel."

Greg felt himself being rolled over onto his stomach. He put his head on his arm and sighed. The world was such a beautiful place, he thought as he felt himself drifting out into space.

Suddenly Greg screamed as Alfredo rammed his cock up into his ass. He felt a hand clamp over his mouth. "No, oh, Christ, no," Greg shouted into the hand. He started to struggle. The pain was unbearable. He fought back with every ounce of strength he could find, but the more he struggled the greater the pain became. He tried to turn over, tried to dislodge the pain that was wracking his body, but every move he made seemed so wasted, so futile. All the beauty he'd seen earlier was gone now, replaced by black, ugly things that were trying to tear his body apart with their sharp, jagged claws. He was sinking into a black pool of mud. He couldn't breathe; something was pulling him down, down, down.

Alfredo had him pinned solidly down on the bed, his cock firmly embedded. He was moving up and down, screwing slowly, brutally at Greg's tortured backside.

"I'll kill you," Greg yelled, but his voice was a blur. He started to struggle again, but something hard and heavy hit him on the back of the head and everything went black. The pain disappeared.

Greg didn't know how long he'd been unconscious. When he came to the first light of dawn was peeking over the tops of the buildings. He opened his eyes and tried to recognize where he was. He looked down at himself and found that he was naked and lying across the front seat of his car. His clothes were in a pile on the floor. For a moment nothing registered.

Suddenly his eyes flew wide open and a gasp caught in his throat. He reached under himself and felt the streaks of dried blood on his ass cheeks.

"You rotten, goddam sonofabitch," he swore as he tried to sit up. He reached for his clothes. His wallet was empty of money.

He started to struggle into his clothes. "I'll kill you, you bastard," he yelled at the top of his lungs. "I'll kill you, you lousy, cocksucking prick, if it's the last thing I do."

He froze, then collapsed on the seat of the car and gave himself up to his tears.

"Phil. Phil," he sobbed. "Help me."

Wednesday

THE BEACH WAS NEARLY DESERTED AS SHEILA and Charlie walked, hand in hand, barefoot across the pale, soft sand. There was a quiet solitude all around them. Even the breaking waves seemed to know that the hour was early and most people were still asleep, and in respect they broke slowly and almost without sound.

Sheila's light, happy laughter floated out across the water as they walked along, mindless of all the troubles and suffering in the world.

"You pick up any more of those shells and we'll have to get a bigger hotel room," Charlie said as Sheila raced toward the water's edge and extracted another colorful shell from the wet sand.

"Oh, but this one is really too pretty to leave behind," she said.

He laughed at her. "What are you doing collecting those things? You can't take them with us when we start out for Cannes." He pronounced the *s*. "Besides, we got lots more beaches to visit before we're done."

"But I thought I'd take them all home when we go."

"We ain't goin' home until I say we're goin'," Charlie argued.

"Hey, look, a fish or something washed up on the shore," Sheila said, pointing and moving back toward the edge of the water.

"Some fish. It looks like a whale."

Cynthia Brandon's body lay face up, staring unseeing at the bright morning sun. The water lapped around her bare feet, her long dark hair floating like seaweed on the surface of the water.

Sheila screamed and covered her mouth with her hands. "Oh, God, Charlie. It's a girl."

Charlie raced to her side and stared down at the lovely, dead face. "Yeah," he breathed. "Christ. We'd better get the police out here." He knelt down and turned Cynthia's head slightly. He saw the huge welt, the opening in the skull. "Somebody cracked this broad over the head, or she hit her head on a rock." He squinted at the ugly bruise. "But, hell, she would have had to hit herself pretty damned hard to get that kind of a welt. Looks like somebody knocked her over the head and tossed her in the drink."

"No, I can't look, Charlie. Oh, God. Let's get out of here,

Charlie. Let's call the cops or something. But take me away from here. I don't want to see any more."

Charlie stood up and put his arms around Sheila, although he was still looking down at the dead body. "Calm down, baby. There's nothing to be afraid of. The kid's as dead as a mackerel. She can't hurt you."

"Oh, Charlie. Look, I suppose you're used to seeing dead bodies, but I never saw one before until now. It's horrible. Please, Charlie, let's get out of here."

"Okay, babe, okay. Come on. We'd better let the dicks know what we found—if they have dicks in this burg."

Inside an hour the beach was dotted with police and curiosity seekers. Charlie had sent Sheila back to their hotel and was with the inspector of police, kneeling down beside the body.

"If you want my opinion, somebody hit her over the head," Charlie said as he showed the inspector the wound on Cynthia's skull.

"You are familiar with these matters, *señor?*"

"I should be," Charlie boasted, pulling his wallet from his pocket. "I've been a detective in New York for the last twenty-three years." He showed the inspector his badge. "See. Charlie Cranston, Senior Detective." He nodded toward the body. "Who is she, Inspector? Anybody you know?"

"This is not exactly a small village, Señor Cranston. Not every inhabitant is known to us personally." He studied the face for a moment. "But I think this girl is known to many people around here. If I am not mistaken she is a member of the Brandon family. They have that big villa just up there," he said, pointing up along the bluff. "It is a very wealthy family."

Charlie whistled. "Boy, aren't they going to be surprised when they find out there's one less member of the family who'll be spending the money."

Charlie started looking over the dead body again. "I'd say she's been dead about twenty-four hours," he said. "Of course I couldn't be certain without an autopsy."

"You seem very knowledgeable about such things, *señor.*"

"Yeah, I know a thing or two. We get a lot of this sort of stuff in New York. They're always fishing somebody out of the river." He glanced back toward the Brandon villa. "You'd better let the family know right away. There is the possibility, of course, that this isn't one of theirs. Somebody'll have to make a positive identification."

"I am afraid we are not as sophisticated about these things here in Majorca," the inspector said. He paused, rubbing his chin. "It would be very helpful, *señor*, if you assisted us in our investigation. Our chief of detectives is on vacation and there is no one in the police department who could come close to your experience in such matters." He cocked an eye at Charlie. "Would you help us, *señor?*"

"Me?" Charlie grinned with pride. "You want me to help you guys?" He looked suddenly disturbed. "Nah, I couldn't do that. I'm here on a vacation myself. What kind of a vacation would it be for me and the little woman if we started messing around with local crime? Nah. But, gee, thanks. I'm flattered at your asking me."

"It is just that we are presently very short-handed, *señor*. And as I said, no one in our department has your qualifications or experience. Are you sure you wouldn't reconsider?"

"Sorry. I'd like to help, but I think the little wife would scalp me alive." He flushed. "This is kinda our honeymoon too."

"Ah, *si*, I understand, *señor*," the inspector said with a grin. "But perhaps we could consult with you if we find we require your expert knowledge."

"Sure, sure. Any time, Inspector." Charlie puffed out his chest and sucked his gut in as far as he could. "The wife and I are staying at the Victoria." He started to back away, afraid he might relent if they tossed any more flattery at him.

"*Señor,*" the Inspector called. Charlie stopped. "I was thinking, *señor*. The Brandons are an American family. Possibly their Spanish is good, but I am not certain. Would you consider coming with me to the villa? Perhaps such terrible news coming from a fellow American and spoken in English without a Spanish accent would help to lessen the blow."

Charlie glanced up at the villa on the bluff. "Go up there?" Damn, he'd always wanted to see what the inside of one of these big expensive villas looked like. Sheila would be impressed if she heard he was hobnobbing with the rich elite of Majorca. But he hesitated. He didn't want to get involved. If word got back to New York, they'd know exactly where he was and they might contact him and order him back home. "Gee, I don't know."

"It would not take very long, *señor*. An hour, perhaps."

Sure, it was only an hour. Nobody would be contacting his superiors in New York if he just helped out the locals for an hour. He looked again at the beautiful villa. "Well, I guess I can spare an hour," he said finally. "But don't inform my chief back home that I'm helping you out. There they call this sort of thing 'moonlighting' even though you aren't paying for my time. Back home they don't like us guys doing that."

"I understand perfectly, *señor*. Come, shall we go? I think the quicker we get this over with the better." He stooped and pulled a scarf from around Cynthia's neck and removed a large ring from her finger. Charlie frowned. Back home they weren't allowed to do that sort of thing. Never take anything off the body until the lab boys had gone over it thoroughly. "We'll take these along to show to the Brandon family. They may be able to identify them."

Charlie wouldn't have noticed Dario Avisa if it hadn't been for the stumpy woman in the outlandish sunsuit who was skipping along beside him. Her high, shrill laughter seemed very out of place as he looked down at the body of the dead girl. He saw the woman point at them and hurry in their direction. A policeman stopped them before they got too close. Charlie watched them converse for a moment, then the cop motioned and he brought them over to the inspector of police.

"They are from the Brandon villa," the policeman told the inspector.

"Good heavens," Maggie gasped. "Look, Dario. Someone's drowned."

"Are you members of the Brandon family?" the Inspector asked Dario.

"No, just houseguests. Why?"

"Would you mind stepping over here, *señor*?" He touched Dario's elbow and led him over to where Charlie was standing beside the body. "Do you recognize this girl?"

"*Madre de Dios,*" Dario gasped.

Maggie was hanging on to his arm. "Cynthia," she said, surprised, as if the girl had come to her door unexpectedly and she didn't particularly want to see her. "What is she doing there?"

"You know her?" Charlie asked.

Dario was simply staring in disbelief. There was a blank, dead look in his eyes. He nodded.

"Of course we know her," Maggie said. "That's Cynthia Brandon. Is she dead?"

"*Si, señora.* She is quite dead," the inspector said.

"My heavens." Maggie rolled her eyes. "Now I know what they mean about not being caught dead without one's makeup. She looks simply dreadful."

Dario swayed on his feet, numb with shock. He felt the nausea heave his insides and clutched his stomach and turned away. "*Madre de Dios,*" he said again, and blessed himself.

"There's no doubt in your mind that this is the Brandon girl?" Charlie asked.

"It is she, *señor,*" Dario managed to say, wiping his mouth with a handkerchief. "How long . . . ?" He shook his head to dislodge the tears that flooded his eyes.

"I'd guess she's been dead for about twenty-four hours," Charlie said. "But it's just a guess."

Dario nodded. "That would seem right."

"What do you mean?"

Maggie interrupted. "Cynthia disappeared night before last and nobody's seen or heard from her since."

"You say you are houseguests of the Brandons."

"Yes," Dario said, regaining his composure. "That is, I slept over at the villa last night. Señora Montgomery," he added, motioning to Maggie, "has been visiting there for the last several days."

"Oh, Elaine will simply be stunned," Maggie said.

"Elaine?"

"The girl's mother," Maggie said. She pursed her little bow mouth. "Ohhhh, will she ever be surprised."

"Is the Señora Brandon at home now?" the inspector asked. He looked at Charlie. "We should go up and notify her of this unfortunate affair."

Charlie nodded.

"Oh, Elaine isn't at home," Maggie said. "She went out real early this morning. She said she was going shopping, but I can't for the life of me know where she intended shopping at that hour, unless it was in the fish markets." She giggled slightly.

Charlie squinted at her. "You don't seem to be very upset about this girl's death," he said to Maggie.

She straightened her shoulders indignantly and gave her head a little toss. "Of course I'm upset," she said in an injured voice. "I'm perfectly devastated." She lowered her eyes and tried to look grief-stricken. However, not knowing how to look grief-stricken—an emotion foreign to Maggie—she came off looking bored.

"When will Mrs. Brandon be back home?" Charlie asked.

Maggie shrugged her fleshy shoulders. "Around noontime, I'd guess. Unless she runs into someone and decides to have lunch with them."

"We will come to the villa at noon," the inspector said. "There are, of course, many questions that need to be answered."

"Just like in the movies," Maggie said, clutching Dario's arm. "Isn't it exciting?"

The inspector ignored her and turned to Dario. "If the *señora* returns home before we arrive, I would suggest you have her telephone me," he said, handing Dario his business card. "The news, of course, would be better coming from someone close to her, but . . . " He let his sentence trail off unfinished. Instead he turned to his assistant. "We had best get the victim to the morgue."

ROD OPENED HIS EYES AND STARED UP AT THE ceiling. Slowly he turned and curled into a fetal position and tried not to think of what had happened last night. He'd been weak and stupid. He should have come right out and told Nancy to get lost, that she was nothing more than a perverted little tramp. But he hadn't. He'd let his disgust cool and then had come out of the bathroom and told her he was suffering from stomach cramps and felt ill, blaming it on the brandies. Nancy had been alarmed and insisted he let her call for a doctor. He had refused, saying it was nothing, that he'd suffered with them over the years and that they'd go away— that he'd taken some medicine for them when he was in the bathroom.

Why had he lied to her? Why hadn't he been straightforward and truthful? He felt ashamed of himself, but he couldn't bring himself to do anything about it.

He felt lost, lost in an abyss with towering walls from which there was no way out. But he had to get out somehow. He couldn't let himself be trapped. Yet he felt trapped. He pinched shut his eyes and saw Nancy's face. It was such a beautiful face.

There was a knock at his door. He glanced at his watch and slipped out of bed. Who in hell would be calling at eight-thirty in the morning? Maybe it had something to do with Lisa. He pulled on a robe and hurried toward the sitting room that separated the two bedrooms of his suite.

Nancy was looking at him with concern. "How are you feeling?"

He felt his stomach began to shake. "Fine, fine," he said, running his hand through his hair.

"Well," she said, "aren't you going to ask me in? I brought you some milk and yogurt. I hear it's good for stomach trouble."

Rod hesitated. "Oh, yes, sure," he said, but it took a second or two before he held the door open.

"You look strange," she said, peering at him. "Are you sure you are feeling okay?"

"Yes, I feel fine."

She put the paper sack down on a table. "Fine enough to finish what we started last night?" she asked, coming toward him.

He pushed her away harder than he had intended.

"Hey, what's the matter?"

Rod turned his back to her and walked toward the window. He drew back the drape and pretended to look out at the square below. "Nothing," he mumbled.

Nancy went over to him and turned him around. "I think there is," she said. She studied his expression. "Something's bothering you, and I get the feeling it isn't your stomach."

Be honest with her, damm it, Rod told himself. Stop being such a sniveling coward and speak your mind. It will be for the best to get everything out in the open and put an end to this. "All right," he said finally. "Something's bothering me. Let's leave it at that." He started toward his bedroom. He didn't want to look at her face, so sweet, so innocent, so pure, knowing that behind all that purity was a girl without morals. He sat down on the edge of the bed and put his head in his hands.

"Let's not leave it at that, Rod," Nancy said as she followed him. "I happen to have spent a rotten night worrying about you, and now I get the impression that you are trying to brush me off. Why?"

"Oh, it isn't your fault, it's mine."

"What's your fault? Hey," she said, kneeling down beside him and brushing away the stray lock of hair that had fallen over his forehead. "How about filling me in? I feel like I just walked in on Act III."

Rod, suddenly realizing he was sitting on the bed, got to his feet and started to pace back and forth. He turned sharply and walked back out into the sitting room. Nancy followed him. "I don't think we should see any more of each other," he said.

"And why not? What did I do wrong?"

"I said it isn't your fault, it's mine. I guess I'm just not used to girls like you."

"What do you mean, girls like me? What am I like? I'm no different from other girls."

"It's just that . . . " He found he couldn't bring himself to say it.

"It's just that what?"

He felt blocked in, trapped. He kept clenching and unclenching his fists. There was no way out of this, he knew. He'd have to stand his ground and face it head on. "Damn it," he said finally. "Nice girls just don't do what you did last night."

Nancy frowned. She looked totally confused. "What did I do?"

Rod's face was crimson. "You know what you did," he said, hoping she'd go away and leave him alone. He felt utterly humiliated. Talking about stuff like this in the light of day made him feel like the dirtiest pig in the world.

"I'm sorry, Rod, but I haven't the foggiest idea what you're talking about." She put her hand on his arm and interrupted his pacing.

Her touch sent shivers through him. He brushed away her hand. "I'm just not used to sophisticated girls from New York, I guess."

Nancy shook her head in frustration. "What in the devil are you trying to say?" she demanded.

"I've said it. I just don't think I'm ready for a girl like you."

"Ready? What do you mean ready? I'm not putting any ring through your nose, Rod, and I don't want you to think you can put one through mine either. So will you kindly say what you have to say and let's stop all this doubletalk."

"Please, Nancy. Just go away. You're making this very difficult for me."

"Difficult for you? What about me?" She felt a stinging behind her eyes and braced herself against the tears that threatened to run down her cheeks. "Boy, you sure know how to bring a girl down," she said in a choked little voice. "If this is the way you treat your daughter I can understand why she's in trouble." Her voice broke. "Just go away, kid. I'm not sophisticated like you. Get lost. You did something wrong but I'm not going to tell you what it is."

"Oh, God, stop it," Rod breathed. "It isn't your fault, I tell you. You can't help the way you are any more than I can."

"And which way am I?" Nancy asked.

"Look, if it will make you feel any better I think you are one of the loveliest girls I've ever met. I loved having dinner with you, I loved talking to you. Any man in his right mind would be happy to be seen with someone like you."

"But you're not one of them, right?" she asked evenly.

Rod turned away and refused to answer.

"Why?" she asked, stomping her foot. "I think you owe me an explanation at least."

"I don't mind being seen with you," he admitted. "It's just that . . . "

She raised her head slowly and frowned at him. "It's just that you don't want to have sex with me, is that it?" She thought she was beginning to understand when she saw his face grow red. At least she'd hit a nerve, she was sure of that.

Rod bowed his head. He shoved his hands into the pockets of his dressing gown and said, "Yes."

Nancy's breath caught in her throat. "Why? What did I do that was so awful?"

He couldn't look at her. "I'm just not used to what you did to me last night." His whole body felt as though it were on fire.

There was a dead silence in the room. For a moment he

was sure that Nancy had turned and walked out of the suite. Then to his complete surprise he heard her laugh. He spun around.

"So that's it," she said, cutting off her laughter as though it had been sliced in half with a knife. "Oh, Rod, what a poor little innocent boob you are." She walked over to him and gently laid her hand on his arm.

He moved away from her touch.

"Well, it isn't like I have syphilis or leprosy, you know."

"Please, Nancy, let's not pursue this any longer."

"Let's not pursue this any longer," she mimicked in a sing-song voice. "Have dinner with me, Nancy. Let me tell you my troubles, Nancy. Gee, it's nice to be with someone like you, Nancy. Now, get lost, Nancy."

"Stop it."

"You're an ass, Rod Shepherd, a complete unmitigated ass."

"I've been told that before," he said dejectedly.

"And you deserve to be told that." She hesitated. "Why did you lie to me about all the women you enjoy sleeping with?"

"I didn't lie to you."

"Then surely women have done that to you before."

"Common women have, yes," he barked.

Nancy refused to let herself get angry. She liked him too much and wanted to go on liking him. "So you think I'm common. Well, let me tell you something, Rod Shepherd. I've only slept with three guys in my entire life, and although you are not the first one I ever went down on, you're the first I've ever *wanted* to go down on."

"Please," Rod said, waving his hand. "You're being crass."

"Oh, for Christ's sake, Rod. Stop being such a stupid prude. There isn't anything disgusting about doing something like that with a man you like and respect."

"It's the kind of thing women do for money, not out of love or respect," he argued, wishing she'd let the subject drop.

"Oh, you poor little hick from Ohio, thinking that good girls don't do that sort of thing . . . that only whores and prostitutes make love with their mouths."

"You're purposely being disgusting."

"Do you mean to tell me that you and your wife never did things like that?"

"Oh, my God," Rod breathed.

Nancy saw the sudden hurt, the humiliation on his face. Although she couldn't understand all of it, she was beginning to. Rod had told her of his strict upbringing, his puritanical parents, his churchgoing, Godfearing wife. She could almost hear her own father warning her about the sins of the flesh, the hellfire and brimstone bit they always went on about. Rod obviously still had those things deeply ingrained in him. He actually believed God would punish him if he did not conform to the dictates of a good Christian life. Oral sex was an instrument of the perverted devil. She'd performed an oral act on him last night. That relegated her to the bottom of the flesh heap. She felt sorry for him. How his conscience must suffer after he'd left the whore or prostitute he undoubtedly resorted to. He'd admitted that he liked women too much and that because of his liking of them he would never marry again.

How was she going to get through to him? True, he was from the older generation that actually believed in a cruel God always ready to rain His wrath down upon sinners. He couldn't help the way he was. If there was only some way she could change him, make him see that his sexual urges weren't wrong, weren't something to be pushed under the rug until he had a chance to slip away to some prostitute. Unfortunately, she couldn't think of a way.

"Okay, Rod," she said finally. "I won't embarrass you any more than I have. I'm sorry. I'll go and leave you alone. But do me a favor. Ask yourself one question. Wouldn't it be a lot better to have a wife or a girlfriend or someone you love and respect make you completely happy in bed so that you wouldn't have to resort to paying for what you want? And don't tell me you weren't enjoying what I was doing to you last night. I know differently. And I'll bet my last buck that that's why you were visiting prostitutes—because Helen wasn't giving you everything you needed in sex."

"Please, Nancy. Go," Rod pleaded. "I just don't want to talk about it."

Nancy shrugged and heaved a sad sigh. "I'll go. But please think about what I said, Rod. I've really taken a tumble over you, and I'd like nothing better than to show you that you're wrong and I'm right. Don't fight it, Rod. Open your mind and come out of your closet. You'd be surprised at how fresh the air can be." She looked longingly at him for a moment, then turned and slowly walked out of the room.

When he heard the door close after her he turned. He almost called out to her, but her name caught in his throat. He wanted to run after her, but his feet seemed cemented to the floor.

He thought of what she said and shook his head. No, he'd been right in letting her go. For once he had stood up to temptation. Helen would have been proud of him.

Still, Nancy was such a great girl to be with. Why did it have to turn out that she was sexually corrupt and without moral decency? Why couldn't she have been innocent and good like Helen?

Oh well, he thought as he glanced at his watch. Perhaps it was for the best. She was too young for him anyway. Okay, you had a few laughs and she made you feel like you were eighteen again. But you aren't eighteen, you're forty-two. At eighteen you could afford to talk about uninhibited expression and all that junk; people didn't expect too much respectability of you at eighteen. At forty-two it was an entirely different matter. He was old enough to know that at his age uninhibited expression resulted in degeneration of the mind. When he was Nancy's age he could afford to experiment—and had. But he wasn't Nancy's age now.

His eyes were wide open. He must never see Nancy again— at least not alone. She was just a silly, impetuous kid out on a lark. He meant nothing to her except possibly a convenient lay or a challenge.

Yet he remembered how intently she'd listened to his problems and how sensible she'd been. She hadn't been just a silly kid then. He shook his head. No, he mustn't weaken. He mustn't start making excuses. He'd done the right thing in sending her away. It wouldn't work out, and that was all there was to it.

Everything he did that morning reminded him of Nancy. Showering, he felt the scratches her nails had left on his back. While shaving, he saw the hickey and teeth marks on his neck, left there by her sucking. On his way to Miguel Montoro's office, he ran his hand through his hair and remembered how she'd pulled and tugged at it. Even paying Montoro the money he asked for to affect Lisa's release caused Rod to wonder if perhaps he shouldn't have offered Nancy money earlier—that would have hurt her deeply and drawn a definite conclusion to the affair.

No, that would have been cowardly and mean, he thought

as he and Montoro made their way to the jail, a release signed by a local high official tucked securely in his pocket. If he was going to call the whole thing off between them—as he'd done —then he had been right in being straightforward about it.

"I apologize again for all the, how you call it, 'red tape' you had to go through this morning," Miguel said.

Rod hadn't heard him. "Huh? Oh, yes. Thank you." He turned and stared out the window again. He didn't want to talk. He wanted to think of how he was going to keep himself from seeing Nancy again.

Lisa was lying on her cot when they reached her cell. The guard unlocked the door. "You are free to leave, *señorita*."

Lisa jumped up, then saw her father standing on the other side of the bars. She looked at him but did not return his smile. She moved her eyes to Miguel Montoro, who was also looking at her, smiling. "I don't want to go anywhere with him," she said spitefully as she gave her father an angry flash of her eyes.

Miguel laughed. "But you have no choice, *señorita*. Everything has been arranged. You are free to leave."

Lisa looked defiant. "I said I don't want to go anywhere with him."

Rod pushed the guard aside and went into the cell. He grabbed Lisa roughly. "You're going home, young lady, and I don't want to hear any more of your childish nonsense." He took a firm hold on her arm and started toward the door. "Come on. We'll collect your things at the desk and go back to the hotel."

She pried herself free of his grasp. "No. I'm not going."

Miguel laughed lightly again. "But you cannot stay here, *señorita*. The charges against you have been removed. You must leave. You have no other alternative."

Lisa narrowed her eyes and thought for a moment. She stood quite still, then let her shoulders sag. "Okay," she said finally. "Let's go." She went by her father, brushing off his touch, and walked out of the cell without so much as glancing behind her to see if Rod was following.

"Quite an independent young lady you have there, Señor Shepherd," Miguel said. There was something about the way the man said it that Rod didn't like. It was as if he were making fun of all Americans.

"You're not too old to be put over my knee and given a

good spanking," Rod said when they were alone in the taxi, heading back to his hotel.

"Oh, Dad, don't be so archaic."

"And don't you be so fresh," he said, feeling his patience slipping. They fell into silence for a moment. Rod glanced down at the canvas bag at Lisa's feet. "Is that all the clothes you brought with you?"

"It's all I needed."

"We'll get you some."

"Don't bother. I have everything I need."

He looked at her dirty jeans and faded plaid shirt. "You look a mess."

"Well, I am coming out of a jail, not from a beauty contest."

How could he reach her? Everything he said was wrong. If Helen were only here she'd know what to do. Or Nancy. The thought gave him hope. But he wasn't going to see Nancy again. Depression hit him like an iron fist in the stomach.

Neither of them spoke until they reached the hotel and were walking across the lobby. At the desk he saw Paul Verdugo, Jr., talking to the clerk. When Paul Jr. turned he saw Rod and Lisa and called to them.

"Hey, Mr. Shepherd, I was just asking for you. The clerk said you'd gone out."

"Hello, Paul." The two men shook hands the way the youngsters did. Rod found himself falling into the strange handshake quite naturally. "This is my daughter, Lisa. Lisa, Paul Verdugo."

"Junior," Paul added. "I don't like to get confused with my father." He looked at Lisa and put out his hand. "Hi."

"Hi." She took his hand but didn't bother to put much enthusiasm in it.

"Your dad told me about you."

"Oh? I bet that was a gas."

A slight frown creased Paul's brow. He looked from Lisa to Rod, then back to Lisa. He sensed a heavy friction between them. His smile faded and he felt uncomfortable, at a loss what to say.

Lisa shifted her weight from one foot to the other. "Can I have your key?" she said to her father. "I'd like a bath."

Paul Jr. found his voice. "Oh, I didn't mean to keep you. I just stopped by the hotel to invite you both to our house for dinner tonight. Gee, I hope you're free. I realize it's short notice."

"That would be nice, Paul. Thank you. We'd love to," Rod said. "Wouldn't we, Lisa?"

"Sorry, I have a date," she said.

"Yes, you do," Rod said, not bothering to hide his annoyance. "You have a date for dinner with Paul here and his family." He made his voice softer when he spoke to Paul. "What time, Paul?"

"Is seven o'clock all right? Everybody eats late here, I know, but I'm still on New York time, so the family accommodates me with earlier dinners."

"Seven o'clock is fine."

Paul turned to leave but hesitated. "Gee, I mean . . . " he stammered. He looked at Lisa. "Look, if you don't want to come it's okay." He turned to Rod. "You'll come, won't you, Mr. Shepherd?"

"We'll both be there, Paul."

Lisa huffed and went toward the elevator. Both men stood staring after her.

"She's had a rather difficult time of it lately," Rod apologized. "She'll be a little more sociable after she's rested and bathed."

You mean after you've given her a good bawling out, Paul said to himself. "She's very pretty, Mr. Shepherd."

"Yes, she is," Rod agreed. "Well, thank you, Paul. We'll see you this evening."

They shook hands again and Paul went out into the street. Rod narrowed his eyes at Lisa, who was standing tapping her foot in front of the elevator. He went up to her and roughly grabbed her arm and shoved her into the elevator. "We're going to have a talk, young lady," he said sternly as the doors closed and the car started upward. "Paul Verdugo is a nice kid."

"He's a square. You could cut your fingers on his corners."

"Square or not, at least he's polite. Look, it's one thing being rude to me, but where in the devil did you learn to be rude to strangers? You were never like that."

Lisa looked suddenly contrite. "Okay, I'm sorry."

"Being sorry isn't enough. We are going to the Verdugos for dinner, and you're going to apologize to that boy."

She felt ashamed. It was true; she had been rude to the boy

and there hadn't been any reason for it. Her father had been
right on that score. She guessed she was just trying to embarrass him, wanting to show the world that she was independent
of him. Why she'd acted like such a trashy little creep in front
of the Verdugo boy she didn't know. But Paul Verdugo was a
friend of her father's, obviously. She didn't want to have anything to do with her father or anybody who liked him.

She'd go to the dumb dinner party. Maybe there'd be a
chance for her to slip away and go in search of George Petrik.

THE CENTER OF PALMA WAS ALIVE WITH
people doing their morning business before retiring to the cool-
ness of their homes for the afternoon siesta. Elaine had grown
to dislike big cities. Palma, however, although large, wasn't
like any of the others. Here there was a quiet excitement that
was unmatched in all the world, and large as it was, it still held
that mystical atmosphere of closeness. The blending of the
old and the new worked so well. Outsiders mixed comfortably
with the natives; the natives made no man feel alien. There
were other cities equally as beautiful, Elaine remembered, but
if they were all strung together they would resemble a string of
perfectly matched pearls, while Palma would be the diamond
pendant that hung isolated from the strand. Its modern section
melted beautifully into the largely unspoiled medieval and
Renaissance city with its cathedral, its royal palaces, its art
galleries, its girdle of beaches and rolling countryside.

She was glad she'd decided to spend the remainder of her
life here on this island. As much as she disapproved of her past
she had to admit that it had afforded her the luxury of dying
on Majorca. Money had, after all, some rewards. Money
bought people if one wanted people; it bought privacy and
seclusion if one wanted privacy and seclusion. It was these
latter two that she thanked her money for most.

She did not appreciate the other facets of responsibility that
her wealth had brought her, she thought as the chauffeur
pulled the limousine up in front of the National Bank of

Spain. She dreaded these weekly visits, the long discussions, the decisions that had to be made about investments, contracts, mergers, profits. She had once hoped that Miguel would relieve her of these tiresome business affairs, but he had proved totally inadequate and dishonest. Miguel believed money should always be made by the easiest and quickest methods. His methods always failed, and so she resumed handling the larger, more important aspects of her fortune herself, without letting Miguel know that everything he did had to have her approval first.

As she stepped from the car she saw the young girl smile at her. For a moment she could not place the face. There had been so many faces in the past; she could hardly be expected to remember all of them.

"Mrs. Brandon," Nancy said, putting out her hand. "How very nice to see you again."

Elaine frowned slightly, then smiled broadly. "Of course. It's Nancy Winston, isn't it? How delightful to see you, darling." She kissed Nancy on the cheek, then wagged a finger at her. "I'm afraid I'm a little disappointed that you are not staying at the villa with your aunt and me."

Nancy looked embarrassed. "I do appreciate your kindness, Mrs. Brandon, but I thought Aunt Maggie would enjoy herself more without me underfoot all the time. My aunt doesn't exactly approve of me at times."

Elaine laughed. "Maggie never really approves of anyone, dear. It's part of her charm."

Nancy chuckled. "I suppose. But I did find myself a very quiet hotel near here and I'm quite comfortable."

"Which one is that?"

"Jaime I."

"I'm afraid I don't know it."

"It isn't exactly first-class, but it's very nice." She had nothing in common with Elaine Brandon and women of her wealth and position. Their conversation was proving that. She was glad she hadn't gone with her aunt to the villa. "I'll stop by one of these afternoons, though; I'd like to see Cynthia again," she said. She felt guilty at having lied. She didn't care if she never saw Cynthia, but it seemed like the polite thing to say.

"Well, you are looking marvelous, Nancy, and anytime you want to come, please don't stand on ceremony. I'm generally always at home. Today, however, is my day for business."

She glanced at her watch. "I must rush, darling." She pecked Nancy's cheek again. "Please come and visit, and remember, if you decide you don't want to stay at that hotel, there is more than enough room at my place."

"Thank you, Mrs. Brandon. Give my love to Cynthia." She waved as Elaine hurried into the bank.

Elaine wondered why she hadn't told Nancy that Cynthia wasn't at the villa. She didn't have a chance to think much about it, because the moment she entered the lobby of the bank a handsome young man, very tanned, jumped up from behind his desk and hurried over to her. "Good morning, Mrs. Brandon. Mr. Albeniz is in the conference room." He bowed as she swept past him.

It always amused her how the employees struggled with their English when they spoke to her. Money did strange things to people.

The president of the bank, Señor Albeniz, was a small, squat little man dressed in an impeccably wrinkle-free black suit and vest. A thick gold watch chain was slung across his ample stomach—the mark of a successful man on Majorca. He stood when she came into the room. With him, Elaine saw the familiar faces of the other bankers who handled her accounts. She nodded to them with regal dignity, declined the demitasse of thick coffee that was offered her and said she would like to get right to the business at hand.

The looks they gave her always annoyed her, the hidden contempt they held for this American woman who should have a man handling her financial affairs. A woman at the head of their conference table was a sacrilege. Money was a man's business.

"The South American tin mines," she said coldly, looking at the authoritative gentleman seated beside Mr. Albeniz. "Are they back in operation?"

He nodded gravely, holding a cigar poised inches from his mouth. "Full production, señora. The report is there in front of you."

She ignored the report. She would study it later at her leisure. The least amount of time spent with these pompous gentlemen the better. They were almost as incompetent as Miguel, but she needed them to do the dog work. She never allowed them to make decisions. That was her sole responsibility. She knew they resented her intrusions into their business world. She wondered if they ever thought that she resented their intrusion as much. But they were a necessary element in her life and she tolerated them, just as she tolerated so many other things.

They spoke at length about the Brandon wineries in southern France, the oil rights in Saudi Arabia, the inflation in America, the decline of the English pound.

Mr. Albeniz cleared his throat and said, "While we are on the subject of the English pound, *señora,* it has come to my attention that there has been an unfortunate neglect of control over your investments in the Harshaw Textile Mills in Devonshire."

Elaine raised both her eyebrows and gave him an impatient look.

The president cleared his throat and went on. "I realize that I should have been more diligent in my paperwork concerning those mills, but there is so much to be attended to these days, I was wondering if you would consider my employing another representative to assume the responsibility of looking after the financial aspects of Harshaw Textiles."

Elaine sat there, eyebrows raised, waiting for him to continue.

"I have a young nephew who has just returned from school in England," the president said.

Ah, here it comes, Elaine thought. They were always trying to get their relatives in on a good thing. She waited patiently for him to go on.

"My nephew is most expert with the English economy, and I believe he would do an admirable job on your behalf. Being a novice in the business and banking world, his salary would be minimal, but it would, of course, have to be in keeping with the dignity of his position."

"Naturally," Elaine said sarcastically as she led him on. None of them noticed her sarcasm.

"I would like your permission to add him to your payroll."

Elaine sat silent. After a moment she broke her pose and said, "Am I to assume that your work on my behalf is becoming too much for you, Señor Albeniz?"

"Oh, no, *señora.* It is not too much, it is just that there are so many details to be attended to. Everything is becoming more and more complicated each day."

"Well, if it is becoming so complicated, perhaps I should

consider transferring my business management to someone else." She began collecting the papers that had been placed in front of her.

"No, please, Señora Brandon. Please do not misunderstand. It is just that my nephew would be a valuable addition to your organization. I was merely giving you the first opportunity to include him on your staff. He is extremely qualified, believe me."

"If you feel that you are being overworked and are not doing your job to your as well as my satisfaction, perhaps I should consider replacing you with this very qualified nephew of yours," she said coldly. She saw the man's face fall. He lowered his eyes and started to fiddle with his magnificent watch chain.

They were a lazy lot, Elaine thought as she got to her feet. "If that is all of our business, I bid you good morning, gentlemen."

They all got to their feet as she scooped up her reports and swept out of the room. At the door she paused and turned back. "Incidentally, before I leave I would like again to make myself very clear on the matter of Miguel Montoro. He is to have no access to any of the information under your responsibility. If he requests anything concerning my investments you will kindly refer him to me. If I learn that he has gained access to anything I have entrusted to your confidence, the person responsible for that breach in confidence will be dismissed immediately and without notice. Am I understood?"

They mumbled and looked embarrassed. She smiled, tilted her head and walked out of the room.

As she got back into her limousine she began wondering what would happen to all these investments, all this money, after her death. She would have to begin thinking about that. She sighed. What did it matter? With Jorge gone it made no difference who fought over her finances. Her will provided more than enough for Cynthia and Greg. They could do what they wanted with her financial empire. She wished, however, with all her heart, that she had been able to leave it all in Jorge's charge. Young as he was, she was sure he would not let any of it be abused by the greedy businessmen whom she'd just left.

She sighed again. It didn't matter. Once she was dead she was dead and none of it would hold any significance.

She ran her hand over the plush upholstery of the seat and touched the sterling-silver telephone mounted in the armrest. She would leave so many things behind when her time came. Ah well, at least she had had the world while she lived. It hadn't turned out to be a very beautiful world, but she had had it. Yet with all she now owned, the cancer inside her had shattered it all when it locked its claws into her lungs. Nothing had very much importance to her. Jorge was the only one whom she cared about, and now that he was gone there was nothing she had to live for.

The thought seemed to give her a newfound strength. Without a purpose in life, life had no reason. Yes a reason, a purpose, these were the only things that made life move from day to day. If one awoke in the morning with no plans for the day, the day wasn't worth getting up to face. It was only when one had a purpose, a goal, that one should get up to live; otherwise, one should stay in bed. She had no purpose now. There was no reason for her to go on. Now that Jorge had been erased from her life she was almost glad that death was coming. She honestly wished it would hurry up so she could get it over with.

JORGE WAS SLUMPED IN A CHAIR IN THE pleasantly planted garden under the shade of an almond tree. His eyes were fixed on the words of the book he held in his lap, but he wasn't reading. He was thinking of Elaine and of Cynthia and how quickly his seemingly orderly life had suddenly been thrown into disorder. In the background he heard Carlotta humming to herself as she fussed about in the kitchen. He had gone to bed with her eagerly, and he knew it had pleased her. But her gratitude only made him feel more guilty. He had enjoyed it, of course. Nevertheless, he should never have allowed it to happen. Carlotta was vulnerable and naive. She'd read more into the sex act than was there; he could tell that by the happy little tune she was humming. The best thing for him to do right now was to get out of her house. He was only misleading her by staying. But where could he go?

There were lots of places he could go, he told himself. He could think of two or three offhand without taxing his mind. Yet he didn't move. He didn't close the book or get out of the chair. He just sat there staring at the blurred page. What was holding him there? He didn't love Carlotta; he loved Elaine. At least he thought he loved her. But then he'd thought he loved Carlotta once.

He slammed the book shut. Everything was getting too mixed up. He'd come here to think things out and only managed to add another complication to the already complicated situation. He had to start putting things in their natural order, in their proper perspective. He loved Elaine. He loved Carlotta too, in his way. But he was going to marry Cynthia. These were the facts. So what was he making such a fuss about? His path was clear enough. If he was going to marry Cynthia then he should go find her and marry her. It was as simple as that. He'd just have to forget about Elaine. As far as Carlotta was concerned, the love he'd had for her had died a long time ago and he had best set her straight on that count. It was the only fair thing to do. She mustn't start thinking there was more to his lovemaking than pure sex.

"I squeezed you some fresh orange juice," she said as she came into the garden carrying a tray and two glasses. She put them down on the table beside the chair he'd vacated and went over to him. She saw the coldness in his eyes. "You are thinking about her again, yes?"

He dropped his head, looking like a little boy who'd been caught stealing cookies.

"You upset yourself too much thinking about those Brandon women," Carlotta said. "Forget them, Jorge." She wrapped her arms around his waist and squeezed him hard, pressing her cheek against his chest. "Stay here with me. I will make you forget."

He unlocked himself from her embrace. "I am sorry, Carlotta. I have made a terrible mistake coming here to you." He turned away, lifting his head and looking up at the sky. "I made a worse mistake taking you to bed. That was wrong of me."

Carlotta pressed herself to his back. "What are you saying? I did not think it was wrong."

He clenched his fists. "But it was wrong. I am in love with another woman. I do not love you." It came out sounding much more cruel than he thought it would.

Something sharp pierced her heart. She forced herself to smile. "Since when do you have to love a woman in order to take her to bed?" She hugged him. "I love you, Jorge. That is all that is important to me. And if you would give me half a chance I would teach you to love me as you once did."

"That was a long time ago."

She released him and picked up one of the glasses of orange juice. "Not so very long ago. Six months ago? A year? That is not all that long ago." She could tell by the way he squared his shoulders and kept clenching and unclenching his fists that he was fighting an internal battle with himself. She tilted back her head and swept away the years. "Remember when we were growing up, Jorge, how we used to look at the grand houses along the shoreline and dream about how we would live in one of them someday? There was one house in particular that I fell madly in love with. It was the big white one with the yellow shutters near Alfabia. Ah, I thought it was the most wonderful place in all the world." She glanced at his back. "You loved it too, Jorge. Remember? But then you decided you did not like it any more; you preferred the one we saw that day at El Toro. It was bigger and grander and had a large orchard of olive trees. Then you saw another, a sprawling villa overlooking the cove at Santa Ponsa. You liked that best of all." She swirled the glass and watched the tiny pieces of pulp swim in a circle. "You never did make up your mind which house you wanted to live in." She didn't want to be cruel to him, but she felt it was for the best. "You still cannot."

He turned around. "What do houses and villas have to do with anything?"

"Oh, Jorge. You will never change. You could not make up your mind about those lovely houses, and you cannot make up your mind about what woman to marry."

"I know which woman I want to marry. Elaine Brandon."

"And will you still want to marry her this time next year, or next month?"

"Of course I will," he said, looking away. Her eyes were unnerving him.

"Why?"

"What do you mean, why?"

"Why do you want to marry this rich Brandon lady, Jorge? Ask yourself truthfully . . . do you dearly love her?"

"Yes," he said, but again he found he could not look at her. "Yes, I love her," he repeated softly, but not as emphatically as before. "Elaine is rich and beautiful." Slowly he turned back to Carlotta. There was a look of desperation in his eyes. "Oh, Carlotta, I cannot go back to being poor. I cannot. I want money and a big house and cars and servants. I want to travel and forget the peasant dirt that has been worked into my pores."

"You would marry her for her money?"

"Yes!" Jorge almost shouted it. Feeling suddenly ashamed, he added, "But I love her too."

"That is what you said about the big white house with the yellow shutters near Alfabia. You loved it too, once."

"You are making no sense, Carlotta."

"That is because you do not want me to make sense." She put the glass aside and laid her hand on his arm. "Oh, my dearest Jorge. I do not wish to hurt you. All I want in this world is for you to be happy. But first you must know what is going to make you happy." The coldness was back in his eyes when he looked down at her. "Do not marry Elaine Brandon and all her filthy money. You will only be miserable."

He walked away and sat down on the low wall that held back the garden from creeping into the untilled field beyond. "I will not marry Elaine; I will marry Cynthia."

"As opposed as I am to your marrying Elaine Brandon, I am more opposed to your marrying the daughter. Either of them will only make you suffer for the rest of your life."

"That is all well and good. How, may I ask, do you suppose I am to get out of fulfilling my obligation to Cynthia? I am the father of her unborn child."

"Are you so sure of that? Unfortunately, there are too many girls who use that excuse to get themselves a husband."

"Cynthia assured me that I am the only possible father."

Carlotta laughed. "If you had the opportunity, Jorge, then you may be assured that others had the same opportunity. Please do not be so innocent." She fixed her eyes on him.

"Tell me something. Was Cynthia a virgin when you went to bed with her?"

Jorge looked uncomfortable. He frowned. "No."

Again Carlotta laughed. "Then if you were the first, what happened to her precious virginity? Did she give it to the seat of her bicycle? Oh, Jorge. Do not be such a fool."

"Stop this, Carlotta," he said, shaking his head. "You are mixing me up more than I was before."

"Look, my darling. I love you. I have always loved you and I always will. I think you are making a mistake wanting Elaine Brandon, but I think you are making a bigger mistake eloping with Cynthia. Do not do anything foolish right now. Stay with me for a few days and think things out more. Promise me that."

He thought for a moment. Carlotta was right. If Cynthia had not been a virgin when he took her to bed, then there had to be at least one other before him. Cynthia had lied to him. He nodded finally. "I will stay a little longer," he said.

Carlotta took his hand and squeezed it. "Thank you, Jorge," she said softly.

CHARLIE HAD NEVER BEEN IN SO GRAND A house before. He wished Sheila were with him. The Brandon villa looked more like a museum than a private residence. He stared in awe around the vast foyer, cool and subdued and imbued with the sweet, rich odor of wealth. Everything was polished and expensive. He found himself walking more softly over the waxed tiles, feeling like someone who had just intruded upon a holy sanctuary.

The liveried butler ushered them through the drawing room and out onto the terrace, where Maggie and Dario were basking in the sun.

"I'm afraid Elaine hasn't come back yet," Maggie said as Charlie and the inspector of police approached.

Charlie noticed that Maggie Montgomery had her hand on Dario's thigh. What did a young, good-looking kid like him see in a dumpy old broad like her? he wondered. One of those Latin gigolos, he decided.

"She should be back at any moment," Dario said, glancing at his watch. "Unfortunately I will not be able to wait much longer. I must go to the bicycle-race qualifying trials in a little while."

The inspector beamed. "*Si, sí*. I understand you are entered again this year, Señor Avisa. I hope and pray you will add another trophy to the two you already have. I have a small bet riding on you, my boy."

"Then I will try not to disappoint you, Inspector."

Charlie turned when he heard footsteps behind him. He had expected Elaine Brandon to be at least middle-aged and matronly. The woman he saw approaching looked more like a budding movie star.

"Gentlemen?" Elaine said.

"Oh, Elaine," Maggie said in a loud voice. "These gentlemen are from the police. Cynthia—"

"Please, Maggie," Dario said, patting her hand.

Elaine frowned. "Cynthia? What about Cynthia?"

"I am Inspector Delfaro, *señora*. This is Detective Charles Cranston from the New York Police Department."

"New York? I don't understand."

"Sit down, *señora*," the inspector said, holding a chair. "Unfortunately we have come to bring you some rather unpleasant news."

"About Cynthia?"

"She dead, Elaine," Maggie blurted out. "Isn't it just too ghastly."

Elaine's face went white as ash. Her eyes widened in shock as they darted from Maggie to the inspector to Charlie. Maggie's words were echoing around inside her head, but she hadn't quite grasped them. "What?"

"I am sorry, *señora*," the inspector said. "I would have preferred to be a little more delicate, but the truth of the matter is that your daughter's body was found washed up on the beach a few hours ago."

Elaine just stood there staring at them.

"Sit down, Elaine," Dario said, touching her elbow. She wasn't conscious that he'd spoken. Yet she found herself slowly being lowered into the chair. "What are you saying?" she said, her mind suddenly fogged over.

"It is true, my dear Elaine," Dario said. "Maggie and I identified the body. Cynthia is dead."

"Murdered would be more like it," Maggie shouted.

But Elaine didn't hear her. There was a terrible dizziness inside her head. She felt herself swaying slightly. Everything was suddenly spinning around like a mad carousel out of control. Shapes lost all form. She thought someone was talking, but the words were all garbled, all tumbled together into a senseless mass of sound.

She thought she heard Maggie's voice saying, "Good heavens, I think she's going to faint," before everything went gray, then black. She found herself slipping out of reality, losing the firm grip she thought she'd had on herself. She fell into a vacuum and stayed there until something sharp and biting tore at her nostrils and made tears come to her eyes. She fluttered her lids and tried to focus on the tight little cluster of people gathered around her. Someone was holding a vial of ammonium carbonate under her nose. She waved it away and tried to sit up. She felt herself being eased back against the chair.

"Relax, Mrs. Brandon," a man said. His accent was American. "Just take it easy." She felt his hand pat her shoulder. "Everything's going to be all right."

"Cynthia dead?" Where her words came from she didn't know. They didn't even sound as though they belonged to her. It wasn't right. Someone had gotten the plot all mixed up. It wasn't Cynthia who was supposed to die. I am the one who was to die, Elaine told herself. It couldn't be true. Cynthia was alive; it was she, Elaine, who was dead. She closed her eyes and tried to sort it all out. Nothing came clear. Everything was all jumbled together like unmatched pieces of a jigsaw puzzle.

Someone was holding tight to her hand. She didn't know who. "I'm afraid it is true, Elaine. I am sorry." It was Dario's voice, kind and soft and understanding. As her vision cleared a little she saw his eyes. Although his voice seemed sad, his eyes were *cold* as stone.

"How?" Elaine asked in a weak, frail voice.

"She was—"

"Please, *señora*," the inspector said, cutting Maggie off. His voice melted from its brittleness. "We have a suspicion that it was not an accident and are certain that it was not from natural causes."

"Murder?" The word sounded so odious she shrank from it. She'd heard that word before being leveled at her in a court-room.

"There is that possibility."

Maggie slapped her fat little hands down on her knees and stood up. She took Dario's arm. "Well, as dreadful as it is, my dear, we must be off to the qualifying trials. Dario and I will have to leave," she said to Elaine. "And if you had any sense you'd gather yourself together and come with us."

"Oh, Maggie," Elaine groaned, turning aside.

"Don't 'Oh, Maggie' me, Elaine. Everyone knows you never cared for that silly daughter of yours anyway, so I don't see why you are carrying on like this, fainting and all. Really, Elaine. Snap out of it. Let's go with Dario. It will be such fun. And just think of all those lovely young men in their short pants." She rolled her eyes.

Elaine waved her away. "Please, Maggie. Go if you wish, but I want to be alone." She turned to the inspector and then to Charlie Cranston, who she found was eyeing her suspiciously. "You mentioned the New York Police Department," she said. "I don't understand."

"Mr. Cranston found your daughter's body. He is a detective from New York who is visiting Majorca. He was kind enough to come along with me in view of the fact that our chief of de-tectives is presently away on vacation."

Elaine's mind raced over the trouble Cynthia had had with the Immigration Department in New York. "I thought . . . " She let her words filter off. "It doesn't matter."

Charlie touched her shoulder again and let his hand rest there. "Before anyone goes anywhere," he said, "I'd like to ask a few questions on behalf of the inspector here."

"Questions?" Maggie said, arching her brows. "What kind of questions? Dario and I are late as it is."

"It will not take very long," Charlie said.

They all turned toward the inside of the house when they heard Greg's angry voice yelling at one of the servants. Elaine made a feeble gesture toward Dario. "You'd best ask Greg to come out here," she said.

They sat in silence, then heard Greg yell, "What in hell does she want?" Another silence followed. "What?" they heard Greg gasp. A moment later he came hurrying out onto the terrace. He looked at his mother and stared down at her. "Is this true?"

Elaine nodded slowly. "Yes, Greg. I'm afraid it is. These gentlemen represent the police," she said, motioning toward Charlie and the inspector.

"And who are you?" Charlie asked.

"Greg Brandon. Who in hell are you?"

Charlie didn't like the type. Smart-assed and cocky. And the guy looked more pissed-off than sad about the girl's death. "I'm Detective Cranston, and I have a couple of questions to ask, so you might just as well sit down." He narrowed his eyes at Greg when he saw him jut out his chin and remain standing. "Greg Brandon? Then I take it Cynthia Brandon was your sister, is that right?"

"With brains like that you must have graduated first in your class," Greg sneered.

"Greg, please," Elaine said. "Sit down and let's get this unpleasantness over with."

Greg paused, then settled himself in a chair. He winced inwardly. His ass was killing him.

Charlie started with the preliminaries, how he and Sheila had found the body, the blow on the scalp. He showed them the kerchief and the ring and told how Dario and Maggie had definitely identified the body. Out of the corner of his eye he saw Maggie Montgomery glance at her watch and tug Dario's arm. He shook his head at her and took her hand, massaging the fingers as if to say, Be patient a little longer. He didn't like any of the looks on any of their faces. Even the mother—Elaine Brandon—now seemed very indifferent to the whole business. What had that Maggie Montgomery said earlier? Elaine had never particularly liked her daughter anyway.

He questioned them all at length. They were all here when the girl disappeared. They all had the opportunity of knocking her on the head and tossing her into the ocean. Even the flighty, silly Montgomery woman seemed to hold a resentment for the dead girl, so she couldn't be ruled out as a suspect. Whenever he questioned suspects, Charlie made it a rule to pay close attention to their eye expressions. The eyes told him everything.

This group he summed up like this. The mother, Elaine, looked sad enough, but it was a cold kind of sadness, as if a thorn had been pulled from her finger and she was glad it was gone although the hurt still remained. The brother, Greg or whatever his name was, in spite of his antagonism had a genuine look of grief behind his eyes. Charlie guessed that the brother and sister were very close. The Montgomery woman just looked stupid and annoyed. Charlie reminded himself that it was always stupid people who killed. In Dario Avisa's expression there was something that didn't quite add up. The guy looked sorry enough—perhaps it was because he'd been in love with the girl. But there was something lacking in that love. Rejected lovers always made the best suspects.

Then there was this Jorge Aguilar fellow and the lawyer, Montoro, who were both in the house that night. And what about the emerald necklace the Montgomery woman said disappeared at the same time as Jorge Aguilar and Cynthia Brandon?

"Well, that should do it for the time being," Charlie said finally. He turned to Elaine. "I'd like to question the servants while I'm here."

"Certainly," she said, getting up from her chair. "I'll call them together in the library." As she walked from the terrace, Charlie noticed that there wasn't a sign of weakness in her steps. Had the fainting spell been an act? He decided it had been.

An hour later as he and the inspector were leaving Elaine's villa he glanced at the luxury he'd admired earlier and thought of the people who lived here. He shook his head. Regardless of how grand it all was, he wouldn't trade any of it for his life with Sheila.

EVENING WAS JUST BEGINNING TO LAY ITS lovely shadows on the tall mountains as Dario braked his car in front of Carlotta's house. He saw Jorge's car parked on the side and was glad he'd guessed right. He tucked the evening newspaper under his arm and rapped on the door. He hadn't liked the article covering Cynthia's death. It hinted at a connection between the missing Jorge Aguilar and the missing emerald necklace. Dario shook his head. Was it possible that Jorge had taken the jewels? No, not Jorge.

Carlotta opened the door just a crack. When she saw who it was she threw it wide. "Dario! How wonderful. Come in, come in. Jorge," she called over her shoulder, "Look who's here."

"Dario! What happened to you the other night?" Jorge asked as he came in from the other room. "You were supposed to come back . . . " He suddenly noticed the strange look on Dario's face. "Hey, my friend, what's wrong?"

"You didn't see the paper, then?" Dario said as he took the newspaper from under his arm and handed it to Jorge. It was folded to the article about Cynthia Brandon's death.

Jorge scanned the page and when his eyes rested on the headline "Girl's Body Washed Up on Beach," he glanced up quickly at Dario. Dario simply nodded. Jorge started to read. When he stumbled over Cynthia's name his hands tightened on the paper. *"Santo Dios,"* he breathed.

"Jorge, what is it?" Carlotta gasped.

Numb with shock, he handed her the paper.

"This isn't possible," Jorge mumbled.

Dario nodded. "Maggie Montgomery and I were there when they found her," he said. "It is all too true, unfortunately."

"Cynthia dead," Jorge breathed. "I can't believe it." Contradicting emotions swept through him. He felt filled with sadness, of course, and yet he wanted to laugh with happiness. "Cynthia dead," he repeated. He turned suddenly and started toward the little bedroom alcove. "I must go to Elaine. She will be heartbroken."

"Wait, Jorge," Dario said. "Perhaps that would not be wise just now."

Jorge turned back and saw the somber faces of Dario and Carlotta watching him. He gave them a confused smile. "Why not?"

"You had better read the entire article," Carlotta said, handing him the newspaper.

He read slowly. When he had finished he looked up. "So?" He frowned at their worried expressions. "It is natural that they will want to question me about Cynthia. I see nothing wrong with that."

Carlotta went over to him. "They will want to know why you took the emerald necklace," she said.

He gave her a blank look. "What emerald necklace? I know nothing about an emerald necklace."

Carlotta merely studied him, her dark, lovely eyes smoldering with concern.

"Why do you look at me like that, Carlotta?"

She didn't say anything. She simply went into the bedroom alcove and took something from a drawer. She walked back to him. "When I was unpacking your canvas tote bag I found this," she said. She let Elaine's shimmering emeralds drip from her fingers. "Oh, Jorge. Why?" she groaned, then burst into tears.

Jorge stared at the necklace for a moment, then turned and saw the accusing expression on Dario's face. "I never saw that necklace anywhere except around Elaine's throat," he said. "I did not steal it."

Carlotta, through her sobs, asked, "Then how did it get here?"

"I don't know how it got here," Jorge said angrily. "But I did not put it in my bag." He thought they were eyeing him with disbelief. "I am no thief," he shouted. "Surely, you of all people, Dario, know that I would never steal anything from anyone."

Dario's expression softened. He nodded. "Yes, I know you would not, Jorge, my friend. It is obvious that someone planted that necklace on you. Who did you see the night you left the villa carrying your bag?"

"No one." He reflected. "Oh, I spoke briefly to Miguel Montoro and that silly Montgomery woman, but no one else. I looked everywhere for you, Dario, but, as you know, I did not find you. Elaine refused to open her door to me. Cynthia was gone, as was that brother of hers. I saw no one." He grabbed the necklace from Carlotta's hand. "I am going to the police and straighten this out. If they suspect me of murdering Cynthia, then I will confront them with my innocence." He turned to go.

"No, wait," Dario said. "I think you would be making a mistake. Perhaps it would be wise for you to disappear for a while until I have had a chance to do some digging on my own. If you show up at police headquarters with that necklace they will surely lock you up if not on a charge of suspicion of murder then for possession of stolen property. They will put you in jail."

"So they will put me in jail," Jorge said, stuffing clothes back into his tote bag. "I have nothing to hide."

"Perhaps Dario is right, Jorge," Carlotta said. "Why not stay here with me for a few more days? Dario can take the necklace back to Señora Brandon and explain to her."

"And suppose the police stop Dario while he has possession of the emeralds?" He shook his head and zipped shut the bag. "No, I am going to the police. It is the only sensible thing to do."

Dario said, "I think you are making a mistake."

The idea that his problem with Cynthia was now solved and that he could be reunited with Elaine blinded him to any danger. "I have nothing to hide." He kissed Carlotta's forehead. "Do not fret, my pet. Everything will work out just fine." He shook Dario's hand. "You are a good friend, Dario. Thank you."

"But—"

Jorge cut him off with a look. He smiled. "I'll be fine. Really I will." He turned and hurried out. A moment later they heard his car start up, and if Dario's ears didn't deceive him he thought he heard Jorge whistling a bright little tune.

THE VERDUGO DINNER WAS A STRAINED AF-
fair. Lisa was particularly cool and indifferent toward her father; she treated Paul Jr. no more cordially. She picked at her food and answered questions in monosyllables, if she deigned to answer at all. She found the elder Paul Verdugo nice enough but disliked his wife intensely. There was something about the woman that made her skin crawl. She'd met other women like Laura Verdugo. They all had that same hungry look. Every man represented a challenge; every

woman, too, for that matter. She remembered the woman who had picked her up on the road when she first ran away from home. She was missing her mother dreadfully and was starved for feminine affection. She had talked about sex with the girls at school, of course, but was under the impression that women only went to bed with men. This woman, she discovered to her horror, wanted sex with anything that moved, man, woman or beast. She'd fought and clawed her way out of that situation, suddenly wanting desperately to go home to her father. But then she met the owner of that nightclub in Columbus. He'd been kind to her, and he was so much easier to talk to than her father. Jack told her all about women like Laura Verdugo. Nymphos, he called them. Jack wasn't like that. He never once touched her, although she knew he wanted to. Then there was that stupid party where some kid pushed a joint at her and she smoked grass for the first time. Just her luck to have the fuzz bust in and arrest the lot of them.

Her father hadn't understood. He blew a gasket, yelling like a madman and calling her a dope addict and accusing Jack of child molestation. What a row he kicked up. Even subjected her to the embarrassment of being examined by a doctor before dropping the charges against Jack. Life at home was miserable after that. He didn't trust her out of his sight—not that he was at home that much. He had his hired watchdogs take over when he was supposed to be working late. Working late. Ha! That was a laugh. She knew very well where he was, and it wasn't in his office. He was with that Rose Mallory and her cluster of prostitutes. That secretary of his—the one who was so hung up on him and the one he fired—told her all about her father and that Rose Mallory.

Lisa glanced at her father at the end of the table. How she wished he could understand. She wasn't a bad girl. She'd never done anything she was ashamed of. Even with George Petrik she'd never gone all the way. He, like Jack, was more of a father to her than anything else, kind and protective and understanding. Her father was never understanding; not the way her mother had been. She gave her head a little shake when she felt the stinging behind her eyes. She wouldn't think about her mother. It didn't do any good to cry for something that she could never have again.

Her father was a sap about women. Look at him, she

thought. How can he be so dumb as to not see through that ridiculous Verdugo woman. She had never thought of him as weak, but she saw it now. And it was that weakness that killed her mother. Why did he have to be like that where women were concerned? She loved him more than anybody in the whole world, yet that stupid weakness of his was destroying that love.

She let her eyes move to Laura's husband. He seemed like a decent enough sort of guy, she thought. How on earth did he get himself tied up to a woman like that? But then she'd learned that they'd been married a long time, so he certainly knew what his wife was. They were obviously two of a kind, she decided when she saw Paul Sr. glance at the low neckline of her dress. She wished she hadn't worn the silly dress her father had gone out and bought for her. It was just the sort of dress a man like him would buy for a woman—even if it was for his daughter. No, she was judging him too harshly. He had bought a scarf to wear with it, apologizing that it was the only decent dress in her size that he could find. It was her fault for not having worn the scarf.

It angered her to watch her father being taken in by all Laura's feminine charm. Couldn't he see through it? Men were so dumb. The only person she kind of half-admired was the son, Paul Jr. He seemed just about as uncomfortable as she about his stepmother's actions and conversation. The boy was definitely a square, but at least he wasn't as dumb as the others.

"Why don't you take the children into the den and show them that new electronic tennis game that hooks up to the television?" Laura said to her husband. She propped her chin on her hand and smiled seductively at Rod. "Mr. Shepherd has shown an interest in my decorating. I thought I'd give him a tour of the house."

"That's a good idea. What do you say, kids? What do you say we go into the den and I'll show you the latest thing in games?" He addressed his remark to Lisa.

"Sorry," Lisa said at the wink she saw Mr. Verdugo exchange with his wife. "I'm afraid I'm not a very good game player."

"Ah, come on, Lisa. It's fun. Besides, I brought along some great rock tapes. We don't have to play the game. We'll listen

to some rock and maybe dance a bit. What do you say?"
Paul Jr. grinned. "I'll show you all the latest steps."

He'll show me, she thought. That's a laugh. He most likely
thinks the Twist is the latest thing.

He certainly didn't impress her as the type who'd know the
first thing about new rock steps. She liked to dance—in fact,
she liked to dance more than anything else. It was a great
way to get rid of her pent-up energy, and she had plenty of
that right now. She really didn't feel much like dancing, but
she didn't want to sit and watch her father make a fool of
himself over that Laura Verdugo. She tried to look bored as
she put down her napkin and got out of her chair. "Why not?"
she said. "What else is there to do?" She saw the hurt look
on Paul Jr.'s face and was immediately sorry. To soften the
remark she asked, "Do you Hustle?"

"Really," Laura breathed, looking aghast.

Paul Jr. rolled his eyes. "Oh, Laura. It's the name of a dance.
It isn't the kind of 'hustle' you think." He smiled at Lisa.
"Yeah. I learned just about a week ago. Do you?"

"Sure. It's old hat to me."

"Great. Come on." He took her by the hand and went toward the den.

"I think I'd like to watch this," Mr. Verdugo said and followed after them.

Laura gave a tight little laugh. "My husband is really a
teen-ager at heart, Mr. Shepherd." She put her hand over his.
"Or may I call you Rod?"

"Call me Rod, by all means," he said. In the background,
loud rock music suddenly split the air. "How about showing
me around? Somewhere away from that racket. Unfortunately
I never graduated into a lover of rock music."

"Me neither," she said, taking his arm. "But it has its place,
I suppose."

Rod felt a little uncomfortable at the way Laura pressed
herself against him every chance she got. She was certainly a
stunning woman, yet there was something disturbing about
her. Everything she said, even the most innocent comments,
seemed to have a sexual connotation. Colors she referred to
as "hard as a man's body," or "smooth as a woman's skin."
Shapes were "sensual" or "voluptuous" or "stiffly erect."

The house was a showplace. It was more like pictures from
a magazine than an actual home. There wasn't an ashtray out

of place or a crushed pillow. Everything was beautifully co-ordinated and in the best taste.

In the downstairs sitting room Laura touched a corner of the molding and a wall panel moved aside. "This is our little retreat away from home," she said, taking hold of his hand and leading him through the open panel. "Paul and I refer to this room as our arena."

At first glance the room looked extremely ordinary, but hardly in keeping with the rest of the house. It was almost stark in appearance, although dimly lighted. "The arena? I assume this is where the family fights take place," he said with a chuckle.

"Not exactly that," she answered, running her tongue over her already glistening lips. "More hand-to-hand combat, if you know what I mean."

He cringed slightly. There was that suggestiveness again. He looked at the several long divans and the huge throw pillows that were scattered over the floor. "Well, there is enough floor space for that," he said.

She lowered herself onto the largest of the divans and pulled him down next to her. "Would you like a brandy? Or perhaps you'd prefer to smoke some grass."

He felt a tightness in his throat. "No thank you. Nothing." To cover his sudden discomfort he added, "I'm afraid the several cocktails before dinner and the wine were about all I can handle."

"Oh, I doubt that very much," she said, sidling closer to him. "You don't look like the type of man who has to limit his intake of anything." She rested her arm on his shoulder and peered up into his face.

"Ordinarily I don't, but tonight I have a teen-age daughter in tow."

"Lisa looks like a girl who can very well take care of herself. A very handsome child, I must admit." She began toying with the lapel of his jacket. She let her hand drop to his thigh.

Rod swallowed hard. He spied a row of decanters sitting on the bar. "Maybe I will have that drink after all," he said, getting to his feet. "How about you?"

"Yes, please. Cognac and soda, please."

He saw the pout of disappointment on her face when he moved away from her. Boy, she comes on like a house on fire, he thought as he fixed her drink and poured himself a healthy shot of straight scotch. He'd never run across this kind of situation. What in hell does a guy do to discourage his host's wife from putting the make on him? And in her own house, too.

Reluctantly he returned to the divan and handed Laura her drink. Her hand immediately wrapped itself around his wrist and she tugged him down beside her again. She took the glass from his hand, letting her other hand slide across his thigh and in between his legs.

Rod splashed scotch down over the front of his jacket. He jumped to his feet, groping for his handkerchief.

"Do I make you nervous?"

He took a deep breath as he blotted the stains. "I guess I'm just not used to this sort of thing."

"What sort of thing? Being seduced by a woman?" She laughed softly. "I would have thought you were very accustomed to it. You are a very exciting-looking man, Rod. Haven't women told you that before?"

"No, I'm afraid not. I'm afraid I don't lead a very sophisticated life." He replaced his handkerchief and picked up his glass. He took another deep breath and tried to calm down. He wasn't conscious of the fact that he glanced toward the secret panel and saw that it was closed.

"We're quite alone here," Laura said, watching his eyes. "You don't have to worry about Paul or the children. Paul will keep them entertained."

What did that mean? he wondered. Christ, was Paul aware that she had him in here and was making a pass?

It was as if she'd read his thoughts. "Paul and I have a very modern marriage," she said, sipping her drink. "We are referred to in the vernacular as 'swingers.'" She winked boldly, reaching out her hand to him.

Rod ignored it. "I'm afraid this isn't exactly my cup of tea," he said.

"What you need is a little atmosphere to help you unwind," Laura said as she dimmed the lights by means of a switch next to the divan. The walls of the room suddenly came alive. Rod's eyes widened as he saw the forms and shapes materialize as if by magic. An ultraviolet light bathed the room, revealing walls completely covered with the most disgusting erotic art he'd ever seen. In his mind it was far from art; it was pure, filthy pornography. He saw scenes depicting sex acts he never thought about. Women having intercourse with horses and dogs; men sodomizing other men; men defecating on women; people in chains; faces of people contorted in agonizing pain. He looked away in disgust, but wherever he looked he saw more scenes, even more depraved. He tried to keep himself composed. "I'm afraid this kind of thing turns me off." He put down his drink and headed toward where he thought the secret panel was.

The ultraviolet light vanished, erasing the pornographic walls. He heard Laura sigh. "Too bad," she said lightly. The next thing he knew, she was standing beside him and the secret panel was open. "Well, at least I tried. Paul will be disappointed, but then we can't always have everything, can we?"

"It's getting late, Mrs. Verdugo." He noticed that his hand was shaking. "I think I'd better take Lisa back to the hotel."

She blew him a kiss and sashayed around him. "I can understand that," she said. "Especially if you and that pretty daughter of yours are sharing the same room."

It took all his effort to keep from slapping her. Instead he hurried ahead of her and went in the direction of the loud music coming from the den.

All of the resentment he'd held toward Paul Sr. because of the affection his son felt for him had gone. Now he just felt sorry for the son. He wondered about Paul Jr. being exposed to the kind of life his father and Laura were obviously living. But the boy was bright. Rod was sure he'd be able to handle things if Laura got out of line. And she would get out of line; that he knew for certain. Laura wouldn't be able to keep her hands off anyone.

Poor kid, he thought. Wait until he finds out what kind of man his father really is. And he would find out sooner or later. He wondered if he should tell Paul Jr. himself. No, keep out of it. It isn't any of your business, and the boy isn't exactly a child.

"Ah, back so soon," Mr. Verdugo yelled over the music as Rod opened the door. "I was just making sure the kids were kept occupied before joining you for a drink in the arena. Laura did show you the play room, didn't she?" he asked with a laugh. "Quite a cozy little place, isn't it? Of course I can understand your reluctance to linger, what with the children here and all, but perhaps tomorrow night you'd like to return and the three of us could get better acquainted." He put his arm around Rod's shoulders and grinned into his face. Rod knocked off the arm.

"No, thank you," he said angrily. He put his face close to Verdugo's. "You're sick," he snarled. "Sick!" He fought to control his anger. "Come on, Lisa," he yelled over the music. "We're going home."

He wondered if he should call Nancy when he got back to the hotel. That would be the last thing he'd do, but the temptation remained.

GREG FELT HE SHOULD CRY, BUT THE TEARS just wouldn't come. Cynthia was dead. He'd never be able to hold her in his arms or see her beautiful face. Wild, crazy thoughts gnawed at him. He remembered Cynthia's cruel words. She deserved to be dead. No, that wasn't right. He'd loved his sister. She'd been good to him. He remembered the happy times they'd had together.

He also remembered the party and the rape. His stomach contracted. Maybe he'd be better off dead too. No, the world was too exciting. There was still so much to see and do. There were still so many people who would admire him, want him. Besides, he was too young to die, and far too handsome.

He turned the car sharply and headed back to the seedy bar on the waterfront. Let Cynthia be dead. He had other, more important business to attend to . . . like revenge. He had to settle a score with that Latin sonofabitch if it was the last thing he did. It wasn't the physical pain he'd been subjected to that he minded so much; it was the humiliation. In fact, it surprised him to find how the pain had diminished in so short a time. He felt a soreness, nothing more. And perverse as it seemed, there was a certain kind of pleasure in that soreness.

The thought bothered him. He pushed it aside. It was ridiculous. Guys didn't get screwed in the ass and feel pleasure. Queers did, he supposed, but he wasn't queer.

He thought of Phil, the guy back in military school. Phil

had asked Greg to screw him in the ass a couple of times. And he had. But hell, that was different. Phil was all man. There was nothing queer about Phil.

He felt a sudden warm flush creep over his skin. Sure, he'd enjoyed it at the time. But Christ, he was only a kid then, and there weren't any women around to screw. It was better than beating off a couple of times a day. All kids did stuff like that in school. It didn't make you queer. Oh, his mother thought so, Cynthia thought so, but he knew differently. He thought about all the women he'd laid since then. Didn't that prove that he wasn't a stupid fag?

He found he was getting a semi-hard-on and fumbled it into a more comfortable position in his pants. That was because he was thinking about the broads he'd screwed, not Phil back in school or that Latin bastard. If he had enjoyed what that Latin prick did to him then he certainly wouldn't be out looking for him in order to kill the rotten bastard. That in itself proved that he wasn't queer.

The thought settled him somewhat. His erection started to go down.

There wasn't anyone in the bar when he got there, only the bartender polishing glasses with his greasy apron. He was listening to flamenco music on a battered old radio. Greg was sober tonight. He had resisted the urge to smoke a couple of joints before coming here. He wanted his mind crystal-clear. He didn't want anything to stand in the way of his revenge.

"Whiskey, *señor?*"

"With water," Greg said.

The bartender laughed. "That is not how you were drinking it last night, my friend."

Greg forced himself to smile. "Yes, I suppose I really did tie one on, didn't I?" He had to be pleasant if he intended getting any information out of the guy, he decided.

"I trust Alfredo saw that you got home all right, *Señor*. . ." He gróped for a last name.

"Brandon. Greg Brandon." Immediately he bit his lip. Why in hell did he offer his name? That was stupid. He was being too affable. That was a mistake. He should have smoked that grass or had a couple of shots. When he was sober he was always too damned easy to get along with. "Yes, I got home all right," he said, trying to avoid the accusing smile in the man's eyes. "This Alfredo, does he come here often?"

"You like him?" The bartender grinned and slapped the bar. "Alfredo will like that. He was in a little while ago and told me how much he thought of you. Ah, he is a very romantic man, that Alfredo."

Greg felt his cheeks redden; he also felt the raging anger building up, but he fought against it. "Oh, I don't mean I like him in the way you think," he said, sipping at his drink.

"Oh, I understand, *señor*. Do not be embarrassed. Most of my customers prefer that kind of thing. I myself have weaknesses sometime when I see a pretty young man such as yourself. It is healthy to admire everything beautiful."

Greg squirmed on the seat. "You say Alfredo was in earlier? Do you think he'll be coming back?"

"Aha," the bartender said, grinning still and wagging a finger at him. "You are anxious for another rendezvous, huh?" He laughed suggestively and Greg wanted to plant his fist in his face. But perhaps he'd best play along, humor the pig. If Alfredo wasn't coming back maybe the guy knew where he could find him.

Greg shrugged. "You wouldn't by any chance know where he lives?"

"Alfredo? Nah. I only know he sometimes stays with one of his whores."

"Whores?"

"Sure, didn't Alfredo tell you? He is a pimp. He has many beautiful young *señoritas* who work for him." He laughed again and shook his head. "Oh, that Alfredo. He is quite a man with the ladies as well as with the boys."

"You wouldn't know where I might find him, would you?"

"No more tonight, *Señor* Brandon."

Damn, Greg thought. He wished he'd forgotten his name.

"Alfredo was going to Andraitx. When he goes there he usually stays the night. You will not see him here again until tomorrow perhaps. But stay around, *señor*. There are many other boys who come in regularly, some much more beautiful than Alfredo. Stay around. I will introduce you to some of them."

"Some other time," Greg said. He felt the disgust in his guts and wanted to get the hell out of the place as quickly as he could. "I'll be back tomorrow."

"Tomorrow is my slow night," the bartender said. "Alfredo will stop in briefly, perhaps. Business, you know. I give him a few pesetas to let his girls come into the bar sometimes when I have customers who ask for them. Or if Alfredo is very busy with his business he sometimes . . . " He didn't finish his sentence. He jerked his head in the direction of the men's room. An ugly leer spread over the fat man's face. "In fact, if you are especially anxious tonight there is one of my regular boys in there now."

The glory hole, Greg thought with disgust. The hole in the partition. Yes, sure. Alfredo did mention that he used it sometimes.

Without thinking of how it looked to the bartender, he got up and went into the men's room. He didn't want to avail himself of the built-in service that was sitting on the other side. He just wanted to reassure himself that the hole was still there. It gave him an idea.

He stared at the hole for a moment, ignoring the soft little cough of encouragement that came from the other side of the partition. He snapped his fingers and quickly turned back toward the bar. He knew now exactly how'd he'd have his revenge. Oh, God. It was perfect. Revenge. Sweet revenge, he thought as he felt his steps becoming lighter and started to hum.

"You are leaving so soon, *Señor* Brandon?"

Greg found himself smiling at the man. "Yes. I have an appointment," he said. "Tell Alfredo I'll be in tomorrow night about this time and ask him if he'll please wait for me. It's important that I see him."

"I will tell him, *señor*. Until tomorrow night, then."

"Tomorrow night," Greg waved and started for his car. Yes, tomorrow night everything would be taken care of, and after that he could get the hell away from this rotten island and forget it existed. He'd never come back—never.

Thursday

THE BUS CREAKED AND COMPLAINED AS IT
lumbered over the twisting road that skirted the coast before
swerving inland toward Valdemossa. The beauty of the landscape was so awesome, so dramatic in quality and texture,
that it took the breath away. Rod didn't notice it at all. He
sat silent and unseeing, staring with the backs of his eyes at
nothing but his own thoughts. Beside him Nancy sat equally
quiet, obviously lost in her thoughts too. He wished she
hadn't come along, yet he was glad. Their conversation the
morning before had embarrassed him. He'd thought a lot
about what she'd said, but he still could not bring himself
to see things her way. He told himself that he had no more
respect for her. Hard as he had tried, he could not convince
himself of that, however. In spite of everything, Nancy was
still looking as lovely and as sweet and innocent as she had
when he first met her. He tried to block his mind from the
sight of her making love to him with her mouth. He tried not
to think about that, but it remained indelibly etched on his
brain. Her naked body had been so smooth and young and
exciting. Everything about her was exciting. What she had
wanted to do to him was wrong. He'd have to make her see
that.

At least Nancy wasn't as terrible as that Verdugo woman.
God, how it sickened him to think of that depraved room with
its filthy pornography. What Nancy did was wrong, but at
least she could be saved before she became a woman like
Laura Verdugo.

Okay, he was a prude. He couldn't help it. That was the way
he was brought up. But if he was such a prude, then why did
he feel he had to resort to women like Rose Mallory? That in
itself proved that he really wasn't all that much of a prude.

He rubbed the heels of his hands in his eyes. He felt Nancy
glance at him, but she said nothing.

Nancy. She was such a nice girl.

To force himself not to think about Nancy he looked at
Lisa and Paul, who were sitting directly in front of them on
the stiff leather seats seemingly oblivious of anything but
the music they were listening to. Rod was surprised that Lisa
was paying it any attention; it wasn't the loud, hard rock
music she claimed to like so much. Paul was playing a tape
of classical music, and every so often Rod would see him
turn to Lisa and say, "Listen to this. Moody Blues used the

231

same theme in their last album." Or, "Remember the Bee Gees' last record? They did a keen arrangement on this melody." To his amazement, Lisa was actually listening, both to the music and to Paul's explanation of musical structures and chord constructions.

He was glad that Lisa was acting more like her old self this morning. He wondered if it had anything to do with their conversation on the way home last night. She'd seemed glad to hear him complain about Paul's stepmother. Oh, not that he'd gone into any details. Nevertheless, she'd acted pleased. She'd even condescended to say goodnight before she turned in.

Then, when Paul had called and suggested this trip to the Chopin-Sand retreat at Valdemossa, it had surprised him again to find Lisa accepting so quickly and without complaint. At breakfast they had met Nancy. Lisa had taken to her immediately and she to Lisa. Rod hadn't asked Nancy to join them. He was still harboring misgivings about their night together. It had been Lisa who had extended the invitation, and Nancy hadn't had to be coaxed into accepting, much to Rod's chagrin. He hadn't wanted her to come, and yet he had.

So, the four of them set off for the little Moorish town of Valdemossa, about twenty-five miles from Palma. The bus wasn't particularly crowded; just the four of them, a few native women returning from marketing, a swarthy old gentleman in a wide-brimmed straw hat and an American couple. The man was loud and fat, the woman gum-chewing and flashily dressed. Rod wondered idly why the pair thought it was necessary to talk at the tops of their voices. And they certainly did not mind what they said, reading aloud from their guidebook about the indiscretions of Madame George Sand and her young, foppish lover. A couple of times he was tempted to turn around and tell them to be quiet. Nancy, however, found the couple very entertaining and told Rod they looked like a fun pair.

The bus hit a chuckhole and Nancy landed up tight against Rod. He grabbed her and held her for a moment, then, realizing how close they were, he eased her away from him.

"Gee, for a moment there I didn't know you were aware

that I'd come along this morning. Still holding fast to your puritan morals?"

He frowned at her, held his finger up to his lips and darted his eyes toward Lisa and Paul. After a while his expression softened and he turned and stared out the window. "Something like that," he mumbled under his breath.

Nancy shook her head. "Brother, what am I going to do with you?" she said, half to herself.

She suddenly wished now that she hadn't accepted the invitation to come along. When Lisa had extended it, she'd seen the frown on Rod's brow. He hadn't wanted her to come either.

Outside the window she saw a farmer with one mule plowing a field. The soil looked rich and productive. The man stopped to wipe the sweat from his brow. Nancy felt sorry for him. All his life he had most likely toiled in that field without thought of the world outside. He would be buried in that soil he was turning over, and she wondered if he ever wanted more out of life.

Perhaps she was wrong in her independent attitude. Perhaps it would be better to hide from the world and never know all the complexities of living. She was dissatisfied, with all her education and female liberation; that simple peasant might well be the happiest man on earth.

Had she let herself get too far away from innocence?

Just at that moment the fat man in the wild shirt pointed out the window and said, "Hey, Sheila, this must be Valdemossa."

"Yeah, Charlie," the woman said. "It looks just like what the guidebook said it would."

The bus had rumbled through a narrow gorge into a quiet, broad valley. To their right a stony pine-bordered stream followed along a dividing wall, churning and babbling around massive rocks. The town itself was perched among sunlit mountains; its huddled white houses and central square tower gave it a fairytale quality. The cypresses and green tiled roofs lent an Arab aspect to the place and accentuated its somberness.

"That must be that charterhouse, you know, the one the book mentioned," Charlie said, pointing.

Sheila scanned the pages of the guidebook. "Yes. It was built in 1446 and then rebuilt in the sixteenth and seventeenth centuries when the defense tower, raised as a protection against Saracen"—she mispronounced it— "raids, and the cloister of St. Mary were added."

"Yeah, yeah," Charlie said, waving at her to be still. He looked at the town. "Seems like a nice little place, well built, but kinda touristy," he added, seeing the modern souvenir shops and little commercial-looking cafés.

"But it all looks deserted," Sheila said. "Then this ain't exactly the tourist season," she said, again referring to the guidebook.

"Maybe not," Charlie said, "but there is someone in that ticket booth to the church, or whatever it is."

"So we gotta pay. So what. Nothing in life's free, you know that."

Rod wished they'd lower their voices.

They straggled off the bus, Sheila and Charlie first. Rod waited for the natives before he and Nancy got off. Paul and Lisa trailed, their heads together in deep, serious conversation. As they came up to them, Rod heard Paul say, "Look, I can dig the bad stuff like E.L.O. and Ten Years After."

"Bad?" Lisa barked angrily. "They're the greatest."

Paul shook his head. "Oh, man, are you ever starved." He gave her a patient glance. "Bad means great." Again he shook his head. "Where have you been?"

"Hey, you two," Rod said. "Are you coming with Nancy and me? I thought we'd find ourselves a place for lunch."

"You go ahead, Mr. Shepherd. I'd like to take Lisa up and show her the monastery where Chopin lived."

Rod raised his eyebrows. "I didn't think Lisa knew who Chopin was."

Lisa narrowed her eyes. "That's because you never took the time to find out."

Paul gave a strained little laugh. "She's not as dumb as she looks, Mr. Shepherd."

Lisa glowered at him. "Men," she huffed. "Why do they always stick up for one another?"

Nancy put her arm around Lisa's shoulder. "Because they're men. They can't help it."

"Just like I can't help being his daughter," Lisa snapped.

"Hey, Lisa. Wait up," Paul called as he hurried after her. He grabbed her arm and slowed her down. "What's with you and your dad? He seems like a real great guy."

"You don't live with him."

"That wasn't a very nice thing for you to say. You hurt him, I could tell by the look on his face."

"So I hurt him. He's hurt me a lot more than that."

"Like for instance?" He steered her toward the path leading to the monastery.

"I don't want to talk about it."

He glanced at her out of the corner of his eye. "Too bad the scientists don't perfect a truth dart, something you could stick into somebody and you'd know exactly what they were thinking about. Boy, would that make relationships a lot easier. You'd know right off what someone thought of you at that moment." He thought it might be a good idea to steer the conversation away from her father, because he was troubled about his own father. He was finding out that his father wasn't exactly as he'd expected him to be. The guy seemed to be always leading the conversation around to sex. Ever since he'd arrived, all their talk had been about pussy and orgasms. Christ, it was enough to turn a guy off. The father he'd yearned for for so long was nothing but a cock-hound and as empty as a drum. He didn't want to think about him any more than Lisa wanted to think about Rod. Paul could understand that.

"Why do you say 'at that moment'? Lisa asked. "Why not what people thought of you, period?"

"Because people change from minute to minute. They're merely reflections of their many-faceted personalities. One minute they might be honest, upstanding, dedicated to a cause, but the next minute they may completely reverse themselves in their thinking, their actions."

"What are you, a psychologist as well as a piano player?"

"Pianist," he corrected. When she didn't say anything, he said, "No. I'm just interested in people. I like them."

"All of them?"

He laughed. "I haven't met all of them yet. When I do I'll let you know."

"How about the ones you've met so far? Do you like all of them?"

"No, not all of them."

"How about your father, for instance? Do you like him?"

He flinched the minute she touched the nerve. To hide the

pain he chuckled and said, "I'll take your stand on that and say I'd rather not talk about it."

They walked along in silence for a moment. As they passed under the towering, dark shadow of the monastery, Lisa shivered and Paul tightened his arm around her.

"Cold?"

"No. I think someone just walked over my grave."

He chuckled. "But you aren't dead yet."

"At times I think I am," she said.

"Yes, I know the feeling," he answered, feeling his spirits slip, remembering all the hard work his mother had forced him to do over the past years. No, he wasn't being fair to her. She hadn't forced him to do anything. He'd done it all quite willingly. He forced his spirits up. "Hey, look at the two of us. We're on this perfectly wonderful island of Majorca and we're talking like two old professors at a class reunion. Let's make a pact. From here on we'll be nothing but laughter and gaiety."

"I don't think I want to be laughter and gaiety."

"Ah, come on, Lisa. You make out of this world exactly what you put into it. Give and people will take; take and people will give. Right now I'll give, you take. Later when I'm feeling down you can give and I'll take. What do you say?"

She found herself smiling at him in spite of herself. "You're really a child," she said.

"I'd rather be that than an old lady like you," he said, chucking her under the chin. "Come on. Let's look inside this old barn and see where genius lived."

As they went inside the dreary old monastery, Paul commented, "You know, Chopin and his beloved Madame Sand first lived in Palma. But Chopin had tuberculosis—consumption, they called it then. And the people in Palma were terrified of consumption, so they forced them here to this place, which was once a monastery." He looked around at the dingy little cells and vaulted ceilings. "God, I can almost hear Chopin playing one of his cheery little waltzes trying to get rid of some of the gloom of this place."

"You're a strange one, Paul," Lisa said, looking quizzically into his eyes. "I don't get you at all."

"What's to get?"

"One minute you're all fired up about Elton John or the

Stones and the next minute you're reeling with thoughts of Chopin and his waltzes."

"So what's wrong with that? I like music, all kinds of music, but especially piano music. I want to play, play well. Oh, not for the money and not for the applause—though I admit that's an essential part of striving for success. I want to play well because I love the piano, I love music, and it is the only way I've found so far to express the way I feel, the way I love."

"You know, you're rather like a piano yourself."

"I don't get you."

"Black and white," she said. He gave her a vague look. "Black and white. Aren't piano keys all black and white? They don't have any gray areas, do they? Neither do you. I don't know whether that's good or bad."

He saw that she was slipping back into depression again. "Ah, I may not have gray areas, but I really am like a piano keyboard in that I have a lot of cracks."

It brought a smile to her face, for which he was pleased. They strolled along the open colonnade supported by dusty pillars. Their footsteps echoed like lost souls at the edge of the world.

"Do you really think you have talent, Paul?"

"Sure," he said without hesitation. "If I didn't know it, I wouldn't have any. You see, I want to become a serious success. Semi-talented people don't want that; serious success is too costly to their potential success. Most people just want to make a quick buck, and they don't give a damn about anything else. That's why you have so many flashes in the pan these days. This year's big name is next year's has-been. That's only because they really didn't have any real talent to offer. People don't tire of true talent. As you know, it even lives long after they're dead."

There was a light of admiration in her eyes. "I wish I could be like that."

"No you don't." When she frowned at him he added, "If you wanted to be like me then you would be. It would come naturally. It wouldn't be anything you'd have to force on yourself." He touched her cheek. "But I wouldn't want you to be like me. I'm not pretty like you are."

"But you are—" She blushed, angry at herself for letting that slip out.

It was his turn to blush. "Gee, I didn't think you noticed," he kidded. She stood quite still and he thought she was expecting him to kiss her. He wasn't very good at kissing, he thought, not having had much experience at it. As much as he wanted to, he didn't want to show his inexperience. Lisa assuredly had been around a lot of smooth characters. He didn't want her to think he was virgin woods. He put his arm around her waist and turned her back toward the monastery exit. "What do you really want to do when you get out of school?" he asked, changing the subject away from himself.

She turned it right back by saying, "Nothing. What do you want to do? Become a great concert pianist, right?" She felt disappointed that he hadn't kissed her. She knew he wanted to. So why hadn't he? Maybe she had made it too obvious. That annoyed her. She didn't want him to dislike her.

"Yes. I've never played with a symphony orchestra yet. I'd like to do that one of these days."

"And playing with a symphony is important?"

"Of course it's important. It is to me, at least. All forms of art are important." He sighed. "I want to be good, real good, perfect in fact. Perfection to an artist has to be the ultimate trip. And that goes for all good artists, be it Rubinstein, the Beatles or Elton John. I don't care who you equate it with, perfection is perfection and it must be the absolute greatest."

" 'Equate,' " Lisa put in, turning up her nose. "Snob words like that turn me off."

"Oh, come off it, Lisa. You know damn well what 'equate' means. Why do you play-act sometimes, pretending to people that you're some kind of dunce? Is it because you think it's 'in'? Do you think ignorance is something to be proud of, or are you afraid people won't like you if you're smart? Well, let me tell you something. The people who put down education are the ones who are resentful of it. It's easy to be stupid. It doesn't require any effort at all, so the dumb so-and-so's are the first to scoff. They know they can't climb up to your level, so they try to pull you down to theirs. How many jerks do you know who go around stealing hubcaps or dropping acid or shoplifting just for the fun of it? Do you know why they do things like that? Because they can't compete with people with a little intelligence and they think it is a way of gaining attention."

He paused and looked at her. He thought she was laughing

at him. "Come off it. It's easy to be dumb, but it takes common sense and a little bit of effort to be smart."

She kicked at a pebble and missed. "You sure are a talky one." She put back her head and let the sun beat softly on her face. "Do you ever come down off that soap box?" She cast him a sidelong glance. "Who are you trying to convince of your intelligence? Me or yourself?"

Paul frowned, then laughed. "Myself, I guess," he said.

"I thought so." They strolled on a little farther. She was thinking how old Paul seemed; his maturity attracted her. But he's just a kid, nevertheless, she reminded herself. Yet she found herself being drawn to him. She'd never met a guy who was young and old both at the same time. More important, there was something about him that brought out her trust. He wasn't like Jack or George Petrik; Paul was closer to her own age and he would be able to understand her better than older people did. She was tempted to test her intuitions about him. "You never asked why I was in jail," she said.

"I guess because I didn't think it was any of my business. Besides, it couldn't have been anything too serious, because you're out, aren't you?"

"I was picked up for possession of drugs."

"That happens." He wondered if he should ask his next question. He decided he would, even though Lisa might think he was prying. "Were you pushing?"

"No. Some guy stashed some stuff on me, then took a powder."

"Nice guy. What hole did he crawl out of?"

"He's a great guy, really," she said, taking George Petrik's part. "I can understand why he did it."

"I'm afraid I can't."

"He knew it would be a first arrest for me. They'd lock me up until my father arranged to get me out. He had a lot more to lose. If he were caught they'd check back on his record and put him away for good."

"So rather than take the consequences for his own stupid actions he let you hold tight to the bag and pinned an arrest record on you."

"You don't understand. George did a lot for me. It was the least I could do."

"George?"

Lisa looked a bit disconcerted. "Forget I mentioned that name."

"Okay, you didn't mention it," he answered without hesitating. "I just think the guy was a rat."

"He is not a rat. He's tops in my book, just as I am in his."

"Oh, sure. He arranges for you to be put in the slammer while he flies around free as a bird." He stopped and turned her to face him. "If he's such a great guy, why didn't he arrange to get you out of jail? He could at least have come to visit you or offered to post bail or something."

"They don't run the jails here like they do at home," she argued. "It doesn't work that way." She pouted. "Besides, he's older and I'm a minor. He could have gotten himself into more trouble than just drugs."

"Jesus," Paul breathed. "You were traveling from country to country with an older man. Are you nuts?"

"I don't see anything wrong with that. You have a dirty, rotten mind. You're just like my father." She yanked herself free of his grip and ran on down the path.

"WOW, THIS SURE IS A WRECK OF A PLACE," Charlie said as he peeked into the dusty nooks of the old chapel adjoining the monastery. "Look at this place, Sheila. And to think people used to live here." He turned and saw Sheila still standing at the door. "Hey, come here and look at this joint. That's what we paid for, you know."

Sheila left the door and walked toward him. "I was just eavesdropping on those two young kids. They seem to be having a lovers' quarrel."

"They're just kids. What would they know about love?" He picked up a crumbled piece of molding and examined it.

"You mean you were never in love at that age?"

"I was too busy growing up to be in love."

"I was," Sheila said. "I had the most awful crush on my shorthand teacher in high school." She giggled. "I was so dumb and he used to keep me after school and help me with the lessons. After I got a little older I realized that he was just looking for an excuse to get real close, holding my pencil for me and showing me how to make the figures, and all the while he was rubbing up against me. Oh, he never did anything fresh, but if he had I think, at the time, I would have let him."

Charlie dropped the piece of molding and dusted his hands. "A regular little pushover, huh? Is that why it was so easy to get you?"

"Easy? Why you big lout, I gave you the chase of your life."

Charlie laughed. "Yeah, you sure did, honey. And I loved every breathless step." He pulled her against him and put his hands on her breasts. "I can understand why that teacher wanted to get next to you. You've got the best jugs I've ever seen."

"Charlie," she squealed, pushing away from him. "Not here. This is a chapel we're in. It isn't right."

"What's not right about it? There ain't nobody here to see."

"God's here. He can see."

"Since when have you taken up religion?"

She put her hands on her hips. "Why, Charlie Cranston, how can you ask that? Who was it insisted on a church wedding when you wanted to go to the clerk down at City Hall? And who made you go to the priest and promise to him that you'd see that our kids were brought up Catholic?"

"Yeah, yeah. I forgot."

"Well, I didn't. And I intend holding you to that promise."

"So who said I was thinking of breaking it? Of course there ain't gonna be any kids, so I don't have to worry. At least not right away."

"Who said?" Sheila wanted to know.

"What do you mean?" He found himself staring at her. "I thought we agreed. I thought we were going to wait for a while."

Sheila turned away, looking embarrassed. "Sometimes things just happen and there's nothing to be done about it."

He turned her around. "What things? What are you trying to tell me?"

She couldn't look at him. "It's just that, well . . ." She tightened the lines of her mouth and straightened herself up. "It's just that I've missed my period. It don't mean anything yet, but it might, so you'd just better accept it if anything happens."

His mouth dropped open and his eyes were wide as half-dollars. "A baby?" he breathed.

"Maybe," Sheila said in an offhand tone.

"A baby," he yelled, a happy grin widening his mouth. He grabbed Sheila and swung her around. "A baby," he shouted.

"Charlie, put me down. Stop it." When he did she said, "I'm not saying yes and I'm not saying no. We'll just have to wait and see."

He grabbed her again and hugged her tightly and swung her around and around.

"Charlie," she squealed. "You're making me dizzy."

"Oh, Sheila, I couldn't be happier."

"But I thought you didn't want any kids right away."

"I didn't think I did until now. And they're not just any kids, they're ours, Sheila. Yours and mine." He pulled her into his arms and kissed her hard on the lips. "Oh, baby, you've made me the happiest guy in the world."

"You really mean that?"

"Of course I mean it, doll baby." He rubbed his hands together. "Just think, a baby." He was smiling with joy.

"Now take it easy, Charlie. As I said, I'm not real sure, just a little bit. I'll have to have a doctor check me over to make positive."

"Then we'll find a doctor."

"I thought I'd wait until we got back home. I sorta don't like to trust these foreign doctors."

"What's not to trust? Besides, we aren't going home for a while."

"Well, I didn't mean next week or in the next fifteen days. It can wait for a month, even two months. There's no hurry. It's just that I know this girlfriend who swears by her doctor. She's had four kids so far and never a speck of trouble. I'd like to go to him."

"We'll fly him over here," Charlie said.

"You're crazy. Do you know what that would cost? We don't have that kind of money."

Charlie averted his eyes. "Yeah, maybe you're right. But look, there are plenty of real good doctors over here. Don't all the movie stars come here to have their kids? If it's good enough for a movie star it's good enough for my wife."

"But I don't want to have one of these foreign doctors taking care of me. How do I know they speak English? I won't be able to talk to them."

"Don't be silly. We'll get a doctor who does speak English. I bet they even have American doctors over here. We'll go to one of them."

Sheila looked dubious.

"Look, honey. Remember me telling you about my having to go to the Brandon villa yesterday when we found that dead girl on the beach? Well, the inspector of police was hinting that maybe I would like to stick around here and take a job with them."

"That don't make any sense. You don't know how to talk their lingo. How would you handle an investigation if none of the people involved spoke any English?"

"I'd work through an interpreter until I learned to talk whatever they talk here."

"You're off your rocker."

"I'm not. I can do it. They're short-handed. We can go finish our vacation, then come back here and settle down. There's plenty of nice places we can live in."

Sheila caught his eyes and looked directly into them. "I asked you this once before, Charlie, but I'm asking again. Is there any reason you are so set against going back to New York?"

"Of course not," he said. He was thankful for the dimness of the chapel that hid the flush that was creeping over his cheeks.

"I get the feeling that there is."

"Ah, Sheila. I'm just sick and tired of New York. This would be a much better place to raise kids. They'd be real continental when they grew up, speak lots of languages and be well traveled. They'd turn out to be real nice kids, believe me."

"They could learn lots of languages and be well traveled back home too," she argued.

"Ah, Sheila," Charlie whined as she turned and left the chapel with him close behind her.

MIGUEL DECIDED TO INDULGE HIMSELF WITH
a second cigar as he entered Elaine's villa. The butler told
him the *señora* was in the morning room with her friend,
Maggie Montgomery. Miguel was a little nervous about his
visit and felt the cigar would help keep his hands occupied.

Elaine was pacing before the windows when he entered;
Maggie was stuffing toast and jam into her plump face.
"Miguel," Elaine said, hurrying toward him. "Any news?"

"Yes," he said, "but I think you'd better sit down, my
dear."

"Why, what is it?" She fought back the tears. "Oh, Miguel,
not more bad news. I don't think I can take any more. Is it
about Jorge?"

He nodded gravely and felt her hand tighten on his arm.
"Sit down, Elaine. Please."

"Tell me."

He raised his arm and puffed on his cigar, dislodging the
grip she had on him. "Jorge gave himself up to the police late
last night. He's in jail."

"Oh, no."

Again Miguel nodded.

"But why was he arrested? Surely they don't think he was
responsible for that happened to Cynthia."

"They are holding him for questioning on that score. Unfortunately Jorge admitted to having your emerald necklace."

Elaine's hand went to her throat.

"See?" Maggie put in. "What did I tell you? I said that that
young scoundrel took the emeralds to finance his elopement.
Didn't I tell you, Elaine?"

Elaine swayed. "Please, Maggie. Don't." She watched Miguel's eyes, pleading for an answer she wanted to hear. "Did
he admit to stealing my necklace?" She held her breath.

"No. He said he found it in his satchel and didn't know how
it had gotten there."

Elaine let out her breath. "Thank God."

"That's what they all say," Maggie said. "Certainly you don't think he would admit to being a thief."

Elaine was finding it easier and easier to block Maggie's remarks out of her mind. There were moments, however, when she was tempted to tell the gossipy woman just what she thought of her, but after thinking about it nothing Maggie said or did mattered very much. Everyone knew her for what she was, so it didn't matter much what she did or said. Still, it was annoying at times.

"I want to see him," Elaine said, again gripping Miguel's arm.

"I'm afraid you can't," he answered.

"Why not?"

"Jorge gave specific instructions that he wanted to talk to no one but his attorney. He gave the police my name."

"Guilty conscience," Maggie interjected. "He can't face the kind people who were nice to him and who trusted him. Oh, he's guilty as sin." She made a face. "Just like that niece of mine. Imagine her calling to say she was taking off for Valdemossa—wherever that is—without so much as a by-your-leave. God only knows what kind of people she's hooked herself to this time. Sinful, just sinful." She bit into another piece of toast. "Where do you get this delicious jam, Elaine? It's simply heavenly. It reminds me of those lovely English jams I used to have sent to me from Dundee."

Elaine ignored her. "But surely Jorge will see me," she said to Miguel.

He shook his head. "He said specifically that he did not wish to see you." He saw the terrible hurt expression and softened it by saying, "He's very upset and confused right now, Elaine. Be patient with the boy. He's frightened and annoyed. He told me about the argument you and he had the other night, and he's still a bit angry with you."

Elaine's whole body sagged. "But I wish to explain to him."

"I think you'd best wait for a few days, my dear. Jorge is in a very foul mood. He has even refused my help after having sent for me."

Elaine straightened. "Well, I'm going to see him regardless," she said firmly. She started out of the room.

"I wouldn't advise that, Elaine," Miguel said, stopping her in her tracks. "I didn't want to tell you this, but Jorge gave the jailers very emphatic instructions concerning you."

Elaine turned slowly. Her face was a grayish color, her lips thin and colorless. "Yes?" she said, feeling every muscle in her body grow taut.

Miguel lowered his head and hesitated. He puffed deeply on his cigar and finally looked up at her. "Jorge told the jailer that he absolutely did not wish to see that *lying old woman*." He fanned out his hands in apology. "There you have it."

For a moment he thought Elaine was going to faint. He took a step toward her. She was breathing very hard and her grayish pallor had turned ash white. Her lips trembled and her eyes were dead. She raised her hand to ward off his assistance. "I'm all right," she said softly.

"A lot of good all those face lifts did," Maggie said spitefully. "You could have saved yourself a bundle of money."

Elaine couldn't control herself. She broke into deep, throaty sobs and turned to leave. Upon turning she collided with Greg just as he stepped into the room. He had a glass of whiskey in one hand.

"Still crying your eyes out over the little stud who abandoned you, Mother dear?"

"Greg," she stammered. "Excuse me," she said, skirting around him. The pains in her breast were worse than they had ever been. If only she could die now—this moment. She prayed she would.

"Elaine. Please, there is something else you must know," Miguel called.

Elaine kept her back to him. "No more, Miguel. Not now. I don't think I could take any more right now." Yet she found she could not move. A little voice told her to get it all over with. If there was more bad news, at least hear it all and be done with it. It was like the advice a physician once gave her: If you have several bad habits, break them all at once. Don't drag them out one at a time. It only prolongs the agony. She lifted her head high and stood with her back to them.

"There is no doubt now that Cynthia died at the hands of a person or persons unknown. The autopsy proved that it was no accident. Splinters of wood were found in the scalp. There was a deep puncture, like that made by a rusted spike or nail.

She'd been struck. She did not hit her head on the rocks as was first thought."

"Oh, my God," Elaine groaned, still unable to move from where she stood. It was as if she were standing in a vacuum.

Miguel took another drag on his cigar. He blew the smoke up into the air. "The autopsy showed also that Cynthia was four months pregnant."

Greg grunted and rattled the ice cubes in his glass. "Most likely by that Jorge fellow."

Elaine swayed dangerously on her feet.

Maggie slapped the top of the table. "Why that little devil," she said. "So that's why your young Casanova needed the jewels. But at the last minute he decided he'd rather have them to himself than waste them on a kid, so he knocked Cynthia on the head."

Elaine did not hear. Everything went black and she slumped to the floor before Miguel could reach her to break her fall.

ROD AND NANCY WERE SEATED BENEATH AN old olive tree. They stumbled upon a delightful little tavern tucked inside a courtyard and shaded by a cluster of gnarled olive trees. The proprietress was as old and gnarled as the trees. They had ordered glasses of the local wine and had settled themselves to wait for Paul and Lisa.

Rod hadn't spoken more than ten words since the kids had left. Nancy cocked her head at him and sipped her wine. "Did you give any thought to what I said the other morning?"

Rod nodded. "I don't want to talk about it."

"That's dumb. But regardless of how you feel, I think we should talk about it." Rod kept his eyes trained on his wine glass and tried to block out her words. He didn't want to discuss it, but he was beginning to know Nancy and he knew that the more he objected the more she'd insist.

Nancy put down her glass and said, "You still think it was wrong for me to try to do what I wanted to do with you the other night."

He started to object again but changed his mind. He nodded but said nothing.

"Why?"

He heaved a sigh and turned toward her. "It disappointed me."

"How?"

"It's not the kind of thing a nice girl like you should do," he said, again glancing around to make sure no one could hear them.

Nancy shook her head. "If you would throw away those stupid old-fashioned ideas about what nice girls should and shouldn't do, you'd be a much happier man, Rod. You're frustrating yourself, don't you see that?"

"It's immoral and it's illegal."

"Wow, are you messed up." She thought for a moment. "If it's so immoral and so illegal, how come you paid prostitutes to do it to you?"

"Please, Nancy, let's not pursue this."

Nancy wouldn't be put off. "Maybe if your wife—"

"Leave Helen out of this," he said sharply.

"Okay, okay. But believe me, Rod, what I wanted to do doesn't make me a bad girl. Everybody does it today." She thought again, then said, "Your wife couldn't have children, right?"

He hunched uncomfortably over the table to hide his discomfort. He nodded.

"But you still had sex with each other, right? Well, according to what I was told in Sunday school, the church frowns on that. It's called a sin of the flesh. Married couples are only supposed to have sex in order to increase and multiply. Sex for sex's sake is a sin. So if you think oral love is a sin, then so is fucking for the fun of it."

Rod wished she'd stop. His face was flushed and hot.

She patted his hand. "You're just a regular old fuddy-duddy, do you know that?"

"I admit that," he said, looking hurt. "That's the problem, I guess."

"It doesn't have to be. Look, if you didn't like what I did, just tell me to get lost and I won't see you again. Personally I think you were enjoying it. What I can't figure out is why you stopped me. Why didn't you just pretend I was one of those 'common ladies' you seem to put so much store in?"

"You are not one of them, that's just it," he said, again making sure they were not being overheard.

"We're back to that, huh? Nice girls don't do that, but it's okay for one of the so-called 'ladies of the evening' to do it. That's being hypocritical, and you know it."

"I just don't want to think about you like that. I like you too much. I just want to be friends and pretend it never happened."

Nancy laughed softly. "You are really a case, Rod. Am I to assume that you like being with me but you won't ever take me to bed again?"

"That's right." His face was screwed into tight determination.

"But suppose we see a lot of each other and we fall in love and get married? Then what am I supposed to do, just perform the way Helen did? Oh, no. Then I'd be the one who'd be frustrated and hypocritical."

"I see no danger in that. I like you, sure. In fact, I've grown very fond of you, but I have no intention of ever falling in love with you. I don't intend falling in love with anyone ever again." He felt the dampness on the palms of his hands and remembered how difficult it had been to put Nancy out of his mind the last day or two. He hadn't been able to. Even after that disgusting bout with Laura Verdugo he'd wanted to see Nancy and tell her about it. He felt he needed her understanding. He hadn't, of course, but the fact remained that he'd wanted it.

He took a deep breath. "Look, Nancy, you're trying to change me into something I'm not."

"That isn't true. I just want you to become aware of who and what you are. I don't want to change you. I wouldn't do that for anything. I like you too much to change you." She laid a gentle hand on his sleeve. "If you'd only be honest with yourself you would be a much happier man, Rod."

Rod felt himself weakening. "Oh, I don't know," he said. "I'm getting too old, I guess."

"Oh, so you're getting old. Who isn't? Is that what's back inside your head, that you're getting too old?" She saw the hurt and truth on his face. "You don't have to get old," she said quickly. "Just get it out of your mind and join with the young people and you'd be surprised how it strips off the years. Of course, if you enjoy getting off being old, then stay with your old ways and old ideas and get old with them. No one is really going to care. You older people put too much emphasis on youth and smooth skin. Younger people never think of things like that because they never think they'll get old." She gave a little laugh. "We all think we're going to die before we're thirty."

Out of the corner of his eye Rod saw Lisa coming toward them. He was glad for the excuse to change the subject. "Here's Lisa," he said as if speaking a word of warning.

Nancy shrugged.

"Where's Paul?" Rod asked as Lisa sat down on the wooden bench beside Nancy.

"He's coming. Man, what a bore. He sure loves to listen to himself talk," she said.

"I thought him very nice," Nancy said.

"Oh, he's all right, I guess. It's just that he's such a child."

"Child?" Rod laughed. "He's several years older than you are, young lady."

"You don't understand anything, do you?" she said hatefully. "I wasn't referring to years."

Rod felt stung, but tried not to show it. "Whatever you were referring to, Paul seems a lot more mature than you," he said sternly.

"There you go again," Lisa said. "You don't even know the guy and you're taking his part over mine."

"Oh, that isn't true and you know it," Rod answered, annoyed. Why did she always fight him at every turn? It was like reading a book with mixed-up pages . . . frustrating and lacking in sense.

Nancy toyed with her wine glass, knowing it would be wrong for her to get involved. She smiled at Lisa and said, "I thought you and Paul were hitting it off rather well."

"We were until he started sounding like him," she sneered, poking a thumb at her father.

Nancy was tempted to say that she rather liked the way Rod sounded, but Lisa would interpret that as everyone being against her, so Nancy kept still.

"Here comes Mr. Intelligence now," Lisa said, jerking her head toward where Paul was coming down the path.

Nancy waved at him when she saw him start to turn in the opposite direction. "Paul. Over here. Lunch."

She saw him hesitate, then turn toward them. Trotting

along behind Paul they saw the fat man and the flashy woman who'd ridden with them on the bus. They were holding hands; he kept reaching over and pecking her on the cheek every so often. They turned and started up another path toward the central part of town.

"That's cute," Nancy commented, smiling at Charlie and Sheila. "They must be terribly in love."

"They're a little old for that kind of love," Rod objected.

"How would you know?" Lisa snapped.

He ignored her. So did Nancy. "The only people who can judge a love affair are the people involved in it," Nancy said.

"Then I take it back," Lisa said spitefully, glaring at her father. "With as many as you've had you should be an expert."

"Lisa, stop it," he said sharply.

"Hi," Paul said, relieving the tension around the little wooden table. "I'm starved. What's for lunch? I hope not stuffed grape leaves."

"Stuffed grape leaves are a Greek dish. This is Spanish country, or didn't you know?" Lisa said.

Paul refused to be ruffled. "That's very intelligent of you, Lisa. I like intelligent people—even when they're stupid."

Lisa wouldn't be put off. "And an intelligent man on one level can be a fool on another."

Paul winked at Rod. "See, I told you she wasn't as dumb as she looks." He turned to Lisa. "Who said that? Or did you make it up yourself?" He knew she didn't like being teased, but he couldn't help it.

Lisa tossed her head and refused to answer.

"That was very good. I'll have to remember it."

"You aren't the only smarty in the world, you know," Lisa said.

"Gee, I hope not," Paul kidded. "I'd be terribly lonesome if I were."

"You could always live with tape recordings of your own speeches," Lisa said.

"Lisa, behave yourself," Rod warned as he sipped his wine.

Lisa turned to Nancy. "See what I mean, Nancy? Anyone can say anything they like, but when I open my mouth I'm reminded that I must behave myself. Paul insults me and gets away with it; I'm told to behave myself."

Paul looked genuinely contrite. "I didn't mean to insult you, Lisa. I was only joking; surely you know that."

"I don't know anything of the sort," she said, refusing to be placated.

"I'm sorry if you took me wrong, Lisa," Paul said. "I apologize if I hurt your feelings. I didn't mean to."

Lisa fumed for a second or two, then fumbled with the pockets of her jeans and said, "Oh, that's okay, I guess."

One could almost feel the tension lifting from the table.

Rod clapped his hands. "How about lunch, everybody? I don't suppose they have a menu, so we'll have to take pot luck."

"That's fine by me," Nancy said.

"Me too," Paul echoed. "Anything at this point in the game."

"I'm not too hungry," Lisa said. "I'll just have a glass of the wine."

Rod frowned at her. "You'll have a glass of milk or tea or something. No wine."

Nancy put her hand over his. "Let her have some wine, Rod. What can it hurt?"

"She's only fifteen."

"Surely if she wants wine she'll have it one way or the other. Isn't it better if she drinks a small glass of wine with you rather than with strangers?"

"Mother used to give me sips of hers at home," Lisa said as she lowered her chin and pouted.

"We'll share a glass," Paul offered. "I'm not all that nuts about wine, but I like a taste of it now and then."

Rod found himself outnumbered. Rather than chance antagonizing Lisa anymore, he relented. "Okay. But just one glass."

Lisa stuck out her lip. "I didn't ask for a whole bottle," she said petulantly.

To get out from under his daughter's angry glare, Rod motioned to the fat old woman in the apron who'd brought their wine. "Lunch," he called. "For three."

She made a gesture that showed she did not understand him.

"*La comida para tres,*" Paul said. He squirmed slightly when he noticed their admiring looks. "I brushed up on my Spanish before I got here." He made a face. "I'm lucky she understands Spanish; I understand they speak nothing but Majorcan out here in the country."

"Is there anything you don't know?" Lisa asked, lacing her words with sarcasm. She was peeved at herself for showing her admiration.

"Lots of things. I don't understand the binomial theorem or how to get those little fish eggs to distribute themselves evenly through tapioca pudding." He crinkled his nose at her. "And I don't understand why you're so angry at the world."

"Because I'm only a child of fifteen. If you don't believe me, ask my father."

A strained uneasiness settled over the table again. Nancy picked up her wine glass and watched Rod over its rim. He looked miserable; she wished she could touch his cheek and tell him she understood.

Rod sat there biting down on his lip. After a moment he said, "No one has to ask me, Lisa. The way you're behaving proves what a child you are."

A dark shadow came over Lisa's face. She slumped on the bench and went into a pout.

Nancy and Paul launched into small talk and tried to draw Rod and Lisa into their conversation. They succeeded with Rod; they failed with Lisa. The old woman served large, leafy salads and a loaf of crusty brown bread. When she placed a glass of wine in front of Paul, Lisa reached for it and emptied half the glass in one swallow. She banged the glass down on the table and gave her father a defiant look. He shook his head and began eating his salad.

"It's good," Nancy said. "Lisa, are you sure you don't want any?"

"No thanks." She picked up the wine glass again, but Paul took it out of her hand.

"Hey, remember, we were supposed to share this." He took a deep swallow, almost draining the glass, then handed it back to her with a smile. "Here, you can be the old maid," he said.

"What does that mean?" Lisa asked, refusing the glass.

"The one who takes the last of anything winds up an old maid. Haven't you ever heard that before?"

"That's dumb."

Paul took her hand. She pulled it away with such force that she almost toppled the glass. "So are you," he said. "Here, try some of my salad. It really is good."

Again Lisa shook her head. But Paul held out a forkful and said, "Open up. It's some kind of fish." It surprised him to see her obey.

"Not bad," Lisa said. She took Paul's fork and helped herself to some more. You could almost hear the sigh of relief as the tension eased again.

The talk grew less strained as Lisa and Paul started their own private battle over the salad. They wound up ordering a second one. Nancy and Rod had somehow gotten themselves embroiled in a discussion of the pros and cons of abortion. Nancy was for it; Rod definitely against.

"I agree with Rod," Paul said. "Abortion is just another form of murder."

"You would," Lisa said. "That's because you men don't have to bear children."

"Right, Lisa," Nancy said. "My mother once told me that if it were possible for babies to be borne equally between husband and wife, the man having the first child, the woman the second, there'd never be more than two children in any family."

Lisa laughed. Rod looked up in surprise. It was the first time he'd heard that delightful laughter in a long time. It sounded more beautiful than any melody he'd ever heard.

Rod smiled. "Your mother may have had a point."

Nancy looked wistful. "My mother is a sweet, dear woman, but I'm afraid she's the weakest woman I've ever known. She's a little like you, Rod, in that she lives in a sort of dream world."

"Dream world? Me? You don't know me very well." He knew what she was referring to and found he couldn't look at her. His face felt hot again.

She propped her arms on the table and leaned toward him. "I think I know you better than you know yourself. You want everything to be pretty and proper; you close your eyes to true reality."

Rod found himself fidgeting nervously. He toyed with his wine glass. It was empty, but he picked it up and pretended to drink from it.

"You're like a fly who's fascinated by the wispy beauty of the spiderweb—pretty but deadly. And once the fly is caught in that web it is the first to complain about the spider."

"I don't think I'm like that at all," Rod said, looking most uncomfortable. He glanced at his watch. "It's getting late. We'd better start back." He got to his feet.

"Hey, I haven't finished my salad," Paul complained.

"Men," Lisa huffed, looking up at her father. "Why are they always so good at criticizing but can't take criticism themselves?"

Nancy laughed. "That doesn't apply only to men, Lisa. Everybody is pretty much like that."

"Not me. I'm always being criticized."

"And you are always criticizing," Paul said, quickly finishing the last of the lettuce. He dabbed his mouth with his napkin. "Come on, lovely lady," he said, helping Lisa up. "Your dad's right. It's getting late and I still have several hours of practicing to put in today."

"Yes, my lord and master," she said. Lisa rolled her eyes at Nancy. "Men," she breathed. Nancy laughed.

JORGE SAT HUDDLED IN THE CORNER OF THE cell. It was hot and damp and he kept rubbing his palms on his pant legs to wipe off the clamminess. He wondered why Elaine hadn't come. Surely she'd heard by now that he was there, had given himself up, even though he didn't know what he was supposed to have done. He had explained about the necklace and knew that they did not believe him, but he had expected Elaine to come and straighten them out. Surely she knew he was not a thief. There had been too many opportunities for him to steal from her before this.

Was this how he was going to end up? All his life he had vowed he would not end as his father had, a prisoner behind bars, given a release only because the prison officials knew he was dying. They let him go home so that his family would have to bear the expense of burying him. If Elaine abandoned him, then he would share his father's fate. Everything would have been for nothing. All his clawing to climb out of that hole of poverty would have been wasted effort.

Elaine had given him up. He had to face that fact. He was

back where he had started, only worse. Without Elaine to intercede for him, he knew he would never be a free man again. He knew only too well the minds of the Majorcan officials. They hated the poor peasants who tried to better their lot by attaching themselves to the rich, especially the rich foreigners. They would have their revenge on such traitors. In their eyes, the poor of Majorca must remain poor. All of the officials considered themselves Spanish nobility who had conquered, and the poor of Majorca must bow to their will. What chance did any poor man have, except to leave the island and try to make something of himself outside, where he would always be a stranger? Some had left only to spend their lives trying to earn enough money to come back. Every true Majorcan wanted to be buried in the soil of his native land. Even those that left always took with them a small packet of Majorcan dirt to be sprinkled on their grave if they died elsewhere. It was a custom for the loyal Majorcan.

But he had no fear of being buried other than here. Now that he was alone he had no cause to think of anything but a life of darkness and confinement in a Majorcan prison. All his hopes and dreams had been shattered. He had tried so desperately to avoid all the problems of being poor. It had all been in vain. Everyone said he would wind up as his father had; he'd sworn that he never would.

Jorge slammed his fist against the rough stone wall. They had all been right after all, he cried to himself. Fate, they called it.

And if by some miracle his fate was changed and he was freed, what would he have without Elaine? Still nothing. He would end up like Alfredo Lorenzo—a pimp, a drug pusher, anything to keep from sinking into the slime of the gutter, to forget the stench of poverty in which he'd been baptized.

He covered his eyes with his hands and tried not to cry.

"Want your lunch, Jorge?" the jailer asked as he unlocked the door and carried a tray into the cell.

Jorge knew the man well. They had come from the same small town in Andraitx. He was a distant cousin of Dario's and knew all about Jorge's father. "Thank you, Carlos, but I am not really very hungry," he said, fighting back the tears of frustration.

"You must eat, Jorge." He swept the napkin away and put the tray down on the cot beside Jorge.

"I do not want it," Jorge said, pushing himself up from the cot and going to stand at the window. Outside the sun was making long, dim shadows on the courtyard floor, resembling specters with outstretched arms, beckoning to him.

"Then you will not mind if I eat it?" Carlos said as he began helping himself to the food. "It is good." He studied Jorge's back for a moment, then asked, "Do you want to talk to me, Jorge?"

"There is nothing to talk about, Carlos."

"Why not talk about the Cynthia Brandon woman, to start with. You did not have anything to do with that, did you? You know they found she was four months pregnant. Was the baby yours?"

Jorge turned sharply. Four months pregnant. She had told him she was three months pregnant. But what difference? Maybe it would help to talk about it. He nodded. "She told me it was my child," he said sadly. "Of course there is no way of knowing for sure. Cynthia was a very popular girl. I found out she liked sleeping around. But whether it was my child or not isn't important. The important thing is that I did not have anything to do with her death. We were going to run away that night and get married."

"So you took the emeralds?"

"I did not take the necklace," Jorge barked, spinning around. "I told you all that last night. I found that necklace in my satchel. When I saw in the papers that it was missing I came to turn it in."

"Just as your father tried to return the money he took from the Labraggio family?" Carlos smirked. "Why did you not just go back to the Brandon villa and give the emeralds back to Mrs. Brandon?"

Jorge's expression went sour. "Elaine ordered me out of the house. She said she never wanted to see me again."

"Elaine? Oh, yes, the other Brandon woman."

"Cynthia's mother," Jorge corrected. He did not find it painful to refer to Elaine as that. He thought he would at first, but it did not bother him at all now.

"Look, Carlos. Regardless of what I have been in my life, I have never stolen anything. You know that."

Carlos shrugged. "That may be, Jorge, but I am not the one you have to convince."

Jorge ran his hand through his hair. "I do not know why I

am being held here. Why do you not get in touch with Mrs. Brandon? She will clear me of this necklace thing. She knows I did not take it."

"If she knew that, then why is she not here to say so?"

"Perhaps no one has told her."

"Miguel Montoro said he was going up there to talk to her. That was hours ago."

Jorge's heart started to sink in his chest. It had been hours since he'd spoken with Miguel and told him to bring Elaine to see him. Why hadn't she come? Was she still angry? He sighed. He supposed she was. But it wasn't like Elaine to let her anger stand in the way of what was right. Perhaps she really did think him capable of stealing her jewels. He found it difficult to believe, but her absence was beginning to give him doubts.

He watched Carlos finish the last of the food. "Elaine didn't file any formal charges against me, did she?"

"No. All we know is that Montoro filed a report about a stolen necklace. Then we discovered that the Brandon girl was found dead. The autopsy showed that it was murder. According to the people at the house, the last person seen with her was you, and you had disappeared."

Jorge stared at him. "Who told you I was the last person seen with her?"

"Miguel Montoro, for one."

"But that isn't true. I saw Miguel at the house that night, and he said he thought Cynthia had gone off with Dario." Again he pushed his fingers through his hair. "This is crazy." His thoughts spun out of control. If Cynthia had gone with Dario, was it possible that Dario and she had had an argument and Dario had lost his temper? He had seen evidence of Dario's temper on several occasions. He was prone to flying off the handle. "No, that can't be," he said aloud.

"What can't be?"

"Oh, nothing. I was just thinking." He tried to get his thoughts straight. "Carlos, look. Would it be possible to put in a telephone call to Elaine Brandon?"

Carlos shook his head. "You know that isn't possible. It's against the rules. No phone calls other than to your lawyer, and that's limited to one call."

"Then how about taking a message for me?"

"You know I can't do that. If they thought I was being

friendly toward you or doing you favors they'd have my job."

"But if I got this emerald-necklace thing straightened out, then I'd be free to go, wouldn't I?"

Again Carlos shook his head. "There seems to be too much evidence building up against you on the murder. If some of that could be cleared up then yes, I suppose they'd let you go."

"Like what kind of evidence?"

"From what I heard, the people who were at the villa said they saw you and the girl having a heated discussion in the garden that night. Then they heard the other Brandon woman shouting at you. Next the emerald necklace disappeared, and you had it. Your lawyer claims you were the last one seen with the dead girl. Now if you could disclaim a lot of that with proof, then you might get yourself out of here until the trial."

"But how am I going to do that if I'm kept penned up in this lousy cell?"

"That's what you got a lawyer for, isn't it?"

Jorge agreed, but his heart wasn't in it. For some unknown reason he just didn't trust Miguel. He couldn't put his finger on it, but Miguel was dead set against his marrying Elaine. He didn't think Miguel meant him any harm, and yet there was a tiny nagging voice that kept telling him not to trust Miguel. Perhaps he'd made a mistake by calling Miguel. But that was the first name that had come to his head when the police told him he could call a lawyer. He had made a mistake. He should have called Elaine. He sighed. But perhaps Elaine would have hung up on him before he could explain. That is why she had not come to the jail. She was still upset about the scene she had stumbled upon between him and Cynthia.

He wished with all his heart she would get over it. She had to get over it, he thought as he pounded his fist against the wall.

THEY WOULD LEAVE TOMORROW, ROD DE-
cided as he stretched out on the bed. Tomorrow he and
Lisa would go home. There was no reason now to think
about taking a vacation with her. She didn't want to go anywhere with him, so it would be senseless to waste the time
and money convincing her that he loved her and wanted to
be with her.

He was too tired to think about it now. He had to get
some sleep. When he got home with Lisa he'd give it some
thought then. Right now he wanted to sleep.

Lisa eased her father's door open and looked into the bedroom. The shades were drawn, but there was enough afternoon light to see that Rod was sleeping. She closed the door
and tiptoed across the sitting room toward the door to the
hall. She opened and closed it without making a sound. Once
in the corridor she speeded up her escape, hurrying toward
the elevator and out onto the street.

The avenue was almost deserted. Everyone was sleeping
away the hotter hours of the day, she remembered, and
hoped against hope that she wouldn't have any trouble finding
a cab or a bus that would take her to the airport.

She was surprised that it had taken her so long to decide
to run away when her father told her he was going to lie
down. She'd found herself fighting with her conscience. She'd
been rude and spiteful toward him. Regardless of what he'd
done, he did not deserve to have his daughter prove her dislike in front of strangers. She had allowed her personal
feelings to show in front of others. That was unmannerly.
Her mother would have been ashamed of her for behaving
like such a spoiled little brat. She knew better. But she
hadn't been able to stop herself once she'd gotten started.
George had taught her to speak her mind. He had told her
never to be a phony, to say exactly what she wanted to say
just as long as it was the truth, regardless of whom it hurt.

At the time she thought it was good advice; now, she wasn't too sure.

She turned her head and saw Paul Verdugo, Jr., hurrying toward her. On blind impulse she started to run. Behind her she heard Paul call out and heard him start to run after her. She ran as fast as she could, but she knew by the sound of his footsteps that he was gaining on her.

"Hey," he said as he grabbed her arm and pulled her to a halt. He was panting. "What's with you? Why didn't you stop when I called to you?"

She let her anger show. "Did it occur to you that I might not have wanted to stop?"

"Why not? Since when are you avoiding me?"

"I thought you were supposed to be home practicing the piano."

"That's where I'm headed now. I ran into my dad and I had a second lunch." He saw the satchel she was carrying. "Where are you off to?" A look of annoyance creased his face. "Don't tell me you're going to that George character?"

She glowered at him. "I told you not to mention his name." She shifted the satchel from one hand to the other. "It's none of your business where I'm going." A taxi started toward them. Lisa raised her hand and hailed it.

"I guess you're right," Paul said, feeling helpless. "It's none of my business."

As the cab drew up to the curb, Lisa began fumbling in her bag. "Drat," she said as Paul opened the door for her. "I forgot to bring money. Could you loan me some, Paul? I'll send it back to you, really I will."

Paul eyed her for a moment. "On one condition," he said. "If you have coffee with me and tell me what's going on. As long as I'm expected to finance your little expedition I think I should know how my money is being spent."

Lisa felt trapped. She certainly couldn't go without money. She had no other recourse but to accept his offer. "Okay, but let's make it fast. I'm in a hurry," she said, glancing up and down the street, expecting at any moment to see her father rushing around looking for her.

Paul slammed the door of the cab and apologized to the driver. He handed him a bill and the taxi drove off.

"Now what's happening?" he asked as he led her toward a deserted little coffee shop that was directly across the street.

He ordered two coffees and sat down across from her at one of the sidewalk tables.

"Can't we sit inside?" Lisa asked, watching the street with apprehension.

The waiter overheard her as he put the coffee in front of them. "Sorry, *señorita,* but we are cleaning the floors." He gave a little bow of apology and walked away.

"Now where are you off to? Where's this George fellow you think you're so crazy about?" Paul asked.

"Barcelona, I think. The air fare isn't much. If you could lend me a hundred that would be plenty."

"Barcelona, you think! Don't you know?"

"I'm not positive, but I'm pretty sure I know where I can find him. If he's not there, then there are people there who know where to send me."

"How do you know he wants to see you?"

"Don't be stupid. Of course he wants to see me."

He leaned across the table, folding his hands in front of him. "Listen, Lisa. I'd be only too happy to give you the money if I thought it wouldn't bring any kind of harm to you, but I can't be sure of that."

"Harm? What kind of harm could it bring? I'm only going to Barcelona, not to the Black Hole of Calcutta."

"This isn't the United States, you know. Suppose you get yourself lost. Do you speak any Spanish?" He saw her lower her eyes. "I didn't think so."

"So what's the big deal?" she argued. "I've hitched around before, lots of times, both here and back home. I can take care of myself."

"I doubt that very much in view of what's happened to you already." She opened her mouth to argue, but he hurried on. "You get mad when your dad calls you a kid, a child, and then you turn around and start acting like one. Why don't you listen to him and let him take you back home where you belong?"

"I've gone that route. I don't have a home anymore."

Paul just looked at her.

She let out an exasperated little breath and leaned back in her chair. "Okay, so I'll tell you." She rushed through her father's indiscretions with Rose Mallory and her mother's fatal accident. "He killed my mother just as sure as if he'd pushed that car into the tree."

Paul shook his head. "Your poor father."

"Poor father! What about poor me!" she shouted, jabbing a thumb into her chest.

Paul looked sad. "Okay, you lost your mom. I agree, that's a bummer. But think what your father's lost . . . not only his wife but his daughter. That's a double bummer."

"He doesn't care about me. All he cares about are those whores he likes to shack up with."

"That's why he flies to Majorca or runs after you whenever you disappear. He doesn't care, huh? I think he cares more than you know."

"Believe me, if I were of age he wouldn't lift a finger to help me. He thinks it's his parental duty, so he does it."

"I can tell by the way he looks at you that it's much, much more than that, Lisa. Your father loves you very much, and you hurt him every chance you get. Don't you think he's suffered because of what happened to your mother? Was he heartless and uncaring, as you claim he is, before the accident?"

Lisa refused to answer.

"I thought as much." He smiled at her. "I'm just as guilty as you for putting the blame on someone else rather than on myself. I really hated my mother for keeping me and my father apart. But she was smart enough to make sure we were kept apart until I was old enough to see things for myself. When I was fifteen I must have run away at least a dozen time, hoping to get over here to Majorca somehow. My mother had custody of me then, and she, like your dad, always brought me home. Wait a couple of years, Lisa. Believe me, things will seem different then. You're running around half-cocked, looking for someone to latch on to, because you really want your father—the father you had when you were a little girl. This George guy isn't the answer. None of them will be the answer. You'll learn that in time."

Lisa tightened her lips. "Is the lecture over? Are you going to lend me the money, or aren't you?" she asked, pushing back the chair.

"Do you have any relatives in the States?"

"Yes, why? I have an aunt in Ohio."

"Okay. I'll give you the money if you promise me you will go home to your aunt, but I won't finance your trip to meet George whatever-his-name-is. He smells like bad news."

"Well, if you won't give it to me, then I'll find someone who will." An English-looking tourist in a bowler hat and dark suit happened to be strolling past the café. Lisa called to him. "Hey, mister. Can I speak with you a moment?"

Paul stayed put and let her approach the man. He saw them whispering together and then saw the horrified look on the man's face. Paul quickly went over to them and took Lisa forcefully by the arm. To the man he said, "Excuse her, mister. My sister." He pointed to his head and made tiny circles. "Just a little crazy." He pulled her back into the café and pushed her into her chair. "Very good," he said to her as she sat there pouting. "You hate your father for picking up women like that; is that why you're trying to turn into one?" He grinned at her. "You're sick, do you know that?"

"I don't need your money," she spat. "If that man wasn't interested, I'm sure there are lots who will be. Men like young virgins, I hear."

"So you're a virgin," he said, arching his brows. "I thought as much."

"I've been around," Lisa said, looking contrite.

"Not as much as you would like people to believe. Ah, come on, Lisa. Why don't you get rid of that chip on your shoulder and start being the girl you want to be? Why throw your life away just because you want to spite your father? It isn't his life you will be ruining, it will be your own."

"You should be a preacher. You sure like to talk, but that's all it is, talk, talk, talk."

"Okay, if that's the way you feel. Go ahead, become a whore or a dope addict or whatever you feel you are compelled to become." When he saw her hesitate he said, "Go ahead. I'll give you some money so you won't starve, but I won't pay for your fare to meet George."

"Lisa!" Rod came running across the street.

Lisa shook her head in disgust.

"Hi, Mr. Shepherd. I just bumped into Lisa when I was on my way home and we decided to have some coffee. Want some?"

"No, thanks, Paul." Rod's face was lined with worry. He saw the stachel sitting alongside Lisa's chair. "I woke up and found you gone. I thought—"

"You thought right," Lisa said. "Paul's lying for me. I was on my way to the airport, but I found I didn't have any money. I asked Paul to lend me some." She gave Paul a weak smile. "Thanks for trying to cover for me, but there's one thing I don't do and that's lie. A friend of mine once told me to tell the truth regardless of whom it hurts."

One look at Rod's face told Paul exactly whom she'd hurt. His eyes were so pained it hurt Paul to look at them.

Lisa stood up. "Paul wouldn't loan me any money, so I was going to come back to the hotel anyway."

Paul thought of the incident with the Englishman, but when he saw Lisa's face he knew she was telling the truth. She really had intended going back to the hotel.

"Well," Paul said, "I've got to go home and practice. I'll be in touch."

"How about having dinner with us tonight, Paul? Nancy is joining us. What do you say?"

"Let me check and see what they have planned at home. I'll call you later if that's okay."

"Sure, the invitation is open."

Paul waved as he walked away. He hesitated and turned back. He didn't know what possessed him, but he came directly up to Lisa and kissed her square on the mouth. Lisa's eyes flew wide open. Rod grinned and looked the other way. "That makes up for this morning," Paul said. He gave her a quick two-finger salute and walked away.

THE AFTERNOON SUN THREW A STAB OF LIGHT across the floor of Jorge's cell. He judged from the diagonal slant of the sun's ray that the afternoon was well on its way toward evening. He'd slept, but it had been a troubled sleep. Elaine's face kept drifting past his eyelids, a haughty, angry face. He supposed he couldn't blame her for being angry with him. Too bad she had stumbled upon him and Cynthia at the end of their conversation. Why hadn't she heard all of it? Better still, why had she heard any of it? If she had only listened to him none of this would have been happening. He would have explained why he had to marry Cynthia;

Elaine would have understood. She might even have come up with a solution.

In that restless sleep he had heard Elaine's voice cruelly accusing him of killing her daughter. Surely she didn't believe him capable of such a thing. Of course they hadn't known each other all that long, so perhaps she did think him capable of murder. Miguel had told her by now the results of the autopsy. She knew Cynthia had been pregnant. That's why she was refusing to have anything more to do with him. He too had been guilty of lying, remembering he had told her he'd never slept with Cynthia. They had both played their games of deceit, so the score should be even. It wasn't, however. Elaine was a woman, and lying was an expected part of a woman's nature; it was unforgivable for a man.

"You have a visitor," Carlos said as he unlocked the cell door.

Jorge jumped to his feet. "Elaine." But it wasn't Elaine. When Carlos stepped aside to let the lady enter, it was Carlotta. Jorge's disappointment must have shown; Carlotta wore an injured expression. "Ah, Carlotta," he said, hugging her tight. "It is good of you to come."

"Five minutes," Carlos said. "I'll let you alone." He relocked the cell door. "Rattle the door if you want to leave earlier." He disappeared into the shadows of the corridor.

"You were expecting the Brandon woman?" Carlotta asked. "I had hoped."

"If it weren't for her you would not be in this trouble."

Jorge turned from her. "None of this is Elaine's fault."

"Then why did she not come and say it was not you who took her precious emeralds?" She wrapped her arms around him and pressed against his back. "Forget her, Jorge. You know that I love you. I will make you happy."

"I can't forget her, Carlotta. I'm sorry. I love you too, in my way, but I think I love Elaine more." He turned and faced her. "I do not mean to hurt you, but I can't help myself. I am in love with Elaine."

"You are in love with Elaine's money, nothing more. It has blinded you. She dangled wealth and luxury before your peasant nose and you got the smell of it in your nose and you cannot shake free of it." She was angry, but she did not care.

"You may be right," Jorge admitted. "I do not know. To be honest, I admitted to you earlier that I am attracted to her wealth, but I do not think it is just that. Elaine is a very fine, beautiful woman."

"Yes, a fine, beautiful woman who is old enough to be your mother. Oh, Jorge, I do not wish to hurt you, but can you not see that you are looking for a rich mother and not a wife." She looked pleadingly up into his eyes. "You love her as you would love your mother if she were still alive."

Jorge's expression went stern. "I do not want to fuck my mother," he said, pushing her away. He rubbed the back of his neck to relax himself. "Oh, I am sorry, Carlotta. I am upset and disappointed."

"That is all right, Jorge. I guess I can understand. I just wish you had never met these Brandon women."

"I am not sorry. Even with all these troubles I do not resent having met Elaine. She is worth the misery I am suffering."

"You mean she *was* worth the misery. I believe she has abandoned you, Jorge. I think you should face that fact and stop hoping for the impossible." She smoothed back his hair and smiled at him. "But I did not come to talk about Elaine. I came to see if there was anything you needed, anything I could do for you."

"No, nothing, Carlotta. I have already spoken to a lawyer. He said he will do everything he can to get me released."

"Money," Carlotta said. "I have a little. Perhaps a bribe."

Jorge smiled kindly. "No, I think not. The charges against me are too serious to be bought off. I asked Miguel about that. But I appreciate it, Carlotta." He gave her a brotherly kiss. He thought for a moment, then said, "There is one thing you can do, if you will."

"Anything."

"Ask Dario to come to see me. There is something troubling me about him."

"About Dario?"

"Yes. I know it is crazy, but somehow I think Dario is more involved in this matter than I thought."

"What are you saying?"

"I know I should not be suspicious, but I was told that Cynthia went off with Dario that night. Miguel said he thought he saw them leave the villa together. Dario told me that he never saw Cynthia. Someone is not telling the truth. I want to confront Dario with it."

"If Dario said he did not see the girl, then you can believe him. Dario does not lie, especially to his best friend."

"I know, I know," Jorge said. "It is just that I am all mixed up and perhaps Dario can help shed some light on the subject. Will you ask him to come to see me? But please do not tell him why."

Carlotta hesitated. "All right. I will try to find him for you."

"Try the training area. He is most likely working out on his bicycle. If he is not there, he may be at Elaine's villa. He wanted to marry Cynthia, you know."

"Yes, I suspected as much."

Jorge shook his head. "Knowing Dario's terribly blind temper I was wondering if he and Cynthia had quarreled . . ." He let his sentence trail off. "No, I do not think Dario would do anything to hurt her."

"And he certainly would not let you take the blame for it if he had," Carlotta said. "Cynthia Brandon," she said bitterly. "I wish she had never been born."

PAUL JR. SAT HUNCHED OVER THE KEYBOARD working on left-hand octaves. He was so engrossed in the exercises that he did not hear his stepmother come into the music room. She stood in the doorway for a moment, then came up behind him and put her hands on his shoulders.

Paul jumped. "Oh, Laura. You startled me. I didn't hear you come in."

"You know what they say about all work and no play, Paul."

He smelled liquor on her breath. It was overpowering.

"Why don't you and I have a little drinkie together before dinner," Laura said. Her words slurred together. She was quite drunk, Paul decided.

"I really have neglected the piano too much already today," he said, returning to his exercises.

Laura reached down and lifted his hands from the keyboard. "But Laura is lonesome. She wants some company. Besides, I have something to show you."

"What?"

"It's a surprise. Your father didn't think we should show you, but I got him to change his mind."

Paul let himself be pulled up from the piano bench. "Dad did mention something about a surprise at lunch. He wouldn't say what, though. But shouldn't we wait for him to get home?"

"No, now. I want to show you now." She held tight to his hand and pulled him across the room and into the little sitting room on the other side of the foyer. She fumbled with the piece of molding and the panel slid open. *"Voilà,"* she said with a flourish. "Enter, proud gladiator. Welcome to the arena."

Paul looked at her apprehensively.

"Come. Your surprise is in here," Laura said as she stepped through the open panel.

Paul hesitated for a moment, then followed her. He looked around the room, not understanding what was going on. "What is this? Why the secret room?"

Laura touched a button and the panel slid closed. "You are now my prisoner, young knight, and you must do everything I command."

Paul was nervous and decided he'd best humor her. It was obvious that she was very drunk. "I am at your service," he said, trying to smile.

"How about a little smoke?" Laura said as she picked up two neatly rolled cigarettes.

"I don't smoke, thank you."

"But this is very special grass. All the way from Jamaica." She handed Paul one of the cigarettes. He waved it aside. "You do smoke dope, don't you?"

"Sure," he said, trying to sound worldly. "But I never touch it if I have work to do. I find it interferes with my fingering."

"But you're finished for today. Relax and forget about that old piano." She struck a match to her cigarette and sucked the smoke deep into her lungs. She held it for a long time, then exhaled slowly. She extended the cigarette to Paul. Again he declined. "How are we going to show you your surprise if you aren't relaxed?"

Paul glanced toward the closed panel. "Perhaps we'd better wait until Dad comes home."

"He knows where to find us. He should be along soon. I'm sure he won't mind if we start without him." She walked over to him and started to unbutton his shirt. Paul clutched at his shirt front. "We've got to get comfy first," Laura said, struggling to get the buttons undone as Paul tried to push her hands away.

"Please, I think we should wait for Dad," Paul protested. He buttoned the buttons as fast as Laura unbuttoned them.

"Oh, don't be such a little prude," Laura pouted as she gave up her struggle and dropped onto the divan. She pressed several buttons on the control box.

Paul spun around as the room went dark and a movie flickered on a screen that appeared from nowhere. It took a few seconds before everything registered. "Good God," he breathed. On the screen two women, naked, were servicing an extremely well-endowed youth with their mouths. One was licking the guy's testicles; the other was moving her mouth up and down the length of his cock. Paul took a couple of steps backward and collided with a chair. He moved back with such force that the chair seat connected with the backs of his legs, shoving him off balance. He fell backward into the chair. Laura pounced on him like a tigress on her prey. Before he knew what was happening she'd plastered her mouth over his and pushed her tongue into his throat. Her hands dug into his crotch and squeezed the mound of cock and balls.

"Good God," Paul breathed under her mouth. Then with a forceful shove he toppled her down onto the floor and raced toward the panel. He pounded on it, trying not to look at the erotic pictures that showed so vividly under the ultraviolet lights. There was the taste of bile in his mouth. His stomach wanted to vomit. Laura was on his back, ripping at his clothing, pinching his nipples. He shot his elbow hard into her ribs. She doubled up with a groan of pain. He didn't care if he'd hurt her or not. He had to get out of that room. He felt so dirty and sick that all he could think about was escape. He remembered the little control box on the table next to the divan. He hurried toward it and began pushing all the buttons, banging them hard with the flat of his hand. Lights went off and on, the fuck-movie flickered on and off, on and off, the screen started to move, stopped, then started to move again. Paul kept his eyes glued to the panel. It finally opened just as Laura straightened up and started toward him again. There was a wild look in her eyes and she was grinning like a starving vampire. He didn't know what possessed him. If he had been in a rational frame of mind he would never have thought of doing such a thing, but he was far from rational. The minute she got close enough his hand slashed out and he slapped her as hard as he could across the face. "Pig," he shouted, his face red with rage. "You fucking pig."

He stumbled blindly out of the room and ran as fast as he could toward the front door. He could hardly see the knob through his tears, but he groped for it, then threw open the door and raced out into the dying afternoon.

He didn't know where he was going. All he knew was that he had to get away . . . as far away as he could. A single thought kept echoing inside his head. It was his father's voice saying, "Laura and I have a surprise for you. We thought tonight would be a good time to show it to you."

That sick sonofabitch, he thought. That horrible, sick bastard. This was the father he'd longed to be with all these years. His mother must have known. That was why she'd tried to keep them apart. That was why she'd sent him away so early in their marriage. Oh, God, he thought, shaking his head. Where could he go? What was he going to do? He didn't have answers to those questions, but he knew one thing: He would never go back to that house ever again, not even to get his clothes. He never wanted to see his father again as long as he lived.

He found himself at the end of the street. How far he'd run he didn't know. He leaned against a lamppost and found that he was panting heavily. His heart was pounding, tears were streaming down his face. Several passersby glanced at him with queer expressions. He pulled out his handkerchief and wiped his face. There was sweat on his brow and his hands were trembling like leaves.

He knew he must look bad. His shirt was torn in two places and his back pants pocket was ripped. He took his wallet out of his pocket and thumbed through the bills. He had enough money, thank God. He'd get a hotel room and try to calm himself down.

"Hotel," he said, and suddenly he thought of Rod and Lisa Shepherd. Mr. Shepherd was a good sort of man. He'd help, Paul thought. He was sure of it.

He straightened his clothing as best he could and started toward Rod's hotel.

"What in Christ's name happened to you?" Rod asked as he stared at the young man standing outside his hotel-suite door. "You look like you got mugged in the subway." He was smiling.

Paul looked embarrassed. "May I come in, Mr. Shepherd? I'm afraid I've had a bit of trouble."

"Come in, lad," Rod said, letting his smile fade when he saw the serious, hurt look on Paul's face. "Come in." He motioned toward a chair. "Sit down and I'll get you a drink. You look white as a sheet."

"No drink, thanks," Paul said, falling into the chair and wiping his hand over his face. "A glass of water would help if it's not any trouble, sir."

"No trouble at all." Rod went into the little kitchenette and brought back a glass of icewater. "Now what's this all about? What happened?"

Paul gulped down the water and handed the glass back to Rod. "I've had a little trouble with my stepmother." He swallowed the lump in his throat. "I'm afraid I hit her." The tears sprang into his eyes again.

"Hit her? Why? What happened, Paul?"

"I couldn't help myself, Mr. Shepherd. She was horrible. She was all over me like a cat in heat. I couldn't get away from her. I slapped her as hard as I could. I didn't know what I was doing." He tugged at his torn shirt. "She had me locked in this room downstairs."

The arena, Rod thought with horror. Oh, Christ, she really did try it with her own stepson. He was afraid she might.

"They have all kinds of pornographic stuff in there. I couldn't get out. She kept clawing at me." He made a vague gesture toward his torn clothes. "I kept pounding the buttons on this control-box thing until I finally got the door open. I just ran out. I hadn't any place to go. Then I thought of you. I had to talk to someone."

Rod put his arm around the boy's shoulder and seated himself on the arm of the chair. "You did right, Paul. I'm glad you came to me. I've seen that room."

Paul looked up through his tears. "She showed you?"

Rod smiled. "Yes, I had a pretty similar experience last

night when you and Lisa were in the den dancing. I'm afraid I didn't get violent, though."

Paul lowered his head. "I couldn't help it. It was disgusting. She was drunk, of course, but that doesn't excuse anything."

Rod nodded. He thought for a moment. "Was your father there?"

Again Paul looked up in surprise, then looked down again and shook his head. "No, but he knew about it. That's the filthy part. He's as sick as Laura. What kind of man is he, anyway?"

"Well, you must remember, Paul, you're practically a stranger to him. He really doesn't look upon you as a son."

"But surely he wasn't intending to participate."

"No, I don't think so. From what your father hinted at last night, I got the impression that he likes to watch. A voyeur, I think it's called."

Paul grimaced. "Ugh," he said with a shiver. "That's the sickest thing I've ever heard. His own son."

"I don't think he looks on you as a son, merely as a sex partner for his wife."

Rod patted his back. "These things happen, Paul. I'm just sorry it had to happen to you. I was tempted to warn you about Laura last night. I knew it was just a matter of time before she tried to seduce you."

"Seduce. Hell, it was rape, pure and simple." Suddenly he started to laugh. It was an uncontrolled, almost hysterical kind of laughter. "I bet I'm the only guy in history who was raped by his own stepmother."

Rod smiled. "I doubt it, Paul. You'd be surprised what goes on in this old world of ours. I know of a couple back home in Ohio who make it a regular practice to carry on with their own kids. They have two girls and a boy and they all participate with Mommy and Daddy."

"That's sick."

"Sure it is. But from what I understand their parents were playing around with them when they were little tiny kids, so you can't blame the kids. They just don't know any better. No one ever told them it was incestuous and not only wrong but illegal." Rod stood up and went toward the window. He looked out, struggling for something to say that would remove the tension Paul was under. He glanced at the boy, sitting with his head in his hands. "I think you'd better stay here to-

night, Paul. There's room in my bed, if you don't mind sharing." He laughed and held up his hands, palms open. "I
promise I won't make a pass."

Paul grinned. "Why not? Everyone else has."

They both started to laugh. The tension was broken.

"Hey, we've got to do something about those clothes of
yours," Rod said, noticing the rips and tears.

Paul fumbled in his pocket for his wallet. "I have money.
Is there a men's store around that you know of?"

"There's one just around the corner. Come on. We'll pick
you up some duds and then we'll all have dinner together." He
put his arm around Paul's shoulders and shook him gently.
"Put it out of your mind, son. Tomorrow things will look a
lot different."

"I'm never going back there," Paul said, his head bowed.
"Never." He clenched his fists and tried to keep himself from
breaking into tears. He didn't succeed.

Rod pulled him close. "Go ahead and cry it out, Paul.
That's always the best way."

Paul let himself go. After a moment he eased himself out
of Rod's embrace. "I feel like such a stupid kid," he said,
wiping his eyes on the sleeve of his shirt.

"There's nothing stupid about crying. I've done a hell of a
lot of it myself lately."

Paul looked at him, and he could tell that Rod was thinking of Lisa. Everyone had their own problems, he thought.
He guessed that no one ever escaped them.

"ELAINE," MAGGIE SAID, LOOKING UP FROM
her collection of hatpins. "You look simply dreadful in that
black dress. It washes you out. My dear, it adds twenty years
to your age."

"I am in mourning, Maggie," Elaine said sadly.

"Well, you look dreadful. I don't care who died, I certainly
would not make myself ugly for a corpse."

"Maggie, please. You're being thoughtless."

"Thoughtless? Me? Heaven forbid, Elaine. How can you say that about me? I'm the most thoughtful person in the world. I never think about myself. I'm ashamed of you for saying such a thing."

"Yes, all right, Maggie. I'm sorry." When would this ridiculous woman leave? she wondered. But from the looks of things and the way Maggie talked, she was afraid she was stuck with Maggie Montgomery for quite a while. "They've suggested that the funeral be held tomorrow," Elaine said as she stared out at the garden and remembered the last time she'd seen Cynthia was the night in the gazebo.

"Funeral? Oh, Cynthia's. Well, isn't it a bit quick?" She polished the stone of one of her pins. "I do hope you don't expect me to attend, Elaine. Funerals are always so depressing. I just couldn't bring myself to go. Besides, you'd most likely expect me to wear black." She made a cute face. "But then I don't mind wearing black. In fact I look rather good in it; not like you. I must say, Elaine, that dress is positively horrible."

It wasn't a particularly attractive dress, Elaine knew, but she didn't care. Since resigning herself to the loss of Jorge, she didn't care about anything. The cancer pains had become much more severe in the last few days. It was as if Jorge had kept her suspended in a dream world where reality had no place. Now the dream was over and the hard, cold light of actuality had taken its place. She had had her taste of happiness, brief as it had been. At least she could be thankful for that. Unfortunately the taste had only whetted her appetite.

She caught a reflection of herself in the mirror as she went toward the window. Maggie was right; she did look dreadful. She looked as old and unattractive as she felt. As she peered at herself she suddenly noticed a lot of Cynthia in her face. Cynthia, dead. It didn't seem possible. The spoiled little girl she'd tried to provide for and protect would be lying in a grave tomorrow. There was so much she wished she could change now. A tear ran from the corner of her eye. She let it stream down her cheek unchecked. Despite the problems she had had with Cynthia, she felt genuinely grieved at her death. It wasn't right for one so young and beautiful to be denied life. Regardless of the differences they'd had, it wasn't

fair that she should continue to live and Cynthia die. She
wished with all her heart that they could trade places.

"Of course I could always wear white," Maggie mused.
"White is always acceptable at funerals, isn't it, Elaine?" She
didn't wait for an answer. "Yes, white. I bought a new
sheath before leaving Paris. It will be perfect. And I saw the
most divine wide-brimmed hat in one of the boutiques in
Palma. Very wide-brimmed, darling, so I needn't wear a veil.
The faces of mourners must be covered, you know. People
so like to gawk at mourners' faces. I suppose there will be
simply scads of people there . . . photographers and all.
Dario will escort me, I'm sure. I must telephone him." She put
her hand to her mouth "Oh, dear. The bicycle races. When
are they? Tomorrow? No, I think the next day. It would be
a pity if I missed Dario's races. He looks so cute in those
little tight shorts. He has the most divine legs." She got up,
leaving her hatpin collection on the table. "Yes, first telephone
Dario and then I'll have your chauffeur drive me into Palma
for that hat." She hesitated. "I guess I should call Nancy too.
After all, she and Cynthia were in school together. Strange,
Nancy hasn't made a condolence call. Of course, what with
her gallivanting all over the countryside with her weird
friends, she most likely doesn't know. But then she hated
Cynthia, you know. Simply hated her. That's why Nancy
refused to stay here with you. She couldn't tolerate the
sight of Cynthia. Jealous, I suppose, what with Cynthia having
all that beauty and money and Nancy so plain and poor.
Wicked girl, that Nancy. I don't know why I am so kind to
her."

At the door she met Miguel. "Can't stop to chat now,
Miguel. I simply have a million things to do."

Elaine extended her hand to Miguel as Maggie fluttered
away in a trail of pink chiffon.

"Any news, Miguel?"

He held both her hands in his. "I just came to discuss the
funeral arrangements. I assume you want Cynthia buried
here?"

"Yes," she said sadly. "I've already spoken to the church.
There is more than enough room in the crypt I bought last
year for myself."

"Now, now. Let's not talk about you dying. That won't
be for a long, long time."

"You know better than that, as do I." She withdrew her hands from his. Trying to sound unconcerned, she asked, "What of Jorge? Have you talked to him again?"

"No, but I'm afraid things do not look good for the boy." He sighed. "The laws here are so strict. There is very little I can do for him right now. Perhaps when the excitement of the affair dies down a little, the officials might relax the rules a bit. For the present he will have to stay in jail. I tried my best to have him released into my custody, but they would not hear of it. They would not even turn your emerald necklace over to me. I explained that you would like to have it returned to you, but they said it is material evidence and must remain under their protection until after Jorge's trial."

"Trial?"

"Well, not a formal trial as you have in America. It will be like an inquest. You will not have to appear. I will represent you."

"But I want to appear. I want to do everything I can to clear Jorge's name. He didn't take my necklace. I'm sure of that."

"Then how did it come into his possession?"

Elaine found she had no answer for that. "If I could only talk to him."

"But you can't. He won't see you."

The butler came to the door and waited until he caught Elaine's eye. "Pardon, *señora,* but there is a young lady here to see you. She says she is looking for Señor Avisa. When I told her Señor Dario was not here she asked to speak with you."

"Show her in here, Jaime."

A moment later Carlotta walked into the room. She eyed Elaine coldly. How could Jorge claim to love this woman? She was old and plain. She glanced at the opulence of furnishings. She had been right; it was the woman's money Jorge loved.

"Yes?" Elaine asked.

Carlotta held her head at a defiant angle. "I am called Carlotta," she said haughtily. "I have come only because Jorge has asked me to."

Elaine caught her breath. "You are a friend of Jorge's? You have seen him?"

"I have seen him," Carlotta said.

"Is he well?"

"He is well." Her voice was like ice crystals. "He wanted me to deliver a message to Dario. I understand he is not here. I was wondering if you knew where I could find him." Carlotta had not intended asking to see Elaine Brandon, but her curiosity about the woman had gotten the better of her and she found she could not leave the villa without at least getting a look at her rival. Now that she saw her she knew she had no competition as far as the woman herself was concerned. How she could compete with the woman's wealth was something else. She would find a way, she decided.

"No, I'm afraid I do not know where Dario is. Perhaps at the race course."

"I have been there. Do you expect him?"

"No." Elaine shivered slightly under the girl's cold, appraising stare.

"If I may, I would like to leave a message for him if you see him." Carlotta stared directly into Elaine's eyes until Elaine looked away. Ah, she was weak as well, Carlotta thought. All the better.

"Of course," Elaine answered meekly. Who was this girl, she wondered. A friend of Jorge's. She was so young, so beautiful. Yet there was a hard quality about her. She seemed so coarse and callous. There was hatred smoldering in those dark, lovely eyes. What had Jorge told her? She was tempted to ask, but she knew the girl would give her no satisfaction. "What is it you want me to tell Dario?"

"Jorge would like to speak to him."

"Speak to him?" Miguel asked. "I understood he wanted to see no one."

"He wishes to speak with Dario."

Elaine brightened under the spark of hope. "Perhaps I could speak with Jorge," she said.

"No," Carlotta snapped. "You stay away from Jorge. You are bad for him. If it weren't for you he would not be in the trouble he is in. Stay away from him."

"Did Jorge tell you to say that?" Elaine asked, straightening up under the onslaught. She saw the way the girl's eyes softened when she spoke Jorge's name. She was in love with him. Elaine was her rival. She would not let herself be browbeaten. "I demand to know," Elaine said in a firm even voice. "Did Jorge say he did not wish to speak with me?"

Carlotta lowered her chin, looking like a young bull getting ready to charge. "Stay away from him," she threatened.

Elaine refused to be intimidated. "But did he say he refused to see me?"

"Yes," Carlotta shouted. "He said he would kill you for all the trouble you have caused him," she lied. The lie embarrassed her. She turned quickly and ran from the room.

"Well," Miguel breathed. "Quite a little spitfire." The tenseness began to leave him. "There, there," he said, seeing Elaine's misery. "It is all for the best, my love. Forget Jorge. For your sake. I will do everything I can for him, but you must put him completely out of your mind."

The tears came in a flood. "I have tried, Miguel. I have honestly tried, but I cannot. I love him, regardless of how he feels about me."

She felt his arms go about her and did not fight to get away. She needed a man's strength and leaned against him. "If you would only let me, Elaine, I would make you forget your love for Jorge." He smoothed her back with his hands. "We were happy once, Elaine. We can be again. Marry me. We will go back to that quiet hotel in Cannes where we spent our first honeymoon. We will forget the villa and all the unhappiness it reminds you of. We'll sell it and move away."

She found she felt uncomfortable in his arms. His body did not have the youthful firmness of Jorge's body, and there was a lingering odor of stale cigar smoke on his breath. She could never love Miguel. She doubted now that she had ever loved him. She wanted the fresh, clean smell of Jorge, the smooth, muscled tone of his body. She patted Miguel's chest and moved away from him.

"No, Miguel," she said. "A long time ago I made a promise to myself that I would never go back to something I once had. Going back was just another way of escaping; it accomplishes nothing." A pain shot through her. She gasped and clutched herself.

Miguel took hold of her. "The pains again?"

Elaine waited for it to pass, then nodded. "I think I should lie down for a while. They are coming more frequently of late." She smiled, thinking back. "When Jorge was with me I hardly noticed them at all."

"Marry me again, Elaine. I will make you forget the pains."

"No, Miguel. I know that I am going to die soon. If I cannot die in Jorge's arms than I prefer to die alone."

Greg stood framed in the doorway. He clapped his hands when Elaine finished her little speech. "Very dramatic, Mother. You should have gone on the stage. Of course you've had a lot of practice during your courtroom scenes. When, may I ask, is this tearful day going to be?"

Elaine frowned at him as he staggered over to the couch and threw himself down on it.

"You've been drinking," she said.

"Not this time, Mother dear. Just a few joints and a pill or two. It makes everything rosier." He giggled like a schoolgirl.

"Really, Greg, you must start taking better care of yourself."

"Why?" He swung his feet off the couch and hunched forward. "Who's to care? The only one who ever cared was Cynthia, and she's dead." His expression was sad, yet he kept on smiling.

Elaine went over to him and put her arm around his shoulder. "I know how much you cared for Cynthia. You shouldn't be ashamed to show your grief."

He shoved her away. "Grief?" He threw back his head and laughed. "I don't grieve for Cynthia. She only pretended to like me. I found out she despised me as much as you do."

"Greg, what are you saying? Cynthia was extremely fond of you, as I am."

"Lies. All lies. Just like all the lies you told about me when they kicked me out of school."

"You don't know what you're saying, Greg." The pains were getting worse. It was as though long, sharp needles were being jabbed into the nerves of her body. A hot, seering flame began to scorch her skin. The room was suddenly spinning around at a dizzying pace.

"Lies," Greg shouted. "Neither of you told the truth in your whole lives."

Miguel saw Elaine turn deathly pale. He went over to her and helped her to her feet. "Come, my dear. I think you had better lie down."

"Yes, yes," she said, passing her hand in front of her eyes to remove the cobwebs. "I think I had."

Greg continued to rage at her as Miguel helped her from the room. At the doorway Miguel turned around and said,

"You are a very selfish, heartless boy, Greg. You always were."

"Go fuck yourself," Greg spat.

Elaine groaned and staggered against Miguel. He supported her weight as he hurried her toward the stairs.

"Fuck them all," Greg said to the empty room. He stood up and pressed his forehead against the mantlepiece. He pounded it with his fists, trying to get rid of all his frustrations. He wanted to kill everything in the world. "Everybody in the whole fucking universe is a lousy bitch."

He heard voices in the foyer and straightened up. He quickly pulled himself together when he heard Maggie Montgomery's shrill voice announcing that she was going into Palma. The sound of her voice drew his attention to her collection of hatpins lying open on the table before him. He gazed for a moment at the daggerlike pin that he'd admired before. He reached for it, letting his fingers caress the long sharp blade of the pin before picking it up from the velvet-lined box. He held it up to the light and watched it flash and sparkle. He smiled, recalling the words of Siegmund when he pulled the sword from the tree. "Needful, I name this sword," he said. Then in a smaller voice he sang the words from *Die Walküre*. He sang slowly, menacingly, as though in a trance: *"Nothung! So nenn' ich dich Schwert!"* He gazed lovingly at the long, deadly pin, then, hearing Maggie's voice nearing, he quickly stuck it under the lapel of his jacket and hurried out of the room.

"Oh, it's you, Greg," Maggie said in a rush. "Where is everyone? I can't find anyone anywhere. I just wanted to see if Elaine wanted anything while I was in town." She shook her head. "And she had the nerve to accuse me of never thinking of others. Oh, well," she said in a flutter, "she always was a selfish woman. Tell her I've gone." She had changed from the pink chiffon to white. It made her look even fatter.

"Ta-ta," Greg called cheerfully after her as he fingered his lapel. The long, stiff strength of the concealed pin seemed to pulse under his touch. "Don't forget to write."

Maggie giggled. "Oh, you," she gushed. "Don't forget to write," she repeated. She thought it was the funniest thing she'd heard in ages. She liked the sound of her laughter. That's what this place needed, more laughter. Everyone was

so serious. She shook her head, wondering how on earth she
could stand much more of it.

THE STREETS WERE BUSTLING WITH TOURISTS
when Sheila and Charlie came out of their hotel and started
along the sidewalk. High above the city, the Cathedral of
Palma stood against the black sky, its walls and spires bathed
in glaring floodlights. The glittering lights of the city reflected like sparks in the water of the bay. The modern line
of hotels glowed like cheap plastic cubes. There was a liveli-
ness in the night air, electric and contagious. They passed two
bearded youths with straggling hair who whistled when
Sheila went by. She gave a little toss of her head and exaggerated the swing of her hips.

"Hey, behave yourself," Charlie chided. "You want to
hurt my kid you have in your oven?"

Sheila laughed. "Oh, Charlie. We don't even know if the
dough is baking yet."

"What street is this?" Charlie asked, looking up at the sign
when they came to the intersection. "Christ, why don't they
print their street signs in English?"

"Because this is Majorca, not New York." Despite all his
correcting, she still sounded the *j*. She glanced at the slip of
paper she had in her hand, then up at the street sign. "This is
the one. It should be down there," she said, pointing along
the line of old, rickety buildings.

"If we had old buildings like this in New York they'd tear
them down."

"No they wouldn't," Sheila said. "They'd rent them out to
the blacks and Puerto Ricans."

"Very funny." He scanned the barely distinguishable numbers. "What's the address again?"

"Seventy-two. It's that place over there with the sign over
the door."

Charlie frowned at the place. It looked more like an

abandoned cellar than a restaurant. "Are you sure? Hell, it's nothing but a cellar with a crooked building on top of it."

"That's why they call it the Cellar. The guidebook said the food's great and there's lots and lots of atmosphere."

"Atmosphere," Charlie sniffed. "That's just another way of saying they're going to charge us an arm and a leg." He frowned at the place. "It don't even look safe."

"Stop your griping and come on. I'm starved. I hope they have steak and french fries. I'm dying for a good thick steak and french fries."

"This ain't the Bronx, you know. They'll most likely have more of that fish and greasy pork."

A dark-skinned man in a gypsy costume bowed to them as they entered. The room was large, with long wooden tables and benches crowded with Majorcans, all jabbering away in their own tongue. The ceiling was vaulted and hanging with pots and pans and every sort of kitchen paraphernalia. A trio of gypsy violins wandered among the customers, smiling and bowing to the diners as they passed.

The man in the gypsy costume asked, in perfect English, "Do you wish to dine family-style, or would you prefer the private dining room in the back?"

Charlie grimaced at the crowded tables, the unscrubbed customers. "We'll eat in back," he said as he gripped Sheila's elbow.

"But Charlie. We came here for the atmosphere," she objected.

"Atmosphere is one thing, but a loss of appetite is something else. These people look as if they hadn't had a bath in weeks. I couldn't sit with them and keep my stomach."

"Who are you to talk? You eat at those flop joints over on Ninth Avenue all the time and I never heard you complain."

"That's different. Unwashed Americans are cleaner than unwashed Europeans."

"You're a bigot, do you know that?"

"So, I'm a bigot. I'm also hungry."

They were ushered toward a small, high-ceilinged room just off the main dining hall. There were only four tables in the room, three of them empty. Charlie stood for a moment in the wide archway looking at the room. It had three square pillars that ran from the floor up to the beams across the ceiling. The overhead beams were very wide and thick and heavy-looking, so wide and thick and heavy that he felt over-powered by them. He'd hate like hell to have them crash down on top of them. There was something very "touristy" about the room, he thought. He noticed the candlelamps on each of the tables, and upon closer examination he saw they had light bulbs for what should have been flames. The wall torches were the same way. Instead of a flicker flame, they had flame-shaped bulbs that flickered a dull orange. The place was a tourist trap, he decided; but he didn't care, his stomach was screaming for food.

Charlie glanced at the other diners. "Hey, hello," Charlie called, recognizing the four seated at the table nearest the back wall. "Hey, look, Sheila. They're the ones who were on the bus with us." He waved. "Nice seeing you again," he called as the gypsy seated them at a corner table.

"Hello," Rod called. He didn't bother getting up to shake hands. After all, these two were complete strangers until this morning, and he hadn't particularly liked the way they behaved.

"I see you all heard about this trap too? I guess they put all us Americans in one room because they only got one menu in English." He didn't pay any attention to the sour look the gypsy gave them.

Through his sour look, the maitre d' asked, "Would *señor* and *señora* care for a cocktail before dinner?"

"Cocktails, huh?" Charlie said, amused. "Gee, maybe this place is a little classier than it looks. Yeah," he said to the gypsy. "We'll have a couple of double martinis, very dry, with twists of lemon. You got that?"

"Yes sir." The man bowed, handed them each a menu and started to leave. He'd learned through long years of experience that Americans needed to be humored and ignored. "Be careful of the menu, please," he said at the doorway loud enough for everyone to hear. "We have only a limited number printed in English." He put on his most superior expression and walked out through the wide archway.

Charlie hooted and banged the table. "See, what did I tell you, Sheila?"

"He's puttin' you on, Charlie."

"Yeah?" He was going to yell something caustic after the man but caught himself. He reminded himself that he had to sell Sheila on the idea of settling down here. "Well, maybe

I was a little rough on him about the menu." He glanced around. "Actually the place ain't half bad. At least it's nice and clean."

"How about those great unwashed out in the other room?" Sheila asked, raising a questioning eyebrow.

"Ah, I was only kiddin'. You're right. There're a lot filthier apes in New York." He knew Sheila was going to start in on him again about his not wanting to go home. To avoid it he motioned over to Rod. "Are you folks from New York?"

Nancy turned around. "I am. First and Fifty-fifth."

"Classy neighborhood," Charlie commented.

Sheila poked him. "Charlie, don't be rude. Can't you see they're talking? You're interrupting."

Charlie looked sheepish. "Sorry," he called over to them. "The little woman says I'm interrupting. Sorry."

"That's all right," Rod called back, then leaned back into their conversation. "I really think you're being too hard on your father," he said to Paul.

"He's sick," Paul said with an ugly twist of his mouth.

Lisa made a face. "Just because . . ." She let her words dwindle off as a low rumbling sound made the floor quiver; the brass caps on the candlelamps started to jiggle. A fine dusting of plaster sifted down from the ceiling. Everyone sat bolt upright, looking upward, wondering, waiting. Then, far off in the distance, there was a heavy thud, like the firing of a distant cannon. Almost immediately after there was a second boom, this one louder. The room started to rock more violently. Outside in the main dining room, people were shouting, chairs and benches were scraping on the floor, there was a busy shuffling of feet. Nancy found herself gripping tight to the edge of the table, looking wildly about, not knowing what was happening.

The explosion came so suddenly, so violently, that no one had time to move. Lisa screamed and threw herself against her father. Sheila was thrown backward over her chair; Nancy was pitched sideways and heaved against the wall. People were screaming at the tops of their lungs. The walls cracked. Lisa screamed again, but her scream was lost in the multitude of screams and screeches coming from the larger dining room outside. Plaster and dust billowed down over them. The timber roof supports of the little room groaned and creaked, but held. The wall sconces flickered out.

Another explosion shattered their ears as the brick arch of the doorway collapsed, cutting off the shrieks and cries of the patrons in the larger room as its vaulted ceiling roared down on top of them.

The deadly silence that followed was horrifying. The little room was enveloped in a thick cloud of powdery debris, making it impossible for them to see. Rod found Lisa clinging to him as they waited, terrified that the roof would collapse on them also. Although they could not hear, they well imagined the screaming and sobbing of the injured and dying on the other side of the pile of debris that completely covered the doorway. Lisa was crying hysterically. Rod shook her. "It's okay, honey. Get hold of yourself." He hugged her tight. "I think it's over, whatever it was," he said through his coughing. His eyes burned, his mouth and throat were clogged with dust.

"Sheila! Oh, my God, Sheila. Are you okay?"

There was a silence, then Sheila gave a little laugh and said, "I guess the Almighty just wasn't ready for me yet." They heard her give a low whistle. "They sure do put a wallop in their drinks in this place."

Charlie tried to laugh. "Yeah, and they didn't even serve 'em to us yet." Then in a more serious tone he said, "Are you sure you're okay, sweetheart?"

"Yeah, I'm okay. What in hell happened?"

"An explosion of some kind. Several explosions." Charlie squinted and tried to peer across the room. "You folks all okay over there?"

Nancy rubbed the ache in her shoulder. She felt it gingerly. Nothing seemed broken or out of place. She was coughing uncontrollably. "Rod?"

"Here," he answered. "Are you all right?"

"Yes, I think so. Where's Lisa?"

"With me," Rod said. "We're fine, I think. Paul? Where's Paul?"

"Over here," Paul said, untangling himself from two overturned chairs.

"Are you okay?"

"I cut myself on some broken glass, but it isn't serious," he said as he groped for his handkerchief and started to wrap it around the heel of his hand.

The dust was beginning to settle as they cautiously began

moving about, finding one another, looking each other over for signs of injuries.

"What happened, do you think?" Nancy asked. She looked at Lisa, who was still clinging desperately to her father. The girl's eyes were wide with fright; her mouth was open but she couldn't utter a sound.

"Something blew up outside. The ceiling must have collapsed."

"Oh, my God," Nancy gasped. She put her hands over her face and shook her head. "Those poor people out there."

As if on cue, the six of them turned toward the blocked doorway. There wasn't a sound to be heard through the thick pile of rubble. They easily visualized the carnage beyond the rubble. The dining room had been mobbed with men, women and children. Their little room was still as a tomb. It was as though they'd been interred in a sepulcher, but they knew that just beyond there were screams and cries and death was running rampant.

Lisa put her hands over her ears and let out a blood-curdling scream. Rob grabbed her and started to shake her. The more he shook her the louder she screamed. He held her away from him and slapped her across the face. Lisa froze, staring at him, then she collapsed against him and began crying quietly. He put his arms around her and rocked her back and forth, thinking, in spite of their terrible predicament, how wonderful it was to hold her in his arms again.

Paul and Charlie had moved over toward the doorway. "It looks like we're trapped in here," Paul said, pushing at the pile of bricks and beams and crumbled mortar. "There must be a ton of this stuff came down."

"Yeah," Charlie said. "One hell of a lot of stuff fell out there. I wouldn't be surprised if the whole building that sat on top of this place caved in."

Sheila looked up at the ceiling over their heads. "How come this roof didn't fall?"

"This room was most likely an add-on, not part of the older building," Charlie said, examining the cracks in the walls and testing the supporting pillars.

"What do we do now?" Nancy asked, trying hard to keep calm. She was shaking violently.

"There's not much we can do," Charlie said. "We'll just have to sit here and wait until somebody digs us out."

"THIS PLACE IS NOTHING BUT A DEN OF thieves," Maggie shrieked, waving her hands wildly in the air. "What kind of people do you entertain, Elaine? First your jewels, and now my rarest hatpin. Thieves, robbers, murderers. My God, it's like living with seasoned criminals."

"Are you sure you didn't just misplace it?" Elaine asked.

"Misplace it? Are you mad? It was right here in its case when I went into Palma this afternoon. It was thoughtless and cruel. You have nothing but thoughtless, cruel people around you."

Elaine was tempted to say she knew, referring to Maggie herself, of course, but she held her tongue.

"Did they let Jorge out of jail? Has he been here today?"

"No, Jorge has not been here," Elaine said, feeling her patience slipping. "Please try to stay calm, Maggie. I'm sure the pin is around someplace."

"You're sure. You're sure. Well, I'm not so sure, my dear. The pin was stolen. I'm going to notify the police." She stomped toward the telephone. "This is unforgivable."

"Maggie, what is the matter?" Dario asked as he came into the room.

"Oh, Dario. The most dreadful thing has happened." She pouted prettily, went over to him and laid her head on his chest.

"One of Maggie's hatpins seems to have been misplaced," Elaine said after greeting him.

"Misplaced. It was stolen. This house is absolutely riddled with thieves."

"There, there, Maggie. I'm sure it will turn up. Don't worry your pretty little head about it." He slipped his arm around her plump shoulders. "Come, I'll help you make a thorough search."

"Dario," Elaine said, stopping him as he and Maggie started out of the room. "There was a young girl here today asking for you. She said her name was Carlotta. She had a message for you."

"Yes, I know. I stopped at the jail to see Jorge. He told me he had sent Carlotta to fetch me."

"You spoke with Jorge at the jail?" Elaine asked.

"Yes."

"How is he?"

"As well as can be expected. He's angry and upset, of course, but that is understandable."

Elaine nodded. Angry and upset. With her, no doubt. The pains were starting to gnaw at her again. She forced herself not to think of them. "I am surprised that he wants to see anyone after what Miguel told me," she said, feeling ill at ease.

Dario looked at her curiously. "I'm afraid I do not understand what you mean, Elaine."

She tried to appear nonchalant but her heart was beating rapidly. "Miguel informed me that Jorge was refusing to speak with anyone, including himself," she said.

Surprised, Dario said, "But that is not true. Jorge is particularly upset because you have failed to come to see him. He has been pacing in his cell all day, feeling that you have deserted him."

Elaine's heart leaped with joy. "Deserted him? But Miguel said Jorge wanted nothing more to do with me."

"Where on earth would Miguel get such an idea? Jorge himself told me that he had specifically sent Miguel here with a message for you to come to him so that he could at least explain about the emerald necklace."

Elaine was at the door in a flash. "Come on, Dario. Would you drive me to the jail? I want to talk with Jorge immediately." She could not describe the happiness that was coursing through her. All thoughts of pain or grief were miraculously forgotten. Jorge wanted to see her; he wanted to talk to her. It was as if spring had burst upon her and a whole new life had opened up. "It will take only a moment to get my coat." She didn't think of the drab black dress she was wearing or that her hair wasn't looking its best or that her makeup wasn't expertly applied. She didn't care how she looked. She had thoughts of nothing but that she would see Jorge. He wasn't angry with her. Her bliss was almost too much for her to bear.

"But what about my stolen hatpin?" Maggie called as Elaine and Dario hurried out.

"To hell with your hatpin," Elaine shouted over her shoulder. "We'll take my car," she said to Dario as they rushed out.

She was glad the top of the Rolls convertible was down. The clean night air felt wonderful on her face, bathing her in a freshness she thought she'd lost. She laid her head on the back of the seat and gazed up at the shimmering stars. She picked out "her" star, the one Jorge had given her that first night they'd fallen in love. It seemed to shine more brightly tonight.

She didn't want to think about why Miguel had lied to her. She understood, however, why the girl—Carlotta—had lied. She turned her head toward Dario and studied his chiseled peasant profile for a moment. "Carlotta," she said finally. "Is she in love with Jorge?"

"How did you know?"

"Women have a way of knowing those things. She hates me, doesn't she?"

Dario kept his eyes fixed firmly on the twisting road. "Carlotta has been in love with Jorge all her life. She feels that you have taken him away from her. She is a simple girl who feels her only happiness in life is Jorge."

"Yes, I can understand that."

He expertly maneuvered the car around a particularly sharp curve. "Carlotta does not understand Jorge. She feels that he is only attracted to you for what you can give him. In her heart she believes that you will only cause him misery. She was once deeply hurt by a man with money. She never forgave him and blames wealth for all the trouble people are made to suffer."

"And you, Dario? Do you believe he loves me only for what I have to give?"

Dario shrugged. "I cannot answer that, but from all Jorge has said I think he is genuinely in love with you."

Elaine wrapped her arms around herself. "Yes, I think he is. I think he loves me as much as I love him. I am not deaf to what has been said about me. I know I am much older, but where Jorge and I are concerned that doesn't seem to matter."

"You knew, however, that Jorge was planning on marrying Cynthia?"

Elaine grew sad. "Yes, I overheard them talking in the gazebo that night."

"Did you know why?"

"Not then, but I can guess the reason now. Cynthia was pregnant."

"Yes. Jorge told me that night. He wanted to explain to you, but you were extremely agitated and I suggested he let you calm down before explaining to you. I am sorry. I should have interfered and perhaps none of this would have happened. Cynthia might still be alive."

"I wouldn't be too hard on yourself, Dario." She watched him for a moment. His eyes had grown sad. "You liked Cynthia, didn't you, Dario?"

Again he shrugged. "Yes, I did. I was very attracted to her, but I am afraid she was not too impressed by me."

"Poor Cynthia. She never knew what was best for her. Did you tell her you liked her?"

"I wanted to ask her to marry me that night. After Jorge told me about the expected child I wanted to tell her I would marry her and bring Jorge's child up as my own."

Elaine felt a sudden pang in her breast. "Then it was Jorge's child she was expecting?"

"Jorge believes it was. That is the only reason he was determined to marry her. He told me that Cynthia threatened to kill herself if he refused her."

Kill herself. The words echoed around inside her head. She suddenly remembered Cynthia's words aboard the yacht several days ago: "You'll never have Jorge. You'll see me dead first." Perhaps it wasn't murder after all. Perhaps Cynthia, in a fit of rage, had thrown herself over the cliff. No, she knew Cynthia too well. She was not one to take the coward's way out. Besides, she certainly would not do away with herself and leave the field clear for her mother. Her spiteful selfishness wouldn't have permitted her to do that.

"I feel so guilty about it all," Elaine said, pulling her coat tighter about her.

"Guilty?"

Elaine sighed. "I know I should be grief-stricken over Cynthia's death, and I am, in my fashion. I miss her, of course, yet it's as if it all happened for the best. I think Cynthia is

happier where she is, whether she realizes it or not, and for
that I'm glad. My only regret is that she never knew how
much I loved her. She was a very difficult daughter to love."
Referring to Cynthia as her daughter seemed right and natural now. No more lying, no more pretending. She saw Dario's
eyes flicker toward her for an instant, then return to the road
ahead. "She was my daughter, you know."

"Yes, Jorge told me."

"Was he very angry with me for having deceived him?"

"I think he was only angry because you had placed him in a
position where Greg and Cynthia could laugh at him. He understands now. Jorge is a very understanding man."

She patted his knee. "And so are you, Dario. I will never
forget what a good friend you are both to Jorge and to me."

"I am very fond of you both, Elaine . . . more fond of
Jorge, naturally, because I have known him longer."

Not wanting the conversation to become maudlin, she purposely moved it to a brighter level. "And what of Maggie
Montgomery? You two seem to be in each other's company
quite a bit lately."

Dario laughed. "Maggie is a silly, foolish woman, but she
is fun to be with. Nothing is ever serious with her. I would
propose to her in a minute if I thought she would have me."

"Propose? To Maggie? You must be joking."

Dario did not seem embarrassed. "No. I do not delude myself. I have always wanted to live in a style which I could
never afford. Maggie has much money, I have none. Opposites
should be put together."

"Dario, you surprise me. I never took you for a materialistic
individual."

He gave her a sly grin. "Why do you think I have worked
so hard to win the bicycle races here on the island? It is the
only way I could think of to draw attention to myself."

"But you are an attractive man, Dario."

He shook his head. "Not so attractive. I am not handsome
like Jorge. I do not have his charm or his intelligence. Those
are necessary talents to have if one is to rise above his position."

Elaine reflected. "Jorge never talked about his background,
his growing up. I asked him if he was poor. He would not
answer me directly."

"He was very poor," Dario admitted. "We both were. It is
not a very pleasant existence here when one is poor. The

wealthy natives resent any poor devil who tries to rise above his station. Things are changing some now that Majorca is becoming more modern, more in tune with the twentieth century. You have lived here only a few years, Elaine. You do not know what it is like to have been born here in utter poverty, as Jorge and I were. If one was fortunate, he might inherit land from a relative, land he could sell to the land developers. But chances such as that are slim. And so the more ambitious, dissatisfied peasants like Jorge and me are forced to fight to live down our peasant background." He sighed. "It was all right, I suppose, before the outside world discovered our wonderful climate, our beautiful scenery, our lovely beaches and coves. Back then if one was born a peasant one was content to remain a peasant; one knew no different. But the outside world infringed upon us. Spain expects us to continue under its domination and remain docile and poor, just as the poor on the mainland must remain. But there is too much discontent among the younger men. The women have not yet raised their fists as the young men have, but time will change that too. Majorca was once the most prized island in the Mediterranean. That is why it was fought over by so many for so many centuries. But everyone forgets that Majorca should belong to the Majorcans, such as Jorge and myself, and not to those overlords who stormed our shores, invaded our land and put our necks in yokes. Unfortunately too many German and Italian and American land developers are putting millions of dollars in resort hotels and land developments. They are polluting our air and destroying our waters with their filthy industries and commerce, and the time will come when Majorca will be nothing but a squalid resort community rather than the paradise it was meant to be. Majorca is a living museum which should be preserved. But time will sack its treasures." Again he sighed. "Ah, but perhaps that will be for the best. Perhaps then the outside world will leave us with our dust so that we can start from the beginning again."

Elaine looked at him as if she'd never seen him before. "I never realized you were so deep a young man," she said.

He didn't bother to look at her. "No one does," he said. "I am not the type of man people think of as having depth, only muscles and the frame of an athlete. People only want surface appearances. No one wants to look beneath those surfaces for fear they might see themselves, and no one wants that," he added with a chuckle.

"I take back what I said about you being materialistic, Dario. You aren't. You are more idealistic."

"You are wrong," he said, shrugging off his mood. "I am very materialistic. Idealism is for those who will come after me. I do not love anything or anyone. I do not think myself capable of falling in love in the way you read about in books. Cynthia was the closest I came to that kind of love, but even then it was her wealth and her position that first attracted me to her."

His brutal honesty took her slightly aback. She found she could not answer him.

"Jorge and I are very much alike on that score," Dario continued. "Beautiful women were never a problem for us, especially Jorge. Women had to have more than beauty before either of us became interested."

She wondered what he meant by that. Was he saying, after all, that it *was* her money Jorge loved? She was tempted to ask, but Dario pulled the car up in front of the jail.

"I hope they will let us see him at this time of night," Dario said.

"They'll permit it," Elaine said, letting Dario help her from the car. "I intend camping on their doorstep until they do."

There was a lot of discussion back and forth before Elaine and Dario were escorted to Jorge's cell. Elaine erased all hesitation on the part of the jailer by pressing a wad of bills into his palm.

They stared at each other through the bars, saying nothing. The moment the door was unlocked Elaine flew into Jorge's arms and broke into tears.

"I didn't know. I didn't know," she kept sobbing as he held her close and comforted her.

"I thought you had abandoned me," Jorge said, his eyes closed, rapture racing like a forest fire throughout his body. "Oh, Elaine, my darling." He took her face in his hands and kissed her softly on the mouth. "My beautiful Elaine," he whispered, then crushed his mouth hard over hers.

Neither of them heard Dario say, "I'll wait for you outside, Elaine."

Elaine thought she would never be able to stop kissing him, touching him. Pure ecstasy engulfed her. "Oh, Jorge, forgive me, my darling," she breathed. "I've been such a stupid old fool."

"No, do not blame yourself, Elaine. I too have been stupid and thoughtless."

"Miguel never told me," she said. "I thought you hated me and never wanted to see me again."

"But I sent Miguel to bring you this morning. I knew if I explained to you about the necklace you would not think I stole it."

"I never thought for a moment that you took the necklace." She kissed him again. "I don't care about the necklace, my dearest. I don't care about anything now that we are together again."

"You have heard that they are going to charge me with Cynthia's murder," he said grimly.

"Miguel hinted as much."

"I didn't kill her, Elaine. Do you believe that?"

She framed his face with her hands. "Of course I believe it, Jorge. I never doubted you for a moment."

"Then who? Why?"

"Dario told me on the way here about your conversation with Cynthia that night. Oh, how I wish I had listened to you then."

"What did Dario tell you?"

"That Cynthia threatened to kill herself unless you married her for the sake of the child." She smiled at him through her tears. "I thought at first Cynthia might have thrown herself from the cliff, but I do not think she did. She never intended for you and me to be together, so she would not have removed herself from her position between us."

"Yes, I thought that too. But who then?"

"I don't know."

"Miguel told me he saw Cynthia go off with Dario that night. I asked Dario about it. He never saw Cynthia except briefly in the upstairs hall. I believe him. Dario would not lie to me."

She remembered suddenly the strange confession Dario had made about himself on the drive in. A disturbing thought caused her to wonder whether or not Dario would lie to his best friend. Contrary to her thought, she found herself saying, "I'm sure he wouldn't." She frowned. "You say you spoke with Miguel after I'd retired to my room."

"Yes. Remember, I pounded on your door and wanted to explain, but you ordered me out of the house."

"Oh, forgive me, my darling. I was jealous and hurt. I didn't know what I was saying."

"I realize that, Elaine. I realized it that night. I was confused and angry also. I wanted some time to think things out by myself, so I drove to Carlotta's house and stayed there."

Another sting of envy bit into her heart. Had he slept with Carlotta that night? He probably had, angry and upset as he was. It didn't matter. She didn't care.

"Miguel was in the hall when I went to my room to pack."

"Miguel," she mused, remembering now his lies, the lengths he had resorted to to keep Jorge and her apart. She began to wonder.

LAURA WAS LYING ON THE DIVAN, NAKED. HER eyes were glassy and her hair disheveled. On the movie screen a man in a policeman's uniform was standing over a nude girl. Her hands were tied to the headboard of a bed, her legs spread wide apart, the ankles tied to the footposts. The man in the uniform greased his long, black nightstick and began working it gradually up into the girl until the entire length disappeared inside her cunt.

Laura reached down and tangled her fingers in her husband's hair, pulling his face tight against her crotch. She moved against his mouth, trying to quench the fires that were burning deep inside her. She moaned and writhed, as if in torture. Suddenly she pushed herself up and shoved him away from her.

Irritably she reached for a cigarette and stuck it in her mouth.

"What is it, Laura?" Paul Verdugo asked as he frowned up at her.

"It just isn't any good. I'm burning up inside and nothing is satisfying me. I bored, bored, *bored!*" she shouted, as she got to her feet, stretching her lovely arms over her head and shaking her fists at the ceiling.

"I could call that young Negro I brought home last week."

"No, I don't want him. I want Paul."

Verdugo bowed his head. "Well, I'm afraid we struck out on him. I wonder where he is?"

"He isn't here, that's all I know," she said angrily.

"I suppose he must hate us both after this afternoon," Verdugo said.

"What does it matter? We both agreed that neither of us could look upon him as a son. He was a stranger to us. You don't know him any better than I."

Mr. Verdugo grinned. "I was sure he'd have inherited some of my traits. I'm afraid he has all of his mother's puritanical traits." He sighed. "Oh, well, we tried, my love."

"Oh, go call that black stud and get him over here. This itching in my pussy is driving me nuts." As Paul went toward the telephone, Laura called, "Tell him to bring a couple of buddies. I'm really on fire tonight."

The movies were still flickering on the screen an hour later when Paul Verdugo ushered three giant Negroes into the arena. Laura merely looked them up and down and spread her legs. She began fingering her vagina. "Come on, boys," she said in a lust-filled voice. "Hurry it up. I'm dying."

The three men looked at Mr. Verdugo. He smiled eagerly and nodded his head a few times, coaxing them to hurry.

Minutes later Laura was being ravaged by the three strangers. Her head was thrown back, her mouth open. They were pounding at her unmercifully. Mr. Verdugo sat quietly in a chair, leaning slightly forward, staring at the orgy that was going on before his eyes. Slowly he inched his hand toward the erection in his trousers. He felt its length and thickness; it had never seemed so hard before. He licked his lips and felt the heavy pounding in his chest. With what sounded like the cry of a wounded animal he ripped open his pants, exposing his erection. He rushed over to the divan, forcefully shoved the Negro away from between Laura's legs and buried himself to the hilt.

"Laura," he moaned as the sperm shot out of him. "Oh, Laura, what would I ever do without you."

SHEILA WET A NAPKIN AND CLEANED THE CUT
on Paul Jr.'s hand. She tore a strip from her half-slip and tied
the wound tightly. "There, that should do for now," she said.
"Does it hurt much, kid?"

"No, not much."

"Anybody else need attention?" she asked brightly. "I took
a nurse's course once."

"You never told me that," Charlie said.

"Well, it wasn't really a regular nurse's course; more like
first aid," she admitted with a sheepish grin. She looked suddenly wistful. "You know, I've always thought it would be
great to have been a doctor."

"A doctor?" Charlie said, aghast.

"Yeah. Ain't it the pits? Me, a doctor." She shrugged, embarrassed. "But I always thought it would be great helping
other people and all."

"That's crazy," Charlie said and turned toward Rod.

"Are you all right, Mr. Shepherd?"

"I'm okay. Not a scratch on me."

They had introduced themselves after stumbling around,
trying to see if there was any other way out of the room.
They found that there wasn't. The walls were faced with
solid brick, some of which had broken free of their mortar
seams, but none had fallen. The ceiling looked steady enough,
at least for the present. The thick beams seemed intact, but
they knew another explosion would surely bring the ceiling
down on their heads.

After searching for an exit they had busied themselves
righting chairs and tables and brushing up broken glass to
keep themselves occupied.

"Anything I can do for you two?" Sheila asked Nancy and
Lisa as they sat huddled together at one of the tables.

Nancy rubbed her shoulder. "I have a bruised shoulder, but
it doesn't feel like anything's broken."

"How about you, kid?" Sheila asked, addressing Lisa.

Lisa had gone into a sulk immediately after the immediate danger was over and had refused to take part in any of the activities of the others. "I don't need anybody's help," she said, pouting.

Nancy put her arm on Lisa's shoulder, but the younger girl shook it off. Nancy said to Sheila, "She's been badly frightened; she'll be all right."

Sheila noticed the smudges of dirt on Lisa's face. She dipped the napkin in the water glass. "Here, honey. Let me clean some of that dirt off you."

Lisa slapped her hand away. "I said I don't need anybody's help."

"Lucky you, kid," Sheila said sarcastically. "With that kind of attitude you ain't bound to get anybody's help. But you're going to grow up to be a pretty lonely person."

"Grow up?" Lisa shrieked. "I'm not going to grow up. We're all going to die in here."

"Nobody's going to die," Rod said, trying to comfort her. "All we have to do is to stay calm. Surely somebody knows we're in here."

"Who?" Lisa shouted. "Who knows we're here? Everybody out there is dead, can't you understand that?" She burst into tears again as Nancy tried to console her.

"Listen, kid," Sheila said sharply, addressing Lisa. "We're all in this thing together. It's tough enough on all of us to be cooped up like lambs going to slaughter, so we can do without the hysterics." Lisa glowered at her through her tears. "Now you snap out of it, kid, and start acting your age. This ain't easy on any of us, you know."

"We're going to die!" Lisa screamed.

"You cut that out or so help me I'll belt you one," Sheila said, brandishing her fist.

"Leave her alone, Sheila," Charlie said softly. "The kid's frightened."

"We're all frightened," Sheila said. "But you don't see the rest of us crying in our beers." She turned back to Lisa. "I mean it, kid. Turn off the waterworks and settle down. We'll get out of this thing okay."

Their eyes met in silent conflict. After a while Lisa sniffed and fumbled in her purse for her handkerchief. She blew her nose and wiped her eyes. She got up and went to one of the other tables and sat down by herself.

Nancy started to go to her, but Rod stopped her. "Leave her alone, Nancy. Sheila's right. We can't afford hysterics."

"See, there you go again," Lisa said angrily. "Taking the part of a stranger over mine."

Paul said, "He isn't taking anyone's part; he's just being sensible."

Lisa stuck her tongue out at him and started to sulk again.

Charlie rubbed his chin. "Now let's settle down and think this thing out. The girl might be right that nobody knows we're in here, so maybe we should start tapping at the walls or something just to call attention to ourselves."

"Tapping is out," Rod said, glancing at the cracked ceiling. "Any kind of banging might bring that roof down on us."

"Yeah, I guess you're right, Mr. Shepherd."

Rod sat down beside Nancy. "No, I think our best bet is to sit quietly and wait. We can't dig through that debris," he said, nodding toward the archway, "and there's no other way out, so we don't really have much choice but to sit tight."

"Did anyone examine the floor carefully?" Paul asked. "Maybe there's a trap door or something."

"Nah, I looked real good," Charlie said. "There's nothing."

"So we wait," Sheila said brightly. "Big deal. I've been stuck with a lot worse company before."

"Too bad we didn't bring a deck of cards, huh, Sheila?" Charlie said.

"Too bad they didn't bring the food before this happened," she answered. "I'm starved."

Charlie patted his stomach. "Don't mention food." He picked up the cruets of oil and vinegar from the table. "I wonder how dust would taste with an Italian dressing?"

Nancy smiled. "We hadn't ordered yet either, so I know how you feel, Mr. Cranston."

"Charlie. Call me Charlie."

"Okay, Charlie," she said with a smile. Her eyes drifted over to Paul, who sat hunched over the table staring at the brass-capped candle lamp sitting before him. "What are you thinking about, Paul?" she asked.

The mention of his name yanked him out of his thoughts. "Oh, I was just examining this little lamp and thinking how lucky we are that they're operated by batteries and not candles. Candles burn out after a while; at least we're pretty sure of not being left in the dark. I wouldn't like that very much."

"Oh? Why, are you afraid of the dark?" Nancy wanted to know.

Paul looked embarrassed. "My mother locked me in a closet one time because I wanted to run away from home. I was only a little kid, and the darkness scared the pants off me."

"We have something else to be thankful for about these lights," Charlie said, picking one up and seeing that they were battery-operated as Paul had said. "Usually with blasts like we just had, there are gas leaks. We could all be blown to smithereens."

"At least it would be quick," Lisa said, coming out of her pout.

Sheila laughed. "Yeah, that's what they call going out with a bang."

Paul went back to staring at the candle lamp. "I wonder if my dad is wondering where I am," he mused.

"From what you told me, I'm surprised you care," Lisa said, flipping back her hair from her shoulders.

"I don't," Paul said. "I was just wondering, that's all."

Nancy said, "You should have at least called him from the hotel, just to let him know you were all right."

"I thought of it, but I just couldn't bring myself to talk to him. I don't ever want to talk to him again," he said bitterly.

"Your own father?" Sheila asked. "That ain't right."

"It is in my case," Paul said.

"Why, is he a real S.O.B.?" She laughed again. "I had a father like that, but I still thought of him as my old man, rotten as he was." A wistful softness came into her eyes. "I wonder where that old coot is? Most likely still trying to hump chicks in the park." She caught herself and threw Lisa an apologetic look. "Sorry, kid, that slipped out."

"I know what 'hump' means," Lisa said.

"Don't be vulgar, Lisa," her father reprimanded.

"Oh, boy, there you go again. Mrs. Cranston can say 'hump' but I can't."

Sheila admonished her with, "Mrs. Cranston is a tough old war horse and you're a refined young filly. People don't expect no better from me, but for you it's different."

"Some old war horse," Charlie said, clucking his cheek. He patted her soundly on the backside.

"Charlie," she squealed. "You're as bad as my old man, always pattin' and grabbin'."

"The last time I saw your father was when you first got out . . . er . . . when we first met."

"Go ahead, say it, Charlie. I'm not ashamed." She turned to the others. "Charlie here is a detective in New York. We met at police headquarters. I'd been in the pokey for taking something they said wasn't rightfully mine, if you know what I mean."

Nancy was smiling at her. She nodded when Sheila looked at her.

"Well, my old man was being hauled in for making a pass at this young chick in the park. Our paths crossed, you might say—him goin' in, me comin' out with Charlie as an escort. It wasn't what you'd call a tearful meetin'." She looked around the room and then at Lisa. "Honey, if you think this place is bad, try spendin' time in the slammer."

"I have," Lisa said, tilting back her head.

"You? Ah, go on."

Rod felt red-faced by the gist of conversation, yet Sheila's open admission about herself seemed refreshing somehow. "Lisa got herself mixed up with the wrong kind," he said to Sheila. "She spent some time here in the local jail, I'm afraid."

"Oh, kid, that's a bummer. I understand these foreign jugs are a whole lot worse than the ones we have back home."

"It wasn't so bad," Lisa answered.

Sheila eyed her for a moment. "What kinda trouble did you get messed up in?"

"Sheila!" Charlie cautioned.

"I don't mind," Lisa said. "Drugs," she said, almost sounding proud.

"Wow, that's big stuff," Sheila said. "How much time did they give you?"

"I was only in about a week. My dad came over and got me out."

Sheila looked confused. "From what I hear, on a drug bust over here they lock you up and throw away the key," she said to Rod.

He grinned coyly. "Over here the American dollar is a lot more important than an American prisoner."

"Ah, I see," Sheila said.

"How about you, Sheila?" Lisa asked boldly. "What were you in for?"

Rod shook his head at her. "I don't think that is any of our business," he said kindly.

Sheila laughed. "Like Lisa here, I don't mind, Mr. Shepherd." She winked at Lisa. "We old seasoned convicts grow tougher skins than you all." She put her hand affectionately on Lisa's shoulder. "I got caught the first time for shoplifting. It seems I've always had sticky fingers. I never could understand why I was always winding up with stuff that didn't belong to me. But that's all changed now. Charlie here came on the scene and straightened me out smooth as a ramrod." She pursed her lips and threw him a kiss. "I know better now. I'd no more take somebody else's bread than cut my own throat. Charlie showed me the difference between right and wrong."

"Don't give me all the credit," Charlie said, feeling his cheeks heat up. "Nobody can change the leopard's spots but the leopard himself."

"Maybe," Sheila admitted. "But I never wanted to change until I met you. I wouldn't go back to that kind of stuff if my life depended on it." She cocked an eye at Paul, who was still sitting morosely staring at the candle lamp. "Hey, Paul," she called to him. "As long as we're all stuck here baring our souls, what's this about you and your father?" She almost said "old man," but Paul had an element of class about him, so she changed it to "father" before it slipped out.

"He's a sex pervert," Paul said disgustedly.

"A fairy? So what's the big deal? What did he do, make a pass at you?"

Paul squirmed in the chair. "No, his wife did."

"Your old . . . your mother?" She looked amused.

"My stepmother," Paul corrected.

Lisa leaned into the conversation. "Paul is sexually immature," she said.

Sheila raised her eyebrows. "Sexually immature. Hey, that's quite a mouthful."

"I am not sexually immature," Paul hissed. "I'm a devil of a lot more mature on that score than you are," he said to Lisa.

"Then why did some woman's sexual advances make you

all uptight? You've been acting like some little schoolgirl who's just been raped."

Rod opened his mouth to reproach her, but Nancy shook her head at him and he kept silent.

"Because the woman was my stepmother, that's why, and she did it with my father's endorsement." He grimaced and banged the brass cap on the candle lamp. "In my book that's sick."

Sheila's voice was soft and understanding when she asked Paul, "But does your father love you?"

Paul was slightly taken aback. "What does that have to do with it?" She didn't answer him; she merely looked kindly into his face. "I don't know whether he loves me or not; we hardly know each other."

"I don't get you," Sheila said.

Paul hurriedly explained about his separation from his father and how his mother had tried so hard for so many years to keep them apart. His hands began to tremble slightly when he rushed through the part of Laura's seduction.

"And you think your father and your stepmother were going to share your body?"

"That's the impression I got," Paul said, his face crimson.

"No, I think you're wrong, Paul," Rod said. They all turned to him. Rod gave Sheila a boyish grin and said, "Paul's stepmother made the same kind of advances to me when I was at their home for dinner the other night."

Sheila's brows shot up. "A regular little nympho, huh?"

"I believe so," Rod admitted. "But although her husband—Paul's father—knew what was going on, I don't think he intended participating. I got the impression that he merely wanted to watch."

"Yeah, I've known lots of guys like that," Sheila said. "In fact, I knew this couple once who had me over to their apartment. The guy told me they were brother and sister, but I found out different. They were married to each other. Well, the guy wanted to make it with me and I found out the wife was behind a curtain preparing to watch. I got out of there only because I didn't like being treated like a piece of furniture."

"Sheila," Charlie rebuked. "I don't think you should be talking like that in front of the kids."

"Like what?" she asked innocently. "I didn't use no dirty words or anything."

"It's not that. I mean the—you know—the sex and all. They might get the wrong idea about you and me."

"What idea? Anybody can tell by looking that you're the only guy in my life."

Rod felt uncomfortable. "I'm sure he is," he found himself saying and not knowing why he said it.

Sheila glanced at Nancy and thought she looked disapproving. She leaned close to Nancy and in a half-whisper said, "You don't think much of my Charlie, do you, kid?"

"That isn't true," Nancy said.

"Ah, I know he ain't much to look at through your eyes, but through mine he's the greatest."

"I'm sure he is," Nancy said.

Sheila glanced at her again. "Ever have any trouble with John Law?"

"No, I'm afraid I haven't." Nancy laughed. "I guess I live a very unexciting life."

"Jail's no fun. You can't imagine what it is like to be in a prison with a bunch of clawing cats. The best of them were pigs, using everything they had to survive, including their own bodies, selling themselves off to the bulls. Nothing but dirty prostitutes, the whole pack of them," she said in a confidential whisper. "I never liked pros; they're the laziest kind of woman I know."

She watched Nancy cringe. "Yeah, jail's pretty disgusting. But the disgusting stuff ain't all in there. Inside at least they were open and honest about what they wanted and what they were. But all animals are like that, open and truthful, not phony and play-acting with people's lives and emotions." She paused, staring fondly at the fat, sweaty Charlie Cranston whom she'd married. "After the pigs I lived with for a time, Charlie was like a rich farmer who slopped and slaughtered those pigs." She glanced at Nancy again. "You'll meet your share of pigs, honey. Believe me, everyone does sooner or later. You don't have to spend time in stir to meet pigs. They're always hanging around, even in the best places." She laughed. "They're mostly in the best places," she emphasized.

She noticed the look of doubt Nancy flashed at her. Sheila gave a little chuckle. "You don't believe me. You think you'll escape all the ugliness by hooking up with some nice guy—

like that Mr. Shepherd over there. But take my word for it, kid. The pigs will come. Even that great big handsome brute who calls himself Rod can turn into a pig before you know what's happened. And you wind up slopping him every day but never get to meet the gentleman farmer. So take my advice, kid. Get a long deep look inside the hide before you make a coat out of it, if you get my meaning. Even ermine smells if it comes from a rotten animal." She sighed. "Yeah, you'll meet your share of pigs; and when you have, you'll realize that guys like my Charlie are real treasures—not much to look at but definitely priceless. You'll see. Only a whole lot of bad luck and heartache can open a person's eyes to the really great people in this world."

She shook herself, as though shedding her reverie. "Hey, look at me getting all philosophical and all." She gazed across the room, seeing nothing. "I've been feeling like that ever since Charlie and I found that dead girl washed up on the beach yesterday."

"Dead girl?" Nancy asked.

"Yeah, one of those high-class kids who lived in a villa. An American girl, Charlie told me."

Nancy frowned. "American?"

"Charlie talked to the kid's family. Brandon, I think he said their name was, or something like that."

"Not Cynthia Brandon," Nancy exclaimed.

"Yeah, that's the kid. Hey, you look kinda strange. Do you know the girl?"

Nancy's face was chalk white. "Are you sure it was Cynthia Brandon?"

Sheila shrugged. "That's what Charlie told me. He went up to the house with the inspector of police." She looked across the room at her husband. "Charlie," she called. "That dead girl, didn't you say her name was Brandon?"

Charlie was checking the bandage on Paul's hand. "Yeah, Cynthia Brandon. Why?"

"Dear God," Nancy breathed. So that was how girls like Cynthia ended up . . . washed up on a beach. She sat there, stunned. "Drowned?" Nancy asked almost without feeling. It was difficult for her to feel sympathy for the girl who had taken so many of Nancy's boyfriends away by impressing them with her money.

"Charlie says they think she was murdered."

"Good heavens," Nancy breathed. Yet her shock was a bit artificial. She disliked Cynthia Brandon. She wasn't genuinely sorry for the fact that she was dead . . . murdered. It was odd, but to Nancy the Cynthia Brandons in this world seemed to deserve an early death. Nancy felt she would be a hypocrite to say she was sorry. She wasn't. She'd always despised Cynthia—actually hated her at times.

She sat there stunned, yet unconcerned. It was as if a distant relative—one she'd never known—had passed away and she was expected to mourn. She couldn't mourn for Cynthia. She couldn't feel sad and knew it was horrible to feel glad.

She would have to pay a condolence call, of course, and would be expected to attend the funeral, much as she did not want to. It was times like these when she wished social etiquette had never been invented.

"You knew her, huh?" Sheila said.

"We went to school together. We were never very close, though." Nancy shrugged. "To tell the truth, I never liked Cynthia very much."

"Well, if she was done in, then you weren't the only one who didn't like her."

"Do they know who did it?" Nancy asked.

"Nah. Charlie was up at the house questioning everybody. He said, in his mind, any one of them is a likely suspect."

Nancy shook her head. "The Brandons always had a lot of scandal in their family. We're related in a very distant way, but I never socialized much with them."

"Yeah, from what Charlie said, they must be rolling in dough."

"They are, but they've never been a happy family."

"Lots of money don't always bring happiness," Sheila said. Sheila laughed and purposely changed the subject by turning to Rod. "You say you're from Ohio, Mr. Shepherd. That's farm country, ain't it?"

"Yes. I was born on one."

"Gee, that must have been real great."

Rod shook his head. "Being on a farm is either one's first exposure to life or one's last. It has been my first; it will not be my last."

"In other words, you'd never want to go back?" Charlie asked.

"Never. I moved to Dayton as soon as I was old enough to make my own way in life. Farm life just wasn't for me. It's not a very broadening kind of life."

Sheila's eyes left Rod, glanced at Lisa and then came back to Rod. "You two don't seem to get along too well, do you?"

"Sheila!" Charlie said. "I don't think you should be prying into people's personal business."

She lowered her eyes. "I'm sorry, Mr. Shepherd, Charlie's right. I'm a regular little old busybody." She paused. "It's just that I can't figure your kid out. When that cave-in happened the first one Lisa made a grab for was you, and she hung on to you for dear life. Now, she treats you like you didn't exist or something. I just don't get it."

"I wish he didn't exist," Lisa lashed out at her father.

"See what I mean?" said Sheila. She turned to Lisa. "You love your father, everybody can see that. Why are you trying so hard to pretend you don't?"

"I don't love him." Lisa felt a clogging in her throat. She had wanted to say she hated her father, but the words just wouldn't come out. Hate was such a terrible word, yet she felt she hated him, even though she couldn't bring herself to say it.

Paul jumped to his feet suddenly, turning all heads toward him. "What's that?" he said sniffing the air.

Everyone smelled it at the same time.

"Good God," Nancy breathed. "Gas."

The instinct to survive hit them individually and as a whole. As if on signal the six of them rushed toward the heap of debris blocking the doorway. They began digging at the rubble, throwing it behind them as they tried to clear the way. A cracking, wrenching noise made them freeze in their various attitudes. Rod looked up at the ceiling. An obvious bulge had appeared near the center, and the several cracks that were there earlier had widened slightly. One of the support pillars had splintered and was bowed. There was another grinding sound and the ceiling began to sag.

THERE WASN'T A SINGLE DOUBT IN ELAINE'S mind that Miguel was responsible for having kept her from seeing Jorge. Although she was beside herself with happiness, her happiness was coupled with anger. How dare Miguel interfere in her life the way he had? He had purposely prevented her from helping Jorge. But why? He claimed he loved her, but deep in her heart she knew that he loved her no more than she loved him. He was in financial trouble, and marrying her again would give him access to her fortune. She'd made that mistake with Miguel once and she did not intend repeating it.

She was fully aware that Miguel was a very mercenary man, but she really had not thought he would purposely try to destroy her happiness and her life—what she had left of it —for his own selfish gain. She admitted that he was weak and devious; she had never thought him capable of turning against those who liked him.

After leaving Jorge's cell, her feet several inches from the floor, she spoke to the policeman in charge about Jorge's predicament. He told her there was very little she could do until the charges against him were dropped.

"But I am dropping the charges," she told him. "It was my emerald necklace Jorge had in his possession. I gave it to him," she lied.

The policeman shook his head and riffled through some papers on the desk. "But according to the report filed by your attorney, you stated earlier that the necklace was stolen."

Elaine giggled, trying to sound flighty and frivolous. "Oh, that. I'd forgotten that I gave it to Jorge. I'm afraid I am a bit scatterbrained at times."

The policeman was not taken in. "Scatterbrained enough to forget giving him the jewels a few short hours before your daughter was found murdered?"

The smile vanished from Elaine's face.

Americans, the policeman thought. They are as cold and heartless as stones. Her own daughter killed, possibly by the young gigolo back in the cell, and she's trying to protect the man. Rich women such as she shouldn't be let out of their cages. They were dangerous, all the time trying to corrupt the young men on the island. Buying what they could not get otherwise. He had seen a lot of such women on Majorca, and he had no intention of being the least bit accommodating.

"Jorge Aguilar is charged with grand theft and suspicion of murder. Even your own attorney has requested that he be kept under custody until answers are found to the many questions."

"That's ridiculous. Jorge had nothing to do with my daughter's death, just as he had nothing to do with the disappearance of my jewels. He was with me in my villa the night my daughter disappeared."

They'd even perjure themselves, the policeman thought with disgust. Again he shook his head. "This report was filed by Miguel Montoro on your behalf. There is nothing we can do for Jorge unless directed by Señor Montoro."

Elaine's anger grew. "How much did Miguel have to pay you to keep Jorge here?"

"*Señora*," the policeman said, narrowing his eyes. "Your position in this matter is questionable enough without adding to it. I would suggest, if you have any questions to ask, that you ask them of Señor Montoro."

"I intend doing just that," Elaine said as she drew herself up and walked quickly away.

Dario was seated in the convertible, smoking a cigarette and listening to music on the radio. He got up with a start when he heard the clicking of Elaine's heels on the sidewalk. He hurried around the front of the car and held the door open for her.

"Do you know where Miguel lives?" she asked as she dropped into the low-slung seat.

"Yes. It is not far."

"Would you go there with me?" she said. "There is something very strange going on."

As Dario started up the car she began telling him of her conversation both with Jorge and with the policeman at the desk.

"But why?" Dario asked when she finished.

"That's what I intend finding out."

"But I thought Miguel approved of Jorge."

Elaine bit down on her lower lip. "I'm beginning to find out, Dario, that you never know exactly what another person thinks regardless of how long you've known them or how close they are to you."

The Montoro mansion was just on the outskirts of Palma. As they drove up to it they saw that the house were ablaze with lights. There were several cars parked in the garage, but there was a strange silence about the place, even though one would think a party was in progress.

Elaine had been here before, of course, but it had been a long time ago. She had forgotten how splendid the house was, pale and pink like a lovely pearl shimmering under the light of the moon.

"At least he's home," Dario said, nodding toward the cars. Miguel's Rolls Royce was parked a little apart from the others. He parked Elaine's car as close to the main entrance as possible and went with Elaine up the steps. He pulled the bell cord and listened as it resounded inside the house. There wasn't any other sound except the echoing of the bell. No one came. They waited a few moments. Dario pulled the cord again. They exchanged wondering glances.

"There must be someone here," Elaine said. She motioned for Dario to ring the third time. Again they got no response.

"Come along," Elaine said, tugging Dario's sleeve. "We'll go in through the French doors on the terrace."

"But we can't just barge in, Elaine."

"Why not? I came here to get things straightened out with Miguel, and I have every intention of doing just that. Come along."

The terrace doors were wide open, their sheer curtains moving gently under the night breeze. Elaine did not hesitate stepping through and into the sitting room. The place was deserted, but there were half-filled glasses of liquor and champagne scattered everywhere. Elaine's foot caught in something as she started across the room. She looked down and frowned. Her shoe was tangled in a woman's silk dress.

When Dario picked it up he smiled and rolled his eyes. "Maybe we've come at an inopportune time."

"No," Elaine insisted. "I think we've come at the precisely correct time. Come on."

They walked across the living room and out into the marble foyer. As they started to cross it they heard a little squeal coming from above them. At the top of the stairs a naked girl started down at a run, a naked man hot in pursuit. When they saw Elaine and Dario they stopped short. "Hey, look, Philippe, new recruits," the girl said. She waved at Dario. "Come on up, lover. Leave the girl there. There are too many up here as it is."

Elaine's mouth was slightly open; Dario's face was beet-red. The two at the top of the stairs retraced their steps and disappeared down the upstairs corridor.

Elaine and Dario exchanged glances. Dario tried to smile. "I think if you want to talk with Miguel it might be necessary for us to untangle him from a few bodies."

"As I was saying a little while ago, Dario, you never really know a person, regardless of how close you get to them. I never saw this side of Miguel before."

As they stood there trying to decide what course to take, they heard a loud groan followed by girlish shrieks of laughter. The sounds came from the room directly ahead of them. As they approached the door, moving more by instinct than motivation, the groan was repeated, this time louder, as though a man was in great torment. There was the sound of something like the cracking of a whip, and again peels of girlish laughter followed.

"No, enough. I can't take much more," a man said.

"That's Miguel's voice," she said, her face suddenly contorted with disgust and anger. She twisted the knob and threw open the door. It banged back hard against the inside wall.

Elaine and Dario stood there paralyzed by the shocking scene before their eyes. Elaine's hand flew to her mouth. Dario's breath caught in his throat as he stared, then quickly averted his eyes.

Miguel was tied spread-eagle to a long table in the center of the room. Margarita was standing over him, dressed in a leather mask, spiked boots and gloves but little else. She had a long, vicious-looking whip raised over her head. Another girl, young and blond and voluptuous, was sitting astride Miguel's chest. In her hand was what looked like a bottle of syrup which she was pouring generously over Miguel's obvious erection. A huge dog was standing between Miguel's outspread legs, lapping hungrily at the syrup that coated Miguel's genitals.

Elaine's stomach gave a lurch as she pressed her hand tighter over her mouth to keep from vomiting. The trio at the table stared at them when the door banged open. There was an awful silence punctuated by the sickening slurps of the dog's tongue. It was the only member of the tableau that hadn't turned to look at them.

Elaine stood, struck dumb. She swayed on her feet and felt Dario's hand steady her.

"Untie me, goddammit," Miguel cursed as he struggled with his bindings. "Untie me!"

"Oh my God," Elaine gasped. She turned quickly and ran stumbling out of the room with Dario close behind her.

"Elaine, wait! Wait!"

They were getting back into Dario's car when Miguel caught up with them, hastily tying the sash of the dressing gown he had shoved himself into.

"Elaine, I can explain," he babbled, spittle running from the corner of his mouth.

Elaine had regained some of her composure as she hurried out into the night air. She was seated in the car waiting for Dario to start the motor. Looking contemptuously up at Miguel's ashen face, she said, "Are you completely mad?"

"Please, Elaine, let me explain."

Years before if she had come across such a situation she would have been so crushed that she doubted if she would have recovered. But that was at a time when she was emotionally involved with Miguel. That emotional feeling toward him was dead. Now all she felt was utter and complete disgust. She pitied him, in a way, but not because of the trouble he had caused her; rather because of the perverted maniac he had become. She had always known of his perversity as far as his financial appetite was concerned, but his sexual perversity was something she had never reckoned with. It was inconceivable to think she had been married to this man and had never seen an inkling of his true self.

"I am afraid I tried a new kind of drug," he apologized, looking ridiculous in his bright-red silk dressing gown. "I got carried away, I am afraid. I have never done anything like this before."

"You are disgusting," Elaine said, turning her eyes from him.

"I am sorry, Elaine. You should have telephoned." He leaned toward her, fixing a worried expression on his face. "Has anything happened to bring you here at this time of night?"

Dario sat behind the wheel looking very uncomfortable.

Elaine's first impulse was to speed away from the house as fast as possible. Jorge drifted back into her thoughts, making her pause. Her mind cleared, remembering Jorge's fresh, clean face, his innocence and honesty. It gave her the courage to confront Miguel.

"I came to talk to you about Jorge," she said. Her mind began clicking into motion. "I suggest you get dressed and come with us," she said evenly.

Miguel's eyes widened. He made a hopeless gesture back toward the house. "But I cannot leave now."

"You will do as I suggest, Miguel," Elaine insisted, her mouth drawn into a tight, angry line. She noticed his indecision. "I have just spoken with Jorge. He told me he sent you to tell me he wanted to see me this morning. Why didn't you deliver that message? Why have you purposely tried to keep Jorge and me apart? I want answers, Miguel, truthful answers, or so help me . . ." She looked back toward the house. "So help me, I'll have you put in jail for what Dario and I have seen here tonight."

Miguel's jaw dropped. "Jail? What are you talking about?"

"Oh, don't play innocent with me, Miguel. You are an attorney. You know the penalty for bestiality here on Majorca. You could easily go to jail for several years if Dario and I testify as to what we saw tonight."

"Bestiality." He tried to laugh. "But it was nothing of the sort. Margarita brought her dog with her and we were only having a little fun, that's all."

"A little fun. Sex with animals is a serious crime." She saw the fear come into his eyes. "I mean every word I say, Miguel. I will stop at nothing unless you tell me exactly what has been going on between you and Jorge."

"But nothing has been going on."

Elaine eyed him with revulsion. "Very well," she said finally. "All right, Dario. Drive me to police headquarters again."

Dario started the car.

"No, Elaine, Dario. No, wait," Miguel blabbered. When Dario shut off the car, Miguel said, "All right. Come, let's go inside. I will tell you everything."

"You can tell us right here," Elaine said. "I have no intention of setting foot inside that house again."

Miguel looked beaten. "All right, Elaine, but please don't go to the police with this. I would be completely ruined."

"What of Jorge?" she asked evenly.

"I didn't want him to marry you," Miguel said after deliberating with himself. "I am having financial difficulties, as you know. I thought if I could get Jorge put in prison on a charge of grand theft that you might come back to me."

"You should have known better than that," she said bitterly. She kept her eyes fixed firmly on his face. "Then it was you who stole my necklace?"

Miguel sighed and nodded. "Yes. I heard you and him arguing outside your room. I heard you ordering him out of the house. We bumped into each other in the upstairs hall. He asked me if I had seen Cynthia. I told him I'd seen her drive off with Dario."

Dario's head snapped around. "But I did not," he said angrily.

"Well, I saw her leave with someone; I thought it was you."

"It was not."

"It doesn't matter," Elaine said impatiently. "Go on, Miguel." Her voice was like ice.

"Jorge went downstairs. I slipped into your room. You were in the bath. I saw the necklace lying on the dressing table and put it in my pocket, then slipped it into Jorge's bag when I saw that he had started to pack. It was my plan to see that the newspapers got news of your stolen jewels. I figured that Jorge would see it in the papers and would try to see you to return it after he found it in his bag. I paid your guards to watch for Jorge. They had instructions to bring him to me and not permit him to communicate with you. I would then have him arrested for possessing stolen property."

"You are a stupid man, Miguel. Now, I suggest you get your clothes on and arrange to get Jorge out of jail."

"But I can't do that, Elaine. The situation has become much more complicated since Cynthia was found murdered."

"Jorge had nothing whatsoever to do with Cynthia's death," she said.

"That may be, but the police believe otherwise."

"Only because you wanted them to believe otherwise." She shook her finger at him. "I'm warning you, Miguel. I want Jorge out of jail immediately or you'll be in there beside him, I guarantee it."

"But Elaine, be reasonable. There is no doubt that I can arrange to have the theft charge dropped against Jorge. But this other matter is completely out of my hands." The fear started to build in him again when he saw the fury in Elaine's face. "I swear to you, Elaine. I will do everything I can for the boy. I will speak with the inspector tomorrow morning, first thing. It would accomplish nothing if I went to the police station tonight."

She could tell he wanted to get back to his orgy; the thought sickened her. However, she knew that Miguel was speaking the truth. It really would not do any good for him to go to police headquarters at this time of night. It would only be through the authority of the inspector that the charges against Jorge could be dropped.

"All right, Miguel. But I expect to hear from you early tomorrow. I want Jorge out of prison. I will stop at nothing to accomplish that. Do you fully understand me?"

"Yes, Elaine. I will try."

"You will not only try, you will succeed, if you know what is good for you." She turned to Dario. "Drive me home, Dario. I'm feeling tired."

THE GAS SMELL HAD BECOME NOTICEABLY stronger as they scurried about trying to find out where it was coming from. Nancy was crawling on hands and knees along the far wall when suddenly her head started to reel. "It's stronger over here," she called to the others.

Charlie got down beside her, his huge stomach almost touching the floor as he crept on all fours, sniffing at the cracks in the bricks. His eyes started to tear as he sniffed at a fissure near the corner. "Here it is," he said, couching and wiping his eyes. "It's coming through this crack near the floor." He glanced over his shoulder at his wife. "Give me some more of that torn slip, Sheila, so I can stuff this up." Quickly Sheila hoisted her skirt and ripped away several strips of silk. "I don't think it'll hold it back for long," Charlie said, "but at least it'll cut down the output for a while. It's most likely building up on the other side of this wall. I just hope there's lots of empty space out there. Otherwise . . ." He didn't finish.

"Otherwise it will continue to build until it explodes," Lisa said, horrified.

"Let's not think about that," Charlie said as he finished stuffing the rags into the crack. "I'd prefer to think there's nothing on the other side of these bricks but open space."

He lumbered to his feet and wiped the sweat from his brow. His eyes stung and his breathing was labored. Sheila took out a handkerchief and wiped his brow. "You okay, love?" she asked.

"Yeah, I'm okay, but I think we'd all better keep to the other side of the room." To Rod he said, "And let's not forget ourselves, Mr. Shepherd, and light any matches."

"Believe me, I won't be that careless," Rod assured him.

"I think our best bet would be to sit on the floor and try to move around as little as possible. If it gets too strong we can wet our handkerchiefs with water from the carafes that didn't break."

They all sat down, their backs to the wall. Lisa put her head on her knees and began to sob. Rod, sitting next to her, reached over and put an arm around her. She straightened up and shook herself away from his touch.

"This is all your fault," she snapped. "If you hadn't interfered I wouldn't be in this lousy place."

A pained expression came into Rod's face. He put back his head and stared up at the ceiling.

Nancy, sitting on the other side of Lisa, patted her knee and said, "You shouldn't be so hard on your father. He's only doing what he thinks is best for you."

"Since when did he start caring about me?"

"You know better than that, kitten," Rod said. "I've always cared for you."

"The only ones you ever cared about were yourself and that Rose Mallory."

Rod blanched and turned his eyes up to the ceiling again. "You just don't understand," he said.

"What's to understand? Mother understood. She knew all about you and that woman."

Nancy leaned forward and looked over at Rod. "Oh, why don't you tell her the truth, Rod?"

He stubbornly shook his head and closed his eyes.

Lisa frowned at Nancy. "Tell me the truth about what?" She searched Nancy's face. "Don't tell me he told *you* about Rose Mallory." She gave her father a disgusted look. "Are you so proud of her that you brag about it?"

"Drop it, Lisa," Rod said, trying not to let himself become riled.

"I won't drop it. I think it's disgusting." She let her eyes slide toward her father. "Boy, I can just picture you picking up some young girl, like Nancy here, and telling her how you were never understood at home and how your family forced you into the arms of other women." She laughed viciously. "Isn't that the way the story goes? Men always toss out the same line."

Nancy tried to calm her. "It wasn't like that at all. First of all, your father didn't pick me up, I picked him up. And secondly, yes, he did tell me about this Rose Mallory, and personally I think he should tell *you* the truth about her."

"I know the truth about that woman. My father's secretary told me all about how he used to have her make telephone calls to the house to explain to my mother that he was tied up in meetings and stuff, but actually he was going out to Rose Mallory's roadhouse."

"Georgette said that?" Rod asked, shocked.

"Georgette told me everything at Mother's funeral."

"Told you what? There was nothing to tell. It's true I used to ask her to call home whenever I was tied up in evening meetings. But believe me, Lisa, I really was tied up in conferences. I wasn't lying to your mother, and I certainly was not visiting Rose Mallory."

"A likely story," Lisa said.

"It's true," Rod answered, but he saw that she didn't believe him and didn't want to believe him.

So that was it, he thought. It was Georgette who had told

Lisa about Rose. Remembering back, it was on the way home from the cemetery when Lisa's attitude toward him had changed so drastically. Georgette had been there; he'd seen her and Lisa talking together. That little bitch, he cursed, remembering Georgette's sly little wink when they were leaving the gravesite. For years Georgette had tried to get him into bed with her. At first he thought her harmless enough and discouraged her as tactfully as he could. She had been an excellent secretary and he hated to lose her, but her advances had become so overt, so annoying, that he found himself with no alternative but to discharge her. He supposed she was more bitter than he thought, and in order to get her ridiculous revenge on him she told Lisa those lies about him and Rose.

Still, he could never bring himself to tell Lisa the truth about Rose. At least not until she was older.

"Look, kid," Sheila said, addressing Lisa. "So what if your dad—"

Charlie cut in with, "Stay out of it, honey."

Sheila gave a shrug and leaned back against the wall. "That gas doesn't seem to be getting any stronger," she said. "Or maybe I'm just getting used to it."

Lisa refused to let the subject drop. "You all may think I'm just a stupid kid, but I happen to think a man's place is at home with his wife and family."

"And what about a daughter's place?" Rod asked caustically.

"If you mean me," she answered angrily, "I had no home to go home to after my mother died."

"You had a perfectly nice home," Rod insisted.

"Ha. Some home. You were never there. You were either at the office or at Rose Mallory's."

"I saw Rose only two or three times. And as for my not being home a lot because of business, that couldn't be helped. Someone had to pay the bills." His voice went softer. "Look honey. I know I may have spent too much time at the office, but I just wanted the best for you and your mother. I wanted to make sure you both had everything you wanted, a nice home, clothes, everything. Surely you can understand that."

Lisa remained petulant.

"We used to be pretty close, you and I, Lisa," Rod said. "Why did you let Georgette's lies change you so and turn

you against me? Surely you didn't really believe all those
things she told you about Rose and me."

"Why shouldn't I believe her? Wasn't it because of your
precious Rose Mallory that mother died?"

"Of course not."

"Do you mean to tell me you weren't with that woman that
night?" Before he could say anything, she added, "I know
better. Mother told me she was going to meet you at the
roadhouse, and then when Georgette told me about Rose
Mallory I put two and two together. Mother was trying to
keep us together, and she died . . . died trying to keep you
from leaving us." She broke into tears.

Again Rod tried to touch her, but she pushed him away.
"It wasn't like that at all. I wasn't trying to leave you or your
mother. It was just the opposite. I was trying to keep us together."

"Oh, for God's sake, Rod, tell her," Nancy urged. When
he shook his head at her, she added, "If you don't, I will."

"No, you will not," he said firmly. "Just keep out of
this, Nancy."

"You're a fool!"

"That may be, but this is my problem and I intend handling
it in my own way."

"Your way is killing the both of you, can't you see that?"

"Lisa has just got to learn to trust me. I have never lied to
her in my life, and she should know that I would not lie to
her now."

"She's fifteen," Nancy argued. "What do you expect of
her? She blames you for something you had no control over,
and I think you owe it to her to tell her the truth."

It was as if Helen were talking to him, not Nancy. Helen
used to admonish him in the same way for his stubbornness.
But he couldn't tell Lisa the truth; he hated to admit it to
himself, but he didn't trust her with the knowledge of the
true relationship between herself and Rose. There was so
much of Rose in Lisa; the same arrogance, the same inde-
pendence. God knows what Lisa would do if she discovered
the truth. No, he could not trust her with that knowledge.
There was a lot of himself in Lisa too. How blind he had been
to his own father's advice when he was Lisa's age.

Lisa cut into his thoughts. Turning to Nancy, Lisa said,
"He had control over what happened to my mother. He didn't

have to be with Mrs. Mallory. Because of his stupid obsession with that prostitute, my mother is dead."

"Your mother is not dead." The words just tumbled out of Nancy's mouth unchecked. She saw Rod's furious look, but she didn't care. She kept her eyes fixed on Lisa and repeated herself. "Your mother isn't dead."

Lisa was staring at her, not understanding. "What . . . what do you mean?" she stammered. Her eyes moved quickly over Nancy's face.

"Ask your father," Nancy answered, refusing to cringe under Rod's indignation.

Lisa turned toward her father. "What does she mean?"

But Rod was glaring at Nancy. "How dare you. I told you to keep out of this."

"What does she mean?" Lisa said, pulling hard on her father's arm. There were tears in her eyes again.

"Nothing," Rod said stubbornly. "She doesn't know what she's saying."

Nancy knew she was taking the chance of destroying her relationship with Rod. But he was wrong. Lisa was no child. She would understand. She had seen too much discord within her own family because of the lack of communication. She didn't know why she felt that Rod's problem was her own as well; she attributed it to the growing love she felt for him. She knew too that she was treading on very dangerous ice, but she could not help herself. She had started the avalanche and there was no turning back.

"I'm sorry, Rod," Nancy said. "Someday you'll thank me for this."

"Nancy, I'm warning you. Keep out of this."

She shook her head. "I can't." She put her hands on Lisa's shoulders and gently turned her toward her. Through her blind determination she heard Rod objecting, but she blotted him out. "I know this isn't going to be easy for you to take, honey," Nancy said softly, "but Rose Mallory was your real mother."

"Nancy!" Rod was on his feet, his fist clenched. "I forbid this."

"Sorry, Rod," she said, looking up at him. "I really think Lisa has the right to know."

Lisa was staring at him. "What is she saying, Daddy?" There was a pleading tone to her voice.

Why, oh why did Nancy tell her? She had no right. This was his problem; she should not have interfered.

"What is she saying?" Lisa insisted, tugging at his pant leg.

He inhaled deeply and slowly dropped to one knee. He took Lisa's hands in his. "Try to understand, Lisa. I didn't want you to know, at least not yet. I intended telling you someday, but I wanted you to be old enough to understand."

"Rose Mallory was my mother?" Lisa almost shouted.

He hesitated for a long moment, then nodded his head. "Yes, that is true. Your mother and I took you the day you were born. Rose never saw you, not even for a moment."

Lisa sat there letting the words filter into her brain, but it was as if someone were speaking a foreign language, one she did not understand. Slowly her head began moving from side to side. It moved very slowly at first, then moved faster and faster. "No!" she wailed. "No, you're lying. My mother is dead." She collapsed on the floor in a flood of tears.

Rod gathered her up into his arms. "I didn't want you to know, Lisa. I never wanted you to know." In spite of what he was saying, he felt as if a tremendous weight had been taken from his shoulders. Even the air in the room was fresher to breathe. The lie was finished. But a new fear clutched him. Although his conscience was at last at ease, the price he had had to pay might prove to be too much. If he had lost Lisa, his world was finished. He smoothed her lovely soft dark hair. "I'm sorry," he said simply. "I'm sorry, baby."

He let her cry, rocking her gently. After a while he felt her stiffen and straighten up. "I'm adopted." She said it flatly, without malice, without resentment.

"Not exactly, kitten. Rose was leading a kind of life that did not include a child. Your mother and I weren't married at the time. It was your mother's idea—Helen's—to go to Rose and ask her to give you up to her. I knew nothing about it at the time. I had broken off my engagement to Helen when Rose told me the circumstances."

"Then you're my real father?"

"Yes. And Helen was as real a mother to you as you could ever have. We both loved you very, very much."

"But why did you begin seeing Mrs. Mallory again?" Lisa asked in a tiny little voice.

"Because she wanted you back. Helen and I decided we'd

do anything she asked if we could just keep you from finding out the truth. We finally agreed to buy her silence. I went to pay her the money she demanded. Your mother—Helen—wasn't supposed to follow me, but she wanted to give Rose a piece of her mind, so she started for the roadhouse in a terrible temper."

"Poor love," Sheila breathed, wiping away the tears that were rolling down her cheeks.

"We didn't want you to find out about Rose Mallory," Rod told Lisa. "Helen and I agreed that we'd keep it from you until you were old enough to understand and to forgive us for what we did."

"Rose Mallory, my mother," Lisa breathed. It was true. She could see it in his eyes. And yet this terrible truth was made tender by something she couldn't see. He was pleading with her, pleading with her to understand. The softness of his features which she remembered as a young child had returned. He seemed so humble, so vulnerable, so handsome and kind. He was begging her with all his heart. She'd seen the same look in her own eyes when she had looked into the mirror after her mother died, when she'd come home from the cemetery and had decided she hated him. She had begged herself then to be kind and to try to understand, just as he was begging her now.

"Don't think about Rose as your mother, Lisa. Your mother is dead, kitten. Rose was never your mother and she never will be."

Paul moved to his feet. "Hey, does anybody notice anything?" he asked, looking around and sniffing. "The gas. It hasn't gotten any stronger. It hasn't been building up." He rushed over to where Charlie had stuffed the crack with rags. "It's still very strong over here," he announced. "But it hasn't gotten any stronger. It must be escaping somewhere."

"Gas rises, at least natural gas does. It's lighter than air, so it goes up," Charlie said as he got up and started to study the ceiling overhead. "Does anybody see any kind of vent up there?"

They all got to their feet, everyone except Lisa and Rod, who kept sitting against the wall, holding tight to each other.

"There," Paul said, pointing up at one of the beams. "There in the side of that center beam. Isn't that a grill of some kind?"

Charlie started to pile tables under the beam. He put a chair on top of the tables and began to climb.

Paul laughed. "Hey, you'd better let me. If you fall off you might bring the rest of the ceiling down on us."

Charlie stepped aside and helped Paul climb up on the tables and chair. The air near the ceiling was thick with gas fumes. He started to cough and finally put his handkerchief over his mouth and nose as he inspected the beam.

"Yes," Paul called down to them. "It's an airshaft of some kind. I can't tell where it leads until I get this grill off." He examined it. "It's bolted to the beam." He grinned as he ran his hand over the beam. "This thing is plastic," he said.

"What, the beam?" Sheila asked.

"Yes. It sure does look like solid wood from down there, but it's phony. Just a plastic false beam that was laid against the ceiling."

Charlie shot Sheila a look and said, "And you said the place had authentic atmosphere. Plastic." He grunted.

Nancy handed Paul a fingernail file she'd extracted from her handbag. "Try unscrewing the grill with this."

They all stood tense and anxious as Paul labored with the screws. He struggled, breaking the end of the file, but after resorting to using the side edge of the file he found he could loosen the screws. After a few moments he handed the grill down to Charlie and stuck his head into the hole it had covered.

"Yes, it's an airshaft all right. It gets a little wider on the other side of the grill." He glanced down at Charlie. "Shall I climb through and see where it goes?"

"Be careful, kid," Charlie said, not wanting to encourage him and yet hoping he'd be willing to explore. "Don't get stuck in there."

"No way. It gets wider," he said as he pushed himself into the mouth of the shaft and started to wriggle himself inside it.

They watched his feet disappear through the opening. Even Rod and Lisa had stood and were looking at the empty vent, watching intently, listening for any sound.

Far in the distance overhead they heard a dull clang. There followed a long, deadly silence. They looked at each other, then returned their eyes to the opening in the beam. Charlie strained to hear. He thought he heard voices coming down through the vent, but he couldn't be sure. After another long, anxious moment they heard the sound of something moving. Minutes later Paul's feet appeared, then the rest of him. In his hand he held a thick piece of rope. He dropped cautiously down onto the chair, pulling the rope after him. There was a happy grin on his face.

"It goes up to the street," he said. His grin faded. "God, it's terrible. The whole building came down on the restaurant. There's a rescue team up there, but they aren't doing anything but standing around. From what I could understand, they're waiting for some kind of expert demolition crew. They're working on removing the debris from the front of the building, where everything has already collapsed, but there's still a part of the building left standing. It's just above us. They're afraid to do anything for fear the rest of it will come down. They know about this smaller dining room but were afraid to try to get to us because it might cause another cave-in."

"Dear God," Nancy breathed.

Paul fingered the rope. "We'll all have to be very careful moving out through that shaft. It isn't very sturdy. I borrowed this length of rope to help us pull ourselves out."

Charlie grimaced. "That's foreigners for you," he said. "If we were home they'd have sent guys down here to help us, instead of them standing around up there with their fingers up their ass." He flushed slightly. "Sorry for the language," he said to Lisa and Nancy. Then he took the rope from Paul and glanced up at the opening. He studied it a moment, touching his hand to his huge stomach. He'd never fit through, he knew that, but he wanted to make sure nobody else realized it, especially Sheila. "Okay," Charlie said quickly. "Women and children first. Sheila, up on the chair."

She hesitated. "Let the kid go first," she said, nodding to Lisa.

"No, you first," Charlie insisted. "I want somebody up on top to help pull the others out. Those characters topside aren't going to lift a finger to help us, especially now that they know we're Americans."

"But—"

"No buts. Up you go, Sheila. Shake a leg."

Sheila wasn't thinking about anything but escape. She willingly let Charlie help her climb the table and chair, and then, holding tight to the rope, she climbed up into the shaft.

"Now be careful and don't rock the boat," Charlie called up to her.

As her feet disappeared Charlie breathed a sigh of relief. He waited until she was well out of sight. Turning to Nancy and Lisa, he said, "Okay, you two. You're next."

Sheila found it difficult to breath. The smell of gas was thick and strong. She wished she had tied a handkerchief over her mouth before climbing into the shaft. But it was too late now. There wasn't any room to turn around, and besides she heard someone shuffling up the shaft immediately behind her.

"Who's back there?" Sheila called.

"Lisa."

"Good girl. Just remember what Charlie said—'Don't rock the boat.' This airshaft is pretty flimsy. I just hope it holds up until we all get through."

She froze. "Oh my God," she breathed. She stopped climbing, causing a blockage. "Charlie!" she yelled.

Lisa bumped against her feet. "Sheila, go ahead. What's wrong?"

"Charlie," Sheila shouted. "He'll never fit in here. He won't be able to get out."

"Please, Sheila. Don't stop now. Go ahead."

"No, I gotta go back." She started to struggle, but couldn't move backward with Lisa directly behind her and the others behind Lisa.

"You can't go back now," Lisa said. "You've got to go on, Sheila. Please. Nancy's right behind me. We'll suffocate in here with this gas. Please, go ahead, Sheila. Please."

Unconsciously, Sheila, shaking with fear, started to pull herself along the shaft. She felt the clean evening air on her face as she moved upward. High above, faces were peering down at her. "Pull me up, you bastards," she screamed, hysteria threatening her as she realized that Charlie would have to remain behind until he could be dug out . . . *if* he could be dug out.

Hands reached down for her and lifted her out, clear of the vent. She gulped down huge lungsful of air and tried to shake off the dizziness in her head.

Down below, Paul's feet again disappeared into the airshaft. "You next," Charlie said to Rod, handing him the rope. He dug in his pocket and handed Rod the claim check for the suitcase at the air terminal. "Do me a favor and give this to Sheila for me," Charlie said.

Rod frowned, glanced up at the opening of the vent and then back at Charlie. "Damn, I never thought," he said to Charlie.

"I'll never fit through there." Charlie laughed sadly. "Sheila always said I should go on a diet. I guess this is my penance for not listening to her."

"Don't sweat it, Charlie. Once up on top I'll get them digging for you right away. We'll have you out of this hole in no time."

"Well, just in case anything happens, I want Sheila to have this," he said, giving Rod the claim check. "When you get upstairs, just hand it to her and tell her to use it if anything happens to me." He patted Rod's shoulder. "You heard her yelling when she was in the vent. She knows I won't fit through, so try and keep her calmed down. She gets pretty hysterical sometimes."

"Sure, Charlie, sure. I'll take care of her. But don't you start worrying, now. We'll have you out of here in no time at all."

"I ain't worrying," Charlie lied. "Go on. You'd better shinny out of here." As Rod climbed up onto the table and chair, Charlie said, "And for God's sake, Mr. Shepherd, see that Sheila don't do something stupid like trying to climb back down here, okay?"

Rod smiled. "Okay, Charlie. See you in a little while," he said as he climbed into the shaft and started to climb up toward the street.

The climb through was more difficult than he'd expected. He scarcely fit in the vent himself, and the air was so clogged with gas fumes that he could scarcely breathe. He marveled at Lisa's and Nancy's courage, especially Lisa's. Maybe things would be all right between them now. Perhaps Nancy had been right. Perhaps he had underestimated Lisa. She didn't seem bitter. She seemed to have taken the shocking news well enough. Of course, he told himself, it was very early in the ballgame. He'd just have to wait and see.

IN THE SEEDY CAFE DOWN NEAR THE WATER-
front, Greg Brandon was sitting in a dark corner watching
and waiting for Alfredo. There were only three or four
customers in the place, busy talking about some restaurant
that had collapsed, from what he could understand of their
gibberish. They were waving their hands in the air and gesturing wildly, telling how dozens of people had been killed.

Greg shrugged and gulped down his drink. What did it
matter that some loudmouthed tourists and Majorcan peasants
were dead? They were most likely better off.

He emptied the glass and sat there, reflecting, breathing
into the glass and watching his breath fogging its sides. He
was tempted to order another drink, but decided against it.
No, tonight he wanted to be sober and conscious of every
moment. His revenge was going to be sweet, something he
would relish and cherish. Revenge is a kind of wild justice.
He'd read that somewhere, and for some reason the words
had stayed in his head.

He sat there, wondering why he had remembered those
words. Was it true—as some say—that people's lives were all
predestined, all laid out on a blueprint, all charted well in
advance, and people unconsciously did things in preparation
for their then-unknown destinies?

And what of his destiny? What lay in store for him? He
knew the answers to those questions, because he was writing
out his own destiny. He wasn't going to leave that in the
hands of some uncaring God who was a stranger to him. The
only God he knew was himself; he made his life the way he
wanted it and not the way someone else wanted it. What did
he care what others thought or did? People only made a
pretense of being good. Basically everyone else was exactly as
he was—selfish. And who could blame them for their selfishness? Everyone had only one life; they didn't get a second
chance. So it was only right that everyone should look out for
himself.

The door swung open, and Greg's thoughts scattered when he saw Alfredo walk into the café. He stayed quietly in his corner and watched Alfredo go over to the bar. The bartender leaned toward him and whispered in his ear. He saw Alfredo turn toward him, smile and start toward the table.

"Hello," Alfredo smiled. "I hear you were in last night looking for me."

Greg hated the sight of him, but he returned the smile and motioned toward the empty chair across from him. "I decided I wasn't mad," Greg said, hoping he sounded flippant.

Alfredo winked. "I thought I had you pegged right. No hard feelings, then, I assume."

"No hard feelings. In fact," Greg said, leaning back, balancing his chair on the two back legs and rubbing his crotch, "I was wondering if you ever did return engagements."

Alfredo's grin broadened. "Not ordinarily," he said, "but in your case I'll make an exception." He stood up. "Come on. I have a little place not far from here."

Greg forced himself to laugh. "No, I was thinking of something else," he said, feeling the underside of his lapel to make sure Maggie's daggerlike hatpin was still securely pinned there. "To be honest, I'm still a little sore back there from the other night." Greg purposely let his eyes move toward the men's room. "I thought . . ." He winked and jerked his head toward the men's room.

Alfredo laughed heartily. "Well, I see you are more educated than I thought." He rubbed his crotch. "Sure, why not. I'm hot as hell tonight. I haven't gotten rid of a load since the one I gave you the other night, so I'm busting at the seams." He sat down again.

"You want a drink first?" Greg asked politely.

"Maybe afterward, if you're still in a friendly, talkative mood. I've found that some guys just want to go off and hide themselves afterward. Guilty conscience, stuff like that, I guess."

"I don't have a guilt-ridden bone in my body," Greg answered.

"Glad to hear that. Come on, then. I'm really hot."

When Alfredo stood up, Greg saw the evidence of his arousal. The front of his pants tented outward. Alfredo gave it a little feel and turned toward the men's room. He glanced over his shoulder and saw Greg fumble with the lapel of his jacket, then stand up and follow him.

There wasn't anyone inside the lavatory when they entered. Alfredo brazenly leaned up against the sink and unzipped his fly. He pulled out his cock and shook it at Greg. Greg stared at it for a moment, feeling the waves of disgust rising up inside him. But he forced himself to keep smiling. He winked again and nodded toward the glory hole in the partition separating the urinal from the toilet seat.

"I never tried it through the hole," Greg said. "It might be kicky. Do you mind?"

Alfredo grinned. "No. In fact I like it that way. As I told you once before, I come in here regularly for that."

"Good," Greg said as he opened the door to the stall and went behind the partition. He sat down on the toilet and let out his breath. What a pig, he thought. What in hell kind of creep would get his kicks from sticking his cock through a hole and getting it sucked off? As he thought about it he guessed it did have an element of fantasy about it. Reality was removed from both participants. The one "doing" had a male penis detached from its body. He could fantasize anything or anyone he wanted. The same would hold true for the one being "done." He could visualize anything as he was being serviced by an invisible warm, sucking wetness.

He looked down and saw Alfredo's feet coming up close to the partition. "Here, man. Take it," he heard Alfredo whisper in a tight, urgent voice. Then Greg saw Alfredo's penis, hard and erect, being pushed through the hole. He stared at it for a moment, unable to move. The thing filled his vision. The long, thick shaft, its head peeking through the puffy lips of the foreskin, quivered before his eyes. Greg found himself unable to move.

"Go ahead, man, take it in your mouth." Alfredo started a fucking motion, screwing the hole itself.

As Greg gazed at the bodiless penis, something way back in his past rushed back to him. He remembered his first night in military school and the night Phil came to his room. It seemed so long ago, and yet the sight of the erection inches from his face brought it all back into focus. He'd been so miserable that night, feeling that his mother had sent him away, hadn't wanted him anymore. And he'd felt ashamed for having done those things with his stepfather and Cynthia.

And Philip had been so kind, so understanding when he told him all about what had happened at home. Greg couldn't remember exactly how things had gotten started with his instructor. Phil had touched his cock and it had gotten hard.

Without realizing it, Greg moved his hand upward. Slowly he wrapped his fist tightly around the base of the shaft that seemed suspended in front of him. It felt just the same as Phil's had felt that night, he thought, as he started to move his hand over it, pulling the foreskin back and forth, covering and uncovering the blood-filled head.

Tears came to his eyes when he remembered the rest of it. He remembred how Phil had urged him to kiss it, touch it with his mouth, suck on it, while Phil was doing the same thing to his own teen-aged cock.

Greg found himself in a trance, sitting there, fondling Alfredo's shaft, staring at it. He leaned closer, his eyes veiled over. His nostrils picked up the strong, heady sex smell. He could almost feel the heat of it against his face. His tongue moved slowly over his lips, moistening them. He was breathing hard.

"That's it, man. Go ahead and take it. Hurry up," he heard Alfredo whisper harshly, anxiously.

Greg tightened his grip on the shaft. You're queer. Although his mother had never actually said those words, he knew she thought them. He remembered seeing her face and the disappointment in her eyes when they'd sent him home from school the day they caught him and Phil in bed together.

Greg felt the beads of perspiration on his forehead. Tiny rivers of sweat were running from his armpits.

"God, man. Hurry."

"Faggot."

"Suck it, man. Christ, hurry."

"Just like his stepfather."

"Take it in your mouth."

"Perverted."

"Suck it. Suck it."

"Perverted."

Greg was shaking from head to foot. His hands were quivering, his whole body was bathed in a horrible film of sweat. He felt trapped in a cage that had no door. He felt as if he were suffocating.

Shakily he reached under the lapel of his jacket and withdrew the long, sharp hatpin. He kept his hand tight around the base of the cock, holding it slightly upward, pointing it toward his parted lips. He kept staring at it, as though it were a powerful magnet dragging his mouth toward it. He tried to shake his head to clear his thoughts, but he found himself hypnotized by the sight of the long, thick, heavily veined shaft. Phil's shaft.

If he could only go back to being fifteen and innocent again. He wanted to be back at military school with Philip, who'd been so kind, so understanding. He wanted to have again all the fun and games they used to play, the hikes they took, the camping out, the swimming naked in the pond. He wanted to forget his mother's dislike of him, Cynthia's disdain, the demands everyone had put on him. If only he could return to Phil.

Maybe he could, he thought, as he gazed longingly, almost lovingly at the quivering shaft of flesh directly in front of his eyes. Perhaps he could recapture all that happiness again.

He moved his mouth closer to the swollen head. Again he licked his lips and closed his eyes and tried to conjure up Phil's handsome young face. Perhaps he could go back after all.

"Go ahead, for Christ's sake. Suck it, man. You know you're queer. You want it badly, don't you, queer?"

Greg's eyes flew open. Alfredo's words started to echo around inside his head until he thought his skull would crack. Anger and hatred blinded him. "No," he screamed and rammed the long, sharp blade of the hatpin through the shaft, pinning Alfredo to the partition.

Alfredo let out an anguished scream. He tried to pull himself free and felt something cutting down the length of his cock. "Santo Dios," he shrieked as he grabbed the top of the partition and tried to keep himself from collapsing. He screamed again in an agony of pain.

"Help me, somebody! Help me!" Alfredo shrieked.

Greg was up off the seat and out the door like a sprinter leaving the block. The door of the men's room burst open. Greg knocked the bartender and several of the customers aside as he raced for the street.

"What in hell's going on in here?" the bartender demanded.

"Oh, God!" Alfredo screamed. His eyes rolled back in his head. "Help me, somebody! Please help me! The pain!" He felt his senses weakening, everything going black. He mustn't pass out. Oh, Christ, he mustn't lose his grip and fall. He must hold on.

The bartender and the others couldn't understand what was the matter. They saw Alfredo hanging on for dear life and couldn't understand it.

Alfredo felt the blood pounding in his head. His eyelids drooped. "Oh Holy Mother of God," he breathed as he slipped into unconsciousness. His hands loosened from their grip on the top of the partition and he fell to the floor, the daggerlike hatpin cutting the shaft of his penis into two ragged halves.

THE RED AND BLUE LIGHTS ON THE AMBU-lances twirled like tops. The police were stringing up ropes to hold back the curious as Rod emerged from the air shaft. He saw Lisa and Nancy standing in a little cluster with Paul and Sheila. Paul was struggling to hold Sheila in his arms. When she saw Rod she broke free and ran to him.

"Charlie can't get out," she shrieked as she threw herself at him. "He won't fit through that hole."

Rod grabbed her and tried to hold her. "He's going to be all right, Sheila. Try to keep calm. I'll get the rescue squad to start digging right away."

"But they won't," she said, halfhysterical. "I asked them. They won't. They're more concerned about the damned terrorists who caused it all."

"Terrorists?"

Paul said, "It seems a terrorist group had their headquarters just above the restaurant. They were making Molotov cocktails. Something went wrong and their entire cache of weapons and ammo blew up."

Sheila said, "They told Paul they're afraid that wall is going to fall in. Oh, my God, Mr. Shepherd, it's right on top of where Charlie is stuck."

"Now, now. Don't be afraid, I'll get some action right now

if I have to pick up a couple of these jokers and knock some sense into their heads."

Paul said, "It's no use, Mr. Shepherd. I've tried to reason with them, but they said it is too dangerous to start clearing away the debris and start digging. That wall might come down at any moment."

"But we can't leave Mr. Cranston down there," Rod said angrily. "They've got to do something." He hurried over to speak to the man directing the firemen and police officers, who were scurrying around like hens in a barnyard.

Below, Charlie was pacing back and forth. So this was how it was coming out, he thought. He had a feeling that he'd never get out of this little dining room. It brought a smile to his lips as he thought about his predicament. Who would have thought Charlie Cranston would wind up buried under a pile of old bricks on the island of Majorca? Oh well, it wouldn't be so bad. If this was the end, he didn't mind so much. At least he'd finally found happiness with Sheila.

The ceiling groaned and one of the support columns bent under the weight.

"Go ahead," he said to the ceiling. "I don't mind. I've had it. It's just as well it does end like this. At least Sheila won't have anything to worry about."

He grew wistful when he thought of the child she was expecting. He hoped it would be a boy. She'd name him Charlie, of course. Gee, how he wished he could see that kid, hold him in his arms. Take him around and show him off to all his friends.

But he didn't have any friends over here. They'd find some, he decided. He ran his hand through his thinning hair. What the hell, he said to himself. It's all for the best. He couldn't keep it all from Sheila much longer. He'd tell her eventually and he'd lose her anyway, so maybe it was just as well for it to end like this. He'd never be able to go home to New York, not with them discovering all that cash he'd been ripping off.

Christ, he hoped that Mr. Shepherd remembered to give Sheila the claim check. Sure he would. He was a nice guy, that Mr. Shepherd. He'd look after Sheila until she got home. Naw, nobody had to look after Sheila, that girl could look after herself better'n anybody alive.

Yes sir, Sheila was some girl.

He sat down on one of the chairs and put his face in his

hands. To his surprise he found tears streaming from his eyes. "Sheila, oh goddammit, Sheila, why did it have to end like this," he cried. He sighed and leaned back, looking around at the empty room. Her handbag was sitting on one of the tables. He went over to it, and without knowing why he snapped it open. He picked up her compact, turning it over in his hand. He'd given her that compact on their second date. It wasn't much of a compact; he'd given her better ones later on, but she liked to carry this one. When he clicked it open he grinned, looking at the picture of himself which she'd glued to the inside of the lid. They'd taken that picture at that crummy arcade out on Coney Island. Sheila insisted on a picture of him, and she had complained that both of them wouldn't fit in the booth. It was a lousy picture. He was better-lookin' than that, he thought as he smiled at himself.

Sheila liked it. Sheila liked everything about him. He rubbed his stomach and looked up at the opening in the vent. She never liked the way he put food away. He should have listened to her. He'd be with her right now if he had.

"Oh, damn, Sheila. I sure wish I was up there with you," he said and started to cry.

Sheila was waving her arms and yelling at the rescue workers, trying to get them to do something about her husband, but they merely shook their heads at her, very apologetically, and walked away.

"They can't chance it right now," Rod said, coming back with Paul. "They've got to put some braces against that wall to keep it from toppling before they start digging."

"How long will that take?" Sheila demanded.

Rod shrugged. "It seems they're waiting for some demolition experts to get here. They're trying to round them up right now."

"Christ, where in hell are they, in China?"

"Try to relax, Sheila. Everything is going to be just fine. Oh," he added, digging into his pocket. "Your husband asked me to give you this before I crawled through the vent."

"What is it?" Sheila asked, trying to study the claim check in the dim light of the night. "It looks like a claim check."

"He said for you to use it in case anything happens to him." Rod saw the horror in her face and quickly added, "But nothing is going to happen, so don't worry."

"What kind of crazy people live on this stupid island?" Sheila yelled, waving her arms toward the rescue teams. "Why can't they start bracing that wall or whatever they have to do without waiting for somebody else to do it? I never saw such a place." There were tears running down her cheeks.

"Now just try to stay calm," Rod said. "It may take a couple of hours, but your husband is perfectly safe in that room down there. When we were down there together we didn't think for a moment of not ever getting out, so try to think the same way now. Your husband will get out. I know it."

"Not if nobody does anything to help him get out," Sheila argued. "Come on, Mr. Shepherd. Let's get ourselves some shovels or picks or something and start digging for him."

"That may not be the wise thing to do." He glanced up at the towering, jagged wall of bricks and stone. "These people know what they're doing, I'm sure."

"Well, I just can't stand around doing nothing. If nobody's gonna help me get Charlie out, then I'll do it myself." She pulled herself free of Rod's hand and hurried away from them.

"Sheila, don't do anything foolish," Rod yelled. But Sheila disappeared around the corner of the firetruck. A moment later she reappeared, carrying a fire ax in her hands.

"Sheila, don't be foolish," Rod yelled as he ran to her.

She brandished the ax, threatening him with it. "Please don't try to stop me, Mr. Shepherd. My Charlie's down there, and I'm going to dig him out."

"But certainly you don't think you're going to be able to dig him out. Sheila, listen to reason. There are tons of debris on top of that room. You'll never be able to get through it. Wait for the demolition teams. They'll have bulldozers and things to clear this away. They'll get Charlie out if you'll only be a little patient."

"I ain't waitin'."

She marched away from them and headed toward the opening of the airshaft. As she stepped over the debris she tripped and fell against a standing beam. It swayed and started to topple. Sheila screamed.

Rod raced over to her and yanked her to her feet, almost dislocating her shoulder. The standing beam creaked, then started to fall. It crashed into the base of the high wall.

There was a loud, horrible rumbling sound. The wall started to crumble.

Sheila let out a piercing scream. Rod yanked her to safety just as the wall fell, collapsing the ceiling over Charlie's head.

"Charlie," she shrieked. "Charlie"

Horror etched itself in every line of her face. Her eyes were stretched so wide open that the sockets stuck out. Her hand flew to her mouth and she bit down hard on her knuckles. She stared at the billowing clouds of dust as the stone and brick and mortar fell, sealing Charlie in his tomb.

"Oh, my God, Charlie. What have I done?" Sheila wailed as she stood horror-struck and stared at the rubble. "What have I done?" she repeated softly, then buried her face in her hands and leaned back against Rod. She felt his arms go around her as she started to scream hysterically.

Friday

THE LONG, SLEEK LIMOUSINE, DRAPED IN black bunting in respect for the dead, pulled into the driveway and started toward the villa. It was a bright, lovely morning, a perfect morning for putting things into their proper perspectives. The air was scented with orange and lemon and almond, interspiced with a healthy blend of fresh salt from the ocean. Somewhere in the distance a church bell tolled sadly, its muted mellow tones drifting over the orchards of olive trees like waves of floating gauze.

Elaine sat straight and unmoving in the back seat, flanked by Dario and Maggie Montgomery. She raised her mourning veil and glanced across Dario, gazing out at the neatly trimmed hedges, the profusion of color that burst from the flower beds. She felt a coldness in her heart. It was a strange kind of coldness, not one of loss or hate or resentment. It wasn't even the coldness of Cynthia's grave that she felt. She couldn't explain it. It was as if that small, deep grave on the hill detached her from the rest of the world. She hadn't really left Cynthia there alone forever. She would be joining her before long. Perhaps within the year, if what the doctors said turned out to be true.

Up on a far hillside she could make out a small flock of sheep moving aimlessly about under the morning sun. She had a fleeting urge to burst out of the car and rush up to the top of the mountain and throw herself onto its soft, grassy slope and never come down again.

She was surprised at herself for the lack of emotion she felt as Cynthia was laid to rest. She felt almost happy, not for herself but for the young girl in the coffin. At least Cynthia had escaped the disillusionment that came with age. She had died young, when the world still dangled beauty and irresponsibility before one's eyes. She had missed the torment of growing old, the pains and disappointments which children could bring. She had been spared facing the transition from a world of excitement and activity to one of dull routine and lethargy. Cynthia was better off where she was, Elaine decided as the car swept up the long, curving drive. She wished now that she could have been as fortunate when she was Cynthia's age.

"Greg could at least have had the decency to attend his own sister's funeral," Maggie said, breaking into Elaine's reverie. "After all, since you made it practically mandatory

341

for me to attend, you could at least have done the same for him."

"I haven't seen Greg this morning," Elaine answered, still struggling with her thoughts. "He did not come home last night."

"Shameful," Maggie breathed. "That boy is utterly thoughtless and irresponsible. He takes after you a lot in that regard," she added.

Elaine ignored her. She found that easier to do as the days went by. She wished with all her heart, however, that Maggie would go away. Maggie was right, though, that it was strange indeed that Greg had not attended his sister's funeral. They had been so close, almost to the point of an unnatural closeness. But then Greg had always been an unpredictable type. He never did what was expected. Greg too would go away now that Cynthia was gone forever, and she would be alone again. The thought did not bother her much. She'd been alone before; she was an expert at coping with loneliness. Besides, Jorge was here, and even though he was not living with her she was, at least, close to him and could see and talk to him every day. In her heart she was convinced that it would be only a matter of time before she and Jorge were together again, and once together, nothing and no one would separate them.

The little time she had left she would dedicate to making Jorge and herself happy. Afterward, he would be without her. But at least for a short while she would spoil him. Her past life hadn't brought her happiness, nor had her children or her husbands. She had made them happy at the expense of herself. Now she would think of herself and Jorge. She would be his ultimate happiness, and anything that came afterward would only be a reflection of the happiness she gave him.

"It was a beautiful service, Elaine," Dario commented.

Maggie huffed. "Beautiful? Good heavens, there were hardly any people there. I thought Cynthia had lots and lots of young admirers."

"Only the curious come to funerals," Elaine answered. "Young admirers try to stay as far away from death as possible. For them it does not exist."

"There was a terrible cave-in in Palma last night," Dario said. "Hundreds of people dead. That may account for the small number in attendance."

"Yes, I read about it in this morning's paper," Elaine said.

Maggie wasn't listening. "At least I had my picture taken for the newspapers, so I suppose the morning wasn't a complete waste of time," she said.

"I'm glad," Elaine said solicitously.

Elaine didn't want to think about the funeral or the newspaper people or anything of what she had had to endure earlier. She turned her head and looked at Dario. "What time are your races this afternoon?"

"The first heat begins at two o'clock. Of course the major races are tomorrow."

"Aren't you just a little nervous?"

"Not me," Dario said, pushing out his chest slightly. "This is old hat for me."

"Well," Elaine said, patting his knee, "it goes without saying that I wish you all the luck in the world."

Maggie leaned toward Elaine. "Surely you're coming to the races with us, Elaine."

"I don't think so, Maggie. Thanks just the same. I really have so much to do. I'm expecting Miguel. In fact, I had expected to see him at the funeral."

Dario grinned. "I have a feeling Mr. Montoro has been a very busy man this morning."

"And a poorer one," Elaine said with a smile. "It serves him right."

Maggie made a pretty face. "Then I assume from what you tell me that that young scalliwag of yours will be out of his cage today."

"I am not too certain of that," Elaine answered. "It seems there is still the question of Cynthia's death hanging over his head. Of course he had nothing to do with that, I'm sure, but the authorities think differently."

"You never know," Maggie objected. "Thieves eventually turn into killers, you know."

"Oh, Maggie, how ridiculous."

Maggie pouted. "Well, I still think Jorge broke out of jail, came here and stole my hatpin."

"And put himself back in jail again. Do be serious, Maggie," Elaine said, fighting against letting herself become irritated.

"Anything is possible in this boring place. I'm half tempted to pack my things and go back to Paris before everything I own is stolen right off my back."

"Surely not unescorted, Maggie," Dario said, giving her hand a suggestive squeeze. "I doubt if you would be safe."

"Oh, Dario, you silly boy." Maggie fluttered her eyelashes. "But then I suppose you may be right. A mature woman alone . . . well, she just isn't safe anywhere these days."

"Mature woman?" Dario chided. "You certainly are not referring to yourself?"

Maggie slapped him lightly on the arm. "Dario. I swear you are the dearest boy." She made big cow eyes at him and said, "Of course if I had a big strong man like you beside me I'd be safe just about anywhere now, wouldn't I?"

"I suspect you would," Dario said, again squeezing her hand.

Elaine looked curiously at Dario. There was something in his manner that made her think he was extremely anxious to leave Majorca. Now that she thought of it, he had acted rather oddly at Cynthia's gravesite. It wasn't anything she could put her finger on, but he seemed extremely uncomfortable, almost like a frightened animal. After they left the cemetery, however, he seemed to relax and revert back to his usual charming self.

Elaine said to him, "I think you would miss Majorca very much if you were to leave it."

Maggie shot her a dirty look. Dario said, "With Maggie I doubt if I would miss anywhere."

Maggie made a cute face, pursed her lips and slapped Dario's knee. "Oh, you wicked child," she said, letting her hand rest on his leg. "If you like we can leave this weekend, immediately after the races."

"That would please me very much," Dario said, smiling seductively at her.

"Oh dear," Maggie groaned. "I forgot about Nancy." Her expression clouded over with displeasure.

"Nancy?"

"My niece. She came here with me. Oh dear. I'd forgotten about her. Of course that isn't my fault. The girl never lets me know where she is or what she's doing. Thoughtless, just like all the other young people today." As though talking to herself she continued, "I brought the ungrateful girl with me when I left New York, so I suppose I will have to search her out and send her back home."

"Nancy's called you several times since you've been here. You told me so yourself," Elaine said.

Maggie looked annoyed. "Yes, I suppose she did. Oh well, it doesn't matter. I'll give her some money and send her back to her family. Poor Nancy. She's such a dowdy little thing, and absolutely penniless, practically destitute," she added, hoping to make sure Dario's interests weren't aroused. She certainly did not intend dragging Nancy with them to Paris; she wouldn't be foolish enough to take along Nancy's brand of competition. Ah, Paris, she thought happily . . . and with Dario in tow. Oh, how envious her friends would be when they got a look at her latest prize. She had a sudden itch to get out of Majorca as quickly as possible, but she knew she would have to be patient until Dario's stupid bicycle races were over with.

"Isn't that the inspector's police car parked at the house?" Elaine asked as the limousine rounded the final curve in the drive and came in full view of the villa. Her heart started to pound. Jorge was home. The inspector had driven him home from the jail. Miguel had managed to clear him of everything after all. Her pulse was racing.

"Police car?" Dario asked, stiffening on the seat. He strained to look out the window.

"Good Lord, now what?" Maggie breathed. "I suppose someone else has been murdered." A second later she brightened. "Or perhaps they've found my stolen hatpin."

The inspector of police was leaning against the fender of his car when the limousine deposited Elaine, Maggie and Dario in front of the villa. As Elaine emerged he bowed and took the hand she extended to him.

"Good morning, *señora*. I had planned on attending your beloved daughter's funeral this morning to express my deepest sympathies, but an unfortunate accident occurred in Palma last evening which prevented my doing so. May I express to you now my very deep sorrow at your loss."

"Thank you, Inspector," Elaine said. "I heard of the cave-in. Most distressing."

"The American detective, the one who came with me to question you the other day, Señor Cranston." The inspector shook his head sadly. "I am afraid he was one of the victims buried in last night's cave-in." He sighed. "I pray one day I

will visit you and your charming home without bringing with
me bad tidings."

"How does Mr. Cranston's death concern Elaine?" Maggie
wanted to know.

"That is not why I came," the inspector said. He looked at
Elaine. "May we go inside, *señora*. I fear I have more bad
news for you."

"Jorge," Elaine gasped. "Something has happened to
Jorge."

"No, young Aguilar is all right," the inspector assured her.

"Bad news?" Maggie said with a huff. "See, I told you so.
Somebody else has been murdered," she said as they walked
into the house.

Elaine's brow was creased. "What kind of bad news, Inspector?"

"It concerns your son, Greg. If he is at home I would like
to speak with him."

"I'm sorry, but Greg isn't here." She turned when she heard
Teresa coming down the stairs. "Is my son here, Teresa?"

"No, *señora*. He has not been home all night. His bed was
not slept in."

"Thank you." She turned back to the inspector and asked,
"What kind of trouble has Greg gotten himself into this
time?"

"It is a very serious matter, I'm afraid." He hesitated,
glancing at Maggie and Dario. "Perhaps we should speak of
it in private."

"No, it's all right, Inspector. You may speak freely in front
of my guests."

The inspector cleared his throat. "Your son was identified
by a certain bartender as having committed a rather sadistic
act last night." He fished in his pocket and brought out a
plastic bag in which Maggie's hatpin was contained. "This
does not belong to you by any chance?" he asked, showing
Elaine the pin.

Maggie snatched it. "My hatpin. How in the world did you
get it?"

"It is yours, *señora*?"

"Of course it's mine. It's part of my collection. Someone
stole it from me yesterday."

The Inspector shook his head sadly. "There is no doubt,
then, that it is your son we are looking for."

Elaine tilted her head and eyed him anxiously. "What is this all about, Inspector? What has Greg done? Tell me."

"Permit me, *señora*," he said to Maggie, taking back the hatpin and replacing it in his pocket. "I am afraid your pin must remain in the custody of the police for a little while. It was the instrument of a very terrible crime."

Elaine was becoming very agitated. "Will you please tell me what happened? What has my son done?"

He told them in as delicate a way as he could. When he finished he found he could not look into their shocked faces.

"Dear God," Elaine breathed.

"The young man is in a very bad state. He lost a great deal of blood. All the ambulances and doctors were at the scene of the restaurant cave-in, so there was no one to look after him immediately. There is a chance that he may not live."

Elaine buried her face in her hands. "Horrible," she sobbed.

Maggie suddenly started to giggle. Everyone stared at her. "Of course the young man will live," Maggie said. She clapped her hands together. "My dear, he'll be a sensation when he's healed," she said and started to giggle again.

"*Señora,* I do not understand you. This is a terrible thing."

"Terrible my foot," Maggie said. "Some African tribes do that to certain young males in the tribe as a part of their religious ceremony. Why I saw a young fellow in Casablanca once whose penis opened like a four-petaled flower when it became erect. It was ever so amusing."

The inspector again cleared his throat to hide his shock as well as his nervousness. He put his hand gently on Elaine's shoulder. "I regret, Señora Brandon, having to come here with such distressing news, but your son was positively identified. Knowing the hatpin came from this house is more evidence of his guilt. I am afraid I will have to place him under arrest."

They all turned when they heard the screeching of tires in the driveway. The roar of a car's motor rumbled through the house. The inspector ran to the door and threw it open just as Greg's car disappeared back down the drive.

"Greg," Elaine shrieked.

The three of them stood there dumbstruck as the inspector raced to his car, revved the motor and sped off after the fleeing car.

Greg cursed himself for having been so stupid as not to think the police would be looking for him. He had made a mistake coming back to the villa. He should have followed his original impulse; he would be well on his way to Switzerland by now if he had. But he had needed money.

He rammed his foot down hard on the accelerator as he passed through the gates of the estate and headed toward the road skirting the shoreline. He thought of the exhausting night he'd spent with the prostitute. Christ, he must have come at least four or five times. Surely that proved he wasn't a fag. It was certainly a night the whore would never forget. She was black and blue when he left her earlier.

He glanced in the rear-view mirror just in time to see the car spin out of the drive, throwing up a cloud of dust, and start after him. Greg floored the accelerator, cut hard to the right and started up a narrow winding mountain road. If he could only make it to the other side of the island, he could hole up in Deya and grab a boat over to France. He had a lot of friends throughout France, mostly women, of course. Ahead of him the mountains towered over the plain, their crests lobster-red under the sun, looking like solidified tongues of fire. He glanced back. The twisting road prevented him from seeing whether or not he was still being followed. He had the feeling that he was.

He steered recklessly around the sharp curves, glancing down occasionally at the little sheltered inlets of still, blue waters with drooping trees close alongside far below him. Above he saw the gray and yellow hill towns, clinging tightly to the sides of the mountain.

He didn't hear or see the donkey cart and the children until he rounded the curve. It was too late then to stop. He yanked the wheel hard to the right, throwing the car into a dangerous spin. His front wheels hit a cluster of rocks at the side of the road. The car leaped forward as if on its front legs and catapulted him through the windshield and into a tight grove of thick trees. He lay there feeling the intense pain that wracked his body, tasting the flow of blood in his mouth. Then everything went mute and still. Darkness drifted over him like a cloud. He thought of how unattractive he must look lying there, then he closed his eyes.

THEY TOLD SHEILA THAT IT WOULD BE SOME
time before they could recover Charlie's body from the rubble.
She had spent the night crying; she couldn't cry anymore.
Her grief had brought in its wake resentment, then anger, then
hatred. She hated everything. In particular she hated the world
and God, especially God, who had taken from her the only
true happiness she had ever known. What kind of heartless,
unfeeling thing must He be to bring this about?

"God in all His mercy," she said. "Ha," she breathed.
"Mercy indeed."

Her anger seemed to ease her grief somewhat. She knew
it would be only a momentary easing, but she welcomed it.
Charlie wouldn't want her wallowing in tears, drowning herself in sorrow. She stood up and looked at herself in the
mirror. She brushed back her hair and studied her face. She
looked all bloated and red. She noticed that she was still wearing the same dress she'd worn the night before. She couldn't
remember how she'd found her way back to the hotel. Rod
Shepherd must have brought her here. She didn't know.

She had to pull herself together. She had to change her
clothes and freshen herself. There was so much to be done, so
many details that would have to be taken care of. Of course
she would go home. But how did one go about traveling with
a deceased husband?

As she turned from the mirror her eye caught sight of the
small claim check that Rod Shepherd had passed on to her
last night. She remembered him saying, "Charlie said for you
to use this in case anything happens to him." Tears bubbled
out of her eyes again as she remembered his other words.
"But nothing is going to happen." She felt the pains in her
stomach. "You promised," she sobbed. "You promised nothing would happen." She staggered back to the bed and threw
herself down, covering her face with her hands.

"No," she said, admonishing herself sternly as she pushed
herself back up. "You are not going to cry anymore. You've

cried enough. Charlie wouldn't like it. Pull yourself together and start acting like somebody with some sense." She could almost hear Charlie saying that.

She looked down at the claim check clutched in her hand. She turned it over in her fingers, wondering what it meant. On one side were the words "Palma Airport"; on the other side was a number. It was definitely a claim check, but a claim check for what? Charlie hadn't mentioned his checking anything at the airport. Maybe it was a beginning, she thought as she got to her feet and started toward the bathroom. Maybe it would give her some idea what she was supposed to do now that Charlie wasn't here anymore.

She couldn't help it. She started to cry again as she went into the bathroom and turned on the shower.

A half-hour later she was still fighting back the tears as she sat before her dressing table. She carefully applied a heavy coating of mascara to her lashes, telling herself the heavier the coat the more insurance against her crying. She couldn't afford black streaks down her cheeks. The strange psychology seemed to work as she finished applying her cosmetics.

"Okay," she said to her reflection. "Now another little bit of lip rouge and I'll be all set." She felt that talking to herself kept her mind off her grief.

Her hand froze. "But I'm not all set," she said. "Money. I haven't a red cent. Charlie . . . " she said, almost choking on the name. "He has my purse with him." She frowned at herself in the glass. "Now don't cry, dammit. Stop it."

She forced herself to her feet and started to pace the room. "Maybe Charlie stashed some extra cash here someplace." She began pulling open dresser drawers and rummaging inside them. Under a neat stack of undershirts her hand touched a thick envelope. She took it out and looked inside. Her eyes widened as she flipped through the bills. "Holy Mother," she said. "There must be close to three thousand here," she breathed, staring at the pile of American currency. "Where in hell did Charlie get this kind of bread? And why didn't he tell me?" Then she remembered him telling her about the money he'd won at the races. It had been more than a couple thousand, she saw.

She smiled down at the money. "Good old Charlie," she said. "You never did let me down when I needed you." She reminded herself of her mascara and refused to cry.

Her first stop was at a bank to exchange the American bills she took from the stack into local currency. Her second stop was at the baggage-claims counter at the airport. When the clerk handed her the satchel she frowned at it, then took it from him and started back toward where the taxi cabs waited. Inside the cab she tested the locks and found them fastened. Charlie most likely had the key, or perhaps it was somewhere in the hotel room.

There wasn't any key anywhere, she found after a thorough search, but she did find a pocket knife among Charlie's belongings. She used it to pry open the locks.

When she lifted the lid of the case her mouth fell open. "Oh my God," she gasped, staring at the stacks of American bills, each stack carefully labeled and held with a rubber band. She labored with adding the figures together. Arithmetic was not one of her better subjects.

A long, low whistle escaped her lips. "There's almost a hundred thousand dollars here," she exclaimed. "But where . . . " Her head felt as if it weighed a ton. Her eyes were stretched open so wide they hurt. There had to be some kind of a mistake. "They gave me the wrong bag," she said. Quickly she checked the number on the ticket tied to the handle. It was the right number. It even had Charlie's last name printed on it.

She sat there trying to think, trying to make sense out of it all. It was as if she had suddenly opened an old photo album and the pictures made her remember things she'd almost forgotten.

"Oh, no, Charlie," she said. But thinking about it, it all made sense. Charlie kept hounding her about staying over here, never going back to the States. She looked at the money. "This is why he didn't want to go back. He couldn't go back." She shook her head. "Oh, Charlie," she sobbed, saying to hell with the mascara. "You didn't have to do this for me." But perhaps it wasn't for her. There was an awful lot of money in the case. It must have taken him years to rip off this much dough. "He must have ripped it off," she said. "Nobody can save this kind of money, especially on a detective's salary." She thought perhaps she was jumping to conclusions, but she doubted it. Everything made too much sense all of a sudden. There was that business about the counterfeit airline tickets, which Charlie got replaced so quickly, so easily. She wondered then how he could possibly have put in a call to New York so quickly. He hadn't called New York; he'd come to the baggage claim and taken some money out of the suitcase.

Again she looked at the money. One of the stacks was less tidy than the others. She checked the numbers of bills with the amount written on the top. They didn't tally.

"Well, there's one way of finding out for sure," she said as she started for the telephone. She picked it up and in a strong, determined voice said, "Operator. I want to place a person-to-person call to New York City. I'm calling Detective Sergeant Tony Gaventi, 17th Precinct in Manhattan." She gave the operator the number. After being told it would take a while, she hung up and went back to sit beside the money and wait. She glanced at her watch and started to figure the nine-hour difference in time. Counting backward on the face of her wrist-watch, she found it would be four o'clock in the morning in New York. With luck Tony would be working the night shift, which meant he'd quit about five.

About twenty minutes later the telephone rang. There was a lot of crackling on the line, but after a moment she heard Tony's familiar voice. "Hey, Charlie, is that you, old buddy?"

"It's Sheila, Tony. How are you?"

"Sheila, baby. How's the honeymoon?"

She tried to remain calm. "Something's happened, Tony. I need your help."

"Something's happened? We got a lousy connection. Can you speak a little louder?"

"Something's happened," she shouted. "Charlie's dead."

There was silence on the other end. Only the busy crackling sound reverberated against her eardrum. Then Tony said, "Charlie's dead?" as if not believing the last word she'd spoken.

"Yes. There was an accident last night." She started to choke up.

"Oh, my God."

"Yeah, a real bummer," she said, her voice shaking danger-ously.

"How did it happen?"

"Oh, I'd rather not talk about it right now, Tony. I'll tell you everything when I see you. That's what I'm calling about."

"Now don't you worry about a thing. I'll arrange everything. Just tell me exactly where you are and I'll take care of the details."

"No, that won't be necessary, Tony, I can handle it from here. What I want to know is what kind of trouble Charlie was in back there."

"Trouble?"

"Level with me, Tony. Let's not play games. One of Charlie's suitcases has a hell of a lot of cash in it. I want to know how come."

"What are you talking about?"

"I said don't play games with me, Tony," she shrieked. "You and Charlie were too close for too many years. Where did all this dough come from? I want to know." She felt herself near hysteria.

"Okay, okay," Tony said. "Calm down, kid." He hesitated. "Listen, there was some trouble back here just after you and Charlie took off." She could hardly hear him. He obviously was cupping the mouthpiece with his hand. "But it's all okay now. Everything's pretty well cleared up."

"Charlie was on the take, wasn't he?"

"Yeah, okay. But listen, Sheila. There was an investigation and a lot of suspicions were thrown at old Charlie, but there just wasn't enough evidence to do anything, so they're going to drop it for the time being and wait for him to come home."

"Oh, no," she gasped, letting the tears run freely down her face.

"Look, Sheila. Don't make waves. I was in on it too, so don't do anything you might regret later. Keep the dough. With Charlie gone the money belongs to you, so please, Sheila, don't do anything dumb. Just keep your trap shut and it'll all blow over in time."

Sheila wasn't really listening. She dropped the receiver into its cradle and threw herself across the bed. "Oh, Charlie. Why?" She cried until she couldn't cry any more. Her head was all jumbled together inside. As she pushed up from the bed she looked at the money. If she returned it to the precinct, Charlie's name would be dragged through the mud. If she kept it she'd just prove to herself that she was still the thief she once was, and all Charlie's good example and all his efforts to straighten her out would be wasted. He had tried so hard to put her on the straight and narrow; she could not let all that go for nothing.

She stood up and started to pace the room. Again she turned and glowered at the money. "What in hell am I going to do with you?"

ROD ROLLED UP HIS SOILED SHIRTS AND jammed them into the corner of his suitcase. On the other side of the bathroom door he could hear Paul Jr. humming to himself. Lisa had propped herself up near the headboard of his bed and was watching him pack. They had done a lot of talking after they left the cave-in site, and the talking had helped ease some of the resentment she'd felt for her father. Rod noticed the change in Lisa, especially when he proposed that they take a little vacation before heading home, just the two of them. Lisa said she was tempted, but that she'd had enough traveling for a while and wanted to go home, that she had a lot of schoolwork to catch up on.

"Are you all packed?" he asked Lisa as he checked the drawers to make sure he hadn't overlooked anything.

"I didn't have much."

"You were smart. I always pack too much when I go on trips."

When she didn't answer he looked at her. She was sitting quite still, staring off into space. "I'm sorry you had to find out about Rose Mallory the way you did last night. I hadn't wanted you to know just yet. I wanted to wait and explain when you got a little older."

"Yes, we went over that all last night. But it's okay, Dad. I understand."

He smiled at her. "Nancy said you were a lot more grown-up than I gave you credit for."

"I just feel funny, somehow, like I didn't belong to anybody at all anymore."

Rod went and sat down beside her. "You'll always belong to me. Nothing's changed. You made me promise last night that I'd start treating you like a grown-up, so I'm going to start right now." He paused. "All Rose Mallory ever did was bring you into this world. That's all. For her it was just a physical thing. She didn't love you and she doesn't love you now; she proved that when she accepted the money Helen and I offered her to stay away from you. Helen and I are your real mother and father. We're the ones who raised you and loved you and did everything in our power to make you happy. You belong to Helen more than you belong to anyone, including me, and don't you forget that," he said sternly. He kissed her on the forehead. "Now let's make a pact. Let's start caring about each other the way we used to care and forget all about Rose Mallory."

"It's not Rose that I feel so bad about, it's me."

"You?"

"Oh, I've been such a rat. I shouldn't have listened to all that gossip and stuff. I shouldn't have been so quick to turn on you the way I did."

"That's understandable, kitten. You were hurt because you lost your mother. You had to blame it on someone. You've heard that old saying about always hurting the one you love. Well, that's what you did. It's natural."

"Oh, Dad," she said, throwing herself into his arms. "I really didn't mean all those terrible things I said to you."

He patted her softly. "I know you didn't, honey. Everybody says things when they're angry. We're together again, you and me, and that's all that's important now." He hugged her for a moment, then eased her away from him and looked deep into her eyes. "Now I promised that I was going to treat you as an adult, so I want to ask you something—as an adult."

She frowned at him.

"What about this George Petrik character? Do you intend going back to him?"

"Oh, Dad. George wasn't what you think he was. Sure we traveled around together, but it wasn't anything like you think." She smiled shyly. "You forget I had a very good mother and father who taught me values in life. I'm still a virgin, if that's what you want to know." She saw the prudish look of surprise on his face. "Oh, Dad, 'virgin' isn't a dirty word, you know."

After a moment he smiled and hugged her. "Of course it isn't, kitten. In fact it is one of the nicest words I've ever heard."

"And about the drug thing," she added. "To be honest, I've smoked grass a couple of times, but all kids do. I never once got into any of the hard stuff. You can believe that."

"I believe it," he said, bursting with happiness. "But you still haven't answered my question about George Petrik."

"He was nice to me, Dad. I really wouldn't want to rat on him, so I'd just as soon not give out any information about him. He's someplace in Barcelona, but I don't know exactly where. I suppose I could locate him if I wanted to."

"But you don't want to."

She shook her head.

"Petrik is doing a lot of harm to a lot of people, Lisa. Are you sure you don't want the authorities to take him in and put a stop to his drug business?"

"Oh, Dad. There are a lot bigger and more dangerous people dealing drugs. George is just a small potato in comparison to the guys in the syndicate. I'd just as soon forget him. Okay?"

He thought for a moment, then said, "Okay. If that's what you want to do."

"It's just that I feel I owe George something. He was a lot like you in many ways. I guess that's why I was attracted to him at the start. But remember, Dad. If it wasn't for George, none of this would have happened and I might still be running around like a jerk."

"Maybe you're right." He wasn't sure he was doing the right thing not pursuing the Petrik issue, but he had Lisa back, and for the moment that was all that seemed to be important.

The bathroom door opened and Paul came out, tying the sash of Rod's dressing gown around his waist. The robe was just a little too big for him. He looked like a little boy trying to be a man. When he saw Lisa he felt a little embarrassed in the ill-fitting robe. "Your father loaned it to me. Pretty 'chick,' right?"

Lisa eyed him up and down and shook her head. "I'm surprised the people from *Gentleman's Quarterly* aren't pounding on your door wanting pictures."

"Give them time, it's still early." Paul turned to Rod and said, "Speaking of early, what time is our flight home?"

"I made reservations for us on the three-o'clock this afternoon. You'd better get a move on if you're intending to collect your things from your dad's house."

Paul's expression darkened. "I'm not going back there, ever," he said, pushing out his lower lip.

"That's dumb," Lisa said. "You can't just leave and not say goodbye at least."

He turned his back and started to brush his hair in the mirror.

"What about your airline ticket?" Lisa asked.

Paul didn't turn around. "Your father is going to pay for it for me. I'll see that my mom sends him the money after we get home."

"That's even dumber. Why waste a perfectly good airline ticket just because you're p.o.'d at your father?"

"I just don't ever want to see him again, that's all." He turned around. "Now, if you will kindly adjourn to your own bedroom, Miss Shepherd, I would like to get dressed."

"So get dressed. You don't have anything I haven't seen before."

"Lisa," her father warned, arching his brows.

"I said I was still a virgin. That doesn't mean I haven't looked." She scooted off the bed and went to her own room. When the door closed after her Paul pulled off the robe and started to pull on his undershorts. He seemed angry.

"I don't mean to side with Lisa," Rod said, "but she may be right, Paul. It really wouldn't be very nice for you to take off without saying goodbye to your father."

"I just don't want to see him."

"Look, Paul. Fathers are human beings just like you. They have their faults and weaknesses."

"My father is sick."

"Okay, so he's a little strange in his sexual appetites, but that doesn't mean you just cut him out of your life as though he'd never existed."

"Why not?"

"Suppose your father was in a mental hospital. Would you refuse to go and see him?"

"He belongs in a mental hospital."

"You're evading the question. Would you go to see him?"

Paul hesitated. "I guess so," he said as he pulled on his pants and reached for his shirt.

"Then why don't you look upon his attitude about sex as a

sickness and let it go at that? The way he likes his sex has nothing to do with the way he talks or thinks or lives. It's just one small part of him. There are a lot of other parts which you're punishing just because you don't like that one small part."

"How can you stick up for him?" Paul argued. "How can you condone what he is?"

"What is he, Paul? Tell me."

"He's a sex pervert."

"He's a successful man in government service. He is intelligent, sophisticated, well liked, personable and kind. Okay, so he goes in for kooky sex. What of it? He isn't harming anyone. He isn't going around raping little girls in the playgrounds or corrupting anyone's morals." Feeling like a lawyer arguing his case, he continued, "Look, your stepmother—a woman you'd never met and who had never laid eyes on you before—made a pass at you. She saw a good-looking young man and wanted him. Surely women have made passes at you before this. You aren't that naive."

"Not with my father's blessing."

"Okay, let's talk about that. I doubt very much if your father intended to participate with you. I really don't think that was in his scheme. I got the impression that he likes to watch. You come on the scene. He sees a lot of himself in you and at the same time looks upon you as practically a stranger. Being the voyeur that he obviously is, he wanted to know what it would be like to see a younger version of himself making love to his own wife. I admit it's a little bizarre, but it isn't criminal."

"It's incestuous."

"It could only be incestuous if your father was there and got involved directly with you. Where I come from, sex with one's stepparent is not considered incest."

Lisa tapped on the door. "Are you decent yet?"

"Yes," Paul called back. "You can come in." He finished buttoning his shirt and sat down to put on his socks and shoes.

"I was listening through the door," Lisa admitted as she again resumed her place on the bed. "Dad's right, Paul. You're being a real prude about this whole thing." She put her hands behind her head and stretched out her legs. "You have a sex hang-up."

"I do not have a sex hang-up," he argued.

She pretended she hadn't heard him. "You should be a little more broadminded about sex. After all, sex is like a smile—just as easy and just as satisfying regardless how you do it."

"Even if you do it with your own father."

"You didn't do anything with your own father," she told him. She studied him for a moment, cocking her head. "Maybe that's your problem, Paul." When he turned and looked at her she paused, then asked, "Are you gay?" Without missing a beat she turned to her father and said, "That's what they call homosexuals nowadays."

Rod grinned. "I know what 'gay' means. I haven't exactly been in a shell for the last twenty years."

"I am not gay," Paul said angrily.

"Then what's this hang-up about sex with your father? It didn't happen, but you're acting like it did—as though you wanted it to happen."

"Don't be disgusting," Paul shouted as he pulled on his shoe.

"George loaned me this paperback all about sex. I read in there where almost every kid has fantasies involving sex with one or both of his parents." She found herself blushing when she felt her father's eyes on her. "We all grow out of that phase—at least most of us do."

"Well, I never had fantasies like that," Paul told her.

"What kind of fantasies did you have?" she chided.

"None of your business."

"You mean you never dreamed about your father?"

"Of course I dreamed about him, lots of times. But not like that."

"How?"

"What do you mean?"

"I mean, how did you dream about him?"

"Just like any boy dreams about a father he never knew or didn't remember what he looked like." He went back to the mirror and began brushing his hair again, this time much more vigorously. "I dreamed about what a great guy he must be and how we'd travel around together, stuff like that."

"And when you got here you found that he was exactly what you'd always dreamed he would be."

"At first, yes."

"So why destroy all that just because you don't like the way he has sex with his wife?"

Although Rod was tempted to admonish her on more than one count, he kept still, silently admiring her for her sensibility. She had fashioned a clever little trap, and Paul was getting caught in it.

When Paul didn't say anything, Lisa said, "We can't afford to live in our dream worlds, Paul. Dreamers are just lying to themselves."

"What?" Paul turned, holding his hairbrush in his hand.

"Dreamers just lie to themselves. They live in an unreal world and blow that world to such ridiculous proportions that they start believing that it's reality that is false and falseness is real. Their eyes get all clouded over and they can't tell honesty from lies; they finally wind up believing that the lies and the dreams are much more attractive, so they make them real." She paused. "Of course when you come right down to it, lies generally are a lot more attractive than the truth, but you're only hurting yourself by thinking that way."

Rod sat there, his mouth slightly agape with silent admiration of his daughter.

"I don't live in a dream world," Paul argued.

"Don't you? You're living in one right now, as far as your father is concerned. You are pretending that the flaw in him doesn't exist, but you're afraid to find out that it really is there, so you're shutting him out for fear of seeing that flaw again."

"That isn't true," he said, sounding a little shaken.

"Isn't it? Prove it to me, Paul. Walk out that door, hail a cab and go collect your things and say goodbye to your father and stepmother."

Paul clenched the hairbrush tightly in his hand. He stood glaring at her, his mind in a turmoil. Suddenly he threw the brush on top of the dresser and went into the bathroom, slamming the door behind him.

Rod and Lisa stared at the closed door. Then he turned to his daughter and said, "You're quite a little psychologist. Where did you learn all that stuff?"

Lisa gave her hair a flip. "If you'd have spent more time at home you'd have known that your wife was an extremely intelligent woman. Some of that intelligence was bound to rub off on her daughter."

The telephone rang. Lisa picked it up. "Oh, hi, Nancy. Yes, we're leaving on the three-o'clock flight. He's right here, hold on." She cupped her hand over the mouthpiece and handed the phone to her father. "It's your lady love," she said with a wink.

"Good morning," he said, feeling his face blush. "You're up early. After last night I thought you'd sleep until noon."

"I've been up for hours," Nancy said. "But for all I've accomplished I might just as well have stayed in bed. I went out to pay my respects to Mrs. Brandon—you know, the mother of my school friend, the one Charlie and Sheila found drowned on the beach. No one was there. The butler said they were all at the funeral. So then I stopped to see if Sheila was okay. She was out too. Now I hope you aren't going to give me the brush-off and say you can't see me before you leave."

Rod had originally been tempted to stay away from Nancy. It would be easier to forget about her if he didn't see her anymore. "Have you had lunch?" he found himself saying. "The kids and I are going to grab a bite before taking off."

"Have I ever turned down a meal?"

"Good. We'll wait for you here, okay? Paul's just finishing dressing."

Just as he hung up, the bathroom door opened and Paul stood there, his fists clenched, his jaw set in a firm line of determination. He glared at Lisa and said, "Okay. I'll go and get my things." He pulled on his jacket and started for the door. He hesitated, his hand on the knob. He glanced back at Lisa. "I don't suppose you'd like to come with me," he said.

She saw the silent plea. "Sure, why not," she said flippantly. "Nancy's coming to have lunch with my father, and I don't think I care to sit through all that lovey-dovey stuff."

"Lisa," Rod said with reproach.

"You might just as well face it, Dad. You're hung up on her and she's hung up on you. Any idiot can see that."

Paul grinned. "Listen to your daughter, sir. I'm finding out that she usually knows what she's talking about."

"Come on, you," she said, taking Paul's hand. "The only reason I'm going with you is to make sure you don't forget your airline ticket and stick my father with the bill."

Rod found himself smiling as the door closed behind them. His smile faded, remembering what Lisa had said. He wasn't in love with Nancy. Oh, sure, he liked her—he liked her a lot —but he wasn't in love with her. Besides, he couldn't afford to fall in love with a girl like Nancy. He really should have told her he couldn't see her before leaving.

Yet, when she tapped on the door he was off the bed like a shot and smiling at her as he pulled the door open.

"Good morning."

"Good morning." Nancy glanced around the empty suite. "Where are the kids?"

"I'll tell you over lunch. Come on, I'm starved."

Nancy pulled him back as he started to move away. "As long as we're alone and in view of the fact that you're leaving this afternoon, couldn't we have a little talk here where we have privacy? I think we should, Rod."

"Honestly, Nancy, I think we've done too much talking already. I've done a lot of thinking, and I really don't believe things could ever work out between us."

"Look. I've been doing a lot of thinking too. I've been coming on pretty strong with you without trying to see your side of the picture. Maybe if we took things a little slower, one step at a time, they might work themselves out."

"Meaning what?"

"Oh, you dumb lug. Can't you see I want you to take me to bed again before you leave?"

He started to pull away from her. "Nancy, please, don't."

She pulled him back again. "Just nice old-fashioned stuff," she said softly. "No frills or fancy trimmings. Just the way you liked Helen. I want to try things your way too. Maybe then I can understand."

He felt himself weakening, yet at the same time he found himself getting angry. He wasn't angry with Nancy, he was angry with himself for not being able to resist her. "Damn you," he swore as he pulled her into his arms and crushed his mouth over hers. He swept her up in his arms, carried her into the bedroom and threw her violently on the bed, then he leaped on top of her.

"That's what I like," she said with a coy smile. "A nice, gentle, passive man."

"Shut up," he said as he quickly began to undress her and himself. To hell with love, to hell with everything, he thought as he eased himself into her. To hell with being gentle too, he told himself as he shoved hard after having gained entry.

Nancy groaned softly and pushed herself roughly back against him. "Yes, Rod," she moaned. "Make it hurt. I want to remember."

He didn't love her, he kept telling himself. This wasn't love. This was just pure animal need. Lust. Yet he found when he looked into her lovely face that he never wanted to be free of her embrace.

"Nancy," he gasped as he covered her mouth with his.

"Oh, Rod," she gasped as her passions mounted and she felt her climax coming on too soon. "Oh, Rod. I love you, you stupid ape. I love you," she said.

ELAINE SAT QUIETLY BESIDE THE HOSPITAL bed. Greg's eyes were closed, his breathing faint. On the other side of the bed a doctor was bending over his bandaged body. The inspector of police was standing at the foot of the bed.

"He's coming around now," the doctor said as he straightened up. "He is very weak."

"He *will* be all right?" Elaine asked anxiously.

"Eventually, yes, but it will take a long time." He looked at the police inspector. "Make your questions brief, Inspector. You can come back tomorrow. Right now, the lad should get as much rest as he can."

Elaine sat holding tightly to Greg's hand. She gave a little start when she saw his eyelids flutter. She cast a quick glance at the inspector, then looked back at Greg.

"Philip?" Greg moaned as he opened his eyes.

The pressure of Elaine's hand increased. The name was another of the many names that had brought trouble to her in her past. Greg, after all these years, still called out for his friend from military school. She had hoped with all her heart that he would have outgrown that schoolboy crush. Obviously she had hoped in vain. Somehow it didn't matter now. At least Greg was going to live. That was all that was important.

Whatever terrible trouble he'd gotten himself mixed up in, she'd get him out of it. She would let him live as he chose to live. All that mattered was that he would live.

She put her hand on his bandaged brow. "It's Mother," she said softly.

Slowly his eyes turned toward her. She smiled. Greg started to lift up, then fell back against the pillows. He moved his eyes again, looking from face to face.

"It's all right, darling. Try not to excite yourself. You are going to be all right."

"I'm dying, aren't I?" Tears welled up at his lids.

"No, darling. You're not dying. You are going to be fine."

He rolled his head back and forth on the pillows. "You're lying to me. You've always lied to me," he sobbed.

The doctor leaned forward and put his hand on Greg's shoulder. "Your mother speaks the truth, lad," he said. "You are not going to die. Now just relax and don't get upset. All you need is rest and quiet."

Greg stared hard into his face. Then, as before, his eyes moved from the doctor to Elaine and finally to the inspector, who was looking down at him. "Who are you?" Greg asked.

"He's a police inspector," Elaine said gently. "He wanted to ask you some questions. You needn't talk to him today, darling. He can come back when you're feeling stronger."

"Questions? About Cynthia?"

Elaine frowned. "No, not about Cynthia."

The inspector looked at him suspiciously. "Why did you think I wanted to speak to you about your sister?"

Greg looked away. "I don't know. She's dead, isn't she?" He said it so casually, so callously, that it made Elaine wince.

"Yes, she is dead," the inspector said. He watched the nervous movement of Greg's eyes. After a moment he said, "I came here to question you about Alfredo Lorenzo."

"Who?" Greg thought for a minute. "Oh, him. What about him? Is he dead too?"

"No, he is alive. You admit knowing the man?"

Greg's eyes blazed with anger. "Yes, I admit knowing him. I also admit that I used that hatpin on him, if that's what you want to know. But there isn't a court in the world that would convict me of any crime after I explained why I did it."

"Why did you do it?" the inspector persisted.

Greg's mouth was drawn back into a tight, thin line. He

glanced quickly at his mother's shocked expression and then back at the inspector. "He raped me, that's why," Greg rasped. "Rape is a hell of a lot more serious a crime than what I did by way of revenge."

"I see," the inspector said.

Elaine's expression of shock changed to one of horror. Her hand clutched at the string of pearls at her throat.

Greg saw her face. A sadistic smile stretched across his mouth. "You and Cynthia were always telling people I was a fag. Well, now you have proof of it."

She shook her head to hide her tears. "Greg, that isn't true. Neither Cynthia nor I ever—"

"Don't give me that," Greg said disgustedly. "Cynthia told me all about it. That's why I hit—" He cut himself off abruptly.

The inspector leaned forward. "That's why you hit whom?"

Elaine turned frightened eyes on the inspector. "Do you really have to question him any more today? Can't you see he's extremely upset and tired? Can't your questions wait until tomorrow?"

The inspector waved his hand. "One moment, *señora.*" He looked back at Greg, whose eyes were lowered. "Whom did you hit, *señor?*"

Greg didn't answer. The inspector repeated his question more firmly.

"No one," Greg snapped. "I didn't hit anyone."

The inspector narrowed his eyes at him. "I think you were going to say that that is why you hit your sister."

"That isn't true," Greg shouted. Again he tried to rise up from the pillows and again he fell back. "I didn't hit her, she fell," he said feebly.

"Greg," Elaine gasped.

The inspector closed in. "How did she fall, Señor Brandon?"

Greg's eyes darted nervously back and forth in their sockets. "She just fell. She tripped over something and fell."

"Then why did you start to say you hit her?"

"I didn't hit her," he snapped. "She fell, I tell you. She fell. We were arguing and she tripped and fell."

"You argued, *señor?* What about?"

Greg felt himself starting to fall apart. "I don't know. I don't remember. She said something about not wanting her baby to have a queer father, and I slapped her. She fell down."

Tears started to run down his cheeks. "It was an accident. I didn't mean to slap her so hard."

"Greg," Elaine said harshly. "Stop. You don't know what you're saying." She turned to the inspector. "He's upset. You've gotten him all mixed up. He doesn't know what he's saying."

The inspector ignored her. He kept looking intently into Greg's face. "Why don't you start at the beginning, *señor*, and tell me everything that happened?"

"No," Elaine said sharply. She grabbed Greg's hand. "Don't say anything, dear. You don't have to talk to this man if you don't want to. Just calm yourself and get some rest. Everything will be all right."

He pulled rudely away from her. "I'm not like you," he said, hatred smoldering in his eyes. "I have nothing to hide. I didn't kill in cold blood as you did. It was an accident."

"What was an accident?" the inspector asked.

Greg glowered with defiance at his mother, then softened his expression when he turned to the inspector. As if speaking to spite his mother he said, "Cynthia. I hit her that night. She fell on a plank that had a spike sticking out of it. When I saw that she was dead, I panicked. I threw Cynthia and the plank over the seawall."

"Greg!" Elaine gasped, then covered her face with her hands.

"Why?" the inspector asked simply.

Greg saw the man, but he was in too much pain to make out his features, nor did he care who he was. The man sounded gentle and understanding, the way Philip used to sound. "Cynthia was going to give my baby away."

"Your baby?" the Inspector asked.

"She was going to give it to that beachboy, that gigolo my mother wants to marry."

Elaine was positive her heart had stopped beating.

"Why do you say it was your baby, *señor?*" the inspector asked in his quiet monotone.

"Because it was. Cynthia was going to have my baby. We figured it out. It couldn't have been that Jorge's baby; she hadn't known him long enough. It was mine, mine and Cynthia's. She knew that. That's why we started to fight."

Elaine cut in, "He's delirious, I tell you. He doesn't know what he's saying."

Greg took a deep breath and let it out slowly. "When I first arrived at the villa, Cynthia told me she was pregnant with Jorge's baby. She told me she was four months pregnant. I reminded her that she'd been with me four months ago, that she'd only met Jorge about three months ago. I told her the baby had to be mine, not Jorge's."

"Oh my God," Elaine breathed.

Greg looked at her with disgust. "Oh, don't be so damned hypocritical," he said to her. "Surely you knew that Cynthia and Leland Harshaw and I had been to bed together. Isn't that why you kept sending us away, because you were jealous that he liked us more than he liked you?"

"No! Good God, no!" she groaned.

"Leland Harshaw?" the inspector asked as he took out a note pad and began writing in it.

"My mother's second husband. The one she shot through the head. Surely you've had all that in your files ever since my mother came to live here."

The inspector merely nodded. Elaine began sobbing into her hands.

"Leland introduced Cynthia and me to sex when we were just kids," Greg said. He sounded slightly proud of himself. "Sometimes he fooled around just with me. I was only about fourteen or fifteen. I didn't know any better."

"No more, Greg," Elaine begged. "Please, don't say any more."

The inspector waved his hand for her to be quiet. "And you were sleeping with your sister?"

Greg nodded his head. He reflected, then said, "When Cynthia told me about the baby I was sure it was mine and not that creeepy beach bum's. She laughed at me and said it couldn't be mine, that she was bound and determined to get Jorge away from Elaine and intended telling him that she was only three months pregnant, that he wouldn't know the difference." He pressed his head deeper into the pillows and looked up at the ceiling. "Later, I ran into her upstairs as she was getting ready to run off with Jorge. She wouldn't talk to me. She went down to the garage and put her bag in her car. I was furious. I threw her into the seat and jumped behind the wheel and took off down the drive. I knew the gates would be locked, so I took the old road, the one that runs along the seawall and out into the fruit orchards." A strange sort of

smile slid across his mouth. "Fruit," he mused. "I guess I'll
never be able to shake that word." He threw an ugly, defiant
look at his mother.

"Oh, please, Greg," Elaine pleaded. "Don't go on. Don't say
any more."

Again she put a restraining hand on his arm and again he
shoved it away. "I know what I'm saying," he said angrily. "It
was an accident. I have nothing to hide."

"Then why did you try to dispose of your sister's body?" the
inspector wanted to know.

"As I told you, I panicked. Cynthia started struggling with
me in the car. I pulled over and yanked her out and slapped
her. She was getting hysterical and I just thought a slap would
calm her down. She started to beat me with her fists. She said
the baby wasn't mine, that queers couldn't produce children
and even if they could she didn't want her baby to grow up
with a faggot for a father." Greg shook his head. "I never
thought Cynthia knew about me and Philip. Oh, she knew
about the guy in Paris, but she said she knew that I didn't do
anything with that guy. She laughed about it, in fact, and said
I was smart to hook up with a movie producer like him,
someone who might make me into a big movie star someday.
We were always joking about it, always saying how great it
would be when I was making a lot of money in films, how we
would never have to depend on our mother again for her hand-
outs. I never thought Cynthia saw any harm in my living with
that guy. Actually, she encouraged me to stay with the French-
man." He turned his head slowly and narrowed his eyes at his
mother. "But then I should have known my mother would do
anything and everything she could to turn Cynthia against
me. It was she who convinced Cynthia that I was a fag."

"No. Oh, no, Greg. You don't know what you're saying."

"I know perfectly well what I'm saying. Cynthia told me
she knew why I was thrown out of military school, how I liked
guys more than I liked girls. She said that was the only reason
she kept going to bed with me, because she thought it would
help straighten me out."

"No. Never. I never said a word to Cynthia about any of
that."

"Who then? Who knew about me and Phil other than you?"

One name began flashing in Elaine's mind. Leland Harshaw.
So he'd beaten her after all. All those years of depriving herself

of her children for their own sake, and what had it gotten her except her children's contempt. Everything had been wasted. Everything. She felt as though someone had suddenly opened a valve and was beginning to drain out whatever life she had left inside her.

"Cynthia kept beating me, saying over and over that it wasn't possible for a queer to make a girl pregnant. She said that was why I beat up on girls, because I hated all women, and that I should come out of my closet and go with guys, which is what I'd always wanted from the beginning. But she was wrong. Dead wrong." Tears were flooding his eyes. "I struggled with her and said if she didn't tell the gigolo the truth about the baby, then I would. She got even angrier. She said if I told Jorge that she'd go to the police about me."

"Why would she do that?" the inspector asked.

"I hurt a girl bad once. I told Cynthia about it. The police in Torremolinos have their eye on me. That's why I was so anxious to leave the mainland of Spain and come here. I didn't want to come. I had to go somewhere until they forgot about me."

Elaine pinched shut her eyes. She put back her head and breathed a silent prayer.

"Cynthia knew about that, and about other things I've done. She said she'd turn me over to the police, and give evidence, if I told Jorge the truth about the child. We fought about it. I told her she'd have to get rid of the baby, that it would be born deformed or would grow up insane because we were brother and sister." He groaned and tried to stifle a sudden sharp pain that coursed through his body. He waited for the pain to subside. The bandages on his forehead were damp with sweat.

"She wouldn't listen to me. She kept yelling and cursing. I was sure someone would hear her. She kept saying this was her only chance at getting Jorge and she wasn't going to let anything or anyone stand in her way. She was screaming at me. I hit her." Tears were flowing freely down his cheeks. "I hit her hard and she fell down. I hated her then. I hated her," he snarled. "She wouldn't get up. I tried to get her to get up, but she just lay there. There was blood coming out of her head and out of the corner of her mouth. I knew she was dead. I didn't have to listen for her heart to know that. I panicked. I knew I'd be put in jail if anyone found out, so I carried her over to the edge of the cliff and threw her into the sea."

"Oh God," Elaine said, again covering her face with her hands. The room was spinning around. She didn't want to hear any more. When Greg started to rave on, she covered her ears with her hands and ran from the room.

In the corridor she collided with a nurse pushing a rubber-wheeled cart into one of the private rooms a little way down the hall. Elaine sent the cart flying against the wall, spilling its contents all over the floor. The nurse yelled at her, but Elaine kept running as fast as she could.

The nurse began muttering to herself as she regarded the debris. Then she pushed open the door of the private room and put her head inside. "Your meal will be delayed a little, Señor Lorenzo," she said to the patient in the bed. "There has been a slight accident."

Alfredo did not hear her, or if he did he pretended not to. He lay in the bed, his eyes fixed firmly on the ceiling.

The doctor had come out of Greg's room to investigate the disturbance. After the nurse told him what had happened he asked about the patient.

"No change, doctor. He has not spoken a word since he was admitted. His mind seems to have gone. I did as you said and tried to convince him that the operation was very successful and that he would be as good as new again, but something has happened in his head."

"I will go and talk to him," the doctor said.

Alfredo did not acknowledge the greeting. The doctor picked up the chart and scanned it briefly. "Everything will be all right, Señor Lorenzo," he said. "Oh, there may be a slight scar, but nothing more," he said.

Alfredo continued to stare at the ceiling. Slowly he lowered his eyes and fixed them firmly on the doctor's face. He reached down with his right hand and cupped the bandages at his crotch. "I am a woman," he said, almost in a whisper.

"Nonsense. You are as much a man as you have always been."

A sly, impish grin curved his lips. "I am a woman," he said and again raised his eyes to the ceiling. He was smiling.

THE SOUND OF MAGGIE'S HIGH-PITCHED, GIRL-
ish laughter reminded Elaine that there was still a world out
there someplace. She had been sitting in the little sitting room
with the drapes tightly drawn. She thought about all her
wasted efforts, all her useless struggles. It had all been for
nothing. All her scheming, her planning, her clawing, and
what had it accomplished? She tried to smile, remembering
that at least it had gained her Jorge. The price had been
tremendously high; she wondered if it had been worth it. Yes,
she thought, remembering the voice of the policeman telling
her, when she'd telephoned, that Jorge would be released
within the hour. He would be coming back to her.

She had lost Cynthia. She had lost Greg. She didn't want to
think of what was in store for him. She had lost everything
but the potential love of a very young boy. And, she admitted,
it was a *potential* love. How long it would last, if it lasted at
all, she didn't know. But it was all she had now; it was the
only thing she could hold on to, regardless of how weak her
hold.

She got up from the chaise on which she was reclining and
walked toward the mirror. She saw her reflection in the glass.
She saw the telltale lines of age that no surgery, no matter how
expensive, could erase. There was a thin, fragile quality to the
skin. It was as if she were wearing a costly mask over the
wrinkles in her face. She was old, whether she wanted to admit
it or not. The truth of her age was inside her. She was old
and Jorge was merely a caprice that she played with to try to
dispel that fact. Surgery had made her appear young, but
there was no surgery in the world that would put the tucks of
youth in her mind.

Perhaps Greg and Cynthia had been right all along. Perhaps
she was nothing more than a selfish, thoughtless woman. She
frowned at her reflection. Selfish? Yes, why not? Selfishness—
that was the only reason anyone stayed alive.

The door burst open and Maggie and Dario came into the

room. "Good heavens, Elaine," Maggie said, going to the windows and throwing open the drapes. "The funeral was this morning. I told you not to stay home. You're looking more dreadful than you did this morning. The races were so terribly exciting," she gushed. "Dario won today's race, of course. There wasn't anyone could touch him. He was simply sensational."

"Maggie, please," Dario said, blushing with modesty.

"But you were, darling. Heaven. That's the only word to describe you. Sheer heaven."

Elaine smiled at Dario and went and kissed his cheek. "Congratulations, Dario. I'm very happy for you."

"The big race is tomorrow. But I am sure I will not have very much competition."

"I'm sure you won't."

Dario's expression went serious. "What of Greg?" he asked.

Elaine bowed her head and fought against her tears. "I'm afraid he smashed his car trying to run away." She sat down on the chaise and told them everything that had happened.

"That wicked, wicked boy," Maggie said, making a face. "Well, like father like son, I always say." She rolled her eyes. To Dario she said, "You should have known the dreadful man Elaine first married. Simply dreadful. We were only girls at the time, but I was always much more sensible, even then, even though I was years younger than Elaine. I told her all about the man, but she insisted upon marrying him. Horrible man. Simply horrible."

"Maggie, please," Elaine said. "I'd rather you wouldn't pursue it."

"Why not? He was a horrible man. Greg is obviously a carbon copy. Like father like son," she repeated. She sighed. "Well, Greg deserves whatever he has coming. I suppose they'll electrocute him or hang him or whatever they do to murderers here in Spain."

"Maggie, please," Elaine said with a shudder. "After all, Greg is still my son."

"I wouldn't be too proud of that, my dear," she said, undaunted. "A thief and a murderer. No siree, I wouldn't be too proud to admit that he's your son."

Their heads turned toward the open windows when they heard a car come up the drive and stop outside. Elaine was on her feet in an instant, hurrying toward the door. Just as she reached it Jorge burst in, throwing his arms wide.

Maggie eyed them with disgust as they kissed passionately. She looked up at Dario and raised her eyes. "I don't suppose we're wanted here. Let's drive back into Palma and I'll buy you a little congratulatory gift for winning today."

"You are too kind," Dario said, taking her hand.

"I know," Maggie said with a sigh. "That's one of my major faults. I'm always much too kind."

Elaine and Jorge didn't hear them leave. They stood for a long time wrapped in each other's arms.

"I brought you something," Jorge said after a while. He put his hand in his pocket and handed her her emerald necklace. "They cleared me so completely they even trusted me to deliver this to you."

She took it from him and again wrapped her arms around his neck and kissed him on the mouth.

When she looked into his face she found that his expression had gone serious. "They told me about Greg," he said. "I'm sorry, Elaine. I truly am."

"Thank you, Jorge," she answered, turning away from him. "I wish it all could have ended differently."

He took her again in his arms. "You have me, Elaine. You won't need anyone else."

She let him kiss her, wondering if he was speaking the truth. Did she really have him? Was she secure now? Would she be able to be happy and enjoy the little space of time she had left? She would never be happy alone, remembering that happiness is perceived only when it is reflected from another. At the moment Jorge was supremely happy; she, then, was happy basking in his happiness.

"We can be married now?" Jorge asked.

Elaine thought she denoted a strange anxiety in his tone. She hesitated, then smiled at him. "Of course," she said. "Whenever you say, my darling."

She wondered as he kissed her why she had hesitated before accepting his proposal. After all, wasn't this what she had been working for, hoping for? She wondered if the terrible toll it had taken to reach this point was responsible for bringing her doubts to the fore. And she did have doubts now. She admitted that as she felt his lips on her throat.

She tightened her arms around him. To hell with the doubts,

she told herself. She was going to be happy now, regardless of the costs. It wasn't selfishness; she was merely being practical. And practicality was something that only came with age.

THE AIRPORT TERMINAL WAS CROWDED WITH people. Paul Jr. stood deep in thought, feeling very much like a rat contemplating deserting a sinking ship. His father hadn't been at home when he'd gone there with Lisa. He had avoided his stepmother; in fact, he'd been downright rude to her. He didn't care. He never wanted to see that woman again, regardless of how Lisa had admonished him.

When he heard his father call his name, he refused to turn around. He'd expected it. He had hoped the plane would be airborn before his father got here. Perhaps it was just as well to get it over with rather than run away without anything being said.

"Paul, boy," Paul Sr. said, clapping a hand on Paul's shoulder. "You can't go home yet. I thought you were going to stay all summer, and even longer?"

Paul couldn't look him in the eye. "I'm going home," he said flatly.

"But why?"

He found the strength to raise his eyes. He accounted the effort to his anger. "You of all people should know that."

"Surely you're not running away because of that little thing between you and Laura?"

"It wasn't a little thing to me."

"Paul, boy. For heaven's sake. Grow up. You're a man now. Don't take it so seriously." Shaking his head slowly from side to side, he said, "I knew I should have sent for you sooner. This is your mother's doings. She made you into a little prude."

"I am not a prude," Paul argued. "If being decent is prudish," he said as an afterthought, "then maybe I am prudish. But I'd rather that than being like you."

"Paul," his father crooned. "You're letting yourself get

angry for no reason at all. All right, Laura made a pitch. She's a very aggressive woman, you're a very attractive young man—"

"I don't want to talk about it," Paul said, throwing off his father's arm. "I just want to go home and be left alone."

"Oh sure, home. Home to your mother and to your fruit music. I was afraid she'd make a little sissy out of you."

"Shut up, just shut up," Paul said. "I don't want to hear you say anything about my mother or my music. Just stay out of my life and I'll stay out of yours."

"Okay," his father said, slapping his hands on his thighs. "At least I tried. Nobody can say I didn't try. I only wish things could have gone differently. But, if you've made up your mind to go running home with your tail between your legs, there isn't much I can do about it, is there?"

"I'm not running home with my tail between my legs. I just don't belong here." A wave of filial affection suddenly grabbed him. "Look, Dad. I know you don't think too highly of me. Maybe in time I'll learn to be more sophisticated about things, the way you are, but right now I want to go home where I belong."

His father sighed. "All right. Go home. But remember. If there's anything I can do for you, you please let me know, huh?"

"Yes, I'll do that," he said, knowing that he never would. He just didn't want to part in the heat of an argument.

Paul Sr. put out his hand. Paul Jr. shook it. "Have a good trip home, son. Remember. You know where to reach me if you want to."

"Goodbye, Dad."

"Say hello to your mother for me."

"I'll do that."

His father waved and walked away. Paul thought he saw tears in his father's eyes.

"At least you shook hands," Lisa said, coming up to him. "Did everything have a happy ending?"

"Not really. But at least we parted amicably."

"That's something," she said. She took his hand. "Come on, they've posted our flight."

Paul looked around. "Where's your dad?"

"Saying goodbye to Nancy." She nodded toward a corner. Paul glanced over and saw Nancy shaking her finger at

Rod. "It looks more like they're having a lovers' quarrel."

Nancy was frowning and saying, "Will you stop being so damned Victorian?"

"I'm not being Victorian. I just can't help the way I feel." Rod shook his head. "I'm beginning to understand that I can't expect you to change any more than I can expect it of myself. I admit, I enjoyed what happened up in the hotel room, but I don't think you did."

"It was okay, just okay. I enjoyed it, for what it was. But I won't lie to you. I felt inhibited. Sex shouldn't be like that."

Rod glanced around quickly to make sure no one was listening.

Nancy frowned at him. "I really don't think you enjoyed it all that much either, if you'd be honest with yourself."

"This isn't the time nor the place," he said in a low voice. His face was flushed with embarrassment.

"You've got your head on backwards," she said, feeling annoyed. "Turn it around and start looking at today, not yesterday. You're a terrific guy, but you still carry around your grandfather's concepts of morality."

"I don't think it would work out between us, Nancy."

"So it won't work. So what? That doesn't mean that we should cut it off before giving it a try. I'm not looking for any guarantees. There aren't any such things. I found that out a long time ago. I just want to be with you because I like being with you and I think I can help you. And, whether you know it or not, Mr. Shepherd, you make me happy." She gave him a sly wink. "And you really are pretty good in the sack even if you are a bit conventional."

Rod's face flushed a deeper red. Again he looked nervously around to make sure no one had overheard her.

She snuggled up against him. "Come on, Rod, let me call you when I get home."

After they'd had sex in the hotel room he'd gotten up the courage to tell her that he didn't think they should see each other again. However, feeling her body up against his own, he wasn't so sure.

Out of the corner of his eye he saw Lisa motioning to him and pointing to the flight board. "I've got to go," he said, moving away from Nancy. "Call me when you get in."

"You mean that?" Nancy said, beaming up at him.

"Yes, I mean that." He cursed himself for having weakened.

"I'm listed in the Dayton telephone book. It's under Shepherd & Co." He cursed himself again for his stupidity and quickly pulled a business card out of his breast pocket. "You get me all mixed up," he said as he handed her the card.

"I'm glad." Again she winked at him. As he started to move away, she grabbed him and threw herself into his arms. They kissed. "And do me a favor, Rod," she said.

"What?"

"Let up on Lisa. I can understand that you grew up in a strict family and you find it hard to understand that Lisa wants to break away. Just remember that you wanted the same thing when you were her age. So don't try to hang on to her, Rod. She can't live as you do. She has to be herself."

"At fifteen?"

"Yes, even at fifteen. Oh, I don't say let her walk the streets. You can keep a rein on her without it cutting her mouth. Use restraint, of course, but God, Rod, don't suffocate her. That's what you're doing both to her and to yourself."

"Goodbye, Nancy," he said, kissing her quickly when he saw Lisa start to wave more frantically.

"Goodbye, Rod. Remember what I told you in bed earlier. I'm in love with you. Don't fight it, pal. Relax and enjoy it."

As he hurried away she smiled and waved happily. Under her breath she said, "You stupid ape. You're in love with me too and you just don't know it."

SHEILA TRUDGED UP THE SLOPING STREET. Charlie's satchel was clutched tightly in one hand. She saw the little church nestled snugly at the corner of the street and started toward it. She felt guilty for hating God. There had been a reason for Charlie's death. She knew that now. God had done the right thing in taking his life. He was far better off where he was than spending the rest of his life running from the wrong he'd done. Much as she missed him, his death was justified in the eyes of God, she thought.

She pinned a handkerchief on her head and walked slowly

into the dark, cool interior of the church. The altar was a simple affair, yet there was a quiet grandeur about it. She genuflected before the tabernacle, then walked to the side altar and knelt in front of the bank of vigil lights. She deposited several coins in the slot and lit one of the candles. She looked lovingly up at the white marble statue of the Virgin Mary and put her hands together in prayer. The satchel of money was pressed against her leg as if reminding her that it was there beside her. She still had not decided what to do about the ill-gained dollars. Temptations had plagued her, of course. There was so much she could do with the money, especially if her suspicions about being pregnant proved true. Yet, she'd done without for so long she wasn't sure she would feel comfortable in the luxuries it would buy. Common sense told her she'd use some of it to send herself and Charlie back home. Charlie may have successfully converted her to the side of honesty, but there was a limit to honesty. A girl had to be practical.

She heard footsteps on the marble floor and turned slightly to see an old priest dusting the altar railing. Seeing him, bent and old and shabby, gave her a sudden inspiration. She put her hand into the satchel and took out a stack of bills, which she tucked into her purse. Feeling guilty, she looked up at the smiling Virgin. Sheila smiled back, then shrugged her shoulders at the towering Madonna, snapping shut her purse. She blessed herself and stood up, feeling lighter than she had in years.

Her eyes rested on the candle she'd lit. "See you, Charlie," she said, then turned and started out of the church. She hesitated and looked back at the candle she'd lit. "I'll even call her Charlie if it's a girl."

"*Señora*," the old priest called.

Sheila turned toward him.

"Your valise," he said, nodding toward the satchel of money she'd left before the altar.

"It isn't mine, Padre," she lied.

"But I recently finished dusting that side altar. It was not there a moment ago."

"Some short, fat man came in when I was praying," she said. "He left it there. He said that if I saw the padre to tell him that the satchel was for the church."

She saw him look at her suspiciously.

Sheila walked slowly toward the door and the bright, clear sunlight beyond. Her head was tilted a little higher, a little prouder than before. Just inside the door she dipped her fingers in the bowl of holy water and again blessed herself. She was sure God would forgive her for taking the stack of bills. It only seemed right, somehow.

AN AFTERNOON OF SUN, THEN DINNER ABOARD the yacht had been Jorge's idea. Elaine was lazing on a deck lounge with Jorge lying on a mat at her feet.

"Dario seems so anxious to leave Majorca," Elaine commented as she sipped her cocktail. "It surprises me. I thought he would be the last person to want to get away from here."

Jorge chuckled. "Dario is bored. Ever since we were children he was the first to get tired of a game. He will win the races tomorrow and that will bore him all the more."

"I know it wasn't very trusting of me, but I was certain that Dario had something to do with Cynthia's death." Now that Jorge was here with her it didn't hurt to speak of her daughter.

"I was a little suspicious myself," Jorge said. "But then, Dario has never been the violent type. I think Dario wants to run away because his family is insisting he marry Isabella, a peasant girl who claims Dario robbed her of her virginity." He arched his brows. "That, as you know, is a very serious crime here. A girl without virtue must either leave the island or remain and live as a public woman if the man refuses to marry her. Dario's family is wrong. Isabella has been had by more men than I can count, but she has singled him out. His cousin, Carlos, the policeman on duty at the jail, told me that Isabella's family was planning to have Dario arrested if he does not marry the girl." He rolled over on his back and put his hands behind his head, staring up at the bright orange sky. "Poor Dario. He will always get himself into trouble like this. He will run off with Maggie, will get bored after a while and will be off looking for new game. He is not like me. I want to settle down and never have to worry about anything again."

Elaine wondered if he was referring to her money. He most likely was, but it didn't matter in the least anymore. She could not tell him about the cancer. He would only pity her. She did not want that. She had made a clean breast of everything in her past life, and although Jorge had looked shocked when she spoke of shooting Leland, he still did not admonish her. He said he understood. He told her to forget all about the past. They would try to help Greg if he would accept their help. She was glad now that Jorge would have all her money after she died. Giving him her fortune would help make up for not being able to give him children and a home with a young, loving wife. To her, it seemed to be a fair exchange. Jorge would have his problems in time. He had never known real wealth. After her death he would find himself in an alien world, one in which he would be important, of course, but in the minds of others, he would never be able to live down his birthright. Perhaps she was wrong in forcing a man as young as Jorge into joining a life in which he would not be at home, a life completely out of his comprehension.

But when she looked at his beauty, it didn't matter. She was happy and content.

Jorge chuckled. When she glanced at him he said, "Do you know what Dario was doing in the garden before we left the villa? He was putting Majorcan soil into a small leather pouch." He laughed. "Dario, who swears he is the least sentimental person on the whole island, is taking Majorcan dirt with him in case he never returns."

"And will he return, Jorge?"

"He will return. Good Majorcans always return. There is nowhere else they belong. Look," he said, suddenly pointing to the sky. "A plane is taking off."

Elaine glanced up and studied the sleek, beautiful jet liner. Tourists. How good it would be to be able to fly away from all her recent unhappinesses. But as she glanced back at Jorge she smiled. She reached out her hand and tousled his hair. He turned and smiled at her. No, she decided, she'd flown enough. She was ready to stay with her feet on Majorcan soil and bask in whatever happiness Jorge cared to give her. She was an older woman, he was merely a lad. But even that seemed right somehow.

Again she looked up and watched the airplane glide out

toward the horizon. She would have her own private plane refurbished, the yacht repainted, the crew expanded in case they wanted to sail somewhere on their honeymoon.

As she watched the plane soar higher and higher she wondered if the people aboard that plane were as certain as she of what they wanted.

"SUPERFICIAL PEOPLE ARE TOO MUCH IN THE majority," Paul was saying as he and Lisa sat huddled together deep in serious conversation. "The talented few proves that. Mediocrity breeds mediocrity unless you put up a strong defense against it. The masses hate the ordinary, and yet they let themselves wallow in it because they don't know any better."

Lisa nodded enthusiastically. "Yes, I see what you mean. Talent is really rare. It isn't something that one teaches or anything that one can explain. I've met some people who were really talented but they suppressed it because they had other values—lesser values—which they considered more important than their true, innate talents."

Rod sat across the aisle, smiling. Paul and Lisa were so wrapped up in each other that they scarcely knew he was there. He glanced out the window and looked down at Majorca and the glistening bay of Palma far below. He saw the same blue-and-white yacht sitting calmly on the dark waters. It was the one he'd seen when he first arrived. Then it had looked like a sanctuary from trouble. Now, glancing back at Lisa's happy, smiling face, the yacht suddenly looked terribly alone, very forlorn.

He leaned back against the seat and closed his eyes. His palms were still damp from the takeoff, but he found he was relaxing. He wondered where Nancy was right at that moment. She had mentioned that she intended going to the Brandon villa, finding her aunt and trying to coax her into letting her go home. He felt guilty about the strong need to see her again, to hold her, to make love to her.

No, perhaps he'd made a mistake asking her to call him when she returned home. He should have kept to his resolve and made a clean, definite break.

But when he closed his eyes tighter and pictured her lovely face, he longed to see her. He wondered how long it would be before she called.

THE WINDOWS IN THE HOUSES IN ANDRIATX shone dimly out into the night, thin ribbons of smoke coming from the many chimneys. The night had cooled, but Carlotta did not seem to mind it as she sat on her little stoop, wrapped in a thick, woolly shawl. She had just returned from Palma after having gone to the jail to visit Jorge. They had told her that Jorge had been freed. But he had not come to see her as yet. She would sit and wait. If he did not come tonight he would come tomorrow. If not tomorrow, then someday, she told herself.

"Someday," she said to the stillness of the night. Yes, someday perhaps—knowing that without hope life would mean nothing.

ABOUT THE AUTHOR

Scion of a prominent Pennsylvania family, Sam Dodson has lived most of his life in the beautiful places of the world. A graduate of the Julliard School of Music, he planned a concert career that was cut short due to a loss of left-hand dexterity while he was in the Special Services Branch of the United States Army. Later he ran with the polo set in Long Island, the jet set in St. Moritz, the surf-and-sand set of the Riviera, after exploring the world of high finance in Beverly Hills, he traveled again in Europe and then turned to writing. He has always possessed a passion for people and has kept extensive diaries since early childhood.

FUTURA CASH SALES,
110 WARNER ROAD,
LONDON S.E.5

Please send me the following titles

Quantity	SBN	Title	Amount
————			————
————			————
————			————
————			————
————			————
			————
		TOTAL	————

Please enclose a cheque or postal order made out to **FUTURA PUBLICATIONS LIMITED** for the amount due, including 10p per book to allow for postage and packing. Orders will take about three weeks to reach you and we cannot accept responsibility for orders containing cash.

PLEASE PRINT CLEARLY

NAME..

ADDRESS...

....